DEADFALL

A RYAN MOAR MYSTERY

Michael D. Hartley

abbott press

Abbott Press books may be ordered through booksellers or by contacting:

Abbott Press
1663 Liberty Drive
Bloomington, IN 47403
www.abbottpress.com
Phone: 1-866-697-5310

ISBN: 978-1-4582-1725-7 (sc)
ISBN: 978-1-4582-1724-0 (hc)
ISBN: 978-1-4582-1723-3 (e)

Library of Congress Control Number: 2014912576

Printed in the United States of America.

Abbott Press rev. date: 08/19/2014

CHAPTER 1

THE TIME FOR THE DESTRUCTION of the false idol had come.
Habib Kadir covered his face with the back of his hand to
shield his eyes from little dust devils of sand that twisted across the
plain. He passed a dry wadi where two ragged boys fired round
stones with slingshots at imaginary targets and where a small girl
in a cranberry-colored headscarf sat under the shade of the low
branches of an apple tree.

Behind the children, army trucks were parked beside a low-
slung mud-brick house set into the crook of the cliff's wall. A boy
soldier gripped an AK-47 between his legs and lolled on a chair
guarding the door. Beside him, a rust-covered pail lay half buried
in the sand. When Habib waved, the boy didn't smile and continued
to stare at wireless power grids that glinted in the sun.

Habib squinted his deep-set, dark eyes at the giant Buddha
carved out of the distant flesh-colored cliff. Previous rulers had
hacked off the statue's nose, but the legs draped in folded robes of
an ancient Greek origin remained defiant and dignified. This statue
rose a mere fifty feet and lacked the fame of the Buddha Habib had
blasted into fragments in Bamiyan.

As the sun sank behind the low-lying hills, Habib glared at the statue's weathered, slanted eyes and thick-lipped smile. Any traces of paint had long since peeled from the face. He rubbed his beard; the blackheads and dry skin in the folds around his eyes resembled dried snake scales.

On both sides of the statue, Habib had embedded plastic explosives into drilled holes and fused the charges with detonating cord so they would explode at the same time. A slow-burning fuse connected to the detonating cord trailed across plowed fields to a cave that looked like a termite hole in the cliff face. The thought of the imminent explosion when he blew up the Buddha gave him a certain boyish pleasure. He couldn't wait. He ran across uneven ground to the cave.

As he approached, he heard a rattle of small stones run like rats down a narrow channel. He looked up at a goatherd with one eye clouded over and two front teeth missing. The boy sat on his haunches on loose shale. He grinned at Habib before he scampered behind a pile of rocks.

Habib climbed in through the cave's narrow opening and paused to breathe in deep. After the boiling heat, he blinked in the cool darkness. He flinched at the sight of a bucktoothed man seated on a munitions box, holding the end of the fuse in his gnarled hands.

"What are you doing, Jamal?" Habib asked, the skin on the back of his neck feeling flaccid and full of needles.

Jamal avoided his eyes and remained silent. Habib heard a flutter behind him as a flock of doves flew into the distance.

"Give me the fuse," Habib said in the soft voice and seductive tone he used when he talked to women. "I will light it so we can destroy the stone devil."

Jamal's left leg quivered under his robe. He put the fuse down beside him on a munitions box, and he grinded his fingers into his temples. "Spirits from inside the statue bounce around inside my head."

"Are you crazy? That hunk of rock is nothing but sandstone carved by infidels before the whore you called your mother squeezed you from in between her fat thighs."

2

Jamal reached for a Kalashnikov and leveled the assault rifle at Habib's head. "Come closer and I shoot," he said.

Habib stood still, listening to his heavy breathing. He knew Jamal to be a fighter, a former bodyguard to a local emir. He had lost a leg in the war against Soviet troops.

"You are a brave man, Jamal. You contributed to our country's defeat of a superpower. Do not try to stop me. I have destroyed statues in the provinces of Ghazni, Herat, Jalalabad, and Kandahar, even some in Kabul's National Museum." Habib reached down to feel the cool steel handle of his curved knife in a scabbard attached to his belt. "Have you ever seen an edict by the Islamic Emirate reversed?"

Jamal pivoted on his good leg to steady his aim. "I'm not afraid of a bunch of rebellious students who think they know it all."

Habib rubbed his forehead, his skin seared by hot winds from the baked southern plains. He felt the pounding of his heart. Why did the mullah appoint a local commander who spouted insolence?

"What will you do if soldiers come to find out why we haven't blown up the statue?" he asked.

"I will fight until I have no bullets. The war has taken everything from my village, even the last scrap of firewood—only this statue remains."

Habib moved closer and distracted him with soothing words. "I mean you no harm, my old friend. Let me light the fuse. In a few minutes all that will be left of this idolatrous carving is dust."

The sudden crack of a rifle shot in the valley distracted Jamal, and Habib sprang with the speed of a panther. The rage of his attack took Jamal by surprise, and he pulled the trigger. His shots went wild, and bullets ricocheted off the charred ceiling. Habib wrenched the Kalashnikov from Jamal's arthritic fingers and smashed the rifle butt against the side of his face. Jamal cried out and cradled his bloody jaw. Habib grabbed him, pinned his arms to his sides, and held him so close their beards touched.

When Jamal opened his dried lips to scream, Habib clamped a hand over his nose and mouth. He stared down at Jamal's bloodshot eyes turned to wide pools of terror. He felt a rage deep within his being, as though a white-hot poker singed his soul.

A harsh voice inside him screamed, *Kill him! Kill him! Kill him!* He pulled his curved bedouin knife out of the scabbard and pressed the point into the man's jugular. Tightening his grip around the cool handle of the knife, he pushed the blade into Jamal's throat until the old man's scream turned into a choked-off rattle. As the knife sank to the hilt, Habib could feel his hand touch the taught sinews of Jamal's wrinkled neck.

Sweat streamed out of Habib's hair and trickled down to his beard. He twisted the knife before he tugged it out. He pushed Jamal's body to the floor. Jamal's heart still pumped blood that pooled in dust turned black by ancient fires.

Habib strolled to the mouth of the cave. The evening air smelled clean after the musty odor of cooking fat, stale sweat, and moldy blankets. Had he been too hasty to kill Jamal? Had his comrade been suffering from a temporary derangement that made him behave in an erratic manner?

The sight of the Buddha mocked him, and he soon dismissed any thoughts of the man he had killed moments ago. He lit the fuse and laid the burning wire with care on the cave floor. He then ran down the hill to the house nestled in the cliff. He pushed his way past the guard and flung open the door. Some soldiers lay curled up on the mud floor, while others sat in a circle and nibbled bones of a goat's carcass. His wild eyes and bloodstained dishdasha startled the young men.

"Jamal is dead," he said. "I'm in command now."

The soldiers eyed him with suspicion as they would an outsider.

"I've lit the fuse." He took a deep breath, jutted out his chin, and waved his fists in the smoke-filled room. "Go outside and see the foreign devil destroyed."

The soldiers staggered to their feet, shouldered assault rifles, and filed out the door.

Habib followed the soldiers until he had a clear view of Buddha's weathered face surrounded by a dust haze. For a moment, nothing stirred in the valley.

He began to count seconds.

When the explosions came, shock waves reverberated throughout the statue. Dust clouds and stones rattled down the side of the cliff to scatter flocks of goats. The noise echoed down the valley.

"God's will is done. God is great," Habib shouted, the deep lines on his face divided by red sunlight and shadow.

CHAPTER 2

INSIDE THE WEST FARGO POLICE Department, Ryan Moar unzipped his jacket, relieved to get out of the rain. Bleak afternoon clouds had moved in from the west. Even if it still felt like fall, there was an unmistakable feel of winter. He strolled across the lobby and climbed the fire stairs to the second floor.

At a workstation, a thickset woman appeared to answer three calls at once. When she had breathing space, she looked at him with sea-green eyes that belonged to a cat.

"Haven't I seen you somewhere before?" she asked.

"Ryan Moar, I used to be in Homicide," he said.

An experienced eye swept up and down his six-foot frame to assess his leather jacket and thick black hair flattened by rain. He grinned when he recognized her high cheekbones and brown hair, close-cropped around the ears.

"You're Susanne Bandy," he said.

"Easum now, Susanne Easum," she said, smoothing down her dark-gray business suit.

A wry smile flitted around Ryan's mouth. "You're both hitched and promoted. Congratulations."

Susanne squinted at him. "How is it out there in the dog-eat-dog world?"

"I'm doing okay."

Her face turned full of menace. "Is that lamebrain partner of yours, Marleau Belanger, still making a fool of himself?" Her thin lips tightened. "Someone should've knocked out his spokes a long time ago."

"What've you got against Marleau?"

"Didn't he try to cuff the mayor-elect in his home on some phony drug charge?"

"You can't fault an officer for being an overachiever." Ryan glanced over to a corner office with glass windows, facing the squad room. "Is Greg in?"

"He's meeting with the DA for a few minutes." She leaned back and crossed her legs, her eyes moving over his face with an undisguised cold look. "How's Joanne?"

He continued in a matter-of-fact tone, "Apart from coaching drama students at NDSU, she eases the caseload."

She tilted her chin, and a private thought lightened her eyes. "I hear you two share bath towels and bedsheets."

Ryan could feel raindrops from his hair drip onto his neck. He glanced around the room at the solemn faces of police officers in front of computers.

"As we're getting personal, isn't your brother-in-law City Councilor John Easum?"

Susanne pursed her lips. "So what if he is?"

"Doesn't it bother you that to get this job in Homicide, you were helped by a hand the size of a football field?"

Her red mouth turned down at the corners.

Ryan spotted Staff Sergeant Greg Duluth stride down the corridor. Carrying a slim briefcase, he was an overweight police officer in a tan suit with hair as gray as gunmetal. "Excuse me, Susanne, Greg's back."

"Do you have an appointment?"

"I've never made one before."

7

She made a face loaded with disapproval. "You can't see him without going through me."

He gave her a little wave. "Ciao, Susanne."

She lowered her voice. "Any special connection you had to Greg in the past doesn't give you access to him now."

Ryan turned, allowing a trace of a smile. "At least I'm not married to my meal ticket."

He crossed the carpeted floor to the corner office, opened the door, and stuck his head around the jamb. Greg looked up from his cluttered desk and crimped his mouth.

"What the hell do you want?" he asked.

"Is this any way to greet an old compadre?"

"I'm sorry, but you simply can't butt in like this," Greg said, his face set in a stony expression. "Would it help if I told you I'm awfully busy right now?"

"Real police work or interdepartmental politics?"

Greg laughed a dry sound without humor. "As usual, it's a balancing act, a combination of the two. Whatever you want to see me about, make it snappy."

"Have you anything on a Moe Fouzi?"

"Should I?"

Ryan took in a deep breath. "Moe's engaged to Tamara Ravenstein. Moe claims to be Lebanese. His paranoid future father-in-law doesn't believe him. I don't either. Will you check him through your system?"

"What's he supposed to have done?"

Greg hadn't invited him to sit so Ryan leaned on the back of a leather chair. The frosty reception made him uncomfortable.

"That's what I need to find out."

"How did Mr. Fouzi ever get close to Carl's daughter?" Greg asked with a slight amusement in his eyes.

"They met at an office party."

"He made a strong first impression." Greg put both hands on his forehead as though he had a headache. "I presume Moe is the diminutive of Mohammed. Is he here legally?"

"There's no record of his legitimate entry into the US."

"If he hasn't the paperwork, that's of interest to immigration." Greg rose from behind his desk. "Do you suspect he's involved in any criminal activity?"

"So far, I've found nothing."

"Have you ruled out the possibility of a terrorist connection?"

"Right now, everything's on the table."

"If you suspect he's a radical, talk to Counterterrorism Officer Ingrid Krenn. She's our feds terrorism task-force liaison."

Greg breathed hard through his mouth; the skin around his left eye twitched. Heavy rain began to plunk against the window. "What does Moe do other than seduce rich women?" he asked.

"He's a computer geek."

"Tell Corporal Player I said it's okay to run Moe Fouzi's name through the system." His voice hardened. "Next time you want to see me, phone Susanne and make an appointment. Now get out of my office."

The next morning, the sky began to clear, and egrets rose out of the dried cattails beside the Red River and scattered like rose petals over the roof of the boathouse. The steel-hearted wind made Joanne Sutter shiver as she sat on the cedar deck at the rear of the house she shared with Ryan Moar. The one-and-a-half-story log home and landscaped grounds overlooked the river that snaked along the border between North Dakota and Minnesota. Beside the dock, the mast of a dingy nodded in the swell.

From the drive, she heard the sound of her teenage son's Mustang convertible roar to life. Her throat muscles tightened when his tires growled on gravel. Where was he going this early in the morning? She never knew what he was up to half the time.

She had to admire Gary's resilience. In the neighboring city of Marsdon, Gary had faced a murder charge. Ryan had helped her prove him innocent. Following this ordeal, she had asked her son if he wanted counseling, but he had rejected the idea. Despite his wayward ways, she thought the best therapy was to love him more.

Ryan's daughter, Charlene, sat down beside her at the breakfast table. She wore black jeans and a white turtleneck wool sweater and tied her long blonde hair behind her in a rope. She looked older than fourteen, and her smooth skin glowed from a light tan. Charlene drank some orange juice, and her blue eyes stared at Joanne over the glass's rim.

"I know Dad works for Carl Ravenstein, but I've never liked him," she said.

"Does his abrasive manner get under your skin?"

She wrinkled her snub nose. "He makes me feel edgy."

"Carl's one of those in-your-face kind who insults you in such a way that you assume he has nothing to hide."

Charlene laughed. "Joanne, you say the coolest things."

"Why, thank you."

Charlene kneaded the top of her forearms. "Apart from being creepy, Carl's so . . . you know what I'm trying to say."

"Elderly, ancient, or just plain old."

"I mean he's getting on, but isn't it gross that he . . .?"

"Has a much younger fiancée," Joanne offered.

Charlene poured Grape-Nuts into a bowl but couldn't let go of the subject. "I can't imagine him kissing Jacelyn. It's so weird that—"

Before Charlene finished her sentence, the french doors opened. Joanne smiled at Ryan as he strolled onto the deck. Joanne felt his warm breath and then soft lips pressing on her wheat-colored hair.

"What's so weird?" he asked, turning to Charlene.

She started to reply, then looked at her father's face and thought better of it.

"We're discussing the age difference between Carl and Jacelyn," Joanne said.

"He isn't exactly Brad Pitt, but to be fair don't you think he's entitled to happiness with his bride-to-be?"

"I'm glad you like him," Charlene said.

"You think he's too old to marry her?" Ryan asked, sitting opposite her.

Petulance showed on her face. "He should hitch up to someone close to his own age."

"Why is the age difference so important if they love each other?"

"Dad, give me a break."

"That obvious, huh?"

Joanne looked at each of them in turn, considering for a moment. "Is Carl still a curmudgeon, or has an impending wedding and the threat of an indictment mellowed him?" she asked.

"He's as feisty as ever," he said.

"My teacher says he's a crook who steals money from other people," Charlene said.

Ryan shrugged his shoulders. "That hasn't been proven in court."

"Under the circumstances, once they marry, how long will they stay together?" his daughter asked, gazing at racing shadows on the water from elms bending in the wind.

"They both could live in wedded bliss to a ripe old age," Joanne said.

"I doubt it," Charlene said, before gulping down the rest of her orange juice. "Excuse me." She got up and went inside through the glass doors.

Joanne stretched her tanned arms, firm with the kind of muscle tone that came from tennis and workouts on exercise machines.

"I think Charlene's right about the age difference." She hesitated and decided to toss out subtly, "Is Carl up to his conjugal responsibilities?"

Ryan poured black coffee into a mug. "Carl? He's a bull. He jogs a mile every morning."

"Why does he spend so much time at his cottage away from his betrothed?"

"Since he risks an indictment, he keeps a low profile."

Joanne gazed at a tangle of tree roots moving down the river, a frown on her face. "He can't disappear for too long, or people will suspect he's concealing something."

Ryan poured Grape-Nuts and skim milk into a bowl.

In between mouthfuls, he said, "Everything so far that's been said about his involvement in insider trading is hearsay."

Joanne paused to listen to the trickle of water from a miniwaterfall and the rustling leaves of poplars and evergreens. She sensed Ryan didn't want to talk about his client, so she switched to a different topic.

"Did Greg help you find something about Moe?"

"The police ran him through the Automated Fingerprint Identification System. He's clean." Ryan stood up and began kneading her shoulders. "Despite not having a criminal record, his lifestyle doesn't match his income. The guy drives a Ferrari, and when I picked the lock of his upscale condo, I noticed he has a new fifty-two-inch plasma TV, a top-of-the-line treadmill, and a closet full of Armani suits." He squinted at lightning trembling inside a storm bank. "I mean to find out who's filling his tank."

CHAPTER 3

I N A DUSTY MEXICAN TOWN close to the US border, Habib Kadir mopped his brow. He sat near the entrance of a dimly lit cantina. He wore a tan, tropical suit and Serengeti sunglasses. He had packed his patent-leather briefcase with health bars and water bottles to sustain him for his trek across the Arizona desert.

Since the attack on the World Trade Center, getting into the United States had become more difficult for a man with his swarthy complexion and dark-brown eyes. To enter the country unnoticed, he had opted to sneak across the porous Mexican border. He had crossed both Iraqi and Afghan deserts, so the Sierra Madre plateau didn't seem a formidable obstacle. The main hazard would be to avoid border patrols.

A low voice behind him caused a twinge of unexpected fear. *"Buenas noches, señor."*

Habib wheeled around. The voice appeared so sudden as if suspended in cacophony from the street. He scanned the sidewalk and a hardware store opposite the cantina. He half expected to see the glint of an assassin's rifle pointed at his heart.

The moment of panic passed when he felt a tug on his pant leg and looked down at an old man whose wrinkled skin reminded him of a sun-dried melon. The man squatted on his haunches, a thick homemade cigarette burning between his cracked lips. He stretched out twisted hands as if he wanted to bless Habib.

For an instant, the man's sunken eyes below a stained black scarf reminded Habib of his father the day before he died. He dug into his pocket and gave him some coins, and the man's broad grin revealed a toothless mouth. Habib watched the bent figure scamper away to steps leading to a church.

Why had this beggar frightened him? He blamed his moment of terror on being a fugitive for over a year. He frowned at a statue of the Madonna mounted on a marble pedestal. Mary's robe, painted a brilliant blue in contrast to the pinkness of her cheeks, reminded him of a doll in a shop window. Almost by habit, he started to calculate the explosives needed to blow up the statue by placing small amounts of *plastique* inside a series of drilled holes in the Madonna's torso.

He couldn't let go of the feeling of being watched. Fumes from cars burned the inner linings of his nostrils and made him long for his hilltop mansion in Kabul. Surrounded by a high wall, his home had spacious bedrooms shared by his four sons.

After the fall of the Taliban, troops had arrived to arrest him, but his friends had warned him. Days before the soldiers banged on his door, he and his family had scattered to safe countries.

The sound of a bus backfire jolted Habib into the present. His hands flew to his chest to check for a bullet wound. He stared at the sun in a haze of low-lying clouds, the color of pressed roses. In an hour, it would be dark. He had to go. He left the cantina and climbed into a rust-flecked Impala sedan parked in a backstreet.

He drove to the outskirts of town and turned down a gravel road, passing corn and cattle acreages. As the sky darkened, he felt the warmth of the twilight air on his face. Veins of heat lightning flickered through clouds above stark rolling hills. In the dim light, he saw the daunting border fence, a thin, black scar that divided the harsh, dry land.

He made a whistling sound in exasperation.

How hard could it be to walk across Arizona compared to his country's unrelenting deserts? Habib stared at the stars in the night sky above the outline of the vast, dry land. Later, when the moon rose, he had a shimmering pearl to guide him.

That same evening, Ryan sat at a small table in a restaurant named Fu Niu Shan Chicken Pita on St. Letinsky Place. The floor, six feet below ground, allowed a little natural light to penetrate through the grime of a front window that faced an open space known as Joraastad Square.

Across from Ryan sat Moe Fouzi's former girlfriend, Gina, a petite young woman who, even when she spoke, kept chewing her nails. She wore sunglasses, her face as pale as her headscarf and long-flowing dress that extended to her ankles.

"Shortly after I started going out with him, he persuaded me to convert," she said.

"How did your family react to your change of religion?" Ryan asked.

Gina stiffened. He noticed one side of her face was reddish and swollen.

"They freaked out," she said, avoiding his eyes.

Business was slow, and apart from a robust Chinese woman in a stained white apron, they were the only customers. The basement walls, covered in bordello-style maroon-and-gold velvet wallpaper, had over time almost blurred to a universal brown.

"Did he ever talk about extremist ideas?" Ryan asked.

"He used to be serious about founding an Islamic state in North America, but as far as I know he never socialized with the radical element at the mosque."

"Was it easy for you to switch to his faith?"

"It isn't anything like becoming a Catholic. To complete the conversion, all I had to do was read out loud a two-line declaration of faith in front of an imam."

"You must have really loved him."

Her face flushed with resentment. "I gave my heart to him, and he ended up throwing me away like an orange with the juice sucked out of it." Gina sighed and took off her dark glasses and rubbed her green eyes. "He's found someone else outside of the faith."

"What gave you that impression?"

"A few months ago, he stopped being active in the local Muslim community. He and I used to study the Qur'an and take classes at the Red River Mosque."

"What made him change?"

"After he began working at Ravenwest, he started getting restless, moody. He stopped going to religious studies, shaved his beard, and bought expensive suits. He began to criticize my appearance. Why didn't I wear makeup, dye my hair, or go to a nightclub?"

"What did his imam and friends at the mosque think?"

"His mother screamed at him."

Ryan leaned forward. "His mother? I was under the impression he came to the United States alone."

"She's here all right." Gina hesitated. "One day while I cooked his supper, this sharp dresser showed up at our apartment. She had her own key and just stormed in. Without as much as a hello, she slapped me around a bit, pulled my hair, and called me a common whore. Then she accused me of being a bad influence on Moe. She said I encouraged him to drink, smoke, and eat pork." Gina squeezed her fists open and shut. "I'm not even sure she's his real mother."

Ryan heard the slam of a van door and glanced out the side window at a man hauling a wooden crate of vegetables to the back door.

"Can you describe this woman?" he asked.

Gina's face had gone white as though the memory was painful.

"She had black, shoulder-length hair. What was so surprising was that under her leather coat she had the figure of a showgirl."

"How old would she be?"

"Probably in her midforties, but she's remarkably well preserved."

"How do you feel about your new religion now Moe's left you?"

"Lost and confused." She wiped moisture out of the corner of her eyes with her forefinger. "I took his faith, and now I'm in spiritual limbo."

A few streaks of rain ran down the window.

Ryan asked, "Did you know Moe now passes himself off as a Lebanese Christian?"

His question died away, and a lingering silence followed. He expected Gina to react with shock or grief, but instead she glanced at the rain, her face blank.

When she turned back to him, she whispered, flush with resentment, "If he's Lebanese, I'm Saddam Hussein."

"Do you ever see him anymore?"

She shook her head. "He's become so high and mighty now that he lives in a fancy apartment on the other side of town."

"Where do you think he gets the money?"

"His new girlfriend gives him the cash, I'm sure of it." She gave him a quick, derisive look. "It's hard to believe, at one time, he lived and breathed his religion."

"He seems resigned to a different path."

She squinted at cool sunlight after the shower. "He really doesn't love his new girlfriend. He's only interested in her money."

CHAPTER 4

AFTER LUNCH, A HUMAN RESOURCES associate at Ravenwest told Ryan that Moe's boss, Chris Chisholm, was on sick leave, recovering from bypass surgery. Ryan phoned his house, but there was no answer, so he drove to an upmarket suburban address in West Fargo and parked beside a black four-door Ford sedan with tinted windows.

The wind flapped a stars-and-stripes flag from a pole on the front lawn of a ranch-style stucco split-level with white balconies. Ryan rang the bell, and a thickset woman in a flowery muumuu opened the door.

"Is this the Chisholm residence?" he asked.

"I'm Mary Chisholm. If you're from Ranchero Realty, we're not selling. We like it here," she said.

When she smiled, the skin under her eyes puckered like dry paint at the bottom of a can.

He handed her his card. "I'm not here to sell your house, Mrs. Chisholm. Is Chris in?"

She put on a pair of reading glasses. "Come with me, Mr. Private Eye; he's in the greenhouse."

She led the way through the living room furnished with a heavy Spanish-style chesterfield and chair. Copper plates crammed the walls beside gaudy portraits of agile matadors battling bulls.

"Why did you think I was in real estate?" Ryan asked when they arrived at a pair of french doors that overlooked an empty kidney-shaped swimming pool.

"You have that hungry, eager look, young man, as though you're already counting the commission," she said, opening the double doors.

Beyond the empty pool, Ryan heard crows squabble in oak trees.

"I dread the fall," she said. "I'm afraid of rainstorms and the flocks of crackles that invade my garden. The only thing that keeps my spirits up is the prospect of planting spring flowers."

As they approached an overheated greenhouse, they found Chris stretched out on a chaise longue.

"You mustn't excite my husband," Mary said. "His heart can't take it."

"I'll try not to say anything to disturb him," Ryan said.

Mary introduced him to Chris, who wore a white Tilley hat and a tartan shirt. His eyes squinted behind yellow-tinted glasses at a girl of five in a pink woolly jacket with soil on her lips. She concentrated on digging in a flowerpot of asters and tossing soil on the concrete floor.

"Connie, I've told you before to keep the dirt out of your mouth," Mary said.

The girl abandoned her spade and started pulling on white lilies. Chris turned to face Ryan, sitting beside him on a wrought-iron chair. Mary handed him his card.

"I knew a damned good cop named Moar. You related?" he asked, his voice husky from tobacco.

"I'm that Moar."

"Why did you quit the force to go private? More money I expect." He chuckled. "I don't have much of my own except for when I retire and get my Ravenwest pension."

Ryan glanced through steamed glass at two carpenters on a scaffold that surrounded a new gazebo. "You could've fooled me."

Chris's face turned melancholy under his wide-brimmed hat. "We're spending my wife's inheritance. Why do you want to see me?"

Mary sat beside her husband and flipped through the pages of a *Martha Stewart Living* magazine.

"What can you tell me about Moe Fouzi?"

A muscle worked on Chris's jaw. "Who wants to know? Don't tell me Carl is having him investigated. He doesn't think Moe worthy of marrying his daughter." He glared at Ryan. "Are you working for him?"

"Yes."

"He wants you to dig up sewage on Moe, so he can persuade his daughter it wouldn't be in her best interest to get hitched to the boy."

"All I'm doing is trying to get some kind of profile." Ryan stretched out his long legs and gazed at ducks paddling on the surface of a pond. "No one appears to know much about his background, family, and friends. What's he like?"

"He's a computer whiz." Chris examined the inside of an empty mug and grunted. "He's installed new antivirus protection and firewall for the company against the most insidious adware and spyware."

"Who are his friends?"

"He's a ladies' man." He smiled and brought his face closer to Ryan. "When he hired on at Ravenwest, he attracted a lot of attention from the opposite sex, but as soon as he started dating Tamara, he stop flirting." Chris looked away, and his head bobbed like a marionette for no reason. "Let me tell you, when he announced his engagement, he broke lots of hearts."

Ryan leaned forward to snare Chris's eyes, brown predator's eyes, staring out of folds of flesh. "What did Moe do exactly?"

"I can't talk about his work, but you could say it was very sensitive."

"In what way?"

"He handled important clients."

"Did Moe report to you?"

"He did, at first. Then Cole Ravenstein told me Moe reported to him."

"Weren't you upset by being bypassed?"

"What could I do? He's the boss's son, and I'm close to retirement."

Ryan extended an arm behind him on the chair's back, trying to strike a relaxed pose, but he didn't feel comfortable. Chris's fidgety fingers bothered him. They reminded him of the body language of criminal suspects under cross-examination.

"Have you met Moe's mother?" he asked.

"Can't say I have," he replied, slowing the movement of his head as though winding down.

"Did he ever talk about her?"

"He never did."

"When you hired him, did you contact his references or do background checks?"

"Cole told me not to bother."

"Don't you find it odd that no one in the Lebanese community has ever heard of Moe Fouzi?"

Chris took off his hat, scratched his baldhead, but didn't reply.

"Does Moe have any colleagues that he knew well or he went with for a beer?" Ryan said.

Chris hesitated for a moment and then wiped sweat off his face with a monogrammed handkerchief. "He often took long liquid lunches with Cole."

Ryan softened his voice in an attempt to put him more at ease. "Where does Moe get the money for his expensive lifestyle?"

"No idea."

"Surely, you must've been curious. Moe pulls down say about forty thousand, tops fifty. To support his current standard of living, he needs an income of at least one hundred thousand."

Chris squeezed his eyes shut for a moment as if trying to blot out an unpleasant memory. "A couple of days, before my ticker took a wallop, I did find some unorthodox expenses related to software purchases. When I questioned him about them, he called me some rude names and said I had no right to question him. When I mentioned Moe's outburst to Cole, he said he'd look into it, but he never did."

Ryan listened to the soothing sound of water bubble in the Japanese rock sculpture. "Did you report this to Carl?"

He wiped the liner of his hat. "My daddy once told me I would either end up a minister or a drunk. Instead, I went into number crunching. Now, I sometimes wake up and don't have any idea who I am." He replaced his hat on his head that was dotted with brown sunspots like an overripe mango's skin. "I did suggest to Cole that his pal take an anger management course."

He intertwined his fingers around the back of his neck. Mary glanced at Chris, an anxious look on her face.

A hostile light grew in Chris's eyes. "If you're looking for fraud, I suggest you focus your investigation on Carl Ravenstein."

"What makes you so sure Carl is guilty?" Ryan asked.

Chris cleared his throat and spat yellow phlegm onto the concrete floor. "As far as I'm concerned, he's guilty."

He rubbed gray whiskers mingled in among a network of blue and red veins in his cheek.

Ryan breathed in hard the moist overheated air. "When the time comes, he'll have his day in court."

"I doubt it will ever go to trial," Chris said.

"Why not, dear?" Mary asked.

"He never left a paper trail." He shielded his eyes from a shaft of sunlight. "My gut feeling is he dropped any incriminating evidence from his Beechcraft into the middle of the Lake of the Woods."

Chris blew his nose until his face turned red.

Mary cocked her head to one side and frowned at Ryan. "Your questions upset my husband; you'd better leave."

"I've a couple more quick ones," Ryan said, tugging at his shirt collar. "What can you tell me about Aaron Hubbard, Carl's business partner?"

"I can't say for sure if I ever actually met him." Chris sat forward for a moment and brushed his fingertips over a scar embedded in his eyebrow. "Wish I could remember more, Ryan."

"How's your memory of your fellow bean counter George Black?"

"George? He tried to blow his brains out and missed the prefrontal cortex, leaving him paralyzed from the waist down."

"Is he able to talk?"

He chortled. "Yeah, but keep in mind George is one of the meanest outhouse buckets that ever worked for Ravenwest."

"Watch your language, dear," Mary said.

"Where does he live?" Ryan asked, getting up.

"In a nursing home," he said, looking up at Ryan, his face a network of cracks like old wallpaper.

Ryan listened to frogs in the series of pools beside the greenhouse. Mary placed a teapot in front of Chris.

"I brought you green tea, dear," she said.

"Why can't I drink coffee? This stuff tasted like cat's piss."

"Antioxidants are good for your immune system."

"Baloney!"

Mary poured some tea in his mug. Chris sniffed at the contents in the mug and twisted his thin lips. He put the cup down and examined Ryan's card with a left eye that looked bulbous and drooped lower than the right.

"Who is J. Sutter?" he asked.

"Joanne Sutter is my partner."

"A woman, eh, I'd always thought they weren't any good at investigative work."

"They're plenty of them in the Fargo Police Department doing an outstanding job." Ryan let humor creep into his face. "What about Miss Marple?"

"There are exceptions, of course." Chris's lopsided smile crinkled at the corner of his mouth. "In the mysteries I read, the cleverest PIs are men. I'd never worked with a woman, but I'm in no position to tell you how to run your business."

"When he nears the end of a mystery novel, he's right most of the time about who did the murder," Mary chipped in.

"Thank you for your time," Ryan said, getting up and walking back to his car.

When Habib woke up on the shady side of a small hill, he looked ahead and saw nothing but another hillock and hundreds after that. During the previous night, he had walked beside the fence under a crescent moon for several hours until he had found an opening and crawled through.

The morning sky took on the color of old bone, and dust blew out of the flats made hazy by a sun high and fierce. He pulled his hat further down to cover his eyes and settled into a slow, long stride.

When the day cooled into evening, nothing moved in the desert, not even a bird. To the left, the sun sank low and turned to a big yellow melon above the horizon.

He spent the next night in an abandoned house with only the wind for company. Around midnight he heard gunfire to the west. Through a crack in the wall, he watched distant searchlights from helicopters light up the hillsides.

The next day he trudged along a trail in places littered with plastic bags, tattered rags, diapers, and empty water bottles dumped in among the mesquite and rocks. By evening, the temperature dropped and he thought he should rest, but without even a blanket, he had no alternative but to keep going.

Around midnight, too exhausted to go on, he collapsed near an outcrop beside a ravine. He burrowed out a place in the earth for his hip, stretched out his aching legs, and closed his eyes.

When he awoke, the early sun's red light covered broken rocks and patches of dried grass. Little white clouds floated above a distant hill to the northeast. He felt delirious as his mind grabbed snatches of a verse from the Qur'an. "And the life of this world is nothing more than a play and a passing delight; and the life in the hereafter is by far the better for all, who are conscious of God."

In his mind, he became a boy again playing imaginary war games in the narrow streets of Kabul. A tremor ran through his body when he recalled being held down on a bed, while an imam used a knife to slice off his foreskin. When he sat up, surrounded by his older brothers, friends, and relatives, he soon forgot the sharp pain. In the street, a volley of rifle shots marked his entry into manhood.

Opening his mouth in an attempt to suck moisture out of the cool morning air, he struggled to his feet and used his compass to set his bearings. He search for his briefcase of food and water, but it was nowhere in sight. How could he have been so stupid to lose it? While he walked, he chewed to make a small amount of saliva flow on the compass's leather strap. Hunger pangs subsided when his thirst became more intense.

He was no stranger to waterless days during Ramadan, but he blamed rich food for widening his waist and making his muscles flabby. By evening, his saliva had dried up, and he stopped chewing the strap. He sank down on his haunches beside a clump of mesquite and watched the moonrise.

Had he come this far only to die in the desert? A slight movement in the mesquite caught his attention and yanked him out of his lethargy. He focused on a head in a wide-brimmed hat. In bid to catch up, he forced his tired leg to walk faster. As he gained ground, he approached a dark-skinned woman, carrying an infant strapped on her back. He suspected she was an illegal migrant, left behind by the main party.

When she stopped to take a sip of water from a bottle attached to a thong around her neck, his cracked lips puckered, and he felt a spasm in his parched throat. He watched mesmerized as she lifted the top of her blouse and aimed her teat at the baby's mouth. After a few minutes, she uncoupled the baby and sat on a rock.

Habib knew he had to act or die. He spurred his tired legs into a burst of speed. He gathered his strength and grabbed her slender throat. When he snatched her water bottle, he felt a sharp pain as she raked her fingernails across his cheek. He shoved her away, and the baby tumbled from her lap to the sand.

After drinking her water, Habib spotted a small satchel attached to her waist. He tugged at the leather bag, while she used her fists to fight him off her. He rammed his knee in her ribs, and she bent over. He tore her satchel off her waist, shuffled away to behind an outcrop, and gnawed on her beef jerky.

The tepid water did little to slacken his raging thirst. Above him, the suffocating heat of the noon sun shone through a thin layer of cloud like a round chemical flame in a fog.

Just before dusk, Habib tripped on a root and fell. He felt too drained to get up, so he curled into a tight ball and slept.

It was dark when he awoke stiff and thirsty. In the distance, headlights stabbed the gloom. His blurred eyes tried to focus on the car lights.

He limped toward the highway.

The image of the Mexican woman with lustrous, terrified black eyes wouldn't leave his mind. Holding the infant in her arms, she had reminded him of the Madonna statue he had wanted to blow up in Mexico.

From the edge of the highway, Habib could see the lights of a town. The welcoming bright haze on the horizon in the early morning twilight buoyed him up. He imagined the coolness of ice water down his parched throat.

For an instant, a spotlight blinded him. He froze, a deer caught in the headlights. He dived for cover behind a sand hill.

A siren set off alarm bells in his brain. A white van, flashing red and blue lights, lurched off the highway and roared at him at high speed. Beside the sand dune, the van screeched to a halt in a cloud of dust. Overcome by shakes, Habib grabbed his chest and coughed fine grit out of his lungs.

Half blinded by floodlights, he cringed as two deputies, a pair of specters with wide-brimmed hats, jumped out of the van with pistols leveled at his heart. He raised his hands to the dawn sky and waited.

Habib felt strong arms drag him upright and shove him against the side of the van. One of the deputies twisted his arms behind his back to handcuff him. He then pushed him facedown on the hood and kicked his legs apart. While he pressed Habib's cheek on the scorched metal, the other deputy's hairy fingers moved like tarantula legs down his chest, sides, and thighs. The officer found the Swiss Army knife strapped to his leg and handed it to the other deputy.

Habib's mind fell into a murky pit as he realized the full extent of his failure to slip into the country unnoticed.

"Do you have ID?" the deputy asked, yanking Habib's head back by his hair and twisting his neck so the prisoner could face him.

Habib stared at his broad face, seething with resentment.

"I guess not." The deputy leaned close to Habib's ear. "I'm gonna kick your fat butt all the way back to Mexico."

CHAPTER 5

THE NEXT MORNING TURNED HOT and bright when a warm breeze blew in from South Dakota. Joanne slipped out of the bedroom and into the shower. Although Ryan didn't hear her words above the water flow, he found her seductive murmurs enticing. The smell of her aromatic soap and inhaling the steam reminded him of a perfumed Turkish bath.

She turned off the water and peeked at him from around the shower door. Through the pebbled glass, he made out the curved shape of her tanned body. She whipped off her shower cap to reveal the fullness of her heart-shape face framed by her flattened hair.

When she stepped on the bath mat, he admired her feline litheness. She went to the mirror to fluff up her hair. She dried off, pulled on a blue velour tracksuit that matched her eyes, and reclined on the sofa as languorous as a cat asleep in the sun. She rubbed a cluster of crystals over her arms that she believed circulated energy. She handed them to him.

"Did you know crystals have more sexual power than Viagra?" she said.

He rolled his eyes, a whimsical smile on his lips. He loved her bawdy sense of humor.

"I guess that means if I wrap them around my pecker I won't peter out," he said, rolling the stones around in his hands.

She groaned, screwed up her face, and turned her thumb down. "Stop it! That's enough," she said, throwing a silk-covered cushion at him.

He stared out of the window. It had started to sprinkle, and the river became dotted with rain rings. She came up behind him and began to knead his shoulders. She trailed her lips over the back of his neck, and the feeling of her warm breath made him shiver.

"If Chris Chisholm didn't provide many answers," she said, "will I find the working parts of George Black's mind any more lucid?"

Driving along Red River Road to Fargo, Joanne thought about her son, Gary. How would Ryan react if her wild teenager started to show a romantic interest in Charlene? She knew his disapproval would be immediate. The first time Ryan and her son had met, Gary had been a minor drug dealer, who had an underage streetwalker girlfriend.

She tensed as she threaded through heavy traffic on Decanter Street. She never liked driving in this low-rent district. Even though the street thrived during the day, within walking distance of the bustling thoroughfare were derelict buildings, railway tracks, and rows of shadowy, drab houses.

She felt a sense of relief when she passed the glass-and-steel Ravenwest building in Fargo's financial hub. Ten minutes later, she pulled into the parking lot of the Louis Armstrong Nursing Home, a low building surrounded by trees in a neighborhood made up of apartments and motels. In the reception area, a noisy air conditioner did nothing to dispel a smell of disinfectant and unwashed bodies.

She asked a wafer-thin nurse named Ursula with brown rings under her narrow eyes if she could see George Black. Ursula ushered her down a long corridor leading to a patio overlooking the Red River. On the opposite bank, kites in Memorial Park fluttered in a sky dotted with fast-moving clouds marbled orange by the sun.

"George doesn't get many visitors," Ursula said, arching her eyebrows. "Are you a relative?"

She decided to stretch the truth a bit. "I'm a friend of the family," Joanne said.

Ursula blinked and swept back mahogany-streaked hair. "As he's easily tired, you can only visit for a few minutes," she said. "Don't expect him to talk much."

She led Joanne to a thin, bony-faced man with a mat of uncombed white hair seated in a wheelchair on the top of the levee. The river had turned brown from topsoil runoff. As she approached George, mosquitoes rose in swarms from the damp grass.

When she stopped in front of him, she tried to snag his eyes, but he didn't look up. Instead, he stared at a tangle of branches, bobbing in an eddy. When George turned to her, his hair fluttered in a slight breeze.

"My boy's quite alert this morning," Ursula said, patting down wisps of hair. "Aren't we, my dear?"

When he smiled, a scar running down his left cheek made his lips twist.

"You two have a nice visit," Ursula said, heading back down the levee. "Remember, only a few minutes and don't talk about things that'll upset him."

As soon as she was out of earshot, Joanne sat beside him on a bench. He moved his skinny fingers to pull a blanket over his knees.

"My name's Joanne Sutter." She shielded her eyes against the sun. "I'm a PI looking into the background of Moe Fouzi, an employee at Ravenwest."

He stared at her with rheumy eyes. "I always liked Moe, although some of his coworkers called him a pushy Arab."

She gazed at a flooded pool of brown water at the foot of the property rimmed by fat Canada geese on the lawn.

"How would you describe Moe?" she asked.

"He's a bit of a nerd, but he knows more about computers than Bill Gates."

"Did you ever suspect Moe used his computer savvy to illegally make money for himself that the company didn't know about?" she asked.

"If he did, he's too bright to leave any evidence."

George pressed his knuckles into his lower spine as though trying to relieve pain in his back. Ryan had asked her to question him about Chris Chisholm. Carl Ravenstein suspected Chris had ties with organized crime. She didn't know how long she could keep George focused, so she jumped right into asking him about his former colleague.

George coughed to clear his throat. "When I think about him, I want to wash every part of my body in disinfectant. I found out he's so corrupt some of his foul stench even attached itself to me."

"In what way is he corrupt?" she asked.

"I caught him receiving under-the-table cash payments in brown envelopes." George sneezed and blew his nose. "One day, after work, I followed him from the office to the Radisson and saw him in the bar where he met Paul and Peter Sinise. The boss's son, Cole, joined them. I overheard Chris explain to the brothers how to defraud an insurance company in a warehouse fire claim." George's right eye had a nervous tic that made him blink every few minutes. "Paul Sinise used to invite him for weekends at his fly-in fishing lodge north of Bemidji." He clamped his hand on Joanne's forearm. "It's not easy for me to talk about the brothers." He withdrew his hand. The corner of his mouth wrinkled to expose his ground-down, brown-stained teeth. "After a Greek guy talked to a vice cop about the brothers, they tied him down on a table and used cigarettes to tattoo Olympic rings on his backside."

He turned to face the nursing home where patients sat on a patio and a woman in starched whites served coffee and doughnuts from a trolley.

He made a gun out of a finger, placed the barrel to his temple, and pulled the trigger. "Interested in knowing why I tried to shoot myself?"

There was a long moment of silence, while Joanne listened to geese honk over the river in V-shape formations.

George rubbed the stubble on his throat. "Before I tried to shoot myself, I left a note on my desk that outlined all I knew about that bastard Chris and the reason why I felt compelled to end my life."

"How did he react when he found out you had survived?"

"He found the note and destroyed it. He then threatened to finish the botched job if I ever talked to the cops about him."

Joanne allowed a twinge of fear to enter her voice. "Would Chris actually kill you?"

"Maybe not personally; he'd hire the Sinises to do it for him." His lips twisted in a lopsided smirk. "When you first meet Chris, he acts like a real gentleman. Don't be fooled. He's never been good; he is diabolical." He craned a crick out of his neck, and the cords flexed like cobras as he rummaged inside his pocket, pulled out a cigarette package, and ripped off the cellophane. "I'm not supposed to smoke, but the nurses aren't looking."

He lit a filter tip and took one puff after another, as if he was smoking a reefer.

"Anyone else in the company, apart from Cole and Chris, involved with the Sinises?" Joanne said.

He remained silent. He put his cigarette on the armrest of his wheelchair.

"Were you involved in any of Chris Chisholm's schemes?"

His low voice became raspy. "I never thought I'd ever do anything more than act as a courier, but he dragged me in deep." He groaned. "I'm in a lot of pain. I gotta have my meds."

Joanne spotted Ursula striding across the lawn toward them.

"I've one more question, George, and then we're done. What else did you find out about Chris's involvement in organized crime?"

"What do I know? Fargo is a weird town." He rested his smoldering cigarette on the table and clenched one blue-veined hand over the other. "He's mixed up with some Afghans heavy into heroin. They use a warehouse near Hector International." His forehead became shiny with sweat. "I never met them, but by reputation they'd put their beaks in an unflushed toilet someone puked in if they thought they could fish out a buck."

Ursula stormed up the side of the levee and mashed the cigarette stub into the grass with the heel of a white pump.

"Give them to me now," she said.

George handed her the pack, and the wrinkles of his left cheek trembled.

"I need a few more minutes, please," Joanne said.

Ursula screwed up her face. "Can't you leave this poor man alone?"

She wheeled George away from her. Joanne stared openmouthed at the nurse's back as she pushed the wheelchair over an uneven patch in the lawn.

Her notebook hung in her hand like an object of shame.

CHAPTER 6

ARLY THE NEXT DAY, THE river cooled the air, and the dingy
at the dock bobbed in the swell. Ryan stretched out on a chair
to watch the sun come through the red-and-white curtain of clouds
that cast a checkerboard pattern on the deck.

It had been four months since his blended family had moved into
the house on Red River Road. Fronted for its entire length by the ten-
foot-wide deck, the cedar-log house overlooked shrubs, lawns, and
rock gardens at an S-bend in the river. At the oxbow, balsam fir and
Scots pines surrounded the tennis court and the kidney-shaped pool.

The french doors creaked open, and Joanne's cairn terrier, Ivan,
known as "Terrible," bounced onto the deck. Seeing Ryan, he ran
around in circles of pleasure, a dynamic, shaggy black-and-white
ball of fur. Ryan's Alsatian, Roy, lying at his feet, growled before
going back to sleep.

His cell phone chimed, and Ryan stopped scratching the cairn's
crown. He recognized the unique ring tone assigned to Carl
Ravenstein. He hoped the call didn't ruin his Sunday morning plans
to take his family out for brunch at nearby Wallenger's Golf Club.

Ryan heard a low moan and then silence.

"Carl, what's going on?" He didn't reply, and the quiet made Ryan uneasy. "Are you in trouble?"

Then he picked up sharp background voices mingled with the relentless sound of a police siren, spiraling higher.

Carl's reply was a strangled whisper. "I'm at Ravenscourt."

"What are you doing there?"

"Aimée's dead."

"Oh my God, no."

Holding the phone to his ear, Ryan went inside to change.

"Two patrol cars blocking the entrance won't let me in," Carl said.

"How did she die?" he asked.

His client's strangled voice became calmer. "Mrs. Vandels found her in bed covered in blood with five bullet holes in her chest. She phoned the police and then called me." His breath quickened and grew louder. "What the hell am I going to do now?"

"Stay put until I get there," Ryan said, pulling on corduroy pants. "Where are the kids?"

"Cole's on a business trip in Minneapolis. Couldn't reach him at his hotel. Tamara stayed overnight at Moe's condo, and she's turned off her cell phone."

"I'll be right over."

He scribbled a note to Joanne, and he raced to his Maxima parked in the carport.

While Ryan drove south to Fargo, Habib sat huddled in a corner of a holding cell. He glanced at new green paint that covered graffiti and gouge marks on the walls, but the smell of fresh latex couldn't mask the odor of stale sweat and old urine.

His arrest as an illegal migrant caused him to experience one of his blackest moments. He sat soaked in sweat on the cement floor. Having never stepped inside a prison before, he felt an acute loss of control. Being a captive peeled away his identity like skin tugged off an orange. He noticed some prisoners talked to each other, while most remained sullen and silent.

When a young man smiled at Habib, Habib asked him in English, "What are the guards going to do with us?"

"Truck us back across the border," he said, scratching a pimple at the corner of his mouth.

As Habib scanned the crowded room, bleak thoughts flooded his mind. What would the authorities do to him if they discovered his identity?

"Why are you here?" he asked the scrawny young Mexican.

"I came to pick lettuce."

A skeletal man sporting a black eye beside Habib began to snore, his tanned skin as wrinkled as a tobacco leaf.

"Have you crossed the border before?" Habib asked, wiping beaded sweat off his forehead onto his shirtsleeve.

"Many times." He smiled. "For me, it is game. Sometimes I manage to find gringos to hire me, and other times I'm caught." Then the smile faded. "I need the work. I have a wife and three bambinos at home. What am I supposed to do when there's no work in my country?"

"Is there any way they'll let you remain in the United States rather than send you back?"

He rubbed his gnarled fingertips together. "I have heard if you have money, you can persuade the *Americanos* to let you stay."

Habib scanned the corridor opposite the holding cell. What would be the right way to bribe a guard?

The young man tugged his serape over his knees. He studied Habib's eyes in the dim fluorescent overhead lights.

"You're brown-skinned like me, yet you don't speak Spanish. Your English accent is different from the gringos. You talk as if you are a *patrón*."

Habib hesitated. He didn't know if he could trust the man.

"Like you, I also want to remain in the States to work, but I don't have the necessary visa," he said, lowering his gaze to a stain on the floor that reminded him of dried blood. "Would the guards let me use a phone?"

The young man gave him a frigid smile. "Where do you think you are, the Holiday Inn?"

A heavyset man near an open toilet cuffed a thin prisoner on the head until his screams attracted the guards.

"Shut up!" a sandy-haired guard shouted, banging a nightstick on the bars.

Habib wondered if the guard with cruel eyes could be the one to approach. He had always been an accurate judge of character, and this guard did have a weak chin, flushed cheeks, and a bloated stomach, so he probably supported a beer-drinking habit.

A man with a rattlesnake tattooed on his chest hit a scrawny teenager, and a fracas broke out.

"Why did the big guy hit that kid?" Habib asked.

"He refused to give Pedro Gonzales his runners. As soon as the boy goes to sleep, Pedro will have them."

For an instant, Habib forgot all about bribing the guard. He tucked his scuffed tasseled black loafers tight into his thighs. He prayed Pedro wouldn't take a liking to his shoes. Folded inside the heels, he had stashed $25,000.

The young man yawned, curled up in a ball, and went to sleep, while Habib stayed awake by thinking of a workable plan. After an hour of observing guards, he decided on the man with the weak chin and the pronounced paunch. He noticed a curved scar, an angry red strip, threaded through the shadow of a heavy beard on his left cheek. Apart from alcohol dependency, did a tendency to violence also make him easier to tempt with a bribe?

The next time the guard checked on prisoners, Habib noticed he had a bow-legged gait that reminded him of an actor in a western. As he could spot weakness in others, he studied the guard's fleshy face and cobra eyes. Was he in a good mood, or did he feel cranky? If he made the wrong choice, skillful interrogators, in time, could strip away layers protecting his identity. The thought of waterboarding during a long-term prison sentence at Guantanamo Bay made him shiver.

The guard approached the holding cell and ran his nightstick along the bars. When Habib stood up, his cramped leg muscles throbbed from pain. He stepped around sleeping men and headed for the bars. As he came closer, he saw a flicker of a smirk on the guard's thick lips.

"Do you have a moment, sir?" Habib asked.

The guard examined his stained Armani suit. "Who the hell are you?"

"I'm a Canadian citizen," he said.

"What's a polar bear doing this far south?"

"I'm visiting Arizona on business."

"What kind of business?"

"Building supplies, softwood lumber."

"How did you end up here?"

"My car broke down, and hitchhikers stole my wallet along with my ID. A patrol car picked me up by mistake. I'm not an illegal."

The guard examined the lesions on his face.

"It looks like you cooked for a few days," he said.

"After robbing me, the hitchhikers forced me into the desert."

The guard grunted; his scar glowed purple in the harsh fluorescent light.

"What's your name?" the guarded asked, folding his hairy, tattooed arms.

"Roger Bloom from Vancouver."

"Born in Canada were you?"

"Yes, sir."

"If you're on the level, we can get you sprung from here in a day or two, but it'll take some paperwork."

"I would be most grateful." He drew in a determined breath. "I've another favor to ask, sir. Could I borrow a pen?"

The guard hesitated. "What for?"

"I'd like to write you a note."

"Cat got your tongue?"

"No, sir."

"You wanna stab me with it?"

Habib trembled as if the guard had poked him with a cattle prod.

Nevertheless, the guard handed him a ballpoint and a matchbook from a local strip joint. Habib wrote in an elegant script on the inside flap, "I have $25,000. Set me free and the money is yours." He handed the matches back. When the guard read the message, his expression remained blank.

Habib wonder for a moment if the guard knew how to read. While he waited in silence, the guard suddenly thrust an arm through the bars and grabbed Habib's collar. The stubble on the guard's taut skin was speckled with sweat, and his eyes raced with thought. He leaned close to Habib, twisted his fingers into his hair, and jammed Habib's face against the bars. Habib cried out when the guard jabbed his nightstick into his kidney. The guard's eye sockets narrowed like buckshot. His face twitched as he backed away from the bars.

Habib heard him whisper into a mobile phone, "Hey, Jim, it's Brad. I've hooked a big one."

When he disappeared down the corridor, Habib sat down huddled in a corner. Something didn't feel right about Brad, and Habib feared the worst. He heard voices, and his eyes shot across the holding cell to the barred door. Brad, accompanied by a skinny guard, burst inside the cell, both wielding nightsticks. The commotion woke prisoners, and they sat up and rubbed their eyes groggy with sleep.

The two guards used nightsticks to beat men out of the way. When they reached Habib, the guards yanked him off the floor, handcuffed him, and dragged him down a corridor to a windowless broom closet.

Inside the small room, Brad's colleague Jim held Habib's hands behind his back, while Brad punched him in the face and stomach. Habib gritted his teeth to prevent from crying out. When Jim let him go, he crumbled to his knees. He felt pain flood his face from his shattered nose and split lower lip.

"Please, sir, don't kill me, I—" Habib said.

"Shut up, you slimy cockroach," Brad interrupted, kicking him in the ribs.

As Habib lay on the floor, Brad ripped off his jacket and pants, switched off the lights, and slammed the door. In the darkness, Habib's fingertips swept around on the cool tiled floor until he found a metal pail and mop. He pressed down on the pail to hoist himself upright.

He thought the certainties in his life had proved to be as unreal as if he had watched on al Jazeera a bomb explode in a busy subway in Madrid. For a brief moment, he knew the real enemy was a violent monster inside his soul that waited for the right time to unleash his rage upon the world.

CHAPTER 7

O N THE WAY TO CARL'S mansion on Lexington Crescent, Ryan
pictured Aimée's curvaceous body stitched with bullets and
sprawled on tangled, silky pink sheets.

The police had fastened yellow tape around Ravenscourt's
pillars at the front entrance and set up a roadblock along the
winding drive. Dog walkers milled around the wrought-iron
railings, which were guarded by uniformed officers, and television
crews had cameras outside pointed at the mansion.

Built of rusticated stone, Carl's half-timbered Tudor house had
a swimming pool and a ballroom. Behind an old chauffeur's house,
on the stone terrace, Carl waited for him.

A tall man with thinning steel-gray hair and brown eyes, Carl
nursed a mug of coffee.

"Are you all right?" Ryan asked, resting a hand on his shoulder.

"I'm okay, just terribly tired," he said.

His face looked gray with shock.

"Go home and get some rest?" Ryan said, removing his hand.

Carl stared at Ryan, his face showing both anguish and
bewilderment.

"How the devil did this happen?" he asked.

"I'll find out who did it," Ryan said.

Carl shook his head as if to get rid of his torpor.

"Why would anyone want her dead?"

"That many shots indicate extreme rage."

Ryan turned to face the back lawn, a fan of footprints in the dew, the honk of geese fading on the windless air.

"Can you account for where you were last night?" he asked.

"Surely the police don't think I could've been involved in her death."

"Carl, I'm sure you didn't do it, but the police are going to question you."

He looked crestfallen. "Why me?"

"You have the most to gain from her death."

Carl glanced up for a moment at the pale-blue stroke of watercolor sky surrounded by heavy clouds. "I suppose I do. I was at the club all evening."

"Witnesses?"

"Plenty. Even though I don't love her anymore, her death comes as a terrible shock." He clutched his heart, and his voice turned into a pain-filled whisper. "Did you have any inkling someone might want to kill her?"

"None."

"I pay you to provide me with this kind of intelligence." He paused to watch a uniformed detail seal off the back door with tape. "The security system you installed obviously didn't protect her."

"As soon as the cops leave, I'll have an updated one installed."

"Isn't that like patching holes in the chicken wire after the turkeys are loose?"

Ryan had a sinking feeling that Carl wanted to fire him.

"I'll examine the security tapes as soon as Homicide's finished with them," he said. "Do you want me off the case?"

Carl's voice softened. "If I wanted to get rid of you, you would've heard from me by now." He paused to watch two more police cars converge on the drive followed by a white forensic team van. "We need reinforcements to find Aimée's killer. Bring Joanne in on this and Marleau, if he's sober."

"Joanne's on board, and Marleau's on the wagon. Do you want us to continue investigating Moe?"

"I want you to hire another security consultant, someone familiar with the Middle East to find out more about Moe." His hooded eyes half closed as if lost in thought. "Under that easy charm, there is something about him that makes me uncomfortable." Carl thrust his hands deep into his pockets. "I can't help feeling he's in some strange way connected to Aimée's death."

The next evening, Joanne parked the Range Rover in front of a mock Elizabethan house on Cheyenne Street in a tree-lined suburb of West Fargo. She could hear dogs bark, the ruckus carried on a wind that smelled of barbecued steaks and new rain. The moon tinted the front lawn the color of pewter, the sky pinpricked with stars.

A slender young woman in a silk sari answered the doorbell.

"You must be Joanne, Ryan Moar's partner," she said, adjusting the folds of her dress. "I'm Sanjay's sister, Lucinda."

Joanne shook her firm fingers.

"Come this way," she said, leading Joanne to a mahogany-paneled dining room that smelled of curry. "My brother will be with you in a minute."

"Sanjay has an impressive résumé."

Her brown eyes opened as round as quarters. "I'm so proud of him. He rarely tells me what he's doing. I sometimes tease him for being so secretive."

"That's the hallmark of a good security consultant."

She brushed back shiny black hair with her fingertips. "I have to admit I find my brother more attractive when he surrounds himself with a whiff of mystery." She raised plucked eyebrows. "I always worry when he gravitates to trouble spots like Afghanistan or the Middle East. He did a big job last year in Dubai when he protected an important royal family."

"Has Sanjay always been in this line of work?"

She sat down next to Joanne, legs crossed, her elegant hands rested on her knee. "After graduating from Harvard, he did a stint with Britain's special services and then went into his own security and private investigation work."

Joanne heard a door open behind her, and a slight bald man, in a loose-fitting pale-blue suit and white silk shirt open at the neck, entered the room. On his feet, he wore a pair of green velvet slippers without socks.

"Don't believe everything Lucinda tells you," he said, running his hand over his forehead as shiny as a ball bearing. "She likes to brag about me."

Lucinda excused herself and closed the door.

Sanjay sat down, studying Joanne, while he hooked his thumbs in his pockets and drummed his fingertips on his thighs.

"Carl Ravenstein and I are old friends."

"He recommended we hire you to find all you can about Moe Fouzi."

"I presume, while I'm looking into Fouzi, you and Ryan focus on the hunt for whoever murdered Carl's former wife."

"That's the game plan." Joanne opened a briefcase and handed him a slim folder. "Ryan started a file on Moe. This has information on his lifestyle, his spending habits, and his credit rating. His family is a complete blank. He works for Carl as a computer analyst, but he has an extravagant lifestyle well above his middle-of-the-road income."

"Any idea about the source of this extra money flow?"

"We've explored every possible banking and investment angle and come up with blanks. Wherever he receives additional income, he keeps it well hidden. Ryan suspects he has offshore accounts in either the Cayman Islands or Zurich."

"I'll look into it." Sanjay flipped through the file. "How would you describe his personality?"

"He's a congenial young man, who guards his privacy. He doesn't have many friends, except for a few colleagues at work. He practically lives at Tamara's house."

"Do he and Tamara share the same bedroom?"

"They're inseparable."

"Wherever Moe's from, he's adapted well to his new life."

She smiled. "He wears Tommy Hilfiger suits, attends church with Tamara, and has blond streaks in his hair."

Sanjay stuck his hands in his back pockets. "Who is the real Moe Fouzi?"

"He could be almost anyone. His name is as phony as his American passport."

Sanjay leaned forward, his eyes dark and lustrous. "Have you talked to the police?"

"Ryan's had him run through the system, and he's clean. He's also contacted Ingrid Krenn of the antiterrorist unit to look into his possible links to extremists."

Sanjay made a tent out of big hands. "What did Ingrid say?"

"He's not on any lists."

"I suspect she's only done a surface check."

"Ryan's impression is she's a lightweight."

"Ingrid's probably in the dark as to what is really going on except for information that everybody in the antiterrorist business filters out from the media and on the Internet."

Joanne heard a knock, and Lucinda entered. She carried a teapot, cups, and an assortment of sweet Indian cookies on a tray. She had changed into a yellow robe tied around her waist, accentuating her hips against the silk. She wore slippers shaped like tigers.

"I've come to say good night," she said, looking hard at her brother as if to prompt a response.

"How's your headache?" he asked.

"It feels better, but I can't sleep. I keep hearing noises."

"I'm sure it's just the wind."

She appeared to Joanne vulnerable and smaller now, the light reflecting off the reddish henna streaks in her hair.

"If you're cold, turn up the heat," Sanjay said. "It looks as though it's going to rain some more to cool things further."

"Good night to you both," she said, placing the tray on a table.

She smiled at Joanne before she closed the door behind her, leaving behind a faint smell of agarwood oil.

"Lucinda is troubled by nightmares that keep her up a night," Sanjay said.

"I'm sorry they disturb her sleep."

"She often dreams about our dead parents."

Joanne stared through a crack in the blinds at the red Ford pickup she had seen earlier, parked beside the bay's island, opposite the house. In the driver's seat, she saw the outline of the driver. Then, for a moment, a convertible filled with high school students blocked her view. When the car passed, the driver had shrunk down as though he didn't want to be noticed.

She tried to dismiss suspicions about the pickup. The rain began to beat a tattoo on the skylight. She turned back to Sanjay, a pained look on her face.

"I have a bad feeling about Moe that won't go away," she said.

"I speak Arabic, and the color of my skin gives me access to the Islamic Society of the Red River Mosque," Sanjay said. He met Joanne's gaze with a pained look of his own. "There are enemies among us in places you'd never believe."

CHAPTER 8

HABIB OPENED HIS EYES AND rolled over on his back. The sour smell of stale vomit assaulted his nostrils. His fingers explored the cut on his forehead where dried blood had formed a hard crust. He ran his hands down his naked chest to his thighs and genitals. He pushed himself up on one elbow. The guards had stripped away his clothes except for his socks. He heard a click in his throat, and then he let out his breath like air escaping from an ancient tomb.

"God, protect me," he whispered.

He curled his body in a tight ball on the cool concrete floor and tried not to think about torture and death.

A few minutes later, the overhead lightbulb, covered in a protective wire mesh, snapped on, and the harsh brightness seared his eyes.

Brad's eyes had a pinched light. He tossed Habib's clothes on the floor beside him.

"I didn't find no $25,000," he said, stepping close enough to kick him in the ribs with his pointed boots. "Where is it?"

Habib remained silent.

Brad's boot went back, and Habib cringed in anticipation of another blow. "You lying about the money?"

"No, sir."

Brad lowered his boot and ran his fingers through his buzz cut. Habib scrambled to pull on his pants, shirt, and jacket.

"Where're my shoes?" he asked, trembling all over as though he suffered from malaria.

Brad handed him the loafers he had tucked behind his back.

Habib began to feel an old excitement pump him as he tugged open the left shoe's heel. He handed a wad of notes to Brad, who grabbed the money. The more he counted, the wider the grin, turning his face almost boyish in appearance.

Did his pleased look mean he would let him go? Habib's lips moved in a silent prayer.

Brad raised his hand, and instead of hitting Habib, his fingers came to rest on his holster.

"Are you going to kill me?" Habib asked, trembling.

"I could pop you, couldn't I?"

Brad took out his revolver. Habib stared at the muzzle, waiting for the finger in the trigger guard to squeeze and blast him to heaven.

He could hear his coarse breathing as he opened his palms as if to accept a blessing. Brad twisted his mouth; the overhead lights made his lips look as though he had applied purple lipstick.

In an instant, Habib noticed Brad's anger evaporate, and a broad grin crossed Brad's face. He tucked his weapon back in the holster. He counted the money again, before he pocketed the cash. "Enough for a nice down payment on a new Chevy truck."

Brad grabbed Habib's jacket collar and yanked him to his feet. Still holding him by the collar, he hauled him to the back entrance and pushed him into an alley.

"Listen, you worm, I never want to see your pisspot face again, you hear," he said.

In his haste to get away, Habib stumbled, lost his footing and rolled against a garbage can. He staggered to his feet and breathed in the smell of rotten hamburger.

To him, the air of freedom never smelled sweeter.

After Aimée Ravenstein's memorial service at St. Paul's Episcopal Church, Ryan drove to the fitness and tennis club on Brownville Avenue to meet Joanne for lunch. Beside a shady driveway women in whites played doubles on red clay tennis courts.

He was early for lunch, so he changed and went upstairs to the gym and did three sets of bench presses, curls with free weights, and fifteen weight-assisted dips. In the main workout room, rows of exercise machines stood beside a group of pumped-up men and women bodybuilders.

His eyes drifted to Jacelyn, Carl Ravenstein's fiancée. She lay on a bench at an inverted angle, her calves and ankles hooked inside two cylindrical vinyl cushions, while she raised herself towards her knees, her fingers laced behind her head. Sweat glistened on her cream-colored thighs. Her breasts, the size of small melons, strained against her Lululemon singlet.

"Well, if it isn't Carl's private dick," she said, gum snapping in her mouth as she worked out. "The police appear to be stymied by Aimée's murder. How's your investigation going?"

"I'll find out who killed her," he said.

"How can you be so confident?"

"Inevitability," he said, staring at a salamander tattooed on her lower back that appeared to dance in a provocative way above the crease of her buttocks.

"Do you have a suspect?"

"It's early in the investigation to isolate anyone in particular."

"You look tired," she said, her lips parting to reveal even, white teeth.

He grinned. "On the other hand, you look terrific."

"What does a girl have to do to deserve such a compliment?"

"Keep smiling."

She got up and climbed on a glider. Her slender, well-bronzed legs started to pump as she glanced up at a soap opera on a TV monitor.

"I've been meaning to ask you about Moe. Since he's engaged to Tamara, you must see a lot of him."

"He's a Christian, you know, born in Beirut. I like him. He's a young man who says please and thank you, which is unusual."

"Apart from impeccable manners, what else can you tell me about him?"

She stopped peddling for a moment. "Surely you don't think he's a suspect?"

"We're talking to everyone even remotely connect to Aimée."

"He works for Cole, but you probably knew that. He's a genius. He makes the computers in the house do marvelous things."

"What does he do in his spare time?"

"If he's not at work, he's courting Tamara." She chuckled. "That's an old-fashioned word, but at this snooty club I'm sure it's perfectly acceptable. They ride and play tennis."

"A love match?"

Jacelyn giggled and winked at him. "You're a funny man."

She paused from peddling to rest on the handlebars. She picked up a plastic bottle, drank Alpine water, and then pouted her lips, her forehead wrinkled in thought.

"I have something to gain from her death." Her pointed red nails clicked against the handrail as she restarted the machine by pumping her legs. "Are you going to question me?"

Beside them, a tanned young couple came into the gym and worked out on stationary bikes.

"I would like to talk to you in private," he said.

She cocked her head down at him. "I'd love to chat. Make an appointment with Bertrand, my majordomo."

Her eyes were violet from colored contact lenses, her skin shiny from exertion. He folded his hands on the handlebar and then rested his chin on top.

"You have nice hands, like those of an artist," she said.

"If I didn't know you better, I'd say you're flirting with me."

Balancing on the gliders, she leaned over to touch his cheek. Her fingertips felt cool, but the palm of her hand was damp. He could smell her perfume, a mixture of almonds and roses mingled with the scent of her sweat.

When she beamed at him, he wondered if he could have the potential to stray, something he had chosen not to recognize.

CHAPTER 9

A T THE BOATHOUSE THAT EVENING, Ryan watched raindrops form beads on the dock and the brown, dimpled surface of the river. He stepped into the rain and used his Swiss Army knife to cut ten red roses from bushes in Joanne's garden. He needed the flowers to mark the tenth anniversary of his first wife's death. He went to end of the dock and buried his face among the roses, breathing in the scent.

When she was alive, Kathy had been a spirited redhead. A decade ago, an intoxicated hit-and-run driver had knocked her down. The impact had tossed Kathy's half-conscious body into a ditch beside the road. That night, the curious driver came back, and he found her alive and soaked by the rain. He raped her. To prevent her from identifying him, he strangled her and threw her into the Red River. A jogger found her three days later, two miles downriver, her body entangled in branches. Despite an exhaustive police investigation, he and his colleagues had never found her killer.

After Kathy's death, whenever he felt a longing for her, he had searched out bars with rain-streaked windows that overlooked water. In the bars, his pregnant wife spoke to him through the rain. By trapping meaning at the bottom of an empty glass, he had discovered the rain's power allowed him to keep company with the dead.

At the end of the dock, he knelt down to place the roses in the water. He watched the flowers find the current and float north. The roses bobbed in the muddy water, and the petals, as dark red as Kathy's open lips, turned upward as if to kiss him for the last time.

After the flowers disappeared, he walked to his office, attached to the boathouse. Above the gentle murmur of rain, he heard Marleau's black Yukon roar down the drive. From the open door, Ryan watched his business partner climb out of the SUV. He wore a yellow anorak slicked with rain.

When he entered the office, Roy, who had been sleeping under the desk at Ryan's feet, barreled toward Marleau to bark and lick his hands.

"The coffee's hot," Ryan said.

"No thanks." His voice carried traces of his coureur de bois ancestors, the edges of his accent caressing the air like thick pea soup.

Marleau dried rain off his shoulders with a paper towel. "I think I'm out of my depth."

"What is it this time?"

"It's Deirdre. She's talking about us moving in together."

"She's got strong feelings for your Gallic charm, Marleau."

"Yeah, and my mother loves her poodle." He grinned at nothing, while his deep-set eyes stared out at the river through the rain-streaked windows. "You know something, we're happy together, and things have been good between us."

"Do you love her?"

"I guess so."

"What do you want, my blessing?"

"Not necessarily, but I want in on this case you're working on," he said.

"Terrific."

"No, honest, I really want to help solve this Aimée Ravenstein murder."

Ryan gave him a skeptical look. The two men had known each other for over fifteen years. Ryan still had his doubts about Marleau, the serious overdrinking, the high-stakes poker games, the brawls, the women.

When they were rookie police officers, Marleau had pulled Ryan to safety in the middle of intense gang cross fire. Both of them had received slight wounds. Ryan could never forget Marleau had saved his life, and the incident had cemented an unbreakable bond between them.

"Haven't touched a drink in twenty-five days," Marleau said, taking in Ryan's look of approval.

"I was thinking more about the work being hazardous for your noble Métis hide."

"I've never had a problem with that."

His hair had the black sheen of silk, the tips curled and damp around his neck. His pockmarked face softened as he waited for an answer.

"What about the fact you're taking on this new living arrangement?" Ryan said. "Are you sure you're up to handling major domestic adjustments?"

"Right now I feel I can handle anything."

Habib drank for a few minutes at a public water fountain, wiped his cracked lips, and then sat down on a park bench. He slipped off his right shoe as though he needed to remove a stone. Inside the heel, he found rolled-up dollars, a VISA credit card, and a driver's license for a Roger Bloom from Vancouver as well as one for a Jack Mercier with a Fargo address. He stood up and then stumbled half a block to the Alamo Motel he had seen advertised on a billboard.

As he came closer, he was relieved that the motel's mock-Spanish walls had peeling paint that made the single-story structure look shopworn and shabby—a place that wouldn't ask too many question about his lack of luggage. The parking lot was empty except for a few late-model trucks and sedans. He hoped the lack of travelers meant the motel might take in even the most derelict-looking customer.

Inside the cramped reception area, he pulled up his jacket collar to obscure his bruised and sunburned neck. A young desk clerk eyed him as he shuffled to the reception desk.

"Do you have a room?" he asked, hunching his shoulders.

"Let me check," the clerk said, moving a mouse to activate a computer screen.

"Do you have any luggage, sir?" he asked, peering at him closer.

Habib avoided eye contact and shook his head.

"Where are you from?" the red-haired boy asked.

"I'm an American. My name is Jack Mercier."

"Do you have a driver's license, Mr. Mercier?"

"Yes sir," he said.

He handed it to him.

The clerk looked at the license for a few seconds. He then told Habib to wait so he could check on a vacancy. Habib swung around to stare at the motel's neon sign that advertised rooms available.

It crossed Habib's mind that the boy could be contacting the police. For the moment, he was too exhausted to do anything except watch the fresh-faced teen talk on the phone in hushed tones.

What was the boy saying? Things were getting out of hand; he was making too many mistakes.

"You're in luck, mister," the receptionist said with a toothy grin. "We have a vacancy."

"Thank you," Habib said, hoping that after this awkward exchange the rest would be easy.

The lanky teenager continued to gawk at his rumpled suit and bloodstains on his shirt. While filling in the visitor form, he cursed under his breath for not buying new clothes.

"Any vehicle, sir?" he asked, scratching acne at the corner of his hooked-down mouth.

"My car has mechanical problems."

"Well, you're in luck. Alex's Shell across the street has a tow truck."

"Thanks, I'll get cleaned up first, get some rest, and then I'll walk over."

The boy glanced at his watch. "I'd go right away. They close in half an hour."

"Enough time for me to take a quick shower."

"How will you be paying for this room? It's fifty-five a night."

Habib handed him the money. After giving him a receipt, the boy swept a lock of hair that had fallen in front of his eyes. "I'll need the license number of your vehicle."

Habib pretended to cough and turned away to glance at the parking lot. He gave him the number off a pickup truck.

"What? That's my Chevy's number," the boy said, his eyes wide in panic.

He lunged for the phone and punched numbers.

Habib needed to act now. He looked for some kind of weapon in among the travel brochures, soft-drink machines, and tourist knickknacks.

He spotted a half-empty glass Coke bottle on the counter and grabbed it. He raised the bottle and smashed the boy's forehead. The boy cried out in surprise and dropped the phone. He tried to run, but Habib jumped him from behind and gripped him tightly around the throat. At the same time, Habib shoved the teenager's head hard against the counter, crushing bones in his nose. Habib raised the boy's head slightly, slammed his mouth against the counter edge, and heard his front teeth break.

The boy screamed and slumped to the floor, breathing through his mouth like a landed trout. His unbroken teeth stood out like pink headstones. Habib saw a whipped expression on his blood-streaked face. When the boy tried to drag himself away, Habib pressed his shoe on his narrow chest, pinning him. The boy's wide eyes stared at Habib loaded with fear.

Habib longed to have his sharp bedouin knife in his hand. Instead, he broke the mouth of the Coke bottle against a windowsill. He kneeled beside the boy, grabbed his hair, twisted his head to expose his neck, and ground the bottle's jagged edge into his throat until he hooked the jugular. As the razor-sharp glass sank into his soft flesh, the boy's scream ended in a gurgle of blood.

Habib scanned the parking lot, relieved no customers were checking in. The boy's blood had soaked into his suit, so he stripped to his underwear and used paper towels to wipe his hands, face, and hair. Inside a locker, he found the boy's clothes. He had to use a pair of scissors he found in a drawer to widen the waist of the jeans. The T-shirt fit tight around his chest. Inside the dead boy's pockets, he found a set of keys to the truck.

He climbed into the rusty pickup and drove down side streets to the outskirts where he stopped at a run-down used-car dealership. From a thin-faced sales representative with a hooknose, like a bird's beak, he bought a secondhand Honda for cash with no questions asked. After stealing plates off a parked sedan, he drove the Honda until he found a graveyard and pulled up beside a row of neglected tombstones.

For a few moments, he rested his head in his big hand on the steering wheel. In his lifetime, Habib had killed a number of men and a few women, but he never felt comfortable when he killed young people with long lives ahead of them.

Inside the car's protective cocoon, he felt secure for the first time for many weeks, and he fell asleep almost at once.

CHAPTER 10

T HE NEXT MORNING, RYAN'S MAXIMA rattled across a cattle
guard and down a white shale road until he arrived at a
windbreak of poplars. Beside him, Marleau Belanger looked out
at the yellow petals and black inner rings of ripening sunflowers.
His jaw had the sharp definition of a knife, a feature that had made
many female hearts beat faster.

"Ricky's a petty thief, but he doesn't strike me as being capable
of killing Aimée for trinkets," Ryan said.

"We'll find out soon enough," Marleau said, his hands stuffed
into the pockets of his jeans.

The gravel road ended at a bend in the road. Rows of greenhouses
stood behind a faded Lily Vale Home and Garden sign. On a
wooden deck in front of a trailer, a white-haired man sat under a
sunshade, writing in an accounting book.

Ryan parked the car, and they walked in between rows of
gladioli. The fields rippled with blooms of yellow, red, and blue.

They headed to a young man hoeing weeds. Ricky Gomanche
wore a stained white T-shirt with the sleeves cut away. Perhaps
sensing shadows behind him, he stopped work, straightened up,

and turned around. When he saw them, he looked disappointed, but his expression soon changed to irritation.

"How the hell did you find me?" he asked, picking at a mosquito bite on his cheek.

"Hello, Ricky, I never figured you'd take up horticulture," Ryan said.

"I thought skimming pool scum would be the closest you ever came to plant life," Marleau said.

A wide-brimmed hat shadowed Ricky's face, and he twisted the toe of one of his runners into the rich topsoil. "If you're cops, I've told you everything I know."

"We're private investigators."

"Then I don't have to talk to you," he said, flexing a barbed wire tattoo encircling a well-rounded bicep.

Marleau stepped closer. "We want to know about your relationship with Aimée Ravenstein."

Ricky's expression softened. "A good lady. A real tragedy." Ricky turned away and continued to dig in the flower bed. "I got nothin' to say to you." His hoe extracted a dandelion by the roots. "You got no right to harass me."

Ryan pursed his lips and turned to his partner. "Marleau, I think it's time to shake Ricky's tree and see what falls out."

Marleau removed his sunglasses and squinted up at the bright sky. "How'd you like a punch in the old eyeball?"

Ricky laughed in a nervous, jerky fashion. "What, oh yeah?" He glanced in the direction of the trailer and lowered his voice. "What's Lan going to say when he sees me talking to a couple of guys who look like cops?"

"Don't worry about Lan." Ryan waved, and the white-haired man waved back. "The general and I go way back … way back."

Ricky took off his gloves, and his hands looked soft and smooth despite the dirt stains. He scratched his hairless chest through his shirt. "I got work to do."

"Sure you have. What made you disappear in such a hurry? You forgot to leave a forwarding address," Ryan said.

"I wanted to get out of town for a while; that's all."

"If you've nothing to hide, why give up an easy job where most you ever do is pick up a few rays poolside?" Marleau asked.

Ricky put an unlit cigarette in his mouth. The loose soil on his fingers made brown marks on the paper.

"Do you two guys usually work together, or is he some kind of PI in training?" he asked, glaring at Marleau.

"Watch your lip, boy," Marleau replied.

Ricky lit the cigarette, puffed, and rested with his hands on the hoe, while smoke curled up into his face.

"Did you have anything to do with her death?" Marleau asked.

"No way. Carl Ravenstein wanted her dead, not me," he said.

Marleau moved two steps closer, started to talk, stopped, and began again. "Didn't you envy Mrs. Ravenstein for having so much money?"

Ricky looked up at seagulls circling in the sky forming quick-moving shadows on the warm earth. Red veins threaded the whites of his eyes, and he kept blinking his large black lashes.

"You wanted it all, didn't you, Ricky? Is that why you helped yourself to some of her things?" Marleau continued.

"That's a lie."

"The police found the loot in your apartment above the garage."

"She gave me that stuff."

"Tell us the truth," Ryan said. "We know for certain you nicked some of her jewelry."

The heat went to his face, but he remained silent.

"Did you steal something valuable and murder her to cover your tracks?" he continued. "For example, you filched her collection of ancient Greek coins."

Ricky remained silent.

"We found out you tried to sell the coins on eBay," Ryan continued.

Ricky brought his right hand to his forehead and squeezed his temple. "So what if I took them? She ain't gonna miss those coins now."

"That attitude will get you a prison sentence."

"I hate guys like you."

"Oh?"

"Is there anything wrong with wanting a good life?"

"Most people work hard to live well."

Ricky sighed. "Right now, I swelter every night in a hot, stinking attic above Lan's shed."

"You break my heart, Ricky," Marleau said. "I think you killed Aimée, but I can't prove it … yet." He leaned forward and lowered his voice. "Did you and Aimée have a lovers' falling-out that went pear-shaped?"

Ricky started to rock on the balls of his feet. "I never killed her."

"But you were shagging her," Marleau said.

Ricky remained silent. He turned back to glance at Lan, who sat scraping out the bowl of a pipe with a penknife.

Marleau grabbed his right arm and twisted it behind his back to force his head down. Ricky spat his cigarette out, and the butt landed in a furrow.

"You must've been pretty special for her to put out for the likes of you," he said, squeezing his arm until he squealed in pain.

"Okay. She liked me," he said, breathing hard, his face red.

"We talked to Mrs. Vandels, Aimée's housekeeper," Marleau said, easing on the pressure to allow him to straighten up. "She claimed Aimée threatened to fire you."

When he released him, Ricky rubbed circulation back into his wrist.

"If you tell us the truth, we're prepared to overlook your light fingers. Do we have an understanding, Ricky?" Ryan asked.

Ricky leaned over to spit. The wind was hot and smelled of humus.

"I couldn't get any sleep last night," he said. "I had a feeling something ugly would land on me this morning, and I was right."

"Did Aimée have visitors on the day she died?" Ryan said.

"I didn't see anyone."

Marleau faced Ricky, a hard light in his eyes.

"You're lying," he said, driving his fist into Ricky's mouth, snapping his head back as though it were on a spring.

Ricky tumbled onto the flower bed, his knees drawn up in front of him, his face gray with shock, his mouth a round O of incredulity.

Ryan stood in front of Marleau, pressing him back with the palms of his hands. "Back off," he said.

Ricky staggered as he got to his feet and blotted blood from his upper lip with his T-shirt. "You're worse than the damn cops. You all hit first and don't ever listen."

"We're listening," Ryan said.

Ricky ran his tongue over his swollen lip. "Okay, there was this dude who drives a Caddy. He goes over to the gazebo where Aimée is having her afternoon Gibson. After a bit, he starts to yell at her. Then she slaps him, and he hits her back so hard that she flies off and gets tangled in a rose bush."

"What was the argument about?"

"I don't know."

"Can you describe her visitor?"

"He was tall, wore his black hair greased down, and he had on a classy suit."

"Does the name Aaron Hubbard mean anything to you?"

"Sure, that's him." Ricky hung his head for a moment and then met Ryan's gaze. "He said if I told anyone about the argument he'd skin me alive."

While Habib spent the next day driving north on dusty back roads, an odd-looking young man was making his way west on a Greyhound bus bound for Fargo. He had thick black hair tied in a ponytail swept back over his small ears that fitted tight against his scalp. His long beard looked bushy and unkempt. He stretched out his long legs as far as he could and drank from a Coke can, a bland light in his eyes and a half smile on his thin lips. He glanced now and again at the dark outline of thick pines and granite outcrops flashing by in the twilight.

At Minneapolis, the bus stopped and a teenage girl with ruby-red lips climbed onboard. She sat down beside him and flipped pages of *People* magazine. She soon became aware that he watched her with an intense stare that made her fidget. She glanced up and down the aisle for an alternate seat, but the bus was full.

She twisted the side of her mouth and asked him why he kept gawking at her.

"Your face interests me. You wouldn't happen to be a fashion model?" he said.

"Who me? You must be joking." She laughed in a nervous, erratic fashion. "I've never heard that line before."

"My name's Arrak Ahmed," he said, offering his hand.

He shook her fingers, cold and moist as though covered in hand cream.

"Jennifer Rigaux," she said, her eyes glancing at skin peeling off his forehead. "You look as though you've been in the sun."

"Eastern Afghanistan."

"Doing what?"

"Training in the mountains."

She pressed her hand against her lips to curb her anxiety.

"With a name like Arrak, I thought you might be—"

"A terrorist?" he interrupted. "I am Muslim, but you have nothing to fear from me." He unzipped the front of his leather jacket so she could see his waist. "I don't carry explosives strapped to my gut."

She took a quick glance at his empty lap, his back straight, his profile etched against the glare from the setting sun.

"I suppose you're wondering if I've ever considered becoming a martyr, what we call a *shahid*," he continued. He took a sip from his Coke can. "Do you find the whole idea of blowing oneself up difficult to understand?"

"Why would anyone want to kill themselves and innocent bystanders?" she asked, her eyes settling on his face.

"It's a way to gain the respect of your community; think of it on the same level as owning a home."

She rolled up the magazine and squeezed it between her hands. "Isn't it about the promise of beautiful virgins?"

He parted his lips in a lopsided grin. "A martyr has other pleasures to look forward to than seventy-two virginal beauties. You see, anyone who is a martyr can mediate the entrance into heaven of family members and close friends. As long as they live, they'll be honored and, in the second life, assured of entering paradise."

He made a grinding noise in his throat. Heat rose out from the neckband of his black T-shirt as if his faith stoked the fires of his soul.

"You must understand, Jennifer, I am a soldier, preparing myself to make this ultimate sacrifice," he said.

"It all sounds so senseless."

"It's not; it's cool. If I'm martyred, this is my victory. If God keeps me alive, I keep fighting, and I'll be rewarded. So whether it is this life or the second life, I'm always going to be a winner." He pressed his tapered fingers together. "I bet that's something your parish priest can't offer."

His last comment stopped her cold. She cocked her head and glanced into his blue eyes. "I don't mean to be nosy, but you don't look as though you're from an Arab country."

He remained silent, taking his time to answer her. "I'm American-born, and the truth is I've never been farther east than Boston. I've no intention of being a martyr."

"That's a relief."

Arrak looked around the bus at the other passengers and grinned. "Are you traveling to Fargo, Jennifer?"

"I'm going to visit my parents in Moorhead."

He chuckled. "I suspected you're a good Catholic girl. Are you a regular Mass attendee?"

She found his question intrusive, and she turned away from his unyielding gaze.

"Do you ever seek comfort from the confessional, Jennifer?" he asked.

She looked at him sideways, her lips rigid, her brow wrinkled.

"I didn't mean to embarrass you by asking about your religion," he said. "I suppose you're wondering if I was once a Catholic. When I was a small boy, I lived in one of them orphanages." His face flushed as though he had a fever, and he kept jiggling one knee. "Sister Constance, my classroom teacher, loved to beat me with a cane. She was good at twisting arms and stomping toes. Once when she thought I insulted the Virgin Mary, she made me wash my mouth out with soap and water."

"Is that why you turned to Islam?" she asked.

Instead of answering, he gripped her wrist. When she tried to pull away, he tightened his fingers.

"Then she made me swallow the filthy water," he whispered.

"Let me go," she said. "Please, you're hurting me."

"I bet it don't hurt as much as one of Sister's Indian burns," he said, releasing her.

She pulled away from him, her eyes clouding over.

"I promise I won't touch you," he said, gazing at the red mark on her wrist.

"If you do that again, I'll report you to the driver," she said.

He pressed his fist to his mouth. When he turned to her, his eyes glowed with such intensity that she pushed herself up from her seat, her thin arms shaking.

"Where are you going?" he asked.

"To the bathroom," she said.

He spoke as if he could barely contain his delight in teasing her. "Don't forget your rosary."

After washing her hands and face in the small sink at the back of the bus, Jennifer examined her pale cheeks in the mirror. His intense eyes had terrified her. When she calmed down, she opened the bathroom door. As she crept down the aisle, she spotted a roly-poly man wearing a Bavarian hat.

He turned to smile at her.

"Do you mind changing places with me?" she said.

"Is that bearded man bothering you, miss?" he whispered.

"He makes me feel uncomfortable."

"I'd be glad to switch," he said, getting up and offering her his seat.

She sank into the seat with a sigh. She watched him lumber across the aisle and plunk down next to Arrak. Jennifer sat in the semidarkness and listened to the air conditioner's faint hum. She opened her purse, and her frantic fingers sought the familiar comfort of her beads; her lips moved in silent prayer.

CHAPTER 11

THE NEXT AFTERNOON, JOANNE FILLED the Range Rover at a gas station on Main Avenue and tried Aaron Hubbard's home number on her cell phone. The line was busy. She gave up trying and drove to his house in a cul-de-sac off Country Club Boulevard. The property had gray tile over stucco and a double garage with a mounted basketball hoop over the door. When she rang the doorbell, she heard the distinct cheer of Bison football fans at a game telecast.

After waiting a few minutes, Aaron opened the door. He wore an unbuttoned yellow cardigan and tan slacks, and he had a can of Budweiser in his hand.

"Joanne," he said, grinning. "This is an unexpected pleasure."

"They told me at your office that you'd taken the day off," she said, following him into a carpeted living room.

He offered her a beer, and she declined. He twisted the top off a fresh one, turned down the volume on a fifty-two-inch plasma television, and sat down on a leather couch. Joanne removed a pile of men's magazines off a stiff-backed chair and sat opposite him.

"So what's new in the rent-a-private-eye business?" he asked, resting his hands on the back of his head that looked out of place on his narrow shoulders.

"You know, the same old routine, an heiress kidnapped here, a rogue investment banker arrested there. The rest of the time, when we aren't dodging rocket launchers and scud missiles, we soak up sun on our deck."

"I heard you'd bought the Hemingways' house on Red River Road. I bet that set you back well over seven hundred thousand. Is Carl paying you a hefty retainer, so you can keep up the mortgage payments?"

Joanne ignored him and leaned down to stroke a calico cat curled up beside her chair.

"Where's Helen?" she asked.

"She's at the cottage with the kids."

He lifted the can and studied the opening before he took a drink. His pale skin had a rosy tint as though he had soaked up ultraviolet rays without sunscreen.

"What's up?" he asked.

"We're investigating Aimée's murder," she said.

"What bothers me is that there is no robbery, no motive, no clues, a senseless shooting of a defenseless woman. After her death, I was in shock. In what way can I help find her killer?"

She knew Aaron too well to be fooled by his offer to cooperate. He was an opportunist, a smooth operator who had started his career selling high-yielding bonds and moved on to hedge funds. During Ravenwest's takeover heyday, he became Carl's protégé and hatchet man.

"On the night Aimée was killed, you told the police you were home all evening. Can Helen corroborate your story?"

"She will."

Joanne leaned forward to snag his eyes. "The police bought it; I don't. I think you killed her or else you know who did."

His hooded, birdlike eyes focused on her face, his nostrils dilated at some smell in the stale air.

"How dare you accuse me of her murder?" he said. "That's such a ridiculous charge; it's laughable."

The sun filtered through a cactus on the windowsill and reflected off the polished hardwood floor like a cluster of amber needles.

"We've talked to the detectives heading up the investigation," she said, bouncing her fingertips on the top of her notebook as though playing a concerto. "They regard you as a likely suspect."

"They can't be serious," he said, twisting his mouth into a snarl. "Those two detectives didn't strike me as having much between the ears. Dave Marriot went through three wives in fifteen years. Following a nervous breakdown, his partner, Philip Rodgers, had to take a year off work." Aaron's voice took on a hard edge. "Neither of them is capable of doing a competent job investigating this case."

Joanne's shoulders stiffened; a determined look crossed her face. "You got off lightly, Aaron."

"What the hell does that mean?"

"The police detectives investigating this case aren't exactly stellar."

"That's no reason for you to come after me. The police confirmed my alibi."

Joanne stared through cracks of sunlight through a blind. When she spoke, it was with an exaggerated calm. "If you didn't kill her, maybe you know someone who hired the shooter."

Aaron tipped up some beer. "You're being absurd if you think I'd even know the assassin."

She sat back and spread out her hands. "Her killing had all the earmarks of a professional." She examined her notes. "Two shots to the head, the remainder, three to be exact, penetrated the body. A .25 and silenced so the shots wouldn't wake the servants."

Aaron raked his thin hair. "Surely, apart from me, you must have some other leads to follow up on."

"We do. Are you still bitter about Carl firing you for incompetence?"

"I've moved on."

"You've been most fortunate." Joanne waited a moment and finally spoke with some harshness. "After Carl took a hiatus from his company, Ravenwest welcomed you back to bigger and better things, thanks to an unexpected benefactor."

"Cole made me vice president of publishing, so what?"

"To get the job, what did you do? Stroll in, say hi to the troops, go back to your old office, and break out the champagne—"

Aaron butted in. "It wasn't that simple."

"I bet it raised a few corporate eyebrows." Joanne leaned forward. "Why do you think Cole gave you this plum position?"

He smiled at the corner of his mouth, a glint in his gray eyes. "He values my expertise and counsel."

"Don't tell me everything wasn't quite right with the company and only you could fix it."

Aaron took another pull at his beer can. "That sums it up."

Joanne looked up at him, shaking her head. "Carl may have resigned, but he'll be back. As soon as he returns, he'll maneuver to have you ousted."

"I'm not afraid of him."

"Don't underestimate the precarious nature of your situation," she said. She felt uneasy being in the same room with him drinking, but she hoped the beer might loosen his lips.

"Are you and Cole so tight that you feel safe as long as he heads the company?" she said.

"We've an understanding."

"I'm sure you have. I think you've some sort of stranglehold on him that forced him to hand you this senior position on a silver plate."

His penetrating glance made Joanne uneasy. He got to his feet, found his balance, and staggered over to Joanne's chair.

"Are you telling me—?"

Joanne strained to keep her face impassive. "The day before she died, you and Aimée had a heated squabble. What was that about?" she asked.

70

His frown grew more pronounced. A dog barked in the backyard, the call taken up by another before the ruckus died down.

"A witness at the house saw you two quarrelling," she said.

He belched and tapped the beer can with his fingernails. "You've talked to the pool guy."

"You bet we have."

"Look, there's been a misunderstanding about what really happened."

"I'm listening."

"Let's say it was a disagreement between friends."

"It went a great deal further than a mild spat. You hit her so hard you made her fall."

He settled back in his chair and covered his eyes with his hands. "I didn't mean to lose my temper."

"What made you so angry?"

"Aimée wanted me to stay away from her son."

"Did she think you're a bad influence?"

Aaron lifted the can and shook the contents before drinking. "I haven't tried to manipulate him, if that's what you're implying. All I've done is to show the boy the ropes of running the business."

"There must be more to it than that. What made you both so overheated?"

Aaron finished his gulp and slowly put the can down. He hit the top of the coffee table with the flat of his hand. "Look, it was nothing. Don't get all paranoid about this."

"Why did she object to you socializing with her son?" she asked, straining to keep her voice even.

"Occasionally, after work, we'd go out for a few beers, all perfectly harmless and aboveboard."

"Did she object to you introducing him to some of your friends, perhaps?"

"Sure, we'd run into my business contacts. At other times, I'd initiate meetings to help him build his network."

"Would Paul Sinise be one of those—?"

He interrupted. "I resent your insinuation that I'd have anything to do with that cretin."

"The Sinise brothers are precisely your kind of contact."

"Come off it, Joanne; that's a low blow."

"Is it? Is that why you and the Sinises had her killed?"

He tilted the can, foam frothing up to the opening then collapsing. "That's a load of crap."

"I think your quarrel had nothing to do with your dubious friendship with Cole. You more likely killed her over the way she planned to change the distribution of her Ravenwest stock in her will."

"I don't know what you're talking about."

"Isn't it true she gave Cole some shares but not nearly enough to give him control? The balance went in trust to the humane society?"

A tense silence gathered until he got up and propped himself against the mantelpiece, covered his face with his hands for a moment, and breathed hard. "I'm getting tired of your innuendos and false accusations."

Joanne took this as a cue to leave.

"Thank you for your time, Aaron," she said as she slipped out of the chair and headed for the front door.

Habib went for a stroll in Vermillion, Nebraska, until he found a quiet restaurant in a strip mall with an outdoor patio. He sat under a Cinzano umbrella that popped in the breeze. Clouds marbled the paving stones with shadows and light. The brief decoded email from his wife, Zahara, disturbed him.

Who had his disgraced son under surveillance? Zahara had found out from Arrak that Mohammed had someone watching him. If this man tailing him made the connection between Mohammed and his mother, Habib's plans could start to unravel. Habib decided to risk calling Zahara on his iPhone.

When he heard Zahara's low voice at the other end, he asked, "Who's spying on Mohammed?"

He felt a warm sensation as he imagined he was looking into her dark eyes he had once called twin pools of passion.

"He's private, not connected to the police or a government security agency," she said. Her voice sounded thick and husky as though she was a heavy smoker, which she wasn't.

He traced his fingertips over rough scars on his cheeks where the desert sun had burned his skin. "Why is he interested in my son?"

"I'm not sure."

Habib felt rising heat flood his face. "How did you discover him?"

"When Arrak drove by Mohammed's condo, he spotted this same SUV on several occasions parked across the street."

He snapped his finger at a sullen male server.

When the overweight teenager with a ring in his nose appeared at his side, Habib said, "Bring me a coffee, black."

When the server left, Habib gazed at the cell phone as though it were radioactive. He scanned patrons in the restaurant to see if anyone was watching him. No one glanced his way or looked suspicious.

"He will have to be eliminated," he whispered. Habib dreaded the thought that Zahara's network could be compromised. He added, "Has someone betrayed us?"

"I don't think so. Otherwise enemy agents would have swarmed over the ranch and arrested us."

He paused while the server came back with the coffee. Habib dumped three sugar packets in the cup and then drank some dark roast to slacken dryness building up in his throat.

"Is Mohammed still infatuated with this American woman?"

"He's engaged to her."

"What hold does this female devil have on him?"

"She dresses like a harlot."

Habib clenched his fist and drummed it against his forehead. He heard her clear her throat.

"He works for his future father-in-law," she said.

"Is there any way you can extract him?"

"He's lost to us."

"I'm eventually going to need his help."

He heard her sharp intake of breath. "Oh, Habib, please don't—"

"We have to make sacrifices," he interjected.

He was quiet for a short time, until he heard his wife's cough.

"Habib, please don't blame me. I have tried—"

Habib rattled change in his pocket. "What's he done with the money I gave him for education?"

"He spent it on a new Porsche, a condo, and a closetful of fifteen-hundred-dollar suits."

Habib's mouth hooked down at the corners.

He heard her groan. "He no longer attends the mosque."

"Does he still see you, to pay his respect?"

"He only visits on rare occasions. He is ashamed of me."

He pressed his fingers to his lips, and he felt moisture build up in the corners of his eyes. What manner of woman had seduced the boy? How could his youngest son, the light of his life, reject his mother and his beloved faith?

His eyes fixed on a plump blonde-haired woman, who sipped a cola drink through a straw. He could see her chest rise and fall as her cheeks hollowed when she drank. He squeezed his eyes shut until her image disappeared from his mind.

"I travel closer to you every day," he said.

He paused to blow his nose. He could hear the tinkle of bracelets she always wore.

"The good news is Arrak is here," she said.

Habib wiped little beads of sweat off his brow with the back of his hand.

He breathed in hard. "With Arrak at my side, anything is possible."

CHAPTER 12

RYAN SENSED RAIN WOULD SOON come to soothe the parched fields. The air, swollen with humidity and dampness, seemed charged with electricity. When the light changed, he watched Sanjay cross Main Avenue; Sanjay's trained eyes studied pedestrians and the stream of cars, buses, and trucks. Sanjay paused at the entrance of Momma Theresa's to glance up and down the avenue.

When he spotted Ryan seated at a patio table, he waved but didn't smile, his face rigid, his complexion pale. He looked worn out, as though he hadn't slept well.

Sanjay eased himself into a wooden chair opposite Ryan, and Ryan asked, "So who beat you up?"

Sanjay tried to smile. "That obvious is it? I thought I'd disguised my fatigue pretty well."

"You look exhausted."

"It's really frustrating." Sanjay glanced over his shoulder. "I can't shake the feeling I'm being watched by a consummate professional. I spotted him once but lost him." He sat back, yawned, and rubbed bloodshot eyes. "I've tried doubling back, going in circles, but he managed to take off without me seeing his face or the license number of his pickup."

A waiter greeted Sanjay like an old friend, and for an instant, Sanjay's face relaxed into a jovial smile. Ryan ordered a steak sandwich, and Sanjay asked for pepperoni pizza and iced Oolong tea.

After the food arrived, Sanjay leaned forward. "I should've seen you sooner," he said, drinking his tea and stirring the ice at the bottom of the glass. "It's been a hectic few days." His face froze in a frown. "On the surface, Moe appears to be a regular guy, genuinely fond of Tamara. He works hard for her dad's company. Although he claims to be Lebanese, a Christian fleeing from the civil war, in reality, he is no such person. For the most part, a phone tap in his condo recorded pillow talk, but others calls have been coming from a woman who sounds like his mother." Sanjay took some photos out of a manila envelope and fanned them in front of him. "I believe this woman outside his condo is his mother." Sanjay glanced over his shoulder before he slipped the photos back inside the envelope. "She is Syrian, and her name is Mazita al-Battar, which is not her real one. She is from Damascus and trained as a microbiologist at the Sorbonne. As late as last summer, she now lives somewhere on a ranch outside of Fargo."

"Have you found the ranch's location?"

"Not yet." He used his forefinger and thumb to brush down his trim salt-and-pepper moustache. "Mazita's covered her track well. She's a live one all right, planning something quite different from the usual terrorist approach to attack infrastructure projects and scare as many people as possible by blowing up things like buses, subways, and underground fuel-storage tanks." Sanjay bit into his pizza, holding the crust with the tapered hands of a pianist. "A few months ago, Mazita used a Chase bank card to buy night-vision goggles, body armor, and high-tech military equipment from a National Guard turncoat at the Fraine Barracks in Bismarck."

The rain held off to leave the air swollen and heavy with heat. A truck passed the restaurant, belched black smoke, and caused a vibration that rattled wineglasses on tables.

"How did you find out about her?" Ryan asked, the humidity making him feel as if spiders had crawled inside his shirt.

"From sources in Damascus and by searching the desks and computers of local imams, but the Internet is my main conduit for information." He rolled back the sleeve of his shirt to check the time. Not a streak of blue showed in the dung-gray sky. "One stroke of good luck is I'm close to breaking her code, a coded language derived from Islamic theology and history. This is how she signals and reacts to directions within her network."

"How do you determine whether they're real or bogus?" Ryan asked, his hands damp with sweat.

"She uses a set of fingerprints and symbols to identify statements as authoritative." Sanjay paused to emphasize what he was about to say. "It's her husband we should be looking out for. He's a particularly fierce fanatic, a recruiter of disenfranchised and sociopathic misfits."

"Do you know his name?"

"His nickname is Barbar the Pilot."

"The kind that flies into buildings?"

Sanjay's lips cracked a smile. "He grew up in Damascus, moved to Kabul, and speaks fluent English. He's tall, asthmatic, the son of a cleric. At one time, he acted as a link in a chain of al-Qaeda operatives providing the leadership with valuable data. He then fell out with bin Laden, quit the network, and went underground."

"Is he known to the intelligence community?"

"At present, there's no price on his head. He works only with close associates and has allegiance to no one." Sanjay narrowed his eyes and twisted his head. "Did you hear that?"

Ryan eyed patrons in the restaurant. He then squinted out along the avenue at the midday traffic.

"What is it?" he asked.

"Thunder." Sanjay waved to the waiter, who added more tea to his glass. As soon as the waiter left, he said, "After the fall of the Taliban, the radical threat shifted from al-Qaeda to a growing number of splinter groups, including Barbar the Pilot, the founder of one of them known as Winds of Death. They've so far claimed credit for the bombing of a synagogue in Chicago and blowing up a statue of the Virgin Mary in St. Paul."

"Why destroy religious symbols?"

"God only knows what goes on in the minds of these madmen." Sanjay paused to look around at the traffic jammed up in the avenue, a jumpy wariness clinging to him like a winding sheet. "For some time, I've been skeptical about this so-called brigade, and I doubted its existence. I believed it may be a bunch of creepy wannabes, until I learned Barbar the Pilot had entered the States illegally via the Mexican border. At present, he uses a forged passport, and I suspect he's on his way to hook up with Mazita."

When the sun came out, a white orb in a windless sky, Ryan felt heat bounce off the concrete sidewalk like a blast furnace.

"Shouldn't we alert the authorities?" Ryan asked.

"That's not an option. If Moe finds out we're aware of his connection to Barbar, he could warn his mother, and then she'll burrow deeper into the woodwork." A thin sheen of sweat formed on Sanjay's temples, and he wiped it off with the back of his hands. "If that happens, Mazita will change codes, and we'll never find what she's planning to do next." His eyes narrowed. "The uncomfortable truth is that the CIA hasn't been able to unearth all the al-Qaeda operatives in this country. Judging by the amount of military hardware stolen, Mazita's into a meltdown for a major attack. I don't know her target, but she's started recruiting native-born Americans who have converted to Islam. Have you ever heard of the name Omar Yahiye Gadahn?"

"No, I haven't."

"He is an American who wound up joining al-Qaeda. According to the chatter, he's hooked up with Mazita. Omar's life is one of those strange trips that only an odd melding of the 1990s counterculture and the Internet can produce. As a kid, he became obsessed with heavy metal demonic music. He then converted to Islam and hired on as a security guard at a Minneapolis Islamic center. It's not clear what happened to him after that."

"Shouldn't we share this information with Ingrid Krenn?"

"The problem is she thinks I'm nuts. Right now, the feds are preoccupied investigating several prominent Islamic institutes and charities. Agents are looking for evidence that the organizations are involved in possible terrorism funding. They aren't paying much attention to moles."

"What's Mazita's money source?"

"She has access to funds offshore in Caracas." A muscle twitched below his eye. When he spoke, it was with an exaggerated calm. "The reason why Mazita isn't a household name is she works under deep cover, but she's probably one of the most dangerous terrorists alive."

CHAPTER 13

As Arrak drove Habib's rental Buick up to the double gates of Carl Ravenstein's mansion, Habib tugged the light-blue chador down below his knees. Habib had a reputation for being a master of disguises, so dressing as a traditional Afghan woman came easy to him. Under the grill of the thin, ropelike fabric that crisscrossed in front of his face, he paused to blow his beaky nose into a handkerchief. Habib had arrived in Fargo ten days ago, and he had decided to stay in a safe house in the city until the time for the attack was imminent.

"May I speak to Moe, please?" Arrak asked into the speaker box.

"Who shall I say is calling?" a girl's voice replied.

"Galina el Adnan."

"One moment, I'll let you in."

Eye shadow had made Habib's eyes tear, and he hoped the mascara hadn't smudged. He tensed when a blonde girl in a yellow two-piece swimsuit unlocked the gates. He frowned at a ring in her belly button supported by a diamond pendent that jiggled when she walked.

At the open car window, the girl smiled and offered her hand. "Tamara Ravenstein, I'm Moe's fiancée," she said.

"Galina," Habib said, grasping her outstretched fingers.

He hoped she wouldn't feel the roughness of his skin.

While Arrak in a chauffeur's uniform crawled down the drive, Habib kept an eye on Tamara as she relocked the gates. She reminded him of the nearly nude women he had seen on Beirut's beaches. After Arrak parked beside a sculptured hedge, Tamara led Habib to the swimming pool. He followed her at a slow pace, adopting the shuffle of a middle-aged woman.

He tried not to think about meeting Mohammed. He knew his desperate gamble could backfire. Once his son saw through his disguise, Habib anticipated an immediate rejection of his proposal to bring Mohammed back into his family's orbit.

After his son's initial shock, he anticipated tense silences between them, a sound louder than a scream.

Beside the path, he heard sprinklers spray fine particles of water in a wide arc over emerald-green grass. He watched with mounting rage as Tamara lean over to plant a kiss on the top of his son's wet head.

Mohammed looked as sleek as a panther. Habib was shocked by the blond streaks in his dark hair and his chiseled body clean of chest hair.

As Habib approached the pool, he thought, *This carefree young man no longer resembles my son*. In his house in Damascus, Mohammed had often insisted on wearing his dishdasha in the traditional way, a few inches from the floor. Whenever music played on the radio, he would get up and leave the room. If he caught Habib smoking, he used to lecture him about Islam's distain of tobacco.

"Galina to see you, sweetheart," Tamara said, ushering Habib to sit down on a patio chair.

His son looked up from a backgammon board; his tapered fingers held a shaker. His lower jaw dropped as he flicked his neck to shake water out of his hair and grab a terry cloth robe to drape over his body. His hands quivered as he tightened the cord.

"Would you like some tea, coffee, a cold drink perhaps?" Tamara asked, unaware of her fiancé's discomfort.

"No thank you," Habib said in a high falsetto voice.

He sat down and tucked his sandaled feet under the chair.

Tamara was about to pull up a chair beside him, but he held up his hand.

"Do you mind if I speak to Moe in private?" he asked.

The half smile on her red-gloss lips evaporated.

"Of course not," she said. "Are you staying for dinner, Galina?"

"No thank you," Habib said.

When she left, his son looked hard into his eyes, his hair mashed against his forehead like a boy. Moe's throat clicked as he tried to swallow. He let go his breath, the sound like the sudden flare of gas escaping from a new well.

Habib leaned forward and resumed his normal voice. "You saw through my disguise that your mother created."

"Go away," he said, his voice sounding as though it came from deep within a barrel, his youthful face screwed up in furrows on his forehead.

"I'm your father, and you will listen to me."

His son held up his hands. "Please, Father—"

Habib leaned forward. "It's been many years since we last spoke. You've grown into a man."

"I don't—"

Habib interrupted. "Your mother tells me you are no longer a true believer." He glanced at a loaded cocktail trolley. "You drink alcohol. Do you eat pork also? I don't believe you pray five times a day?"

"Have you come to lecture me? Tell me off like a schoolboy?"

"Do you think this decadent society you live in is the true way?"

When his son removed his dark glasses, Habib saw raw fear in his eyes, his smooth face divided by sunlight and shadow.

"You gave me and my mother new passports, new identities, and shipped us to North Dakota so we could have a new life." His son's words were slow and deliberate. "You never told us why we had to leave Kabul. I heard rumors you killed a man and embezzled a large amount of money from jihadists."

Habib's voice lowered to a growl. "How do you think I paid for your expensive lifestyle and helped Hassan start his used car business in Henley-on-Thames?"

"Mother said you coordinated the Madrid train bombings. Aren't you worried about seeing your mug shot on Al Jazeera?"

Habib smiled at the corners of his mouth. "Mohammed, listen to me."

His son glanced over his shoulder. "Keep your voice down."

"Afraid someone will hear your real name?"

His son buried his face in his hands.

Habib leaned forward and touched his shoulder. "Son, I need your help."

He pulled away, balling his fists. "I'll never help you, never."

"You don't understand—"

"What do you want me to do? Fly a 747 into a tall building and kill thousands of innocent people?"

"What I'm planning will change the course of history."

"You're a dreamer, Father."

"Don't you ever wish our people could be free of domination from outsiders?"

"Of course I do, but—"

Habib interrupted. "Our world is under siege from foreign invaders. Our people have always been good at outwitting, outwaiting, and outsmarting others. Never fear, in the end, we come out on top. In the past, our borders have been easy to breach, but strangers find out the alleys inside our walls are where they're taken in, lose their way, or have their pockets picked." Habib's temples hammered, and the inside of his chador was cold with sweat. "We need to bring some of the terror, shame, and humiliation we have suffered to the people who are torturing us."

His son raised his eyes, his face indifferent. "Is this some stupid scheme of yours to blow up statues?"

Shards of color flooded Habib's cheeks and throat. "How dare you speak to me like that? I am your father; show me some respect."

"Show respect. You'd slit my mother's throat to advance your hairbrained schemes."

After a beat, Habib said, "What I'm about to do is written in the stars not in sand."

"Aren't you afraid you'll be hunted down and killed?"

Habib stared at a grackle fly down from an oak tree on extended wings. For an instant, its feathers caught the sunlight. Habib felt a sharp pain in his chest. His son put on his sunglasses as if to shield him from the glare of his eyes, dark and cavernous.

"I never want to see you again," Moe said, his voice even.

Habib struggled with his nemesis, the flame inside him, the obsession driving him, and the ache for his son's obedience. Was his fate just broken glass in his head as he struggled to find a historical context for rage and pain that disturbed him in his dreams?

He rubbed his hands together as though washing them. He decided to tighten the screws on his son.

"If you refuse me, I will leak to the authorities that your passport is forged," he said.

He couldn't see his son's eyes through the sunglasses, but his expelled breath seemed to reach out and touch his cheek like a desert wind that blew over the rubble of a robbed tomb.

"As you entered this country illegally, you'll be deported back to Syria," he said.

The confidence slipped from his son's voice. "Don't do that, Father, please."

Habib pressed down on the chair's arms to push himself up, and spittle leaked from the corners of his mouth.

"You'll be put in a cell in the Adra. They'll beat the bottoms of your feet with a studded whip." He laid his big hand on his son's shoulder for a moment. "There'll be no escape for you this time. Even if you go on a hunger strike, they'll force-feed you."

Moe's skin had turned gray under the tan. "I feel like you've wrapped my soul in razor wire."

Habib got up and walked with wide strides back to the rental Buick. To gain his son back had come at a high price. Mohammed would be compelled to join him or die, but any sense of success of pulling off his plan had turned to ashes in his mouth.

After Aimée's death, Jacelyn didn't waste any time moving into the murdered woman's Tudor-style mansion. Built during Fargo's building boom for a real-estate tycoon in 1910, Ravenscourt had a cast-iron fence that surrounded the grounds and twin gates with ornate scrolling to guard the entrance.

Ryan drove the Range Rover to the gate's speaker box and pushed a button. He heard the whirring of a surveillance camera turn to focus on his face.

"Who is it?" a squeaky man's voice asked through the speaker.

"Ryan Moar and Marleau Balenger to see Jacelyn. We have a ten o'clock appointment."

"She's having her morning massage. Do you want to come back later or leave her a message?"

"We need to see her now."

"You can't, Mr. Moar. She doesn't want to be disturbed. Just leave a message, and I'll give it to her."

"When will she be finished with her rubdown?"

"How the hell do I know? I'm only the hired help, okay. Just leave me the frigging message."

"Listen, buddy, I don't leave private and confidential messages for Jacelyn with her majordomo or whoever you are. Move your lazy ass out here and let us in."

Ryan heard a sigh. "I'll be down in a minute. Park in front of the porte cochere and remain in your vehicle. Is that understood?"

"Why restrict our movements?"

"When madam has guests, she gets upset if she sees strangers wandering around the property."

"Oh, we wouldn't want to upset her, would we?"

"There's no need for sarcasm."

In a moment, a slim man in a checkered business suit, wearing a bronze toupee, strolled down the drive and unlocked the gates. He wore sunglasses and tennis shoes without socks.

He swung the gates open with a flourish, and his wide grin revealed a set of capped teeth. "My name's Bertrand Sapergia. I checked my message board. Jacelyn didn't leave a Post-it note telling me you had an appointment. But I gather you're well acquainted with madam, so I'll treat you gents properly."

"Well, that's comforting to know," Marleau said as Ryan inched through the open gates.

"I'll bring coffee and sandwiches to your vehicle," Bertrand said.

"Whoopee! Drive-in curbside service is back."

Bertrand went inside the house and slammed the front door with his pudgy hands. While they waited, Ryan studied with high-powered binoculars the swimming pool where a party was in progress.

He adjusted the focus on a thick-bodied man in a pair of lime boxer shorts. His tanned skin, the color of mahogany, accented steel-gray curly hair matted to his chest. He recognized the lawyer's pronounced widow's peak.

"What is Mark Sokolov doing here?" he said.

"I don't believe it," Marleau said, reaching for the binoculars. "Let me have a look."

"Since when did Sticky have anything to do with the Ravensteins?" Ryan said, handing over the binoculars. "They're on opposite ends of the society register."

"Business knows no social boundaries."

Ryan took the binoculars back, and he scanned the pool and patio. He recognized Moe and Tamara seated on lawn chairs beside a smoky grill. Cole did a swan dive into the water. A red-haired young woman in her late teens applauded his effort. She occupied a reclining chair beside a portable bar, her full breasts stretching a purple bikini top. In the background, a couple of men in suits sat at a picnic table under the shade of an oak tree. Both had open briefcases, and they were busy shuffling paper.

"Some heavy-duty negotiating is going on among the principle players in the family firm." Ryan handed the glasses back to Marleau. "Check out those two suits behind the woman in the bikini. Do you recognize them?"

"Can't say I do. The redhead by the way is Cole's main squeeze, Caitlin Tyndale. Her father is Chester Tyndale of Tyndico. Almost obscured from view, lying under a sunshade is Roselyn, Tamara's elder sister."

"She's gorgeous."

Marleau twisted his mouth in a smirk. "Keep your eye on the job, partner. Who else do you recognize at this wingding?"

"The man in the green shorts is one of the Sinises, Paul I think. Why are the Ravensteins entertaining bottom-feeders?"

Ryan leaned back and stretched out a cramp from his broad shoulders. "Carl says the *hermanos* have been on the prowl to gobble up legitimate businesses."

"So you think the Sin-easy bros are after Ravenwest?"

"Probably."

"Can Carl stop them?"

"He'll try to head them off, but based on the chummy way his son is chatting it up with Paul, he can't count on Cole's support."

Marleau shifted the binoculars back to the two men in dark suits in the shade of an oak tree. "By the expression on their faces, those two lawyers under the tree are already drooling over the size of the billing."

They watched Bertrand come out of french doors, carrying a tray of silver-topped containers. His shoulder-length hairpiece gleamed in the sunlight. He placed plates of scrambled eggs in front of the guests, and then piled T-bone steaks on the barbecue. Through the binoculars, Ryan watched him screw up his snub nose as smoke rose from the pit.

"Carl's going to spit fire at the prospect of having Paul sit beside him at the next Ravenwest board meeting," Ryan said.

Ryan heard the scratch of sandals on gravel and checked the side-view mirror. He saw a neat pair of ankles below tight pink pants.

"You're spying on my guests," Jacelyn said, her eyes darting sideways to the pool.

She wore a form-fitting white silk blouse, and her lush hair tapered on her neck.

"Excuse me," Ryan said, lowering the binoculars.

"How dare you be so rude?" she said, her fingers pinching hard into Ryan's arm resting out of the car's open window. "You're intruding on my privacy."

"Jacelyn, meet my business partner, Marleau Belanger," Ryan said, shaking loose her grip and getting out of the Range Rover.

She ignored Marleau and led the way through heavy oak double doors into a sunlit room set up like an office that overlooked trimmed hedges that surrounded a wildflower garden.

"I suppose it's what you people do best, peeking inside keyholes and spying," she said, sitting down on a heavy gilt chair behind a pedestal desk.

Ryan and Marleau sat facing her. An ornate candlestick phone rang, and Jacelyn picked it up, as if expecting a call. When she heard a voice that wasn't familiar, she slammed the receiver down.

She rang a bell, and Bertrand appeared with a coffeepot. His tangled blond eyebrows were damp with sweat against his red face. He brushed against Ryan's shoulder as he poured coffee into tiny Royal Doulton cups.

"That'll be all, Bert," she said in a frosty voice. When he left, she added, "Why does it need you all to solve Aimée's murder? Why doesn't Carl leave it up to the police?"

"He wants her killer found soon. The police tend to take their time," Ryan said.

"So what makes you think you dudes can find the murderer faster, when the police have way more resources than you do?"

"We're good at what we do, Jacelyn. We're more flexible, take shortcuts," Ryan said.

She didn't appear to be listening. Her face looked numb, and she had to keep widening her eyes to focus on him.

"Why is Carl also having Moe investigated?" she asked.

Carl must have told his fiancée about the investigation. What if Jacelyn alerted Moe, and he informed his mother? Would this jeopardize chances of finding her and preventing a terrorist attack?

"I'd rather you didn't tell Moe anything about our investigation of him," Ryan said.

Jacelyn opened and closed her mouth like a baby bird in a nest, waiting for food.

Behind her, Ryan heard laughter and the clink of ice on glass float in through the window.

"Bert mentioned a woman in a long robe came yesterday afternoon to see Moe," she said.

"What did she want?"

"Moe said she asked him to donate to a charity to help feed Afghan orphans. Bert overheard them argue, but he didn't understand what the disagreement was about because they spoke in a foreign language."

Jacelyn's eyes seemed to reach out into space, her mouth still slightly parted.

"Did he notice anything else unusual about his visitor?" Ryan asked.

"When she left, instead of taking an elderly woman's short steps, she had the broad stride of someone in a hurry. Bert swears she acted as if she was a man."

The sun reflected off the gleaming hardwood floor and struck Ryan's eyes like broken shards from a mirror.

She glanced at her watch. "Good heavens, I have to split. I've an aerobics and meditation trainer coming in two minutes."

CHAPTER 14

A LIGHT MIST ROLLED OFF THE west shore of Lake of the Woods and collected in hollows as the twin-engine amphibian Beechcraft 18 swooped down to ruffle the glass-smooth water's surface. Carl stood on the shore grim-faced as he watched the floatplane taxi to the dock and the pilot switch off the engines. When Ryan climbed out, he could feel oil drums under the dock rock in a slight swell. A skein of geese, migrating south, flew overhead.

"A windy day for flying," Carl said, greeting him on the dock.

Carl's head topped by a mop of white hair appeared too big for his narrow shoulders. He wore baggy shorts, a yellow turtleneck sweater, and flip-flops. At his feet, his white Scottish terrier, Dixie, barked at Ryan.

"Did you pilot her all the way?" he asked.

"I was at the controls most of the time, apart from a bit of turbulence over Thief River Falls, when the pilot took over," Ryan said, scratching the top of Dixie's head.

They strolled down a path made of fine sand flanked by pines as silent as a cemetery.

"I take it Joanne hasn't given you the green light to buy your own plane," Carl said.

"We're still at the negotiating stage."

Behind a copse of birch trees, Carl's cabin came into view. Overlooking the windswept beach, the cabin was a U-shaped building with a heated outdoor pool nestled in between the wings.

"What's so urgent?" he asked.

Ryan told Carl about the assorted guests at the pool party.

"Why has Cole turned against me?" he said.

"He believes everything Aaron tells him, including doing business with the Sinises."

"He treats me as if I'm a criminal."

"Give him a chance—"

"That's some talk coming from you, Ryan. Are you suggesting I ignore the fact that he's in bed with those sons of bitches who are trying to steal my company?"

"Right now, I think you should avoid a family O. K. Corral–style confrontation. No one wins except the lawyers. Allow for a cooling-off period, and then try to persuade your son to come back on your side."

Carl's face flushed from Cole's betrayal.

"I'm going to talk to my lawyers and stop these bastards from seducing my son and attempting to take over Ravenwest," he said through gritted teeth.

Carl's face relaxed a degree as he paused to introduce Ryan to his caretaker, Kevin Rutley, an aging hippie dressed in jeans and Clorox-stained print shirt with sleeves cut off at the armpits. His stringy, blond hair sprouted out from under a side-skewed Twins baseball cap. A gold religious medallion dangled around his neck.

The sun reflected off Italian marble patio stones where chokecherry bushes groaned with an overload of fruit. Sitting at a picnic table by the pool, Carl's former secretary Megan Mowery munched on tossed salad and pink slices of steak.

"Ryan, I believe you've met Megan," he said, pointing to a buffet. "Help yourself to some lunch."

"Thanks," Ryan said. "Good to see you again, Megan."

She gazed up at him, her shades mirroring the tall pines at the lake's edge. A two-piece bathing suit accented her slim figure. She had wrapped her hair in a towel, and she wore silver-colored sandals on her small feet.

"Will you excuse me? I have a call to make," Carl said, heading inside the cabin.

Sitting beside her, Ryan could hear her coarse breathing.

"Are you close to finding out who killed Aimée?" she asked.

"It's early days, but the investigation is moving right along. We're questioning a number of suspects."

"Forgive me for asking, but have you considered Jacelyn as a possible killer?"

"Why would she want to murder Aimée?" he asked, while eating pieces of steak dipped in HP Sauce.

"Greed," she said, forking a morsel of Angus into the back of her mouth, and then she started grinding her teeth. She put down her knife and fork to slap a mosquito on her wrist. "She wants it all."

"Jacelyn may be interested in Carl's money, but she doesn't strike me as being pathological."

"Don't be fooled by her cool exterior. She's been known to have fits of hysterical rage over trivial matters." Megan paused for a moment to part the red lips of her generous mouth. "I've heard her ball out a hairdresser over a misplaced curl. She exploded in such a fit of rage that the poor girl had an attack of hysterics herself."

"Being angry doesn't necessarily make her a murderer."

"I think you've overlooked the fact that Jacelyn had opportunity," she said, attacking the meat again. "On the night of the murder, she claimed she attended a charity fundraiser for the homeless. I know she didn't." Megan laughed without humor. "How the gods favor those who lie about doing good." She narrowed her eyes. "Did you know she has a handgun without a permit?"

"That's something I wasn't aware of."

"And guess what else. Her prospective stepdaughter says it has an attached silencer."

Ryan drummed his fingers on the table. "Why did Tamara tell you this?"

"When I was at Ravenscourt to pick up weekend work for her father, it came up in casual conversation."

"I didn't know you were still employed by Carl."

"I'm helping him out with legal work."

Neither of them spoke for a few minutes, Ryan just stared at the lake. He had never really liked Megan. After working for Carl for two decades as his confidential secretary, she could be haughty.

"Did she tell you why Jacelyn needed a firearm with a silencer?" Ryan asked.

"Tamara said she wanted the gun for protection against intruders. I've never understood why she should be afraid. You've equipped the house with the latest state-of-the-art security system." Megan started fiddling with her steak knife. "After she and Carl began going out together, Jacelyn could be jealous of the way Carl continued to see his ex-wife."

"They probably talked business. After all, Aimée sat on the company's board and was one of the Ravenwest's larger shareholders."

Megan blew out an impatient blast of air. "Getting rid of the other woman in your husband's life is one of the oldest motives in the world."

"Are you saying Carl's visits to see Aimée went beyond discussions on the latest quarterly report results?"

She sat back, her point justified. "Jacelyn found out they were still romantically involved, and that's reason enough for killing her."

"How can you be so sure?"

"I know my boss well enough to realize he was still in love with Aimée."

"Do you have proof?"

"I overheard odd snatches of phone conversations that were suggestive. When I saw them together, I couldn't ignore unmistakable intense eye contact."

Ryan rubbed his eyes. "I think you've misjudged Jacelyn."

While she poured herself another Bloody Mary, he thought about Megan's reasons for suspecting Carl's fiancée. But even if given the opportunity, he couldn't imagine Jacelyn in a burst of rage shooting Aimée.

"We've talked to other suspects with far stronger motives for killing Aimée." Then he met her eyes across the picnic table. "I don't want to leave you with the impression that I've dismissed your suspicions. I promise you I always keep my options open."

Behind him, he heard the soft sound of Carl's sandals on the patio stones. Carl sat down with a weary smile.

"Would you mind leaving us, honey? We need to talk business," he said.

"I understand," she said. "A girl knows when the big boys want to talk dirty."

Megan refreshed her Bloody Mary from a decanter and added a celery stick in the ice.

When she disappeared through french doors, Carl said,

"I know Megan is brassy and coarse, but she's good company and makes me laugh." His craggy features dissolved into a boyish grin. "And let me tell you, between the sheets she's dynamite."

"I'm glad she makes you happy."

"I don't want Jacelyn to find out she stays overnight at the cabin," he said in a low tone.

"What about the pilot and Kevin? Aren't you concerned about them gossiping?"

"They've signed confidentiality agreements."

The breeze changed direction and blew in from the lake.

"When are you returning to town?" Ryan asked.

He shifted his compressed, hard-muscled frame. "I expect to be back within the week."

Carl rubbed the forehead of his impish face and breathed air like a man out jogging. His eyes looked empty, the anger spent.

He beamed when Megan in a bikini went down the tiled steps and into the water. After wallowing in the pool, she climbed out, picked up a towel, dried herself off, and slapped sunscreen on her thighs.

"I've had a quick conference call with some of my board members and told them about these shenanigans." Carl kicked the leg of the picnic table, shaking the coffeepot, his eyes blazing. "I'm not going without a fight."

"I like your attitude."

"Find out what the Sinises are up to."

"I'll put Marleau onto it."

"He'll blend in well with those buccaneers."

Behind him, Ryan heard the clang of Kevin's ax splitting logs into cordwood.

"Marleau is at times irresponsible and the bane of the West Fargo Police Department, but he's always been loyal, someone I can trust," Ryan said, his eyes squinted at the sun's rays reflecting off ripples on the lake. "Moe remains the enigma."

"What has Sanjay found out?"

"On the surface, he's a regular guy, but his background is full of inconsistencies."

"Isn't he a Lebanese Christian orphan?"

"That's what he claims to be, but there's no record of him entering the States."

Ryan handed him a photo of the woman wearing a headscarf outside Moe's apartment.

"Sanjay thinks she's his mother." Carl examined the photo, and he rubbed his tanned cheek, the color of a weathered razor strop scrolled with gray stubble. "Sanjay put a tap on his phone. She nags him a lot."

"Who is she exactly?"

"Sanjay suspects she heads a sleeper cell of extremists."

Carl wrinkled his patrician nose as though he had smelled something unpleasant. "Are they planning some sort of attack?"

"Sanjay is finding that out by monitoring Islamic websites. He then deciphers their codes."

Carl cleared his throat. "These days nothing surprises me. Did you know the Madrid bombings were part of a far-reaching jihadist plot on the Internet?"

Ryan paused to listen to a loon. "So far, Moe gives the impression he has no intention of giving up his lifestyle or losing your daughter."

The sky began to cloud over; shadows passed like ships of doubt across the wide expanse of lawn.

"Moe's innovative technical knowledge is critical to Ravenwest's Hardware Division," Carl said.

Ryan raised his eyebrows. "Is he that good?"

"He's a wunderkind." Carl slumped down in his chair and crossed his arms over his chest. "If Moe proves to be related to extremists, is Tamara in danger?"

Ryan looked out at the fractured light on the lake beyond banks of impatiens. Given the growing complexity of the case, his expression remained almost serene. "Not unless the terrorists think Moe has confided in her."

"If this woman is Moe's mother, my daughter should be warned." Carl leaned back and laced his fingers behind the sleek curls on the back of his head. "Besides, none of this may be true."

Ryan told him about Moe's mysterious woman visitor, and he described how she walked and talked like a man. Carl rounded his shoulders, while he watched Kevin put on a pair of painter's gloves to split open some northerns' stomachs and half-moon their heads at the gills.

When Kevin finished gutting the fish, Carl swung around. "These people have a history of extreme cruelty that frightens me. Did you know what they did to Turkish prisoners during World War I? They pried open their mouths and poured hot sand down their throats until they suffocated."

CHAPTER 15

T HE NEXT MORNING, GARY CLIMBED out of bed in his small
room attached to the boathouse to watch the sunrise. A warm
breeze picked up, and he could see mating dragonflies rise out of
the reeds with wings turned into rainbow colors in the golden light.
He pulled on a pair of swim trunks and headed for the pool.

After several laps, he hauled himself up on the rim and stretched
out on a chair. A thick mat of his chest hair glistened in the sun as
though slicked down with gel.

He sat up when he heard the soft sound of footsteps. He was
surprised to see Charlene on the deck. She slept late on Sundays.
She wore orange shorts and a matching halter. When she glanced
in his direction, he ignored her.

A moment later, he heard her voice behind him. "Have you been
spying on me?"

He stood up and dried his thick black hair with a beach towel.
"What do you mean?"

"Yesterday evening, I caught you staring at me through my
bedroom window." She placed her hands on her slim hips. "Don't
deny it."

Gary didn't know whether Charlene was really annoyed or just amused.

"It wasn't intentional. I was passing by," he said, grinning.

"I've got news for you, buster. You living here doesn't give you the right to ogle me."

He glanced up at her slim body framed against the glare of the sun, her hair wispy with light.

"I thought you'd be flattered," he said, staring at her beaded moccasins.

She raised her slim eyebrows.

"Well, you did look good in that two-piece bathing suit," he added.

"Is that some kind of compliment or more of your special brand of sarcasm?" She looked him up and down. "The swimsuit you're wearing is so tight you'll soon separate the wiener from the beans."

He laughed. "Aren't you a little young to talk dirty?"

She studied the dark stubble on his face for a minute. In the distance, Gary heard his mother's Cairn terrier bark at seagulls on the beach.

She drew a deep breath. "You must think me absurdly naive if you think I don't know all about male anatomical features."

Gary wrapped the towel around his middle. "I bet you see lots of half-naked guys leap about at ballet school."

Charlene sank into a deck chair and stared at a cabin cruiser head north toward Marsdon.

"Let's get something straight. I'm not exactly ecstatic about being in the same house as you," she said.

"Why did you move here then?"

"If you must know, my mother and I don't get along." She wrinkled her snub nose as if she'd smelled something unpleasant. "I loathe her new boyfriend. Would you believe it if I told you they're talking about having a baby?"

"Well, there you go. You'll have a half sister or brother to play with."

"Don't be ridiculous."

As she watched the morning light spread like a mist over the river, Gary gazed at her, mesmerized by her frizzy blonde hair and full lips. She had put on eye shadow but no lipstick, and she wore dangling earrings set with green stones.

She looked intently at the river, her face colored with remembered irritation.

"I'm curious about something," she said. "When my father worked in Marsdon, weren't you accused of killing and raping a student nurse?"

His eyes grew wary.

"No one wants to talk to me about what happened," she added.

"It was an ugly piece of shit."

"Is that all you have to say?"

His brow netted with lines, but he remained silent.

"What was it like in the juvenile detention center?" she asked.

Gary pressed his lips together, reluctant to talk about his incarceration. Finally, he decided she needed to know. "It was like being in hell with a bunch of rowdy losers."

She chewed on her lip for a moment. "Didn't my dad help prove you innocent? In doing so, he lost his job over some work-related conflict of interest."

Gary stood up and turned his back on her.

"You should be grateful for what he did for you," she said.

"Sure I am," he said in a small voice.

"Then for heaven's sake tell me what happened."

Gary felt uncomfortable as he wrapped his mind around the central issue of his case.

Facing her, he said, "It's about police misuse of power."

"There must be more to it than that."

He turned to face her, hands on hips. "Not when you consider that the cops figured I was an undesirable."

"Surely you don't fit into that category."

"Most people thought prison is where I belonged. You see, the Marsdon cops abused their discretionary powers. They wanted nothing more than to lock me up for the rest of my life, even though I didn't stab or rape anyone." He breathed in hard. "They wanted to be the heroes, who put the bad dude away."

"The police only try to do their job, and it's a difficult one."

"Cops make mistakes. They have their personal demons, you know. On TV, cops wrestle with alcohol, drugs, lousy marriages, and rotten supervisors. What you don't see on TV is cops getting a real rush at playing God by lying and tampering with evidence."

"It sounds too simplistic. You must have been guilty of something, not just the victim of a miscarriage of justice."

"I admit to selling drugs to Marsdon U students."

As the sun rose above the spruce trees, the red light began to flatten like fire inside the wetlands.

"How did my dad get involved?" she asked, watching the sunlight dance on the water.

Her mouth parted in anticipation of his reply, her blue eyes still glossy with sleep.

"He proved me innocent by going after the real criminals—crooked cops, corrupt lawyers, and criminal corporate executives," he said.

"I can understand the occasional bad cop, but lawyers and company big shots?"

"This murder case opened up a can of worms. So-called respectable people wanted me locked away in the NDSP in Bismarck to protect their miserable skins. Some of them, pillars of the community, turned out to be human garbage trucks."

Her expression softened. "I'd call that hypocrisy."

The air turned cool and smelled of damp wood from the river. The eastern light turned the windows of the house gold. He saw her face was calm and ruddy as though she had stepped out of a hot shower.

She said, "I never realized—"

"Don't feel sorry for me." He interrupted her, his face a mask of discomfort. "I'm not the only one who belongs to the walking wounded."

Her expression softened to one of sympathy. "Last summer, my dad had nothing but praise for the way you handled yourself, when you were kidnapped."

"Stick with me kid, and I'll show you adventures that'll knock your socks off."

"I'd rather keep mine on, thanks all the same."

The wind picked up, and Gary heard Ryan's outboard motorboat tied to the dock strain against its painter and knock on the pilings.

"Well, I must go," she said, glancing at a petite wristwatch encrusted in diamonds.

He shivered as she walked away; her dancer's carriage made her glide across the lawn like a wood sprite.

The moon had gone behind a cloud, and rain rings appeared on the river's surface like pickerel rising to feed. Ryan heard a faint scuffle outside the boathouse that sounded as though someone was testing the security of the doors and windows. He took the Magnum from inside his top desk drawer, switched off the desk light, and tiptoed to the door to listen.

Outside was black, the sky overcast with heavy clouds. Through the window, he could see the wooden tower of St. Olaf's church lit up by lightning. The strong wind rattled dry aspen leaves, and he heard his Alsatian barking from inside the house.

When he opened the blinds, he spotted a shadow creep down the path to the boathouse. Who would be out in the rain so late? The figure crept toward the door and kept away from the lights. He thought of threats posed by Moe's parents.

He opened the door a crack and aimed the Magnum at the opening. In the dim light, he recognized Jacelyn's round face surrounded by a hood.

Her mouth froze into a scream when she saw the gun pointed at her heart.

"Never surprise me by coming here late at night," he said, lowering the Magnum.

Jacelyn clutched her hands to her chest. "You got my blood pumping."

"I'm sorry to scare you, but I have to be extra careful."

He opened the door for her to step into the office. She walked so close to him he could smell her perfume.

"Is something wrong?" Ryan asked, his eyes not quite meeting hers.

She remained silent. He locked the door after her and left the gun on the desk. She looked at him with a mixture of anger and annoyance. She removed her cape and shook rain out of her Mackintosh. She tossed her coat on the leather couch and looked over at the coffeemaker's half-full round-glass urn. "Is that brew drinkable?"

"It's reasonably fresh."

She poured herself some coffee. "Have you reported his going missing to the police?"

"I have indeed." She sat on the leather couch, her hand wrapped around the mug and her slender legs tucked in under her. "Tamara thought he was going through some sort of crisis. It began soon after he had that visit from the tall woman a week ago, who talked like a man, trying to speak in a high-pitched voice."

"Did Tamara have anything more to add about his visitor?" he asked.

Jacelyn stiffened, raised her chin, and tilted her head slightly. Her mouth reminded him of a red rose turned toward the light.

"Tamara watched them together from a distance," she said. "Galina kept yelling at Moe in a loud voice. It sounded as though she was scolding him. She acted totally out of character for someone soliciting. Moe shouted back. Their interaction reminded her of a family squabble. Ever since this strange woman visited him, Moe's changed; he gave up shaving. He became moody and distant."

"Prenuptial jitters?"

"Perhaps, but he used to be so polite, attentive, and considerate. To put it bluntly, he became a cantankerous jerk."

"Did Tamara suspect another woman?"

"I don't know if that's his problem. You're the detective, honey." She breathed hard through her mouth. "Where do you think Moe has gone?"

"Bottom line, he's a decent guy, but there's a possibility he's connected to dangerous people."

Ryan's mind began to race. If Galina was a man, he could be Moe's dad, live nearby, and become an even more potent threat. The consequences of him being Moe's father added a dangerous new complexity to the puzzle.

Jacelyn tilted her head back and ran her fingers through her hair. She slipped off her wet sandals and wiggled her toes in the shag rug.

She sipped the coffee and examined his books and computers. "So this is where you solve cases. To quote Hercule Poirot, it's where your little gray cells are hard at work."

She looked into his eyes as the glow from a ceiling spotlight reflected off her hair.

"If you think this business is romantic and riveting, it's the opposite," he said. "It's nothing like the film noir atmosphere of the forties and fifties when gallant private investigators saved beautiful and cunning female clients from the clutches of evil husbands and gangsters."

She got up and peered through the slats at the rain beating on the dock.

"What has your high-priced help found out about Moe?" she said, a look of displeasure and impatience on her face.

"Sanjay Sinha is close to finding out his real identity," he said.

He examined her face, and he realized what attracted Carl to her. Jacelyn was more resilient than other women, more long suffering, and more willing to put up with bad memories and hard desires.

She ran her hands up and down her upper arms over her cream-colored blazer. When Ryan leaned back and rested his hands on his thighs, she fastened her eyes on him.

"Carl comes home soon," he said. She started to speak but gave up. "Are you sticking around?"

"I'm going to marry him; I'll never walk away," she said, folding her arms across her chest. "I don't care what he's done. I want him back."

"So there's no truth to the rumor your relationship is in trouble."

"I wish people would stay the hell out of my private life," she said, a flicker of color rising up into her neck.

Her eyes looked into his, and her expression hardened. "Did you really think I'd leave Carl?" she asked.

"You two belong to each other."

"Well, for the record, I'm sticking by him."

"I'm glad, Jacelyn. You've always been a trooper."

Outside the boathouse, rain blew in sheets across the water. The swollen river had overflowed the sandy beach in front of his property, and the branches of elm trees trailed on the water's choppy surface. The body of a dead walleye floated past the office window, its white bloated stomach bobbing in the waves.

For a moment, she looked up, startled by flashes of lightning coming through the window. Her sun-bronzed skin had the smoothness of soft tallow.

He turned away from her unrelenting stare and looked at the intensity of the raindrops that dotted the river's choppy surface and drummed on the roof.

She got up and came around to the side of the desk to face him. Her mouth pouted as if she wanted him to kiss her.

"I apologize for my rudeness when you came to see me," she said, clicking her scarlet nails on the desktop.

"You were distracted. After all, you had important guests."

She swung around and studied for a moment a watercolor of African buffalos.

"Is that uncouth partner of yours still on Aimée's case?" she asked. "He gave Ricky a black eye and broke his nose."

"Marleau can be overly enthusiastic during cross-examinations, but he gets results."

"You're a great person, Ryan. Why don't you give this sordid business a rest?" she asked, shaking her head to make her looped, purple earrings wobble.

He swiveled round in his chair and made a diamond-shaped opening in the blinds to study the row of aspens in his neighbor's yard. Thunderclouds over the river pulsed and glimmered with streaks of lightning. Facing her again, his eyes narrowed as though buried in private thoughts.

"I make an honest living," he said.

She stood close to him, so he could smell spearmint on her soft breath. She began to stroke his hair with her fingers. She tried to caress his cheek, but he pushed his heels on the carpet, wheeled the high-backed chair against the wall, and laced his fingers behind his head.

Joanne opened the screen door and came in holding a red umbrella over her head.

"Oh, pardon me. I didn't mean to barge into the middle of something," she said. She collapsed her umbrella and speckled the carpet with raindrops. "Clumsy of me, I've made a watery mess."

CHAPTER 16

Later that night, Joanne lay against Ryan, her fingertips tracing a scar on his shoulder from a bullet wound received during a police shootout with a biker gang in North Fargo. Her fingers touched his hair and neck, stroked his chest, while she snuggled her stomach and thighs closer.

"What did *that* woman want this time?" she asked.

"Moe's missing," he said. "I'd like to have talked to him, but now it's probably too late. I'd held off questioning him earlier as I didn't want to spook him."

"Are you going to pursue the angle he's hooked up with terrorists?"

Ryan looked through a gap in the curtains at the branches of oak and elm trees moving against the sky.

"Yeah," he said.

He could feel her press her stomach against his back.

"Will these terrorists put us in danger?" she whispered, her mouth exploring his ear.

"We have to be alert to the threat they pose."

Her fingers trailed over the back of his neck.

"Did Jacelyn try to put the moves on you?" she asked.

He sat up and stared out at the drapes blowing gently in the breeze from an open window. He felt his lips part, but no sound came out. He felt his face tighten with a strange kind of anger mingled with a touch of fear that he didn't recognize.

"I can't imagine her having any romantic interest in an ex-cop and over-the-hill private eye," he said.

"Women seem to be very fond of you; I've noticed the way some of them poured over you."

He rolled over to look at her. She tilted her face on the pillow and brushed hair away from her eyes.

"We have a wonderful family, and I'll never do anything to spoil that," he said.

She pulled him against her and traced her lips across the matted hair on his chest.

"Does Jacelyn have anything to do with Aimée's death?" she asked, looking into his eyes.

"She's not a suspect."

"Why does she hang around you all the time unless she hopes to find out if you're getting closer to the truth?"

"If she is tied to Aimée's murder, I can't figure out how."

The phone beside the reading lamp on the nightstand rang, and Ryan grabbed it, expecting to hear Jacelyn's husky voice. Instead, it was Carl.

"I thought this was too important to wait until the morning," he said. "Someone broke into the cabin during the night."

"Are you and Megan all right?"

"We're fine. Megan's a bit shook up, but she's calm now."

"Where was Kevin?"

"He slept through it all."

"You'd better beef up your security, Carl. How did they get to your place?"

"They came in by air, landed on the far end of the lake, and then rowed in by dingy."

"Anything missing?"

"They cracked the safe but didn't steal cash or papers."

"You can bet they photographed your files. Do you have anything that's sensitive?"

"Unfortunately, they contain an outline of my strategy to prevent a Ravenwest takeover."

"That'll need some damage control. How did they get inside without setting off the alarm?"

"They cut the power lines."

"What about Dixie? Did he bark during the night?"

"For some unknown reason, he didn't."

Ryan could feel moisture building up on his forehead.

"I'd like you to fly in tomorrow morning," Carl said. "I'll have the Beech pick you at your dock at eight."

Early the next morning, the Beech 18 made a wide circle around Winnibigoshish Bay and then dropped through clouds pooled with fire from the sun. The land to the north was flat and dimpled with lakes.

When the aircraft touched down, the floats cut a white swath of surf across the glass surface of the lake. After taxiing to the dock, Ryan climbed out and stretched. He walked along the path to the cabin where the air smelled of cut grass and woodsmoke.

Carl sat in a rattan chair on the deck, his jaw jutted out as though it were made of granite. He wore an Australian slouch hat to keep the sun out of his eyes, a starched checkered shirt, and cowboy boots. He watched Ryan stroll up the winding path from the dock. On his way, Ryan passed flower beds and mowed lawns carved out of high cattails. Before reaching the deck, Ryan paused to examine the churned flower beds where the intruders stamped around while they disabled the alarm system. He also checked the basement window where they had used a looped wire through a window jamb to release the catch from inside.

Carl stood up, removed his hat. "Thank you, for coming straight away."

Ryan followed him inside the cottage and through the book-lined living room to the study.

Carl showed him the safe. "Cash wasn't touched, but someone took a peek at my battle plans to curb those bastards who want to steal my company."

Carl unlocked the door of the wall safe in his wood-paneled office. "I'll let you look around," he said.

When he closed the office door, Ryan glanced at oars from Magdalen College that reminded him Carl was a Rhodes Scholar. Below a wooden propeller from a Fokker Super Universal was a framed photo of Carl, ramrod straight in a tuxedo, beside former president Ronald Reagan. Another photo that caught his eye was a color picture of Carl and Aimée flanked by Cole and Tamara. He was surprised how much Tamara looked like her mother, almost as though she were a twin. She had Aimée's stunning slim figure and photographic features.

He realized that there would be no point in dusting for fingerprints; the intruders left no calling card. Ryan first examined the pile of surveillance photos on the desk that he had faxed Carl. At the bottom of the pile, he discovered a photo of Moe outside a downtown nightclub called Raising Cane. Behind him, the club's signature neon sugarcane stalks surrounded the front entrance. Moe had his arm wrapped around Tamara's shoulder.

Someone had used a knife to scratch out a rough circle around Tamara's head and dig out her eyes.

Did the intruders want to give Carl a message to call off any further search for Moe's identity? Could Tamara's life be in danger? Ryan swung wide the steel door of the small safe. Apart from three slim files, the safe was empty except for several neat piles of new hundred-dollar bills.

Breaking into the safe could mean only one thing. The intruders wanted to find out Carl's strategy to prevent the takeover of his company. Did this mean there was a connection between the terrorists and the dubious attempt to take over Ravenwest?

When he went back outside, bunches of puffy clouds had blocked out the sun. Kevin stood fishing from the end of the dock. The air smelled like rain and roses. On the patio grill, he saw Megan whip up scrambled eggs in a pan.

"Why are these guys messing around in my affairs?" Carl asked.

"I'll find out who is behind it," Ryan said, sitting down beside him. He showed him Tamara's mutilated photo. "For your own safety and the safety of your daughter, you should return to the city."

Carl remained silent, his steel-blue eyes fixed on the Beechcraft rocking in a slight swell. He put on half-lens glasses to examine the photo.

Ryan raised his voice. "Megan, persuade him to go home."

She glanced up from her pan and gave Carl a loving look. "I've tried, but he won't budge."

"I'm not in any hurry to return to town. I like being at the cabin. I walk the dog every day, eat fresh fish, and drink Megan's vegetable-and-fruit health cocktails." He shaded his eyes from the sunlight's glare off the water. "Look at the view. You must admit, Minnesota has its moments."

Sunlight filtered through spruce trees with leaves beginning to turn to gold. Ryan could understand the hold the cabin had on Carl.

"You really think there's a danger?" Carl said, tossing the photo on the table.

"I'm sure of it. I'll hire guards for around-the-clock surveillance here and at Ravenscourt."

"Is that necessary?"

Ryan paused to take a breath. "If you insist on staying, you'll need security patrols as well as guard dogs. Next time, they'll bring sharp knives and automatic weapons."

"I won't agree to security, but I'll have a guard dog to keep Dixie company."

Ryan realized he hadn't seen Dixie since he had arrived. "Why didn't Dixie make any noise last night?" he said.

"I don't know."

"Where is Dixie?"

Carl shrugged his shoulders. "Is there any way of checking with the FAA to find out the identity of these guys?" he asked.

"It'll be almost impossible unless someone saw the plane's identification numbers. Hundreds of private planes and prospectors fly in this area in the fall, and many of them don't file flight plans."

Megan carried over plates of steaming scrambled eggs on toast.

"Dixie hasn't come for his food this morning," she said.

Ryan heard a machine buzz and glanced over to Kevin, who was using a Weedwacker to trim cattails. Suddenly, he cried out and dropped the Weedwacker, while the rotating blades continued to flay the reeds.

"Hey, Kevin! Watch what you're doing," Carl shouted.

Kevin stumbled to the beach and brought up his breakfast on the sand.

Ryan ran across the lawn to switch off the Weedwacker. He saw dog hair enmeshed in the serrated edges. Ryan parted the reeds and found the terrier in a pool of dried blood. His tongue protruded from his mouth.

"Dixie's dead," Ryan said.

CHAPTER 17

T HE KILLER CHOSE A PLACE where old cars came to die, a dank stretch of mudflats bordered on one side by wetlands and on the other by a new upmarket housing project. Behind him, Ryan could smell rotten reeds in a drainage ditch choked by Styrofoam cups and plastic bags.

Harsh light from a video camera spilled out onto the muddy ground. The dead private investigator lay on his back. Greg Duluth knelt down and examined the massive cuts on his neck.

He stood up and took a cigarette out of a monogrammed silver case. The pop and flare from his match made Ryan jump. As Greg set fire to the cigarette, lodged in the corner of his mouth, his fingers had a noticeable tremor.

"You ever see a blood loss like that before?" Greg said.

"This is an execution-style killing, the kind you'd expect from organized crime," Ryan said.

He flinched as he stared down at the body. Sanjay lay on his back, his throat hacked by the deep thrusts of a sharp knife. He also had a bullet wound in the shoulder, and a second shot had grazed his temple.

"Who found the body?" Ryan asked.

"A couple of kids out skateboarding," Greg said. His sharp, harsh voice sounded like tires running over gravel.

Ryan glanced at two boys in jeans and sneakers who squatted on skateboards outside the tape. Crime-scene investigators wearing polyethylene coveralls on their feet and hair were talking to a man and a woman from forensics. Under portable lights, powered by a nearby generator, a photographer crouched down to take flash photos.

A frogman entered the water, and Ryan watched the shadowy movements of his flashlight under the murky surface. A layer of clouds formed above the crime scene, dark and heavy with rain. Thinking like a police officer, he wondered if the team had brought enough plastic to protect the area. Without a cover, they had better work fast, or rain would wash away footprints, blood, and fibers.

Ryan squatted down, eye level with the corpse. Blood was smeared across Sanjay's face and bald head, matted into his chest hair at the opening of his white shirt. The gaping wound in his throat made Ryan's stomach heave. Pushed deep into the neck, the knife had sliced blood vessels and sinews.

Greg snapped on a pair of surgical gloves.

"What time did he die?" Ryan asked.

"How the hell should I know?" He turned to a heavy man with a close-cropped coppery mustache who stood beside him. "What do you say, Roscoe?"

The pathologist's lean, tapered fingers probed over and under Sanjay's body.

"From one or two hours," he said in a mid-Atlantic English accent.

"Did you know the body's been moved?" Ryan asked.

The doctor glared at Ryan. "What is your special knowledge of postmortem lividity?"

"I know that dead people don't usually land on their backs."

"Who are you? I haven't seen you at a crime scene before."

"Meet Ryan Moar, Roscoe Roberts. He's a former member of the WFPD who's gone private," Greg said.

"The problem with you private guys is you always get in the way of the professionals, muddy the waters," Roscoe said, releasing his grip on the body and straightening up.

"I promise I won't mess around in your pond, Doctor," Ryan said.

Roscoe grunted as Greg helped him turn Sanjay on his side.

"Massive neck wound to the throat. From the length of the exit wound, the blade will be about nine centimeters long tapering to a thin point. The bruises surrounding the entry point indicates the knife had a handle or hilt guard. The killer also used considerable force. The wound is at a slight downward angle, which implies the killer is taller than the victim. A closer inspection in the lab may prove different." Roscoe cleared his throat. "Whoever stabbed him is a brutal sadist."

The wind loud in the elm trees bordering the swamp scattered torn leaves across the surface of the open water.

"No apparent signs of defense wounds in the hands and arms, leading me to believe the victim didn't have time to defend himself," Roscoe continued. His knees creaked as he straightened up. "Obviously, the victim's place of origin is East Asia or the Middle East. Do we have a positive ID on this young man?"

"The victim is Sanjay Sinha, a PI working for Ryan," Greg said.

Like a flock of hungry crows, the forensic team moved in on the corpse armed with sticky tape, scissors, and large polyethylene bags.

Roscoe hovered over the technicians, his blue eyes watery under the glare of the strobe lights. "Outsiders at crime scenes make me nervous," he said, pointing at Ryan.

"Is there something wrong, Roscoe?" Greg asked.

"I'd prefer this private investigator stay away until we've done our job."

"I'm sorry to tell you this, old boy, but Ryan's okay. I can vouch for him."

The sky had turned black, the air filled with the drone of mosquitoes. There was a little blood on Roscoe's gloved hand, and he kept opening and closing his fist to look at the stain on the latex.

"He's a bloody nuisance," he said.

The swamp flickered with a white flash as lightning leaped across the sky. The floodlights etched deep lines in Roscoe's bloated face. Ryan realized he had met the pathologist before. Suddenly, he stood inches from Roscoe's face, a flush of color spreading to his neck.

"You're not going to punch me out, are you, son?" Roscoe asked.

"My former partner on the force, Marleau Belanger, once accused you of crime-scene tampering."

Roscoe stripped off his latex gloves; his nails were clean but unusually long.

"As I recall, you and Belanger were a pair of perverse, clumsy officers," he said.

Greg stepped forward, a smile frozen on his mouth. "That's enough, guys. We're all one the same side."

Roscoe glanced at his watch. "I don't have time for this."

He walked past Ryan, up a slight muddy rise to an SUV, and climbed inside. A stab of light from a match in the darkness inside the cab lit up his face as he fired up a pipe.

"What made him so edgy?" Ryan asked.

"Roscoe's been having marital problems."

"That's no reason to take it out on me."

A Cherokee drove by on the highway with windows open, and Ryan heard rap music. Greg turned irritably at the sound and glared at the teenagers leaning out of the car's windows.

A uniformed officer told them to move on.

"How about tire impressions?" Ryan said. "I suspect he was shot first then driven here for the coup de grace."

"Probably every tire in Fargo has been around here at one time or another. This is a prime spot for parking," Greg said, nudging a spent condom with the tip of his toe.

Greg left him and went into a huddle with some of his officers. Ryan stepped outside the crime-scene tape and approached the two boys, who had found the body.

"Before you came across the dead man, did you see or hear anything that might help us?" Ryan said.

The older boy, who wore a reversed baseball cap, nodded toward Greg. "As I told that fatso cop, I did see a pickup drive into the swamp and dump the body where we found it."

"Did you see the driver inside the pickup?"

"Not exactly."

"Can you describe the vehicle?"

"It looked like a regular pickup to me, nothin' special about it."

"Did anything unusual happen?"

The smaller boy wiped his nose with the back of his hand.

"Just as the pickup stopped, someone threw something out the back of the truck," he said.

"You never told the fat cop that, Will," the older boy said. "Are you sure you're not imagining it?"

"Where exactly?" Ryan asked.

"Over by those cattails," Will said, pointing to the edge of the swamp.

"Can you describe this object?"

"It looked like a ball."

"Thanks, guys," Ryan said, smiling. "You've been a big help."

He went back to the crime scene and joined Greg beside the body. A paramedic unzipped a black body bag, and then three of them lifted Sanjay's body. Before placing the corpse on a gurney, one held his shoulders, another carried his legs, and a third cradled his head to keep the tenuous spinal column from breaking.

"What in hell's name did Sanjay do to deserve this?" Greg asked. "How well did you know this guy?"

"We only met a few times."

"What kind of work did you assign him?"

"Keep Moe Fouzi under surveillance, find out where he's from, and determine if he's connected to terrorists."

"Ingrid Krenn claims Moe has no ties to extremists." Sweat beaded on Greg's flushed face. "Did Sanjay find something incriminating about Moe, enough to warrant his murder?"

"Anything's possible."

Ryan could hear lightning pop west of the swamp. In the distance, he could see the grassy slope of a levee already drenched in rain.

"On the surface, Moe is a law-abiding guy, but he seems to have come from nowhere, and now he's missing," Ryan said.

Greg unwrapped a piece of peppermint gum and grinded it with his molars. As he chewed, he watched raindrops form little rings on the surface of the swamp. To protect the crime scene, the forensic team started to pull plastic sheets over the site.

"How could this guy, an outsider, get involved with the class-conscious, tight-assed Ravenstein clan's beautiful heiress?" Greg asked.

"He met Tamara at a company office party. Carl discouraged Tamara from going out with him, but his daughter, like her old man, wanted her own way."

A clap of thunder cracked like a shotgun.

"If he shows up, I'll pull Moe in for questioning. You want to listen in?" Greg asked.

"Thanks, I'd appreciate it."

Greg wrapped his arm around Ryan's shoulder. The cool air smelled of wet reeds and the sulfurous odor of lightning. Rain started to sluice off the plastic sheets.

"If Sanjay's death is in some way connected to your investigation, watch out," he said, wiping rain that had blown onto his face. "You, old buddy, could be next in the line of fire."

Later that evening, Ryan phoned Lucinda Sinha from his boathouse office.

She sounded breathless. "Greg Duluth called me about Sanjay. He told me the details surrounding his death."

"I'm so sorry, Lucinda," Ryan said.

Ryan heard Sanjay's sister sob at the other end of the line. He waited for a moment in silence.

"I shouldn't have involved him in this case," he added.

"You mustn't blame yourself."

"Are you alone?"

"My sister is here. I must face his death on my own terms."

"I'm going to do everything I can to catch his killer."

Ryan glanced out the window. It was still raining, but red sunlight spread out over the lawn. A gale swept through the canopy of a thick copse of white spruce trees on his neighbor's property that made the leaves shimmer as though they were on fire.

She paused to clear an obstruction in her throat.

"I felt nervous when my brother worked in Iraq," she said. "He could have easily died from a car bomb or in a gun battle, but I never suspected he'd be shot and stabbed in Fargo."

"We will find who did it, I promise."

He heard her sigh, a sound like air escaping from a balloon.

"I have to lie down now, Ryan," she whispered and disconnected the line.

Ryan switched off his phone and stared out the window at the river. The bulb on the light post at the end of the dock swarmed with insects in the damp, humid air.

It's time to revisit Moe's pad, he thought. *I'm convinced that's where we'll find the connection between Aimée's murder and Sanjay's killing. I'll look for anything that's been moved or altered in some way.*

Ryan looked pensively at the rain that had soaked the bark of the oak trees near the riverbank. The rain made him think about his dead wife, Kathy, a raven-haired beauty born to smile. He couldn't hide the hurt from his face.

The lights of Gary's Mustang swept the tree-lined drive; the pensive moment broken, but Ryan's face remained as blank as a Lakota Sioux mask.

Early the next morning, Ryan spread out copies, delivered by a police cruiser, of the investigator's preliminary report on Sanjay's murder and the crime-scene photographs. In the report, Ryan learned the killer had stabbed Sanjay in the neck with such massive force that the blade carved nicks out of his vertebrae. Before the stabbing, someone discharged .357 Magnum shells into his shoulder and grazed his temple. A photo showed the bloody interior of Sanjay's Jeep and a bullet hole in the dashboard and another on the blood-splattered seat, indicating the shooter had fired twice to wound him. His killers then dumped him in the back of the pickup and drove him to the swamp to kill him. The crime-scene photographs, stark in color and imagery, showed Sanjay's hands caked with dried blood and his mouth hung open, narrowing his face in a frozen scream.

Ryan locked the files in a wall safe and drove to Moe's bachelor pad on Maplewood Crescent. He took an elevator to the penthouses on the sixteenth floor. It took him a few minutes to disarm Moe's security system and pick the lock.

When he pushed the door open, he pulled back. What reminded him of a booby-trap bomb with a timing device lay on the shoe mat. He shrank away from the door and crouched in the hall. While he waited for the explosion, the only sound inside the apartment was the gentle hum of air-conditioning.

At first, Ryan felt foolish to think Moe or anyone else would blow up his bachelor pad, but after Sanjay's brutal murder, he had braced for the worst. Taking a quick peek around the doorjamb, he soon realized the device was an expensive alarm clock someone had dropped on the carpet.

His first impression of the apartment was that the rooms had lost their Spartan appearance and looked lived-in. Shirts, slacks, and underwear hung over the backs of the black leather sofa and matching chairs. Men's health and fashion magazines no longer lay on the coffee tables. On close inspection of the semicircular bar, the expensive wine bottles had disappeared from inside the cabinets.

In the master bedroom, a backpack lay on the floor half stuffed with jeans, sweaters, casual shirts, and hiking boots. Half-open drawers exposed heaps of shirts and underwear. The armoire that contained Moe's designer suits remained untouched.

Did he plan to go camping? Why had he removed his 1995 Château Margaux and 1996 Château Lafite Rothschild Pauillac from his wine bar?

In the spare bedroom, Moe had piled computers and laptops on top of a fax machine against the wall to make room for a silk mat with an arabesque design in the middle of the floor.

Ryan removed his iPhone from his jacket pocket to call Joanne, but he slipped it back in his pocket when the doorbell rang. His initial instinct was to wait until the visitor went away. When the caller rang the doorbell again, Ryan decided to find out who wanted to see Moe. He glanced into the peephole.

Moe's visitor was a tall, dark-haired woman in her forties, wearing a gray business suit. The first thing he noticed about her was the intensity of her eyes, dark beads of polished coal. For an instant, he froze when he heard a key thrust in the lock. Instead of looking for somewhere to hide, he decided to open the door and adopt a disguise.

When he pulled the door open, she looked stunned.

He put on a false grin. "I'm Nate Sutton from Paradise Realty. Are you here to see the penthouse? It's just come on the market. Believe me, at the listing price of half a million, it's a real steal."

The woman's mouth opened as though she wanted to scream. "Get out! Get out!" she cried.

Her hand reached into her purse for a handgun, which she pointed at Ryan. He leaped forward and grabbed her wrist, twisting until she released her grip on the 9 mm Browning. The handgun clattered to the floor. She hit Ryan in the chin with her fist. He reeled back from her sudden left hook. He reached out to try to grab her hand, but she pulled away and raced down the fire escape stairs.

By the time he arrived at the ground floor, she had disappeared, her vehicle lost in heavy traffic.

CHAPTER 18

EARLY IN THE AFTERNOON, RYAN and Joanne searched the swamp and surrounding park where the two boys had found Sanjay's body. The sky was braided with thick gray and metallic-blue clouds, and the air smelled like rain and dead fish combined with woodsmoke from a smoldering barbecue pit.

Joanne frowned as she poked in among the cattails. She felt annoyed with Jacelyn for dropping in unannounced to see Ryan. She knew Carl's fiancée had a reputation at the tennis club for flirting. Carl hadn't returned home from the cottage, and she suspected Jacelyn had too much spare time to cultivate her habit of chasing men.

She ran her hand through her hair. *Besides,* she thought, *Carl is too old for a woman with her energy and temperament.*

She swung her metal detector over a mound of earth and got a positive reading. She dug into the soft soil with the tip of her runner and came up with a rusty spoon.

The intensity of the case had picked up since the woman, whom Ryan suspected was Moe's mother, had threatened Ryan with a gun in Moe's condo.

After an hour, they had found nothing except discarded trash. She felt frustrated that they didn't have much of a clue about the object the boy had seen thrown from the killer's pickup.

By noon, Joanne had enough of rummaging around in the mud.

"Shouldn't we talk to Ingrid Krenn about the connection between Sanjay's death and his keeping Moe under surveillance? Does she know about Moe's disappearance?" she asked, rubbing her sore back.

"How much more help do you think she'd be?" he asked, probing with a stick at a rusty tin can in a mud pool.

She took in a big breath and let it go.

He shrugged. "Ingrid is preoccupied, as are the feds, in preventing major attacks in North America expected before the presidential election."

"What about involving Greg?"

"By this time tomorrow, he'll have moved on from Sanjay's murder to more urgent cases."

"Aren't we dealing with something bigger than we can handle."

"Yeah, I know. Osama isn't a guy you want to mess with unless you've backed by a squad of special forces."

She lifted a strand of hair from her forehead and rested on the metal detector's handle.

"I feel as though we've covered every inch of this marsh," she said.

"We've overlooked something, Joanne. I know it," he said.

"The police couldn't find anything. What makes you so sure we can?"

The air had turned unseasonably damp from recent rains, but the sky was now blue and cloudless.

"One of the boys was positive he saw some object pitched out of the back of the pickup," he said.

Her eyes drifted to the muddy, uneven ground around her. She stood still, her hair on her neck rustled by a breeze.

"All right, let's continue," she said, beginning to comb again her allotted area.

While she searched, her mind focused on her son. The measure of violence in Gary's existence was as natural in his daily life as his bitterness and sense of failure that greeted him each morning. She couldn't believe how he had managed to mess up his life, yet he had an uncanny way of surviving disasters. She knew his kidnapping and escape last year in the Gulf Islands would've overwhelmed most young men his age.

When she had married Ryan in Seattle, her son had appeared to settle in well in his new surroundings at their house near the beach. Later, he had admitted to meeting some of his old drug-dealer cronies, reigniting his propensity for violence and mayhem.

Ryan had pointed out the irony of Gary's situation. To him, Gary had a great potential and he was one of the most intelligent young men he'd ever met.

As the heat and the mosquito attacks intensified, Joanne became more convinced the search was futile. She glanced at the sun, and then something prompted her to look at a clump of reeds. Lodged in the cattail roots, she spotted a scrunched ball of paper.

"Found something," she said, smoothing out the damp wad on the slats of a bench. The writing appeared to her illegible. "But I can't read it."

"It's written in Arabic," Ryan said, staring at the lined paper that had a jagged edge as though someone had ripped a page out of a notebook.

Ryan hugged her shoulder. "Congratulations, sweetheart, it could be something important."

She sniffed the hot wind that smelled of rotten reeds and dried humus.

"Let's go," he said, opening the car door for her. "I'll ask my Afghan colleague Rafik Shawkat to translate it."

"Doesn't he teach economics at the college?"

"Yes, but I'm sure Rafik would be happy to help."

"If this is what the boys saw thrown out of a pickup, how did Sanjay manage to scribble a message, while bleeding from bullet wounds in the back of the vehicle?"

"It must've taken enormous effort."

"Why write it in Arabic?"

"Sanjay wouldn't want any passerby who happened to find it to know what it said."

"It sounds like something Sanjay would do. Toss us a tantalizing clue and then force us to decipher its meaning."

As they drove away from the park, low-flying geese made quick-moving shadows on the Range Rover's roof, followed by the swish of wings backtracking as the birds landed on open water.

When Joanne parked her van in front of the dead man's house, she glanced at sunlight filtering through the purple leaves of maple trees. On the sidewalk, a group of teenagers listened to white rap music that beat like a fist inside her head. She slipped her .45 in her purse and went up the front steps.

She pushed the bell, and a moment later, Lucinda Sinha opened the door. She wore her long black hair pulled back with combs. Instead of a sari, she had on a black business suit and pearls.

She greeted Joanne with vexed and sullen silence.

"I'm sorry to put you to so much trouble so soon after Sanjay's death," Joanne said.

Although Lucinda had attempted to clean up inside the house, Joanne could see papers scattered on the floor.

"Did you find his laptop?" Joanne asked.

She shook her head. "It's missing. I suspect the cops took it."

She led the way into the dining room, where they sat opposite each other. Lucinda fiddled with matches and lit a cigarette.

"Sanjay had me down to smoking one of these a day," she said. "I usually smoke one just before bed. If he caught me smoking more, he'd confiscate them."

"He was a good brother."

"Indeed," she said in a voice with a soft New Delhi lilt. "I wanted him to follow in my footsteps and become a physician, but after graduating from Harvard, he'd have nothing to do with medicine. He tried to get into the police academy, but they told him he was too short and underweight. I didn't believe them. I think it was the fact that he wasn't a woman. Don't get wrong; I'm glad there are so many females from minority groups who are cops now."

"They make damn good police officers."

She puffed hard on her cigarette and exhaled smoke out of the corner of her mouth. "Look at you. I bet you're an outstanding private investigator, equal to any man."

"I think we're more intuitive when it comes to investigative work. That's what gives us keener insights in the criminal mind," she said, smiling in an attempt to put her at ease.

Lucinda's eyes were bright and hard, the whites bloodshot.

"In medicine—to heal people—we often rely on our powers of observation rather than instinct or skill," she said, tilting back her head. Her thin-rimmed glasses caught a shaft of light as she ground out her half-smoked cigarette in a saucer.

"I felt sorry for Sanjay," she continued. "He wanted so badly to get into law enforcement. That's why he went into security management and started his own business."

Joanne swallowed and took a deep breath. "Did Sanjay say anything to you about his investigation of Moe Fouzi?"

"He never discussed cases with me, but the night before he died, after checking Islamic websites, he kept repeating this phrase about birds dropping deadly eggs on the heads of kings."

Joanne, who had begun to doodle on her notepad, tried to reign in her excitement. It was similar to the Arabic note Sanjay had managed to throw out of the back of the pickup: "The exploding eggs of eagles will destroy infidel rulers."

"Did he tell you what the words mean?" she asked.

"He didn't, but I presume he was deciphering some sort of code."

"He left us a clue of what could be the target for a terrorist attack."

She showed Lucinda a copy of the rolled-up piece of paper found at the crime scene.

"I'm familiar with the Russian double-eagle symbol of the Romanovs, but I've never heard of them using their eggs to kill kings." She shuddered. "Do they mean bombs?"

"We've done a search of Arabic mythology and came up with nothing."

Lucinda sat straight up. One hand dug into the flesh above her heart; the other gripped the hand rest.

"My brother worked all his life with dangerous and violent people," she said, her dark eyes clouded with sadness. "I believe more than ever that his death is somehow connected to his investigation of Moe Fouzi. He referred most of his current projects to other investigators or put them on hold so he could devote time to find out about Moe."

"Did he leave behind notebooks or computer disks?"

"I'm sorry to disappoint you, Joanne, but I can't find anything like that."

Joanne stared at Lucinda's hands. For a moment, they no longer had the smooth, tapered fingers of a physician. Instead, she had curled up her fingers until the knobby bones struck out as though he wanted to crush something inside them.

"Have you done a thorough search of the house?"

Lucinda raised her pencil-thin eyebrows. "Yes, but wait a minute; Sanjay kept valuables in a safe."

She got up and removed a painting of Shiva to reveal a small safe embedded in the wall. She spun the dials, and the door swung open. Inside, Joanne saw piles of euros and US currency. In the back of the safe, Lucinda removed a hardcover notebook.

She handed the book to Joanne, who flipped through the pages, trying to decipher Sanjay's tiny script in Hindi.

"Can you translate it?" she asked.

Lucinda examined the pages for a moment.

"It appears to be meaningless gibberish. He's using a code."

In the middle of the book, Lucinda found a dog-eared photograph of a young Arab man and his wife. The couple stood in front of four preteen boys, in ages about a year apart. Someone had circled the head of the youngest son with a red pen.

Joanne exhaled like the whistle of wind in a chimney.

"That has to be Moe." She stabbed the photo with her index fingernail. "The forehead, the eyebrows, the mouth, they're identical."

Her thin-rimmed glasses caught a shaft of light as she studied the family portrait. She pointed to the thickset man with a pronounced widow's peak, a hooked nose, and a drooping moustache.

"Moe's father," she whispered.

Lucinda's face filled with a level of sorrow Joanne had rarely seen before. "What are you getting yourself into?" Lucinda asked.

CHAPTER 19

I NGRID KRENN STRETCHED OUT HER long bronzed legs to the sun. The walls surrounding city hall's courtyard muted the sound of traffic on Third Street North, and the air was heavy with the smell of freshly watered red and white geraniums. She brushed a thin strand of brown hair from her forehead and watched a shaft of light on the cement tiles. When she spoke, she stared at Ryan through a pair of Bolo sunglasses.

"There's little doubt that al-Qaeda is trying to strike before the November election on a scale as big or larger than 9/11," she said.

"Have you found many active operatives in the state?" he asked.

"We have to assume there are some, but we don't know. The reports are mixed. Certainly, a few have entered the US at some point. That's why agents are fanning across the country to ferret out suspects."

"Do you expect the current crackdown to roll up any sleeper cells?"

"Judging by the extent of the sweep, I'd say that's a strong possibility."

"Do you know if they have targets identified in the city?"

"I don't think Fargo's skyscrapers are of interest. We're too regional, and any strikes would have limited effect internationally. New York and Chicago are far more likely to come under attack.

There's a much greater population and concentration of economic power. A few years ago, al-Qaeda agents cased financial targets, including the New York Stock Exchange, World Bank, CitiGroup, and other sites in Newark and Washington." She leaned forward and pouted her glossy red lips. "One terrorist, Iyman Faris, had a cockamamie scheme to cut down cables on the Brooklyn Bridge." She laughed. "He gave up when the steel strands proved too thick for his wire cutters."

"Are they shifting to a different set of targets?" he asked, trying to keep his voice relaxed and friendly.

She narrowed her eyes and cocked her head.

"We know that high-level operatives have been traveling around the world to the Afghanistan-Pakistan border to meet and plan. These meetings resemble those that took place in Malaya the year before 9/11."

Ryan glanced over her shoulder at a display of quilts that symbolized AIDS victims, filling a corner of the quadrangle in a tragic way to humanize the cold concrete.

"Is it possible Sanjay Sinha's investigation could've come too close to an operative or a splinter group? As a result, they murdered him to protect the integrity of their network?"

"Who knows? Sanjay did security work in Lebanon, Iraq, and Somalia. In these countries, he probably met some cold-blooded, ruthless people. His stabbing has the characteristics of a revenge killing."

"I think his investigation of Moe Fouzi had a direct bearing on his death."

"If you're referring to Moe Fouzi as a possible sleeper, forget it. I've had Moe checked out. As far as we're concerned he's completely in the clear."

"He has an ideal cover, buried deep in the social fabric."

She glanced at her watch. "We have to focus on the big picture. We can't be sidetracked into looking for jihadists under every rock and in every cranny."

Ryan stared at circling seagulls in the clear prairie sky, the color of light-blue velvet. Cooing pigeons roosted and strutted on ledges and abutments, staring down at them like hundreds of eyes from all points on the compass.

"By the way, I've advised Greg Duluth not to call Moe in for questioning," she said, shifting her buttocks to straighten her tight skirt.

Her eyes heavy with mascara took in the disappointment flooding his face.

"We need solid evidence, not just vague insinuations," she added, getting up and extending her fingers.

Ryan stood up to grasp her slender fingers.

"He's disappeared."

"Oh, I hadn't heard. I expect he'll turn up in a day or two." She withdrew her hand, tapped her foot, put her hands on her hips. "We've new evidence from the crime scene and the Sinha home that has thrown a whole new light on the investigation into his murder."

"What new evidence?"

"It's confidential."

She turned on her heel and walked back to city hall's rear entrance.

"Can't you give me some indication of what's going on?" he asked, speaking to her slender back.

She glanced over her shoulder without slackening her pace. "If you're interested, contact Dr. Roberts."

A cement truck passed by and belched a cloud of black smoke into the pristine sky.

He ran to catch up with her. "I still think you're wrong about Moe."

She paused in midstride and turned around. She tightened her lips and spoke in a voice just above a whisper. "Moe belonging to sleeper cell doesn't follow the pattern. Al-Qaeda plans attacks far in advance. So any intelligence we receive, even if it's several years old, is taken very seriously."

Ryan felt frustrated and had to force himself to show some semblance of calm. "I know any evidence connecting Moe to

Sanjay's death is at the moment unclear, but I do have a photo of his father."

After a short and tense silence, Ingrid said, "I'd rather go after the big fish. Fight the fight today so if I have any kids they won't have to worry about being under siege."

"I have two teenagers at home, and I sure as hell want them to be safe in the future. That's why I came to you."

"You must understand that any terrorist activity in this state, against say a military target, could be a diversionary tactic to spread out resistance in several places and then bomb another. Surely, you see my point."

She turned on her high heels, scurried across the paving stones, and disappeared behind city hall's revolving glass doors.

Dr. Roscoe Roberts returned Ryan's call in the afternoon. His voice sounded cold and impersonal. By the crisp, clipped way he spoke, he had clearly refused, since his arrival in Fargo twenty years ago, to give up a sliver of his upper-class English accent.

"I can't give you any information on the phone. I'd prefer to talk to you face-to-face," he said.

"Why's that?" Ryan asked.

Roscoe's answer didn't make much sense.

"Autopsies can tell things about human behavior I don't care to know about," the pathologist said.

An hour later, Ryan walked into his office, an airless room without windows, smelling of formaldehyde. From behind a large mahogany desk, Roscoe didn't look up from his paperwork and didn't venture any kind of greeting apart from "Sit."

Ryan noted that his dyed black hair was too dark for his wrinkled alabaster skin. Beside his desk was a dry fish tank, home to a knot of pet garter snakes.

A silence settled while Roscoe scribbled a notation on the pile of paper he was working on. Finally, Roscoe pitched his head up, a puzzled look on his pale face as if trying to decipher a linguistic puzzle.

"You should know I'm only seeing you due to a big favor owed to Greg Duluth."

He tipped his chair back against the wall, stood up, and stripped off his brown-stained lab coat and hung it on peg. He replaced his work coat with a navy-blue blazer he wore over a white shirt and a striped Regimental tie.

"Thank you for seeing me on such short notice, Roscoe," Ryan said. "When can I see the—"

Roscoe interrupted. "I'm afraid I don't have much time."

"Are you taking me to see Sinha's body?"

Roscoe held up his hand as though asking for silence during a lecture. "Hold on. Let's talk in a more congenial setting."

Roscoe led the way down a narrow corridor that smelled of unwashed bodies and disinfectant. He opened his office building's glass-and-steel entrance doors.

"Why aren't we going to the morgue?" Ryan asked.

Roscoe's melancholy eyes fixed on Ryan. "We're going to sit under the elms. You'll have to excuse my dark mood; my work depresses the hell out of me some days."

They sat on a bench beside a wading pool where a passel of children frolicked in the water. On the lawn, two boys without shirts tossed a Frisbee.

"I want his body examined by an independent pathologist," Ryan said.

"Over my dead body." Dr. Roberts chuckled at his own joke. "You see, he's already been cremated."

"How can you do that when his murder is still under investigation?"

"I completed all the necessary paperwork." His pipe went out, and he went through the ritual of putting new tobacco in the bowl, tamping it down, and relighting. "Besides, his sister agreed to it. She wanted him cremated so she could scatter his ashes in the Ganges River."

From a folder, the pathologist removed a photograph of the back of a man's head and naked shoulders. "The abrasions and scrape marks are more like trauma from a fall than a direct blow." He rested his hands that had long fingernails in the lap of his creased gray slacks. "Of course, you're more interested in cause of death."

"Are you describing the right body—?"

Roscoe interrupted. "I mean these abrasions may have been unrelated to his death. Do you know if he'd been in a traffic accident?"

Ryan snatched the photo from him and examined the bloodstained back of a victim with a full head of hair. "This isn't Sanjay Sinha; he's bald."

Dr. Roberts cleared his throat and looked at a tab on the file. "You're right. This body belongs to a John Doe." His mouth opened, but nothing came out, his eyes searching somewhere within himself. "How perfectly stupid of me." He closed the file and drummed his fist on his forehead. "Let me reconnect. Sanjay Sinha. He's that Asian fellow found in a swamp with two bullet wounds and a slit throat."

"Did you do an autopsy on Sanjay?"

"Of course I did. Stop telling me how to do my job."

"Then where is your autopsy report?"

He opened an expandable file case and started rummaging until he found a slim folder. He put on half-frame reading glasses and flipped pages. "My notes indicate I found evidence of marijuana and heroin in his blood. It's a bit complicated, but there's no question about these substance being there long before he died."

"He definitely wasn't a user."

"Let me finish." He lit a pipe and stretched out his legs as he puffed. "The marijuana is locally grown. It is identical down to the last chemical to the narcotic that's being sold here by city dealers. The heroin is an Afghan import."

His eyes gazed at hanging flowerpots of petunias swaying in the breeze from a shelter where families were barbecuing.

"Do you wish me to confirm this in a formal report?" Roscoe asked. "My findings are conclusive."

Ryan began to form a fist with his right hand, and he could feel veins tightening at the temples. A voice in the back of his mind urged him to avoid a confrontation.

"Even to suggest he had an addiction to narcotics is absurd," he said.

Dr. Roberts took out a pouch and piled a pinch into a pipe bowl, lit it, and sucked in his cheeks at the same time as he tamped down the tobacco until it glowed.

"After examining tissue in his lungs, I'd say he'd been a long-time user."

"Sanjay is an international security investigator. In his line of work, he needed a keen, analytical mind, not one befuddled by drugs."

"When I examined his pupils, they were dilated, a clear indication he's a regular user. We also found a roach in his coat pocket."

Ryan stared up at the sky ribbed with strips of cloud, while a warm breeze began to ruffle the pungent pipe smoke away from him. His throat felt as though he had swallowed a pincushion punched full of needles.

"So what you're saying—"

"I suspect he was not only addicted to these illegal substances, but he also sold them."

"How can you make such a baseless accusation?"

Roscoe expanded his wide chest; his eyes reflected renewed clarity. "After his murder, the police searched his home, and the officers found a stash of illegal substances hidden in the basement. His sister, Dr. Lucinda Sinha, faces charges of possession."

Ryan couldn't contain himself any longer. "She's been framed—"

Roscoe cut him off. "In my opinion, his death is related to a drug deal gone sour." He strained to keep his voice even.

Ryan glanced at a Victorian house at the edge of the park with filigree painted yellow. Roscoe's smug, arrogant attitude and superior manner made Ryan boil over in anger.

Roscoe appeared to be oblivious of Ryan's mounting rage. "As far as I'm concerned, the cause of death relates to one of Mr. Sinha's transactions gone pear-shaped."

Roscoe started to hack with such severity that he knocked off his reading glasses. When he recovered, Roscoe put his finger on a notation underlined in his file. "His skin color could indicate an association with Asian gangs, who are now using our fair city as a focal point to cultivate, market, and distribute drugs throughout the Midwestern states."

Ryan was so angry he couldn't stop himself. "I've heard enough of your lies, distortions, and downright fabrications."

Dr. Roberts ignored him and puffed hard on his pipe, filling the air with renewed acrid smoke. "As a result of my findings, I've included his obvious signs of addiction in my final report."

"His murder had nothing to do with his alleged drug habit. It's related to dangerous terrorists."

"Are you serious?" he asked, a smirk crossing his thin lips. "It's pure and simple a case of trafficking in narcotics. You've been reading too many spy novels, Mr. Moar. You're obsessed by some obscure conspiratorial nonsense."

"While conducting an investigation—nothing whatsoever to do with the drug trade—Sanjay was brutally murdered. How can you even consider this killing related to turf wars between drug lords?"

Roscoe's eyes glistened with a harsh light while he consulted his notes. "I've already received a similar report from another independent lab confirming my findings." He looked at his watch and raised his eyebrows. "Oh heavens, I'm late for a staff meeting."

Ryan felt bulldozed by Roscoe's attempt to pin Sanjay's death on drug wars. He recognized Roscoe as a snob, who treated him and others as being without anything to contribute to his superior knowledge. The pathologist stood up, knocked ash out of his pipe bowl into the palm of his hand, and swept the cinders onto the grass.

"The bottom line is the blood samples. My lab clearly indicated your security adviser is a drug user," he said.

Whistling a nameless tune, the doctor walked away and didn't look back.

The next evening, Charlene was sitting on the patio when she spotted Gary's red Mustang convertible speeding along the drive. He wore a blue-striped dress shirt, starched khaki pants, and sunglasses.

He jogged around to the patio and stood in front of her, his fingertips drumming the tabletop, his face blank.

"Take a ride with me," he said. "I'm meeting friends at the West Acres Mall's food court."

She glared up at him, her voice irritable. "How can you eat that disgusting food loaded with unhealthy saturated fats?" Gary's hands curled into fists. "Plus I'm not sure I want to meet *your* friends."

He leaned toward her, his mouth parted to speak, but then changed his mind.

"Do they resemble the losers you used to hang out with in Marsdon?" she asked, her lips parting in a grin.

"You are seriously pissing me off," he said. "My mom asked me to be nice to you, and you end up insulting me and my mates."

She arched her slim eyebrows. "If I criticized your cronies, it wasn't personal."

He screwed up his face. "The mall serves salads, and they won't spoil your figure."

She couldn't see his eyes behind his dark glasses, but she could feel the heat rising in his throat. He stared down at her, his back against the setting sun, while she looked at her reflection, distorted and diminished in the lens.

"I suppose my friends aren't good enough for you," he said, turning on his heels.

"Wait a minute," she said to his back. "I don't want you to think I'm a snob."

"I'm outta here," he said, looking back at her, his cheek and neck containing shards of red. "You're a stuck-up, skinny bitch."

Charlene waited until he had driven off before she started crying. She wanted to like him, but he seemed moody, easily offended. She didn't want to sound standoffish. Would she be this way with other boys? She went inside. In the living room, Ryan noticed her flushed cheeks and red eyes. He followed her upstairs to her bedroom with shelves lined with Agatha Christie novels, stuffed owls, and framed photographs of ballerinas Evelyn Hart and Margo Fontaine.

After a bit of coaxing, she told Ryan what Gary had said.

"You mustn't take his remarks seriously," he said.

"He's right. I am too skinny. Some of my friends even say I'm ugly."

"Sweetheart, that's not true; you're beautiful."

"Even Mom thinks I should gain weight."

"You're perfect the way you are."

"Because I'm thin and ugly, I don't have many friends."

"Trust me, once you get settled in at Oak Grove in the fall, you'll make plenty of friends."

He handed her a tissue, and she blew her nose.

"I feel so miserable I want to die," she said, sitting down on the bed. Ryan sat beside her and started to stroke her back.

"Sweetheart, you mustn't say that," he said.

"Well, it's true."

"I know Gary's rough around the edges, but please try to get along with him."

"He's the one with the attitude problem."

"He's had a hard time."

Charlene got to her feet and looked out of the bedroom window at the wind rock the dingy tied to the dock.

"That's no excuse for having a foul mouth," she said, folding her arms across her chest.

"Would you like Joanne to talk to him?"

"No, please don't tell her. It'll just make thing worse between us."

Ryan cast his eyes around the room, through the window to the river, back to his daughter. "Just remember, we're the only family he's got."

"I don't care. He needs to get a life."

"He's had problems."

"That's no excuse. Why doesn't he want to get a job? Enroll in college courses or learn a trade or do something?" Her voice took on a hoarse quality. "I know all about his life in Marsdon, breaking Joanne's heart by running away from home and returning to sell drugs to university students. Then the police arrested him as the prime suspect in a rape and murder case. How does Joanne put up with him?"

"He's her only son. That's how." Ryan rested his hand on her shoulder. "Is there anything you like about him?"

"He's goofy sometimes," she said, moving away from him.

"Teenage boys are like that, sweetheart. They go through a stage when they like to rebel and tease girls."

"Thanks, Dad, for the insight." Charlene wiped her eyes. "Are you and Joanne getting along okay?"

Father and daughter exchanged a look.

"I heard you two arguing the other night. What was that about?" she asked.

"We had a disagreement about Jacelyn Temple's nocturnal visit to my office."

"Is Joanne jealous? Jacelyn is a beautiful woman."

"I've given her no reason to be jealous." Charlene felt her father move closer, wrap his arm around her shoulder, and kiss her on the top of her head. "You like Joanne, don't you?"

"She's nice. I never want to live with Mom again."

"You don't have to." He squeezed her shoulder. "Why don't I ask Joanne to take you shopping for some new outfits?"

Her smile gave Ryan a contented feeling.

Habib drove the red pickup down Pelican Hill Road through well-treed acreages under a moonlit sky. The cool air smelled of ripening alfalfa, and moonlight glittered like silver leaf off the surface of the Sheyenne River.

When he turned down the ranch's driveway, he noticed Zahara had made the exterior of the house look ordinary by adding a flagstone walkway, planting impatiens beside a birdbath, and building a fishpond bubbling with koi. Behind the bungalow was the barn where she kept the horse trailers. She had disguised a windowless portion of the stables into a machine workshop. He climbed out of the pickup, and before going inside the house, he stopped to admire a sleek Arabian mare chewing on lush grass in a paddock.

He had to ring the doorbell twice before she answered.

Zahara wore a scarf tied under her chin that pressed her dark, straight hair flat against her cheeks. The whites of her eyes had a yellow cast, and her blouse and long skirt smelled of garlic.

He leaned over to kiss her cheek. "Are they here?"

"All of them, except for Gulbuddin," she said.

Habib strolled down a hall to the living room furnished with a Salvation Army–vintage couch and easy chairs. Heavy black velvet curtains blocked moonlight from coming in bay windows.

She smiled when he carried a suitcase in from the pickup. "Does that mean you'll be living with us?"

"I've moved out of the Roosevelt warehouse."

"That's wonderful." She went to him and hugged him, burying her face into the lapel of his suit jacket.

He wrapped his arms around her, and his lips brushed across her hair. When he released her, she looked up, her eyes wide and watery.

"Until we're ready to leave, we'll use the place in Moorhead as a safe house."

Through the open window in the kitchen, he could make out the paddock fences and woods. He sat at the kitchen table, while Zahara made coffee.

"Has Arrak found anything more about the real-estate agent in Mohammed's condo?" he asked.

"He will not rest until he knows his identity."

Habib sniffed the warm air wafting through the window, the smell of fresh hay and sweaty horses.

"When I was on the run, I sometimes thought about making a career of raising Arabians," he said.

"And abandon our plans?"

A grin flickered across his thick lips. "It crossed my mind."

She sat back, stunned by his admission. "What made you change your position?"

He rubbed the stubble on his cheek. "After I saw those photographs of naked prisoners in Abu Ghraib being tortured and sexually abused by depraved American guards, I wanted to vomit."

Her eyes held his for a moment, and a great sadness swept across her face like that of a child watching melted scoops of ice cream fall off a cone and splat on the pavement.

"I thought about how those young prisoners could have been my sons," she said.

"I take it Mohammed has left his girlfriend but still hasn't come home," he said while he hauled out and examined another AK-47, from behind the fridge.

"Give him time."

"He told me to my face he didn't want to see me again."

Zahara took his massive hands in hers. "For so long, he was ashamed to be seen in my company."

"Does he no longer believe in Islamic causes?" Habib said, breaking away from her.

"Do you remember his devotion to Islam? He didn't want to leave Damascus to study abroad like the other boys." Habib checked to make sure the rifle was loaded. "Anytime I turned on the radio, he'd switch it off." Habib used both hands to wave the rifle in the air. "At least my threats to expose him have forced him to leave his old life and go underground."

"Don't give up on him, Habib. There is still hope."

Habib cradled the rifle on his lap, his face charged with energy.

"What makes you think he'll come back?" he asked.

"In his condo, he made room for a prayer mat."

Habib held up the rifle for further inspection. "God be praised."

The front doorbell chimed, and Habib felt a tightening in his throat. He swiveled his eyes as an indication for Zahara to answer it.

She went to the door; the soft pad of her slippers on the hardwood floor made a raspy sound like sand that wears away the surface of old tombs.

Habib strolled to the spare bedroom. Facing the drive, he opened the curtains a crack. His cheeks stung as though someone had slapped him. A police car had parked parallel to the front door. He went back to the kitchen to pick up the AK-47.

While he waited, his lips moved in prayer. "In the name of Allah, the beneficent, the merciful … master of the day of judgment … show us the straight path."

CHAPTER 20

MARLEAU ASKED A SECURITY GUARD at the entrance of the Blue Wolf Casino where he could find a blackjack dealer named Bonnie Kunst. He accompanied the guard inside the barn-shaped casino, and they strolled by banks of VLTs. At the blackjack tables, the guard pointed out Bonnie, a slender young woman dealing cards in front of a mirror. Her brown eyes registered indifference. She wore a tight black dress and fishnet stockings. She had slicked down her short bleached hair and plastered curls to her cheeks and forehead.

"May I talk to you, Miss Kunst?" he asked.

"Sure, I'm ready for a break," she said, nodding to a sleek young man in a black suit beside her who took over her dealer's position. "Call me Bonnie."

Marleau handed her his card, and she examined it in the dim light.

"I don't mind talking to a private investigator with a French name. It's the cops I can't trust," she said, sitting down at a booth. "What can I do for you, Marleau?"

"Up until a few months ago, you worked for the Sinise brothers. Why did you quit?" he asked, sitting beside her.

Her purple round earrings swayed as she spoke. "After I'd worked in Paul's office for six months, I asked him about some entries, and he went nuts."

"Did you find out he did something unethical?"

She removed a wad of gum from her mouth and stuck it under the table. "When he fixed the books before, I'd overlooked his adjustments, but this time it was too obvious, the amount too big. Then he threatened to can me. The next day, however, he was as sweet and smooth as melted chocolate."

"All was forgiven?"

"You might say that."

"Where is his office?"

"He used this warehouse as a front for a larger operation that he ran at night. Whenever I had to work late, the place was buzzing with these colostomy bags."

"He must've known you were aware of what was going on."

"I think he trusted me to keep my mouth shut. I knew he packed a gun. His goons swaggered after him like bodyguards. They even tried to pick me up, take me out. When I'd had enough of those creeps, I handed in my resignation."

"How did he react when you decided to quit?"

"He offered me a lot more money to stay on, and he promised me an office of my own," she said, leaning closer to Marleau to brush off a spot of dust on his jacket. "He said he'd own a legit business soon, and I'd be like his executive assistant in a posh office in the business district."

"When did he say this universe would unfold?"

"As soon as his lawyers and financial guys got off their butts, he'd take over a big company. He'd make tons of legitimate money." She looked at him with wary eyes that had the bright amber tint of contact lens. "After a few months, he sweet-talked me into coming with him to the Horse Park races, and then he took me out to Maxwell's afterward."

Bonnie's cheeks turned bright red, as if embarrassed by what she was about to tell him.

"When his wife found out about us, he dumped me faster than ice breaks up on the Red in spring," she said.

She clamped her hand on top of Marleau's, and he could feel the sweat in her palm.

"Before I packed my personal things, he warned me not to talk to cops," she said. "To make sure I got the message, a guy in a ski mask popped out from behind a pile of drink cartons at a gas station and slammed his fist in my face. He told me if I talked to the police about Paul, he'd use a razor blade to carve his initials on my face." She screwed up her nose. "He then punched me so hard I needed plastic surgery."

"You look great now."

"Thanks. You look pretty cool yourself." She smiled, displaying even teeth. "I should've sent Paul the bill for the makeover."

Marleau scratched at a scar that ran through his right eyebrow. "You don't sound bitter."

She crossed her legs, pulled down the hem of her short dress, and adopted a wounded look. "At first it generated a large amount of anger inside me, but I got over it. Life goes on, right?" Her eyes narrowed with hate. "I see Paul sometimes at the casino."

"Does he bother you?"

She shifted in her seat. "Even when he's playing blackjack at one of my tables, he doesn't know I exist."

"Do you recognize the people he's with?"

"Apart from his younger brother, Mark, his main bud is that son of a big shot." Her forehead wrinkled in concentration. "This guy's father is supposed to have killed his wife."

"Do you mean Cole Ravenstein?"

"That's the dude. He's so stuck up; you'd think he'd been born with a silver spoon up his butt."

Bonnie looked up at a stolid lantern-jawed man who had a bad case of acne and a paunch that hung over his belt like a wet cement bag.

"Break's over, Bonnie," he said in a booming voice.

He gave off a swampy smell, a combination of underarm odor and testosterone.

She folded her hands and lowered her eyes.

"Relieve Della on table six, and make it snappy," he said.

His voice caused a shadow to climb up her face like bruise.

"Sure thing, Art," she said, getting up.

When he left, Marleau said, "Charming boss you have."

"It's better than flipping burgers at McDonald's," she said, winking at him. "Besides, at the casino, you meet nicer people. See you around."

With Habib praying in the kitchen, Zahara answered the door. Her eyes bulged wide in terror when she had switched on the outside light and seen a uniformed police officer on the front steps.

She had taken in a deep breath and opened the door a crack.

"Good evening, ma'am," the police officer said, peering in at her past the door chain.

She tried to control the panic that had put a stranglehold on her throat. She listened to her ragged little gulps of breath.

"What can I do for you, officer?" she asked, maintaining a tight grip on a Magnum .357 in her pocket.

"I'm Officer Bellord, and my partner in the vehicle is Officer Shandy," he said.

"Yes, sir," she whispered, feeling her knees quiver under her housecoat.

"Do you by any chance breed horses?" he asked.

"Why, yes."

"Well, ma'am, we picked up a young man who claims he's lost, and he's trying to find a ranch where folks breed Arabians." He raised his bushy eyebrows. "Would you mind stepping this way to identify him?"

She unhooked the chain and opened the door, glancing over the officer's shoulder at the cruiser, her eyes blinded by the headlights.

Her hands flew to her lips when she recognized Mohammed in the backseat of the patrol car, the details of his face obscured by the dividing grill.

She cursed him under her breath for not following instructions. When he had decided to join them, she had ordered him to wait at the Roosevelt warehouse for Arrak to pick him up. Under no circumstances was he to come to the ranch on his own. Why had he taken such a terrible risk?

She tried to force her lips into a smile, her thoughts as jagged as shards of glass. She felt a band of pressure tighten at the temples.

This pain felt similar to the night in Damascus when Habib had told her about assassins closing in on their compound. The family had to escape to Kabul or die.

Officer Shandy rested one foot on the police car's bumper. He smiled at her with eyes webbed with tiny lines at the corners. They were as blue as a butane flame.

"We picked him up on the road. He had no identification and claimed he'd lost his way," he said.

Mohammed's eyes lit up when he recognized her.

"That's my son," she said. "He hasn't been in North Dakota long, so he isn't familiar with the area."

"Remind him it's not safe to hitchhike late at night."

When Mohammed climbed out of the back of the squad car, she held him close to her.

"You should've taken a cab," she scolded, releasing him. "Your father would've paid the fare."

Behind her, Officer Shandy said, "My daughter, Doreen, is crazy about horses. Could she come for a ride sometime at your convenience?"

"Bring her over anytime," she said, steering Mohammed by his elbow toward the front door.

"That's very kind of you, ma'am."

Zahara took a deep breath, which she blew out in a rush of relief as the two officers had waved good-bye.

When she scurried inside, she could feel the sweat that had soaked the back of her blouse.

"If those cops came to arrest us, I'd have killed them with the AK-47," Habib said, turning to his son.

Mohammed had avoided his stare. He had looked out of the kitchen window at raindrops on the pond and adopted an uncomfortable silence as though he were a stranger.

He had cringed at his father's livid face.

"Listen to me, Mohammed, and listen as though your life depends on it. If you betray me, I'll strangle you—"

Zahara's eyes had shone with tears. "Habib, you're supposed to welcome our son home. Instead, you threaten him." She had pounded her fists on her husband's chest. "He is your own flesh and blood."

CHAPTER 21

T HE NEXT DAY, RYAN SAT at the kitchen table and examined the family photo from Sanjay's safe. He was convinced whoever killed Aimée had also slit Sanjay's throat and slaughtered Dixie, Carl's Scottish terrier. Ryan didn't want to think about who could be butchered next. He pushed himself out of his chair. Behind him, Joanne put plates in the dishwasher.

"What do you think the phrase about the eagles dropping eggs on infidel kings means?" he asked, referring to the scrap of paper Joanne had found in the swamp where the killers dumped Sanjay's body.

"It may have some bearing on the next target." She closed the dishwasher door and wiped her hands on a tea towel. "Moe's disappearance means only one thing. He's reunited with his parents in some unholy war. Is there anybody who'll at least listen to this idea that there could be a threat to national security?"

Ryan doubted even his former colleagues would give him a hearing. The feds would be reluctant to get involved on such slim evidence. "Even if we give Ingrid Krenn what we know about Sanjay's murder, this photo, the translation from the scrap of paper, and the break-in at Carl's cabin as proof of the buildup to an impending terrorist attack, she'll ridicule us for wasting her time," he said. "Greg isn't interested in anecdotal evidence either."

He scrawled a series of circles on the yellow legal pad in front of him. His doodling kept circling back onto itself, reminding him of a noose. He shivered when images of Sanjay's body in the reeds flashed into his mind. The discussion of Moe's father had left an impression on him of a sharp knife that was now slicing his own viscera.

"We'll tighten security," he said.

His eyes met Joanne's, and he saw her face turn pale.

"When is this going to end?" she asked.

Ryan needed exercise to relieve the tension, so he changed into his tracksuit and runners for a jog along Red River Road. Fork lightning veined the clouds reflecting off the wings of dragonflies skimming on the surface of a pond like the sudden burst of flame from matches.

After completing his run, Gary joined him in the backyard, and they worked out together doing three sets each of sit-ups, barbell curls, and dead lifts.

During the workout, Ryan asked, "How are you getting along with Charlene?"

Gary nodded, his jaw set. "She's okay."

Ryan wiped his brow with a towel.

"Do I take it then everything is copacetic between you two?"

Gary looked at him warily as though Ryan was setting a trap for him. "She's okay."

"You keep repeating that."

Gary put down the weights, sat on the bench, and pressed the heel of his hand to his forehead. "I'll admit she's hard to get along with."

"She has the same complaint about you."

"Look, how about we just skip talking about—"

"You're older and know a lot more about life than she does," Ryan said, interrupting.

"What's that supposed to mean?"

"Try to treat her like your little sister."

"She can be bratty." He shrugged. "Okay, I'll give it a try."

A cabin cruiser went by, and the wake slapped the shoreline and slid along the cattails bordering the river.

"There's another thing I need to talk to you about, and I want you to keep it to yourself," Ryan said. "We have to watch out for strangers on the property."

"Sure, I'll keep my eyes open."

"I'm also going to have to restrict your movements for a while. From now on you don't go anywhere unless you're with us."

Gary bristled. "Why? I've done nothing wrong."

"It has nothing to do with anything you've done." Ryan started putting the weights in bags and collapsing the benches. "We're looking for a dangerous man, whom we suspect is aware of you and Charlene. He's a fanatic who may try to use you both as a means to get at me or your mother."

Gary grinned for no reason and rubbed his chin peppered with stubble. "You're kidding me, right?"

Ryan recalled how Gary had often refused to be serious whenever Ryan showed concern for his reckless and self-destructive behavior.

"I couldn't be more serious," he said.

"Are we gonna be kidnapped or something?" Gary asked.

"That's a possibility, but it could be lot worse. I don't know much about this guy yet, but he takes particular pleasure in slitting throats."

"Why is he threatening us?"

"He doesn't want me to find out his identity and track him down."

"Is he the guy who iced Sanjay?"

"I believe he killed him."

Gary sat on the edge of the dock and pulled a handheld Game Boy out of his pocket and began playing. "The papers said his murder was a drug deal gone sour," he said.

"That's what the cops are saying. Although I can't prove it, I think the coroner deliberately made his death resemble a drug-related killing."

Gary hardly looked up. "You mean like Mitch Glover planting my DNA at the Marsdon crime scene, the evidence that made me the prime suspect in Brenda's murder."

"That's right."

"Why did the coroner want to doctor the crime scene?"

"I suspect the guy we're looking for offered him such a huge sum of money that he couldn't refuse." Ryan hesitated before continuing. "We have to stop this guy before he carries out some kind of terrorist attack."

"Is he a towel head?"

"I suspect he is, but please don't use that pejorative term."

The sun had turned the river yellow, the water swirling with weeds at the edge between the deep shadows of the elms and white-barked spruce along the banks.

"Come with me," Ryan said, glancing down at the base of the levee where he had positioned a row of cardboard shoeboxes.

"Where are we going?" Gary said, reluctant to stop playing.

Ryan removed his .257 Magnum from the holster.

Gary fixed him with a startled look. "What do you want with that?"

"We're going to practice shooting," he said, leading the way to the levee.

Ryan showed Gary how the trigger mechanism disengaged from the hammer. He let him work the slide and slip an empty magazine into the butt.

"The cardinal rule of firearm use is never to assume the gun is unloaded or loaded," Ryan said.

"Okay."

"Now let me see you clear it."

Gary pushed the release button, removed the magazine, and worked the slide twice, before examining the empty chamber.

"Excellent," Ryan said. He then demonstrated the two-hand grip and aim with his legs apart and knees slightly bent. "Remember to maintain a firm grip on the pistol; you don't have to strangle it. And take a deep breath before firing."

151

Ryan handed Gary the loaded handgun. They both covered their ears with sound mufflers. Ryan took a step behind Gary.

Gary took aim at one of the shoeboxes and fired, nicking the top of a box, knocking it sideways.

"Aim lower and to your left," Ryan said.

Gary missed two more rounds and lowered the Magnum.

"Keep firing until you've emptied the chamber," Ryan said. "Try to hit other boxes."

Gary kept firing, reports echoing across the river. In time, he found his aim and peppered the targets with holes. Ryan glanced over his shoulder at the sound of a car. Marleau's Yukon pulled up in front of the house.

Above the roar of his souped-up engine, Ryan could hear the blare of a twenty-four-hour jazz radio station. Marleau strolled down to the levee to watch Gary empty the magazine.

"Good shooting," Ryan said, taking the Magnum back and snapping the gun in the holster.

"Aren't you taking a big risk teaching that child to shoot?" Marleau asked.

"I'm not a child," Gary said, scowling at Marleau. Gary leaned over to examine a peppered shoebox. "I'm not a bad shot either."

"After the break-in at Carl's cottage, I thought it best to acquaint him with how to handle a weapon," Ryan said.

Marleau took a closer look at the bullet holes that had stitched a pattern in the cardboard. The neighbor's wind sock beside a floatplane landing dock hung in the still, silent air.

"Pretty fair for a beginner," he said. "If you ever have to fire in self-defense, assume you only get one shot. Always aim for the heart. Squeeze the trigger in a smooth motion or you'll pull back too fast, jerk the weapon, and miss. Rather than wound your assailant, shoot to kill." Marleau let out a long breath as if to calm himself.

"Ending another person's life, even if he means to harm you is never an easy decision to make," Marleau said.

"That's enough shooting for me," Gary said. "I'm gonna work on the boat."

He headed for the end of the dock to the dingy and started to scrape the hull.

Marleau sat down on a deck chair on the dock, yawned, and stretched. "I've been up all night tracking Paul Sinise to a warehouse in Moorhead. I thought you'd be interested in who is also taking an interest in the creep: Sticky Sokolov, accompanied by a PI named Zoe Dolan. She's somehow related to him, his niece or something."

Ryan stared out at the red glow of sunlight, edging over the trees on the opposite bank and drenching the mirrored river's surface in color.

"It sounds as though there's been a falling out among the raiders," he said. "What kind of warehouse was it?"

"It's a fair-size building called Brookshire Wholesalers. I didn't get a chance to look inside. Paul has the place locked up tighter than Fort Knox."

"Do you think you could find out what he's wholesaling?"

"I'll see if I can get inside and take a look." Marleau ran his fingers through his long, slicked-down hair with gray streaks in his sideburns. "Have you had another talk with the Dragon Lady?"

The corners of Ryan's mouth lifted a smidgen. "Jacelyn's developed an annoying habit of dropping in late at night at the office unannounced." He breathed in hard. "Now that I've persuaded Carl to come home, I hope she cools down."

Marleau's eyes were full of glee. "I'd say she has a crush on you. What does Joanne think of her nighttime visits?"

"She's not amused."

After supper, Ryan drove to town and then went to a small Catholic cemetery on Riverside Drive. The air was humid and smelled of nearby rain. He heard the haunting shriek of gulls in a sky mottled with puffy clouds.

Kate's marble gravestone overlooked the Red River. Standing next to her grave, he could see the boat-launching dock and the thick tree-covered banks of Custer Park on the opposite bank. He recalled that it was in the park as teenagers that he and Kate had first kissed.

He placed a dozen red carnations on the grave and then stood up, listening to the wind rustle dead leaves in the elms. He remained, thinking about her, until it started to drizzle. The swells in the river were dark brown with topsoil, dimpled with raindrops, the headstones haloed with a fine mist that rose from the warm earth.

He let his eyes drop to the rain-soaked grass, losing all expression on his face. He then clenched his hands together like an opera singer. Why was the loss of a first love so devastating?

A car park in front of the cemetery interrupted his thoughts. He recognized Jacelyn's blue Jaguar XJ Vanden Plus. He watched her climb out of the car, angered by her intrusion on his grief.

Instead of the business suit she often wore, she had on a white turtleneck sweater, jeans, and calf-length boots.

"Joanne told me you would be here," she said, opening an umbrella.

Ryan stared at the unlined skin of her face encased in a headscarf.

"Does my presence make you uncomfortable?" she asked, kneading a small purse.

"It does," he said, glancing at the sun break through clouds on the horizon that filled the western sky with a red glow like flames in a field of burning stubble.

"I'm afraid I'm interfering at a time when you want to be alone," she said.

Jacelyn stepped forward, her movement unsteady on high heels on the soft ground.

"Kate was my friend," she said. "I still think about her, but not as much as you do." She dabbed the corner of her eyes with a handkerchief. "Do you sense her presence here by the river?"

"It's hard to explain the unexplainable, but as her body was found by a man walking his dog on the bank near the Custer Park marina, it seems somehow as if she'll be forever part of the Red."

"Kate was such a good person. I find it hard to believe that an evil bastard could end her life in such a hideous fashion. Do you think you'll ever find her killer?"

He stared at an Asian angler on the far bank under an overhanging elm, his line in the water.

"I'll never really be at peace until he's caught," he said.

She remained silent, trying to snag his eyes.

"Do you remember the time we made love under the stars on a blanket in the back of my father's pickup?" she asked.

The muscles in his back gathered and constricted under his raincoat, as though her remark had the power to shrink his physical and emotional presence.

"Neither of us was married at the time," he said.

"After that night, I thought you'd call me, but you didn't. I suppose our lovemaking wasn't important to you."

Her eyes were blue and bright, and her face flushed as if dilated by her own heat.

"Does Carl know you're here?" he asked.

"He thinks I've gone to the club."

She pressed her lips against his cheek for a moment and then walked away from the gravestones. He could smell gin on her mouth.

"You're tipsy," he said.

She turned and smiled at him, blinking her eyelashes.

"Dear God …" she said, but she didn't finish.

The golden light of the sun reflected off patches of rain soaked into her coat. She remained silent as if waiting for an apology or an explanation for his rudeness, but none came.

"In another life, marry me, Ryan," she said finally.

She climbed into the car and before driving away paused to fix her makeup in a compact mirror. Ryan snuffed down into his nose and cleared his throat. He pictured Kate's bloated body stained with mud stretched out naked in the morgue.

He stood for a few minutes before he pressed the heels of his hands into his wet eyes. He hoped the drive home would help to ease the seared memories of his dead wife.

By the time Ryan pulled into his driveway, the sky had cleared, and he joined Joanne on the redwood deck for a snack of turkey sandwiches, romaine lettuce, and green tea. The cattails in his neighbor's property had turned a pale yellow, and a breeze made them wave in the sun's afterglow. Rain up stream had increased the river's level, and he could smell a heavy wet odor of vegetation in the water that was edging up the side of the levee.

"I don't like that woman stalking you," Joanne said.

"Now that Carl's home, Jacelyn should leave us alone."

"Don't count on it. That woman wants to get her hooks in you."

"She knows more than she's telling us about Aimée's death," he said. His voice had a hard edge.

"Really? Aaron Hubbard called. His work number is on your desk."

"I'll ring him in the morning."

"Is he still a suspect?"

"Yes. He's bitter about the fallout after Carl mustered all the support he could from board members and shareholders to have him kicked out of the company."

Ryan stared at butterflies in the air above the roses. Even in the shade, the heat from the day's last light made sweat stick to the back of his shirt.

"Before she died, Ricky witnessed a violent argument between Aimée and Aaron," he said. "I suspect it had to do with her refusing to back him on the Ravenwest board. Aaron knew he was vulnerable, and he suspected Carl wanted to can him, but if he could muster her support he could present himself to the board as a formidable force."

Joanne pursed her lips. "If she turned him down, he had a motive for killing her. In doing so, he could attempt to frame Carl for her death."

Ryan rested his palm on Joanne's neck, felt the silky texture of her hair, her skin that was as warm as if she had been lying under a sunlamp.

"We're going to go after him," he said slowly, "but we mustn't lose focus on the man who plans to unleash the four-headed eagle and rain terror on four kings."

CHAPTER 22

Early the next morning, Ryan woke up from the traces of a dream that lingered behind his eyes like cobwebs. In the dream, he discovered Joanne's Cairn terrier with his throat cut in the rose garden. Although he knew it didn't mean that Trouble was going to die, the dream disturbed him like a bleak fog, hardening around his heart.

After drinking a glass of orange juice, he strolled outside in his pajamas bottoms to the end of the dock and dipped his hands in the water to soak his face and hair. The sun had edged above the opposite bank, a delicate glow of pink lighting up the blue sky. He could smell the wet planks on the dock from a night rain carried on the breeze off the river.

It was just a dream, he told himself, but the feeling that went with the still-clear images of the Cairn's bloody throat festered like the ache of an old knee injury. He gazed into the smooth surface of the water, saw fear in his eyes, and felt the dryness in his mouth.

The residue of the dream hovered on the periphery of his mind and made him uneasy. Angst brought back images from when he was a boy. He had found his father in the kitchen, pounding his mother's face with his fists. Ryan had hit him on the back of his head with a baseball bat. Later that night, his mother told him his dad had left for Calcutta, and he never returned.

Ryan leaned back on the dock and let the river water seep into his eyes, cooling the heated surfaces of his eyeballs, and felt the sun's warmth on his chest.

He told himself to lose the guilt for hitting his father and leaving a bloody gash on the back of his skull. Weren't gargoyles supposed to slink back into the shadows at sunrise? He was wrong. Without thinking, he rubbed the inside of his palms as though he could still feel his hands around the baseball bat that cracked his dad's head.

The dream dregs of the mutilated dog continued to beat him down. He told himself that his biorhythms were low. He was sure to perk up in minutes after a cup of coffee and a shower. Then he heard Trouble's bark as he bounded down to the dock, tail wagging. He gave the dog an extra stroking and petting. When Joanne got up, he knew the sight of her would make his adrenaline kick in.

Later that morning, he expected a grueling session questioning Tamara, who was reluctant to talk about Moe's disappearance.

He shaded his eyes from the sun's reflection off the river. When would Moe's father strike again? Would Carl be safe now he had moved back to Ravenscourt? As a precaution, Ryan had beefed up security at the mansion. Thoughts of the dangers in a modern world crowded his mind. He knew the struggle had no end.

At a little before seven thirty, Joanne joined him on the dock. He told her about his dream. She dismissed it as an overreaction, a result of seeing Dixie's mutilated corpse. He then told her how furious he was for placing them under the threat of violence and terror.

"Ryan," she said softly. She must have seen the rage in his eyes that he couldn't blink away. She stepped inside his arms and locked her hands around the back of his neck. "No matter what happens," she said, "if we stick together, everything will turn out right."

After breakfast, Ryan drove to Ravenscourt for his poolside meeting with Carl at ten. At the house, a crew of gardeners mowed the front lawn and pruned the hedges. The guard Ryan had hired, in a blue suit, had parked a sedan on the drive, facing the iron gates. He nodded to Ryan as he drove to the front of the house.

After parking beside the porte cochere, he went to the pool. He sat down on a scroll-metal chair beside Carl, who lay stretched out on an air cushion on top of a lounge chair. He wore a polo shirt, jodhpurs, and riding boots. The day's humid heat slicked his clean-shaven face with sweat.

"Moe was supposed to go riding with us," he said. His knuckles, wrapped around a coffee mug, were as white as ice. "Tamara is devastated; they're getting married in a couple of weeks. Where the hell is he?"

"Marleau had an eye on him until he bolted out the back entrance of his condo on foot in the middle of the night. His movements up until then indicated nothing that you could call unusual, except for signs of packing. Marleau thought his backpack full off hiking boots and sports clothes indicated he planned to go on a camping trip for his honeymoon."

"Tamara had talked about Bermuda."

"As far as I know, he didn't pack shorts."

Carl didn't react to Ryan's attempt at humor; his face remained set in a stony expression. "Have you any idea where he could've gone?"

"Phone taps didn't hint at where he planned to go."

Carl put his mug down. He tightened his fingers around his chair's metal armrests. "Despite our differences, I was beginning to like the guy; I'd sort of accepted the fact he'd be my son-in-law."

"Before he left, did he give Tamara any idea where he might have gone?"

"Not a hint. He did, however, admit to her that he'd been going to the local mosque. She even talked about converting to Islam if that would make him happy."

Ryan looked at him curiously in the sharp clear light.

"I've always wanted another son, and Moe came close to filling that role." Carl stared down at the mahogany age spots on the backs of his hands. "I can understand why it would be hard for him to resist the attractions of returning to the Islamic faith: a world view, a strict discipline and order to life, a reason to live, and an alluring vision of the afterlife." Carl slammed his fist on the table. "But to leave a beautiful, loving young woman and a challenging job with a solid future is beyond my comprehension."

Ryan shaded his eyes from the sun's glare reflecting off the kidney-shaped pool. "Did Tamara meet anyone else connected to Moe, apart from Galina, the phony fund-raiser?"

"She didn't mention anyone." Carl hauled himself up into a sitting position so he could see Ryan better. "Now, you tell me Galina is a man."

"I'm convinced she's really his father. A photo of the family found in Sanjay's safe indicates the father's first name is Habib. If this is true, he's one of the most dangerous terrorists on the planet."

Carl rubbed the salt-and-pepper stubble on his chin. "Oh my God."

"What precisely did Moe do at Ravenwest?" Ryan asked.

"He was a high-tech trouble shooter for some of our major utility clients, including North Dakota Telecommunications Services, Excel Energy, and Fargo Natural Gas."

"So he'd have intimate knowledge of their computer systems."

"That is true."

"Can you imagine the damage a terrorist could do with this kind of information?" Ryan got to his feet and began pacing beside the edge of the pool. "For starters, he could shut down the power grid. He could disrupt Internet and local and long-distance telecommunications traffic, and blow up gas pipelines."

Carl stared at him open-mouthed. His eyes rounded like ball bearings.

Ryan added, "The first thing to do is to have the company's security codes and locks changed. I'd also hire extra guards and do in-depth security checks on all the people handling sensitive material to do with the state's infrastructure."

Carl's lips parted in silence. Ryan could hardly look at the recognition of defeat spreading across his lined face.

"How close are you to finding his parents?" he asked.

"Marleau taped some phone conversations in Arabic between Moe and his mother. He's having them translated. Right now, he's investigating a lead that Moe's father may have owned a warehouse in Fargo."

Carl looked straight at him with the dead expression of a stunned man. The sound of lawn mowers went quiet.

"I'd like to talk to Tamara, if she's up to it," Ryan said.

"I'll get her. She's just back from riding in the park."

Carl walked to the house, his body bent forward at the middle, his expression as blank as the grated grill on a new pickup truck.

Ryan sat down and stared at the red-tinged light in the sky. He wondered what it would be like to step through a window in time into the barren, rock-strewn Tora Bora range on the Afghan eastern border. He imagined himself plodding like a hooded phantom alongside bin Laden, so devoted to an ideal he chose to isolate himself and his followers in caves away from families, while defying powerful forces trying to hunt him down.

Ryan looked up when he heard the tap of Tamara's riding boots on the stone path. Her eyes were bloodshot and her skin glazed with sweat from riding in the sun. The light reflecting off the pool seemed to frame her silhouette against the green ornamental hedge behind her.

"You wanted to see me, Ryan," she said, sitting beside him. She wore tan jodhpurs and a long-sleeved men's shirt.

"Thanks for taking the time for a chat," Ryan said.

She stretched out long legs; her forehead shimmered with perspiration. "I'm sorry I haven't been more transparent."

"I understand how you feel."

"Do you really know what I'm going through? I've lost the man I thought I'd live with for the rest of my life, my soul mate. I'd planned on having his children, and we'd talked about growing old together."

He waited for her to continue, but she didn't. He expected she had reached the point in dealing with Moe's disappearance in which she had accepted the possibility of him not coming back.

"I'm deeply sorry, Tamara," he said. Ryan got up from his chair, keeping his face empty of expression. "We think we've identified Moe's parents."

"Who are they?"

"My guess is his father's name is Habib, and his mother has a number of aliases. If they are the couple we suspect them to be, they're both dangerous terrorists."

She shivered as if struck by a cold wind. "I can't believe he's the son of terrorists."

"Before Moe left, did you notice any difference in his mood, his attitude?" Ryan asked.

"He seemed jumpy and he had a short fuse," she said, removing her riding cap to reveal her sweat-damp, plastered down platinum hair.

"Did he give you any explanation for his behavior?"

She remained silent for a moment as she watched dragonflies dimple the surface of the swimming pool.

"I didn't understand the reason for his grumpiness," she said. "When I tried to probe, he told me to stop tormenting him. He said it had to do with my rejection of him and his religion. He accused me of laughing at him behind his back and of making fun of God."

"Did he want to call off the wedding?"

"He didn't say that in so many words." She laughed in a hollow, empty way, followed by a loud sniffle. "Before he left, he said I was unworthy to be his wife."

Tamara poured herself a glass of lemonade.

"Apart from a backpack, did Moe take anything else with him?" Ryan asked.

"He left his Porsche in the garage, and his suits, shirts, laptop, wallet, cash, and credit cards are in his room."

"Are you sure he didn't pack anything else?"

"This may sound weird, but his riding clothes are missing."

Behind him, Carl came back and rested his hands on his daughter's shoulders.

"It's best if you try and forget him, sweetheart," he said.

That evening, when it started to rain, water sluiced hard off the boathouse roof. The usual dry fall in the Red River Valley had turned wet, which frustrated farmers from bringing in ripening crops.

Ryan's iPhone rang. It was Marleau.

"I've got a positive lead on Moe's dad," he said, a little breathless. "A guy by the name of Omar Shaker, obviously a phony, opened a fake real estate office near the airport on Armstrong Avenue for a few weeks and then disappeared. I showed the receptionist the photo found in Sanjay's safe, and she swears he looks like her boss."

Ryan pounced on it. "Now we're getting somewhere. So it was a positive ID."

"Not exactly. She claimed Middle Eastern men all look alike. They probably say the same thing about us. She mentioned that Omar hasn't been seen for weeks, no one's been paid, and the money in the company bank account is zip."

"Did you find anything interesting when you searched the building?"

"I went over the whole place. The entire office is spotless, polished so well you could eat off the top of the desks. He didn't leave a fingerprint or a trace of DNA anywhere. Behind the building, he had a small warehouse. According to his assistant, in the evening, he locked himself inside and tinkered with engines. She thought he was some sort of eccentric inventor. Before he disappeared, he shipped everything out and left nothing but an empty shell."

"Damn. I was hoping for some clue to lead us right to him."

"He even scrubbed the trash cans clean."

Ryan felt frustration mounting, the first piece of solid evidence now snatched away from him.

"Behind the building, I did find a brochure on horse health stuck at the bottom of a dumpster," Marleau said, digging in his pocket for a booklet. "This describes medication horses need for colic."

"Doesn't that strike you as odd?" Ryan said. "You'd expect them to leave blueprints on detonating remote control devices or causing meltdowns in nuclear power plants. A remedy for a horse disease doesn't make sense."

Ryan looked out of the screen door at cirrus clouds formed by warm southern winds that mingled with shafts of cold air tumbling down from Canada.

He felt alive with ideas as though jolted by an electric current. "Wait a minute. Moe took his riding gear with him."

"We've found the link."

"We'll start building a profile."

"Every detail will soon fit into a rational framework that will lead us to this killer. Why is he interested in the health of horses? We need to find an Islamic man who owns horses. There're only three thousand Islamic people in Fargo, so it shouldn't be hard to track this horse dealer down."

"If we ask too many questions, won't it raise an alarm?"

"Sanjay obtained information about the local community by attending the mosque."

"Don't suggest for a moment that you want me to blend in with worshippers."

"I was thinking more on the line of hacking into the imam's computer."

Through the screen door, he watched Joanne and Charlene carrying bags of groceries they had bought at Walmart.

"I'll see if I can break in tonight," Marleau said.

The rain eased to a drizzle, and Ryan looked out at the harsh light of the sun's reflection off a house's windows across the river.

"I'm getting an awful feeling in my gut about this case," Marleau said. "It's as if someone put a blowtorch to my stomach lining."

CHAPTER 23

O N THE EDGE OF SLEEP, Habib heard the rain tick on the leaves in the oak trees. Instead of being lulled to sleep by the rain and Zahara's gentle breathing, he visualized a tiger with yellow eyes probe the darkness. He could hear the soft padding of paws inside the cage. He knew the tiger fed on fear, and he felt the big cat's destructive energies pulsate through him.

He knew his destiny was fixed as certain as the movement of the stars. He wanted, at the same time, to safeguard some of those he loved. The tiger's growl blotted out his thoughts of his family's protection. He turned over to avoid the smell of fetid meat from the big cat's breath, until he felt Zahara's warmth next to him.

When she pressed against him, her hand stroked the inside of his thigh and then touched his sex. He pulled off his pajamas bottoms and wrapped his arm around her back. She raised her leg around his calf, pressed her palm on the base of his spine and eased him inside her.

As they made love, Habib never imagined her as one person. She had so many different sides. When they first met as teenagers in a coffee shop in Beirut, he had fallen for the fearful innocence in her dark eyes, the fullness of her mouth framed by her headscarf, and the ripeness of her bosom visible under her form-fitting, modern-style dress.

They both lost their virginities in the beach house of a Christian friend. When the lovemaking was over, he recalled lying back on the pillows feeling spent and happy, listening to the gentle roar of the surf that mirrored the beating of his heart.

He could still see the flood of disappointment mingled with fear in Zahara's face after he told her his father wanted him to marry the daughter of a wealthy Damascus family. He knew there was no way of undoing his youthful mistake. He had wounded her spirit and hurt her pride. His rejection of her filled him with self-loathing and pent-up fury. He sought release from his frustrations in the fiery rhetoric he expressed as a young religious student for the passion of his faith.

He studied with the Muslim Youth Association where he learned to hate the United States for being materialistic, immoral, prejudiced against Arabs, and sympathetic toward Israel.

Later, he believed Allah gave Zahara back to him, after his betrothed died of scarlet fever. It hurt him that his father never forgave him for marrying Zahara. Years later, Habib's dad even refused to meet his grandsons.

He shivered with pleasure when he felt the wetness of her mouth in his ear. She flexed her thigh muscles and held him tight inside her, until he felt a surge ripple through him in a tsunami-force wave of pleasure.

After she got up, he heard her take a shower. When she came out, he watched her while she sat before a mirror in a terry towel robe to apply eyeliner and a trace of purple lipstick.

Outside the window, he saw the hard, thick contours of elm branches wrapped in first light and glistening from raindrops.

Outside the bedroom that Mohammed shared with Arrak, Habib heard boots on the tile floor. He suspected his fiery young recruit of going for an early morning ride.

In the kitchen, Zahara hummed a tune and rattled dishes. He was pleased Arrak had taken his son under his wing and spent hours counseling him. They spoke about Islam. Did Habib dare to believe Arrak could help revive his son's former zeal?

Leaning against the headboard, Habib rubbed his stubby fingers together. He thought it ironic that an American was responsible for bringing his son back to the roots of his faith. Even though Mohammed appeared on the surface to reject his former life in Fargo, Habib didn't entirely trust his son and refused to reveal to him the target of the attack.

Habib stretched and climbed out of bed. He put on tan slacks, polished loafers, and a blue sports jacket. He opened the front door to fetch the morning newspaper, and then he went outside and sat under an umbrella at a metal table on the deck. He ran his fingers through his barbered hair and rubbed his jaw, glowing with aftershave lotion. As the sun broke out of the milk-white mist that hung over the pond, he heard horses stir in the stalls.

When he heard the hooves of Arrak's stallion thud on the moist lawn, he looked up from his *Star Tribune*. He watched Arrak trot beside a flower bed. His shadow flew horizontally along the lawn to blend into the vertical shadows of the elms. He dismounted by vaulting over the horse's back and landing on the balls of his feet. He then led al-Tikriti to the stables. For his own well-being, Habib hoped the boy wouldn't become too attached to the Arabian stallion.

Habib folded the newspaper and strolled across the dewy lawn. He found Arrak grooming the steaming black horse. Habib looked into his protégé's narrow face, his skin glazed with sweat, his eyes blinking out the salt.

"This morning's paper reports a break-in at the mosque," he said.

Arrak stopped brushing and thrust his hands in the back pockets of his jodhpurs, his face tilted up into Habib's, the whites of his eyes shiny and pink. His broad chest rose and fell against his blue T-shirt darkened in patches by sweat.

"That pisses me off so bad I want to stamp the crap out of whoever did it," he said.

Habib glanced down at the paper. "Apparently, nothing was stolen, which leads me to believe the intruder was after information."

"If someone has hacked into Massoud's computer, are we vulnerable?"

Habib's face heated. "The imam has nothing filed that can hurt us, Arrak. I promise."

Arrak forked hay into the stall, the muscles in his arms pumped up like rocks.

"I don't believe you, man," he said. "Massoud knows about Mohammed. Didn't Zahara take him to the mosque to help him reconnect to Islam?"

"They used bogus names."

Arrak threw the rake down on the floor and used a hooked knife to split open a burlap bag of oats. He stood erect, his cheeks burning.

"That kid of yours has a time bomb embedded in his head," he said.

Habib tucked the newspaper under his arm. His starched shirt looked as smooth and white as new snow. The sun went behind a cloud, and Habib shivered as though he could feel a circle of carrion birds close in on him. He could almost hear vultures ripping and gobbling meat.

"Your job is to keep him out of trouble," Habib said. Then he chose his next words carefully. "If he betrays us, he dies."

Arrak scooped some oats and molasses balls into the horse's trough.

"He confides in me about his girlfriend, Tamara Ravenstein. She sounds like a great woman. In fact, she has it all: looks, wealth, and personality."

"I hope you discouraged such thoughts."

"I told him Tamara's vanilla ice cream, but that doesn't mean he can't try chocolate. It's just as good."

Habib's laughter broke the tension. He tried to let go of his worries about his son, let the heat and anger drain out of him. He

169

felt so wired he started to pace on the loose straw on the floor and breathe in hard the fecund odor of horses. In the distance, he heard frogs croak out mating calls in the swamp.

"Do you think the break-in is the work of the private investigator Ryan Moar or his partner Marleau Belanger?" Arrak asked.

"Those devils won't give up," Habib said. He dropped his eyes to the floor. "I've half a mind to pack everything up this afternoon and leave tonight."

"We shouldn't let these guys stampede us into going too soon. Ayman, Nadir, and Gulbuddin need more time for training."

"You're right, Arrak." He sniffed and then wiped his nose with a handkerchief. "This PI is no more dangerous to us than an annoying mosquito."

"But he could become dangerous. Apparently, our visit to the cabin wasn't enough to scare Carl Ravenstein into calling off his bloodhounds." Arrak's voice sounded metallic, as though it originated from a resonator imbedded in his throat. "Let me create a diversion, throw them off balance. Scare them at bit. Stir things up."

"What have you in mind?"

"Let Moar know we're capable of harming his kids," he said, rubbing the stubble on his chin.

Habib pinched his temples with his fingers.

In the line of trees that separated the acreage from his neighbor's fields, he watched an owl swoop from its perch in an elm tree. In a flurry of feathers, the owl snared a mouse in its beak. He could hear in his mind faint squeals as the bird flapped toward the sun.

Arrak waited until Joanne drove down the drive in the Range Rover and headed south on Red River Road. He knew she was on her way to teach an evening class in theater arts at the university's downtown campus. She would be back around ten thirty.

He had parked in among a small copse of white spruce at a riverside park where he studied the house through high-powered binoculars. Earlier in the day, he had watched Charlene climb out of the school bus and wave to her friends, before walking to the front to the house, her backpack bobbing up and down on her back. Gary had arrived half an hour later in typical teenage fashion, his tires spinning on the gravel surface of the drive.

At six o'clock, it began to rain, and Arrak listened to the heavy drops of water *ping* on top of the pickup's roof and *tick* on the dried aspen leaves.

He had the uncomfortable thought of what he would do if he were caught while he broke into the house. If the police arrested him, he knew he would be imprisoned. This possibility filled him with a sudden dread. He took meager assurance from the idea that he would rather shoot himself than be cooped up in a cell. As a teenager, he had served three months in a detention center, and the pain after guards beat him with short sticks had seared his brain.

Confinement behind high walls had driven him close to madness. What helped him out of a black pit of depression was meeting a young Palestinian American, Hussein al-Shayea, who was serving a two-month sentence for writing racist graffiti on the walls of a synagogue. Both he and Hussein came from comfortable middle-class families and attended private schools.

It didn't take long before Hussein convinced him that Islam was better than any other religion. Arrak's spiritual mentor soon converted him into believing the real enemy of Islam was the United States.

After his release, Hussein used his contacts in Afghanistan to send Arrak by air to Kabul. From there, Arrak traveled by bus and on foot to Sati Kundo near the Pakistani border to train in the techniques of terror. As a young jihadist, he learned to make car bombs, fire automatic weapons, and propel rocket launchers. Some Yemenis and Syrians distrusted the color of his skin but grudgingly accepted him for fighting back whenever they insulted him for being an infidel. The trainees also admired him for his devotion to Islam and for never shying from rigorous military exercises in the rugged mountain ranges.

During forced marches in the mountains, Habib acted as the squad's leader. Teacher and student soon became friends, bound by a global struggle that would bring them either victory or heaven.

"If you win a battle, you're a hero; if you die a martyr, you go to paradise. Either way, you win," Habib often reminded him.

Inside the pickup, Arrak wondered if Habib would kill Mohammed if he tried to escape or betray them. Was he capable of slitting his son's throat? He had a terrible temper. Arrak had heard him yell at Mohammed, the sound of his rage reverberating off the ranch house walls. During the tirade, Mohammed had remained stock-still, a hangdog look on his face.

Arrak wished he hadn't told Habib about Mohammed's continued infatuation with Tamara. He knew the young man kept a photo of her under his pillow.

Arrak shifted his train of thought when he saw something move behind the house. He spotted Ryan sprinting down the garden path through the rain to the boathouse. The two dogs scampered after him.

Charlene and Gary were at last alone in the main house.

Arrak pulled on a rain slicker over his black tracksuit and tank top. He climbed out of the pickup and jogged along the side of the road, his sneakers squishing in rain puddles. Taking shelter under an elm tree, he studied the house. Lights were on in the living room, but the rest of the house was dark.

He crouched down while he circled the house. Through a gap in the curtain, he caught a glimpse of Charlene and Gary in the family room. Standing in a flower bed, he swung a rope with a three-pronged spike at the end around the chimney and hauled himself up. On the roof, he pulled a ski mask over his face so only his eyes and mouth were visible. He used a glass cutter to make a hole in the skylight and dropped the rope into the upper-level dining room. He climbed down and landed on his feet without a sound on a broadloom carpet.

From the dining room, he could hear Charlene and Gary arguing. He crouched behind a low partition wall filled with tropical plants.

"I'm tired of wearing this ridiculous thing," Charlene said. She fingered an alarm button hanging around her neck on a gold chain. "I should press it just to see Dad running inside with his Magnum at the ready."

"You think this security business is one big joke, don't you?" Gary said.

"Well, at least you got some target practice out of it." She moved to the window and looked out at branches floating in the fast-flowing river. "I've yet to see one live terrorist. The ones I've seen are on TV and look sinister are like gangsters in ski masks."

"These guys aren't bogeymen in burnooses; they're ruthless killers."

"Maybe in Baghdad, but surely you don't believe they're in Fargo. We're in the middle of nowhere, for God's sake."

"They're here."

Charlene shrugged. "If that's true, why won't the police believe Dad?"

"He doesn't have solid evidence that they exist." He picked up a handful of peanuts from a bowl and stuffed them into his mouth. "Let's face it: both our parents are involved in dangerous work."

"That's something we can't change."

He remained silent for a moment. Charlene popped the top of a diet ginger ale can and poured it into a glass.

"I just want to get on with my life," she said, opening the freezer to add ice to her drink.

"At least we can try and be part of the solution," Gary said.

"What do you mean?"

"Do what they say, and be on our guard," he said in a superior-sounding voice.

"It makes me so mad when you talk down to me as if I'm a little kid."

Gary grinned at her, half covering the smirk with his hand.

Arrak dug deep in the pouch pocket of his backpack and pulled out a leather holster that contained a snub-nosed .38 revolver. He held the pistol in his hand, feeling its familiar heft. Then, with his other hand, he scooped up a knife with a slight curve, designed to both stab and slash. He ran his fingertips over the razor-sharp blade, as if caressing a woman's skin.

From the other room, Charlene was saying, "Another thing that annoys me is that we now share a bathroom."

"What's your beef?" Gary asked.

"After you beat me to the shower this morning, you dropped your skivvies and smelly socks on the floor. Not to mention leaving the cap off the toothpaste."

Gary's laughter froze in midstride. His forehead turned into a mass of wrinkles.

"Did you hear something?" he said. "Turn that damn music off."

"What is it?" Charlene asked, switching off the CD player.

"I thought I heard someone inside the house."

"Come off it; you're just trying to scare me."

"I heard footsteps, honest."

Arrak crouched lower and dropped the pistol into the backpack. He held the knife in front of him and crept toward a short flight of steps that led to the family room.

"Oh, this is so creepy. Do you think someone's here?" Charlene said.

"Hush. Keep your voice down."

"You're imagining things."

Charlene stiffened as though she had heard a noise that catapulted her into a new fear, replacing the fright in her eyes with something alien and more terrifying.

"There's someone in the house," she whispered, reaching for her portable alarm. "Should I press the button and alert Dad?"

Arrak dropped the backpack on the carpet, sprang at her, spun her around, and grabbed her waist. He then pressed the knife's edge into her throat.

"I wouldn't do that," he whispered.

For a moment, Charlene was too terrified to breathe.

"What do you want?" she asked, struggling to control the quaver in her voice.

Arrak used his left hand to wrench the alarm from her neck and break the chain. He stuffed it in his pocket.

"Leave her alone!" Gary shouted.

Gary pulled a brass lamp from out of its wall socket and brandished it above his head.

"Put it down or she dies," Arrak said, pressing the knife into her swanlike neck until the blade nicked her skin. "Sit down and be quiet."

Gary put the lamp back on the table and sat down on the sofa.

Charlene whimpered and tried to wriggle away from him. He exhaled hard as he shoved Charlene down beside Gary. Charlene touched her throat as though half expecting to feel a rush of blood. Arrak sheathed the knife, pulled out the .38 from the backpack, and aimed it at Gary.

"If you want to rob us, go ahead. We won't stop you," Gary said.

"I don't want your money or your things," Arrak said, stepping closer.

Gary focused on the man's dark eyes and a half-exposed tattoo on his left bicep of two prancing horses with Arabic writing scrawled underneath.

"Are you a jihadist?" he asked.

Arrak said nothing but pointed the semiautomatic at Gary's head and cocked the hammer back.

"Do you think by killing us you can restore some sort of injustice?" Gary said.

Both Gary and Charlene were quiet for a moment.

"Aren't you going to set up a video camera so you can tape our execution?" Gary continued.

"Don't tempt me, Gary. Don't make me do it," he said, pressing the gun against his temple. "Believe me; I will not hesitate to shoot you with or without the world seeing you executed on prime-time television."

"How did you know my name?" Gary asked.

Arrak felt his pulse swell in his throat. He removed the pistol from the side of Gary's head, squatted down in front of him, and pointed it at his lips.

"You've got a big mouth, and if you don't stop, I'm gonna blast your lips shut," he said.

Arrak slipped a folded handkerchief out of his back pocket and blotted sweat out of his eyes. When he returned the handkerchief to his pocket, his eyes refocused as though capturing a new thought.

He settled himself on one knee like a football coach about to give his players a pep talk. "You're right in identifying me as a jihadist or what you call a terrorist."

"Are you going to kill us?" Charlene said, struggling to her feet.

"I've nothing to gain by killing you," he said in a low voice.

"What are you going to do?" Gary asked.

"What am I going to do? Tantalizing to speculate, isn't it?"

Arrak got to his feet and tried to suppress a twitch of anger, which invaded his face under the mask. "What I will tell you is I'm a warrior of God, who is fighting to restore the rule of Islam over as much of the world as possible," he said.

"You obviously don't care how many die as long as you achieve your ambition," Gary said.

"I'm leaving now, Mr. Smart-Mouth," he whispered, swiping Gary's cheek with the back of his gloved hand.

He climbed up the rope with the agility of a baboon.

As he disappeared through the skylight, Charlene allowed Gary to take her hand as they sprinted out the back door and raced to the boathouse.

The cairn terrier sleeping at Ryan's feet growled, and Roy pricked his ears. The dogs shot to the door and barked while scratching the woodwork. Ryan got up from the desk, heard pounding feet, and flung open the door.

Charlene's half screams of fear melted with relief as she flung herself into her father's arms. Ryan tugged Gary's arm to bring him into his embrace.

"What's wrong, sweetheart?" Ryan asked, holding them both tight.

While he rubbed her back, Charlene said, "He broke in!" She choked back tears. "He put a knife to my throat."

Ryan examined the nick on her neck. "Thank God it's only a scratch."

"He threatened to kill Gary with his pistol. He pressed the gun against his head, and I heard a click as he cocked the hammer."

Gary wiped blood from his nose with paper tissue.

Ryan turned to his daughter. "Why didn't you press your security alarm button?"

"He ripped it off me before I had a chance to activate it."

"Come on; we'd better go inside," Ryan said, strapping on his Magnum.

As he headed out the door, his heart pumped and his head reeled. Charlene and Gary trailed after him, holding the dogs tight by their collars.

Inside the house, Ryan squinted up at the hole in the skylight.

"He's a clever bastard to avoid the alarm system," he said. "I presume he wore gloves so he left no fingerprints."

"Are you going to call the cops?" Gary asked.

"The police will treat it as a nickel-and-dime B and E. As nothing's stolen, they won't bother with an investigation."

"Is it worth going after him?"

Ryan looked outside through the window and down the drive. The night had taken over, covering everything with a vapor of darkness.

Ryan turned to face them. "He's long gone."

"Will he be back?" Charlene asked, her hands shaking.

Ryan felt a surge of protectiveness and pulled Charlene close to him. "I don't think so, sweetheart."

Still holding his daughter, he turned to Gary.

"What did this guy look like?" he asked.

"I couldn't see much under the ski mask, except he's tall and well-built," he said. "He had plenty of long black hair that stuck out in tuffs. He spoke like an ordinary American."

"Did he have any other distinctive features? Scars? Marks on his face?" Ryan asked.

"He had a tattoo on his biceps of two horses, facing each other, raised up on their hind legs," Gary said.

"Horses? That's interesting. Anything else?"

"His eyes are a bit weird, black and liquid like wet paint," Charlene said. "Sometimes when he spoke, his eyeballs were half hidden by his top lids."

"How old is he?"

"In his twenties, I'd say, his voice sounded young," Gary said.

Ryan examined Gary's face. His nose had stopped bleeding, but his discolored right eye had started to puff up.

"He whacked me good, but I'm okay," Gary said.

"Better put some steak on your eye before you go to bed."

"Why did he break in?" Charlene asked.

"To scare us, keep us on edge. Above all, he's trying to distract us from our job of finding Moe's dad." Ryan could feel his stomach tighten, his insides drain tension. "He knows we're getting closer. This break-in is an indication he's planning to attack sooner than we think."

CHAPTER 24

ONCE IN MARTYRS' SQUARE IN Damascus, during a clandestine
visit, Habib had passed by a blind imam speaking to a crowd
of young men near a mosque under construction. The imam's eyes
had no pupils and were the color of peeled hardboiled eggs that
had turned blue. He spoke to them about *takfir*, an Islamist concept
developed in Egypt that gave jihadists a sacred license to kill almost
any person to achieve their aim of imposing sharia, law based on
the Qur'an. The imam explained that to the *takfiri*, democracy is
a heresy because it supplements the laws of God with manmade
jurisprudence. He claimed that Muslims living in a democracy were
apostates ripe for slaughter.

The idea, Habib thought, gave members of al-Qaeda justification
for flying airliners into New York's Twin Towers and the right to
blow up US embassies in East Africa. In a way, it also gave him the
right to blow up symbols Americans loved.

The imam had emphasized it was their sacred duty to kill
infidels, particularly those who had defiled Muslim lands by
promoting democracy. Habib recalled his words.

"Join with your young brothers with the mujahedeen, fighting against the alliance of the Crusaders and the Jews in Iraq and Afghanistan," the imam had said. "Seek the help of Allah, the Almighty, against his enemies. You are the chosen ones to be in the forefront of this battle. By becoming martyrs, you will be sent to paradise."

Sitting at the kitchen table, Habib wondered if the imam had Arrak in mind when he told his audience they were the chosen ones. In the evenings, Arrak often lectured the pilots and Mohammed about *takfir* and jihad. He also downloaded grizzly videos from the Internet of infidels having their heads chopped off.

Habib took a long drag on his cigarette, puckered his lips, and exhaled. He watched disintegrating smoke rings waft up to the ceiling. He wondered if Arrak's diversion at Ryan Moar's house was enough to keep the PI off his back for a short while until it was time to leave.

A gentle rain was falling when Habib stepped outside on his way to the stables to find Arrak. He came across him grooming his favorite mount, the young stallion, al-Tikriti. It pleased him to see that he was now clean-shaven and his hair cut in preparation for the journey.

"You're become attached to al-Tikriti," he said as the young man brushed the black Arabian until his coat gleamed in a shaft of sunlight.

"He is indeed a noble animal," he replied.

"Are his papers in order?"

"Everything is ready. I hope al-Tikriti doesn't find the trip too arduous."

Arrak finished coaxing a burr out of the stallion's mane, then worked the nozzle loose from a hose, turned on the faucet, and drank, his body bent over, the backs of his thighs tight against his jodhpurs. The water caught light as it arched on its way to his mouth.

"Does my son have any idea where we're going?" Habib asked.

Arrak turned off the faucet and straightened up. "He keeps asking me, but I tell him nothing. He is, of course, aware we are packing."

"We'll keep him in the dark about our destination." Habib's eyes burned as though sand had worked in behind the lids. "Is he still wavering?"

"He secretly pines for his former life."

"Will he betray us?"

Arrak remained silent. He didn't want to get Mohammed into trouble, but Habib's son sometimes appeared so miserable Arrak thought he might bolt at the first chance to escape. It did seem ironic to him that he, an American-born, had embraced the true faith, yet Habib's son craved after the kind of life Arrak had experienced growing up and now despised.

"Zahara is convinced he is loyal to his family and his religion, but I'm not too sure," Habib continued. "Although he tries to disguise it, I see, whenever he gets together with me, hate and loathing in his eyes."

"He has long been contaminated by false ideas. In time, he will purify himself of this pollution."

"Time is something we don't have." Habib opened his cell phone, punched numbers, and talked rapidly in Arabic. He turned to Arrak. "I don't know if you picked that up."

"I understood every word," Arrak said in Arabic. He then switched to English. "Why have you asked Rashid to join us?"

"I need him to keep an eye on my son."

Arrak felt an unknown fear unravel inside him, as though the mounting tension of the moment wanted to break loose.

"Have I not carried out my duties to your satisfaction?" he asked.

"You've done a good job keeping an eye on Mohammed," Habib said, resting his hand on Arrak's shoulder. "But I need you now to put all your energies into coordinating the attack."

Arrak felt a surge of heat to his brow, his head filled with the thought of one day becoming a martyr like the pilots, the thought of dying and then experiencing the delights of paradise.

"It will be an honor, Habib," he said.

"If al-Tikriti had wings like Pegasus, you'd be able to ride him to heaven." Habib twitched his nose as though he had smelled a nasty odor. "Talk about winged horses—"

Arrak shivered as Habib took a wide step toward him, his face grim. He reached to lift Arrak's shirtsleeve to examine the tattoo on his upper arm of two prancing winged horses, facing each other, surrounded by swirling tongues of orange flames. His face darkened as though the sun had gone behind a rain cloud. His mouth became pinched, and his eyes acquired remoteness as though he had drifted into a psychological moonscape no one could penetrate. "I don't recall having seen this before. Where did you get this tattoo done?"

The blood drained from Habib's face as he devoured every word of the Arabic inscription, before reading it aloud, "On the Backs of Allah's Flying Horses, I Will Reach the Light."

Arrak wiped the tip of his nose with one knuckle. He could feel Habib's fingers dig into his collarbone.

"Where did you have it done?" he asked.

"It was designed by Samir in his Minneapolis tattoo shop."

Habib started to rub the tattoo. "You're lying. The ink hasn't had time to dry."

"I paid extra for the best-quality ink. It was done two years ago."

Habib reread every word on his skin a second time. "Can anyone trace this tattoo to you?"

"That's impossible. One of our brothers, Hussan Azzis, did the actual work."

Habib leaned forward and let his eyes rove over Arrak's sweaty face. He rocked back, as if Arrak's lies had slammed him hard in the stomach.

"I don't want you to leave behind any unfinished business, understood?" he said.

"That is clear, my master," Arrak said in Arabic.

Habib positioned his face so close to him that Arrak could smell his lemon-scented aftershave lotion.

"If there are any loose ends, Arrak, make sure you take care of them before we go," he whispered.

An hour later, when Arrak heard Rashid's footsteps crackle on stray pieces of straw on the cement floor, he shuddered. Rashid's face was round as an apple, and he had a purple birthmark as through someone had spilt Burgundy wine on his forehead. His left eyeball was a lighter blue than the other one, as pale and empty as a desert sky. On his right forearm, he had a tattoo of a man nailed to a cross.

Arrak had always regarded this symbol alien to his true nature. Rashid had been an inmate inside the Baghdad asylum for the criminally insane. He escaped during the US invasion by ripping the bars out of his maximum-security cell window. He had then trekked across the desert to Syria.

"Is everything packed and secured, Rashid?" Arrak asked, speaking in Arabic.

"The wings are completely hidden inside the trailer walls, floor, and ceiling," he said. "No one will be able to detect them." Rashid grinned, and his skin rolled back from his yellow, square teeth, his lips turned purple by the overhead light.

"We're taking Habib's son Mohammed with us, and he needs to be watched at all times," Arrak said.

The morning air was sunny and cool, yet Rashid's matted hair was damp from the heat of his body fouled by the smell from his own fluids. Arrak knew he had worked as a short-order cook in a fast-food restaurant named Fat Freddie's, a throwback eatery that served greasy food from the 1950s.

"Have you reason to believe he will betray to us?" Rashid asked, swatting at a fly with his giant hand. As he raised his arm above his head, he revealed his armpit sodden with sweat.

"Mohammed is Habib's own flesh," Arrak said, his face jerking and his mouth flexing, "but I fear he is not completely committed to our cause."

Arrak could feel Rashid's rage fill the stables. He wondered what it would be like to have a son of his own who grew up to disappoint him. He knew now it was too late for him to fall in love with a woman and conceive children with her. The only thing left for him was to put together plans for revenge, a chance to rip the heart out of his rotten country.

"Why is he not to be trusted?" Rashid asked, his yellow teeth chewing a piece of straw.

"He was seduced by a harlot, and he's still bewitched by this whore," Arrak said, pulling out of his pocket a color photo of Tamara in a skimpy swimsuit taken by the pool. "His mother found this when she changed his pillowcase."

Rashid's nostrils constricted as his thick lips formed a smile.

"What does his father want me to do if he screws up?" he asked, closing his hand on a sack of feed on the table as though squeezing the breath out of a large dog.

Arrak didn't reply.

Death is never abstract, Arrak thought. He recalled sitting beside Habib in a limousine parked on a street in Beirut when a car bomb exploded and the roof flew off the van amid flames and black smoke that billowed upward as steel bracing turned into licorice. Inside the van, the bodies of two guards, a chauffeur, and a suited politician turned into charred flesh.

As they drove away from the hellish scene, Habib had smiled like a hungry male lion, licking his chops at the prospect of eating the carcass of a disemboweled zebra, its body still quivering under his paws.

Arrak looked at Rashid's dilated eyes for a moment and then turned away as if swept by an undertow of doubt.

"You will know what to do," he said, his voice barely audible.

Rashid stepped closer to Arrak and grabbed his arm so tight that he cried out. While Arrak squirmed to break free, Rashid examined his tattoo of the prancing horses.

"Habib told me to remind you to take care of some unfinished business. Do it now, or I'll apply the same kind of pressure on your arm to your nuts," he said, releasing him.

CHAPTER 25

"I T SOUNDS INCREDIBLY WEIRD," MARLEAU said, biting into a hot dog from a mobile curbside stand on Main Avenue at noon on the same day that Arrak and Rashid met in the stables. "But we're living in creepy times."

Ryan poured more ketchup, relish, and mustard on his half-eaten dog nestled in a white bun. Around them, the wind gusted paper wrappers along the wide sidewalks and flapped shop awnings in a ceramic-blue sky. The avenue, populated with shops, restaurants, and bars, bustled with a lunch-hour crowd.

"This street really rocks," Ryan said.

"It's the 'go' in Fargo."

Ryan stared out at the city's new, tall buildings and construction cranes. "We're no longer 'Fargo, far-gone.'"

Marleau opened his seal-topped coffee cup and drank from it. "I'm starting to see a pattern here," he said. "There's a kind of synergy in all this. Terrorists have infiltrated both the coroner's office and organized crime. The terrorists do the killing and follow up by supplementing Dr. Robert's pension, while the Sinise brothers provide the drugs for our crooked coroner to plant on Sanjay's body."

Ryan washed the end of his dog down with Coke from a can. "Do you know anybody who fits the description of this guy who broke into our house last night?" he asked.

"Not exactly, but he did it to scare the kids and shake up your cookie jar. He's obviously one of Habib's trusted right-hand men."

Ryan crunched the Coke can and tossed it in a wire-mesh trash container. "We can try to get a positive ID from the artist who did the tattoo of two horses on his upper arm."

"You mean check all the tat parlors that do this kind of work? It may take weeks. I say it's time to twist some arms at the North Dakota Horse Breeders' Association, namely Franklin Barroque."

"When Joanne spoke to him, a couple of days ago, he refused to talk about member lists or anything about their nags."

"Let's go rattle a few oats in his feed bag," Marleau said.

Franklin Barroque lived a short distance outside of Fargo in an imitation southern antebellum house with gleaming white pillars surrounded by a low brick wall. Open wrought-iron gates led to a winding drive beside stables and paddocks. Horses grazing in a field pricked up ears and snorted as Ryan and Marleau drove along the oak-lined drive. Behind a high-wire fence, three rottweilers barked, snarled, and rolled back lips to expose teeth.

"So much for the welcoming committee," Marleau said.

Ryan parked his Maxima in between two terracotta jockeys holding up boots that flanked the front steps. There was no reply to the front doorbell, so they went around the house to the stables.

The inside of the stone building smelled of manure, leather, and moldy hay. The ochre paint on the pressed tin ceiling was blistered and peeling. Sepia photographs of champions, along with rows of faded rosettes, covered one wall. As they entered, a horse rummaged against stall partitions.

A skinny, shirtless boy with a narrow, toylike face sat at a table while he polished a saddle. He said they could find his dad in the paddock.

When they caught up to Franklin, Ryan noticed he had his son's wide blue eyes, a stubby replica of the boy. He wore a Stetson, a checkered shirt, and baggy blue jeans tucked into cowboy boots.

"What can I do for you, gentlemen?" he asked. "If you want to buy horses, I can show you some promising young colts."

"That's not why we're here," Ryan said.

Franklin looked sideways and tried to hide the shine of irritation in his eyes.

"If you're plainclothes police officers, I demand to see a warrant, or I'll have to ask you to leave," he said.

"We aren't cops."

"Well, what exactly are you doing on my property? If you're spying on my thoroughbred racers, leave right now, or I'll call the cops."

Ryan said, "I phoned you around noon."

"Oh, Moar? You said you had something important to see me about, so naturally I assumed you wanted to buy horses."

Ryan handed him his card.

Franklin took off aviator shades and replaced them with half-frame reading glasses to examine the card. "I have no need for the services of a private investigator, thank you very much." He gave the card back. "I told your female associate I'd use my whip on her if she ever came snooping around the stables again. She had the gall to ask me a whole bunch of dumb questions about NDHBA members."

"Those weren't dumb questions, Franklin. We believe a horse owner in this area is connected to dangerous criminals," Ryan said.

Franklin planted four stiff fingers into Ryan's chest. "That makes as much sense as dried horse butt crust. I'm not comfortable with your presence here, so I'm not letting you near my membership roster."

"We thought maybe we could appeal to your sense of duty. You know, in the fight against crime," Marleau said, stepping closer.

Franklin removed his hat and ran a hand through his thick white hair.

"Is there anything else on your mind? If not, I've a ton of work to do. So if you gentlemen will kindly clear off my land."

Marleau opened the flap of his jacket so Franklin could get a glimpse of his .32 Beretta strapped to his side. Franklin craned a crick out of his neck, his tendons flexed like snakes.

"If you think you can push me around by showing me your little pistol, you're mistaken," he said.

"Calm down, Franklin. We're not here to see if you're up to your usual tricks. We know all about how you dope thoroughbreds and fix races," Ryan said.

"What the hell are you talking about?"

"The word on the street is the North Dakota gaming commissioner wants to hang you out to dry."

"That's a goddamn lie. Name your sources, and I'll sue the sons of bitches."

"The Sinise brothers?"

"Do you really think I'd do business with buckets of manure like Paul and Mark?"

"Cut deals with grease bags and some used fat is bound to rub off," Marleau said, knotting his big fist around Franklin's collar. He twisted until the horse breeder's face started turning red. He used his other hand to apply further pressure to his throat.

"Let me go," Franklin said, trying to wrench Marleau's hand from his neck.

"Release him," Ryan said.

Marleau pulled his hands off Franklin, leaving him bent over and clutching his neck.

"You're got some nerve threatening me," he said, spluttering. "You drive out to my farm and lecture me on civic responsibilities, accuse me of meddling in criminal activities, and then you try to throttle me." He turned his head sideways into the breeze. The angry welt on his neck stood out like a red flag. "I go by the rules; I don't break them for anyone. The racetrack has rules, and breeders like me, we have ours too. So I'd appreciate it if you'd just leave."

He walked away bandy-legged as though he spent most of his time in a saddle, his shoulders rolling. His eyes flicked from the stables to a flock of Canada geese dissecting shafts of afternoon sunlight that shone through low-lying clouds.

Ryan heard footsteps behind him and turned to see Franklin's son, his eyes filled with a pained, pinched light.

"What's going on, Dad?" he asked.

"Nothing, son," Franklin said, turning and pushing a knuckle against his teeth.

"I thought I saw this guy grab you around the neck." He said to Marleau, "Are you threatening my dad?"

"Everything is cool," Marleau said, his face still heated and knotted with frustration.

"These gentlemen are just leaving," Franklin said. "If you ever see them again, I want you to set the dogs on them."

"It would be a pleasure," his son said.

In the light from the overcast sky, the skin on the boy's hairless chest looked as smooth and white as alabaster. Ryan stared at his tattooed stomach, a washboard covered with prancing mythical winged horses.

"Who did the work?" he asked.

The boy grinned. "A dude named Frisco. He specializes in horses. He's the best. If you're interested, tell him Franklin Junior sent you. His shop's off Main on Twenty-Fifth North."

Frisco's Tattoo Emporium on the main floor of a drab warehouse building had a shabby torn awning. Sun-bleached posters of various naked women's body parts and biker emblems covered most of the unwashed front window. To Ryan, the shop gave him the impression of an aging stripper, working at a low-class club in the middle of the day. The open door let in cool air after the rain and flooded the street with rap music.

A young woman behind a glass-topped counter had her back to Ryan and Marleau while she applied lipstick in front of a cracked mirror. When she turned around, Ryan noticed she wore bleached jeans, a silk chartreuse blouse with a drooping neckline, and a clunky necklace of turquoise Egyptian scarabs that hung almost to her waist.

"What can I do for you, gents?" she asked, fluffing up her frizzy hair.

"Is Frisco in?" Ryan asked.

She crimped her lips and glanced toward a curtained-off area in the corner of the store, the source of the loud rap music.

"He's with a client right now. Do you want to make an appointment?"

"No thanks," Ryan said. "We're interested in a specific tattoo design of his, one of a pair of prancing horses."

"Oh, Frisco specializes in horses. We have a book of photos, if you'd care to look at them."

"You bet."

She took a binder off a shelf behind the counter and flipped through the photos. She swung the binder around so Ryan could see the pages in the horse section. She turned to a tattoo of two horses engaged in sexual union.

"When some guy flexes his biceps, Frisco knows exactly where to tattoo the horses so they're in sync," she said, giggling.

"I admire a man who knows his anatomy," Marleau said.

She grinned at him and crooked her finger to hook under his chin. "Not bad, big stuff."

Ryan stopped her when she came to a photo of winged horses surrounded by curlicues of fire. "Hold it right there."

She paused while he studied the design.

"Do you have the client's name that had this particular tattoo engraved on his arm?" he asked, trying to make his voice sound casual.

"We don't give out that kind of information," she said. "I could ask Frisco if it's okay, but he doesn't like to be disturbed when he's with a client." She glanced at her wristwatch. "He's been working on this guy for an awful long time." She worked her tongue inside her mouth as though trying to dislodge food caught in the fold of her lower lip. "This is so totally weird actually; he never turns his boom box up this loud."

"We're in a hurry." Ryan slid a pile of notes across the counter. "Give me the client's name, please." She grabbed the money.

"This is where he keeps the names and addresses," she said, opening a drawer and taking out a red covered notebook. "He's Kevin Dyck."

"Can you describe him?"

"He's got the shoulders of a body builder and a black beard."

"Are you sure?" Marleau asked.

"Yeah, I am. He told me he breeds horses. He insisted Frisco draw Arabians."

"Do you have his address?" Ryan asked.

She hesitated, and he snatched the book from her. He made a mental note of an address in Moorhead on Fourth Street.

"Hey, mister, give that back!" She grabbed the book. "You could get me fired." She glanced at the curtained-off corner. "Frisco is gonna be mad if he ever finds out."

She noticed a sudden violent riffle in the curtain and hesitated. "What's going on?"

She crossed in front of storage cabinets to reach the workspace in the rear of the shop. She flung the curtains open. She pressed her fingers to her mouth in an attempt to smother a scream.

Someone had driven a switchblade under Frisco's ribs and into his heart. The blood around the wound congealed into his white cotton tank top as though the killer had splattered him with red paint.

Marleau streaked out the rear door while Ryan leaned over Frisco sprawled on the bed. Ryan put his ear close to Frisco's mouth and didn't hear his breath. The sight of the dead tattoo artist felt like a fist in the stomach. Frisco's sky-blue eyes stared back him as though frozen in terror.

"Call the cops and report a homicide," he said to Frisco's assistant, who used her knuckles to wipe tears out of her eyes.

Ryan ran out into the street and raced for the Maxima parked in front. As he turned on the ignition, he saw a red pickup roar out of the back lane and turn right on Main. He started to follow it and then pounded the brakes hard and flung open the passenger door to let Marleau jump inside the vehicle.

"The bastard has the legs of a racehorse," he said.

Ryan followed the pickup, weaving around horn-blaring oncoming traffic. The pickup cut into traffic with Ryan on his tail.

"Step on it!" Marleau said.

Ryan could feel the Maxima shoot ahead as the modified engine added extra power. Ryan caught up to the pickup on the avenue. Despite the heavy traffic, Ryan in the left lane closed in on him. When he drove parallel to the pickup, he could see the killer's sweat bead on his forehead. The man's dark eyes widened with terror as he squeezed around a slow-moving sedan.

Ryan swung into the middle lane and accelerated until they were inches from the pickup's taillight.

"Ram the bastard!" Marleau said.

Ryan aimed at the pickup's rear bumper and braced for impact. The killer anticipated his move and wrenched the wheel to wedge the pickup in front of a school bus and behind an SUV. Ryan pulled up alongside the pickup now driving east on Main Avenue in front a busload of students waving souvenir flags. The pickup's driver swung out blind on the inside lane and almost collided with a semitrailer. Behind the killer, a truck rear-ended the semi and horns blared. In the distance, Ryan heard the wail of police sirens.

At the Tenth Street and Main intersection, the killer veered right into a warren of narrow streets downtown, and Ryan followed. Ryan threaded his way past the Exchange Building and checked side streets as he roared through red lights. By the time he reached Fourth Avenue, there was no sign of the pickup.

"Damn! We've lost him," Ryan said, banging a fist on the steering column.

"No, we haven't," Marleau said, pointing to the pickup, heading back to Main.

Ryan yanked the wheel hard as he swung back north. Ahead of him, the pickup smashed through a line of cones and construction barriers.

As Ryan turned onto Main, he watched in frustration as a mother pushed a stroller across the street in front of him at a light on the University Drive intersection. He thumped the brakes and the Maxima swerved, skidded, and shuddered as it hit the curb and scattered pedestrians. Ryan reversed his tires, kicking up a blue dust cloud of burned rubber. He flattened the gas pedal, and the Maxima growled like a bear shot in the gut.

"Stop him! Don't let him get away," Marleau shouted.

Ryan avoided the startled mother and the Maxima's side grazed a street barrier. The scream of metal jarred Ryan's senses. He spun the wheel to the left and cannoned off the side of the pickup. As he prepared for another sideswipe, he heard automatic fire tear into metal and reduce the windshield to a glittered spray of glass. Chips stung his forehead and sparkled on the dashboard.

Ryan spun the wheel, slammed on the brakes, fought for control. The sudden deceleration yanked him forward against his seatbelt and drove air from his lungs. He forced himself to breathe in hard and blinked sweat out of his eyes.

Marleau cleared out broken windshield glass with his foot. The pickup speeded up, swung behind a milk truck, and raced across the Veterans Memorial Bridge.

On the east side of the bridge, the Maxima surged and then faltered. When his crippled vehicle reached the Moorhead side, Ryan drove down Fourth Street South, a residential side street and coasted to the curb. As soon as the Maxima stopped, Ryan smelled a faint whiff of gasoline. His brain raced to adjust to the new threat.

"This rig's going to blow," he said, unfastening his seatbelt. He opened the door and stepped clear of the vehicle.

For an instant, he was hypnotized by the flickering of fingers of flames under the engine's hood.

"Run, Ryan, run," Marleau shouted.

After he ran half a block, Ryan glanced back at his burning vehicle engulfed in flames and black smoke. He felt an acute sense of loss. The Maxima had been like a reliable friend that had pulled him out of many scrapes. He felt a part of him broken, gone up in smoke. The fire soon died down, and the smoldering shell attracted a ring of spectators, uncertain what to do next, like picnickers at a barbecue waiting for wieners.

In the distance, police sirens headed their way.

Marleau punched Ryan's shoulder. His dark eyes glowed as though the violence of the car chase had excited him.

"We'll catch a cab to my place and use the Yukon to track this guy down to that address in Moorhead," Marleau said.

Reliving the high-adrenaline car chase, Ryan tried to relax by staring at a riverside park where a teenage boy flew a Chinese kite with a long loopy tail against the backdrop of a blue sky.

CHAPTER 26

I NSIDE THE YUKON XL, MARLEAU'S face was shiny and round in the half light, his mouth half full of a turkey sub. He washed the food down with Subway's coffee and wiped his mouth with a serviette.

"Isn't it time you phoned, Joanne?" he asked Ryan seated beside him. "She's probably seen on the six o'clock news a report of our little caper."

Ryan still appeared to be dazed, but black coffee helped to shake him out of his funk. Marleau's arms looked massive behind the steering wheel of the Yukon parked a few houses north of the address the tattoo parlor's assistant gave them.

Ryan took Marleau's advice and called Joanne.

"Ryan!" Her voice sounded frantic with worry. "Oh God, darling, is that really you?"

"The one and only."

"Please don't joke about this. On the TV news, the police claimed, following a downtown car chase, a driver and passenger escaped from a burning vehicle that belonged to a local private investigator." She paused, and he heard a sharp intake of breath. "I thought you'd be injured or worse."

"I've a few cuts and bruises."

"Tell me everything that's happened."

He told her the highlights of the tattoo parlor murder and the subsequent car chase.

"Now that the Maxima's toast, what are you driving?" Joanne asked.

"We've switched to Marleau's Yukon."

Marleau nudged him when a delivery van nosed in front of the three-story clapboard house.

"We're closing in on one of Habib's men outside a safe house in Moorhead," he whispered. Ryan drained his coffee. "Time to boogie, sweetheart."

"Take care, my love," Joanne said. "Stay in touch."

"Will do," he said and switched off the cell phone.

Ryan focused his night-vision scope on the van as the driver parked in a carport. The driver climbed out of the van and opened the door with a key. Once inside, he turned on a light on the first floor.

"It should be easy to break in through one of the front basement windows," Marleau said.

Through the overhang of the trees, Ryan could see the river and evening fog billowing up from the far bank. The heavy clouds turned the water shiny and black like crude oil as it flowed under the pylons of a bridge.

Once the night had taken over, they climbed out of the Yukon and crept in between houses to the back lane. The temperature had dropped ten degrees, and Ryan could smell a dank odor from the Red River. He opened a squeaky backyard gate, and they took cover behind bushes. He stood up to look through the window of a two-car garage that had the familiar red pickup truck inside, covered in part by a tarpaulin.

Ryan used a scope to spot the van's driver on the second floor. He was clean-shaven and wore tan workout pants and a tight ribbed undershirt. His skin was clear of tattoos except for the pair of horses on his biceps. A weight set rested in a corner in front of him. He got up and stretched before he lay down to start bench presses.

"He doesn't seem to be in any hurry to leave," Ryan said.

"Why don't we take him down and apply pressure?" Marleau said.

"He's not the type that'll talk easy. We should tail him to lead us to Habib."

They didn't have to wait long before he stopped lifting weights. Lights went on in the main-floor kitchen. They crept around to the front of the house. Ryan crawled to the window. Through a crack in the blinds, he watched the man pack supplies in cartons on the kitchen table.

A few minutes later, the man came out the side door and piled boxes into the van. They scooted behind a low hedge, close enough to him to recognize the chiseled shape of his high cheekbones and his pale skin in the light from the open door. He went back in and came out whistling. He paused to grunt as he lifted a wooden munitions box into the back of the van.

A door slammed, and Ryan tensed, a light drizzle sliding droplets down his cheeks. He stood still, ever nerve fine-tuned for any further sounds. From behind the house, he heard the harsh sound of an engine start and the screech of tires that kicked up gravel. The stones bounced off fence posts like buckshot.

"He's switched to the pickup," Ryan said. "We'll follow him."

Ryan started to run back to the SUV. He froze in midstride when he heard a rumble followed by a flash of white light, accompanied by a blast of hot air. The explosion knocked him off his feet, and he landed hard on his shoulder on the road. Burning embers fell around him. He wrapped his arms around his head to protect him from flying debris.

The intense heat forced him to crawl behind a tree trunk. When he looked back, the explosion had turned the van into a molten shell and ripped off the carport roof. The fire had spread to the house, and the blaze began to pop glass out of windows. He saw Marleau sprawled on the front lawn. Marleau clutched his left thigh as blood seeped between his fingers.

"I've got a piece of glass in my left bum cheek," he said.

Ryan tucked his hands under Marleau's armpits and hoisted him upright. Then he dragged Marleau to the SUV. He opened the trunk and folded down the backseat. The light from the blaze reflected off a jagged glass shard wedged in Marleau's buttock. Ryan lifted him inside the Yukon and laid him face down on the floor.

"I'm taking you to emergency," Ryan said.

Later that night, Arrak positioned thick rubber mats on the trailer's floor to provide traction for the horses' hooves. He shoveled in shavings to cover the mats and loads of fresh hay to keep the horses occupied during the trip. He fitted each of the four Arabians with high boots to protect knees and hocks. Before loading the horses, he used a pick to dig out dirt embedded in the hooves.

Out of the corner of his eye, he saw Habib stride toward him, while his flashlight stabbed the darkness.

"What's the holdup? You don't have time for grooming," Habib said.

"I have to clean hooves to prevent the horses from slipping," Arrak said in an irritated voice.

"Get them inside the trailers now," Habib said.

Arrak flipped the pick to the ground.

The horses sensed a change in routine, and they started to fidget. He led them one at a time out of the stables and tied them up beside the trailer. He coaxed al-Tikriti to the trailer door and gave his bridle a gentle tug. Behind the horse, Habib pounded his fists on the stallion's rump. The horse snorted, pawing the ground.

"Never force a horse that is afraid to move," Arrak said.

"Give him the whip."

"Let me do it," Arrak said, giving the horse a light tap with his whip on the rump.

Reassured by Arrak's familiar presence, the stallion inched forward. Once al-Tikriti was inside the trailer, Arrak fastened the butt chain, closed the door, and tied the stallion with a rope at his eye level. He left enough slack so al-Tikriti could move his head.

When he started to rummage inside the stall, Habib demanded, "What's the matter with him?"

"He'll settle down once the other horses are inside."

He used the whip on the hindquarters of the mare, Euphrates, to straighten her body to ease her into the trailer.

"Hurry up. It's taking all night to get them loaded," Habib said, checking his watch.

"You can't rush horses."

"Damn the horses. They're just cover."

"Aren't you planning to sell them? You told me you had a buyer and a bill of sale."

"It's a fabrication. The papers are forged."

"What will happen to them?" he asked, stroking the narrow blaze on Euphrates's forehead.

Habib remained silent.

The mare started to crowhop, so he spoke soothing words to her in Arabic. He rested the whip on her tail to discourage her from stepping backward. Being as gentle as possible, he led her inside the trailer. As soon as she was in her stall, Arrak loaded in a bag of bran he would feed the horses during the trip as a mild laxative.

"We will have to stop every three hours to walk the horses, give them water, and a chance to urinate," he said.

Habib's face was all rage. He looked like a man who had lost his soul.

He stepped closer, his face inches now from Arrak's nose. "No more demands, no more delays. Just load the rest as fast as you can."

Arrak shivered as silence slivered between them to envelop him like a suffocating vine. He experienced a sinking feeling that Habib had an alternate agenda for the horses Arrak had grown to love and respect. He loaded the other two as quickly as he could without spooking them.

How did Habib intend to get rid of the Arabians? Arrak went inside the trailer, his mind alternating between frustration and utter fury. His nerves were already raw after having to stab the tattooist and experience the terror of the downtown car chase, followed by the tension of blowing up the Moorhead safe house.

He could hear the horses snort and shift in the stalls.

The Arabians trembled as the truck that pulled the trailer started with a roar and headlights cut through the afterglow of the fast-descending fall night.

CHAPTER 27

LATER THAT NIGHT, A NURSE closed the window blinds in Marleau's hospital room in the redbrick Stanford Health medical center. Lying on his stomach, stretched out on a pillow, Marleau had an IV drip needle attached to the back of his wrist.

"I can't say with any certainty when he'll be able to go home," the nurse said to Ryan.

She was in her forties and had dyed auburn hair and a figure like the Michelin Man.

"Could you leave us alone for a few minutes, Julie?" Ryan said.

"Okay," she said, "but not for long. My boy needs his rest; he's lost a lot of blood."

She gave Ryan a hard stare before closing the door behind her. Marleau shifted his weight and settled himself more comfortably on the cushions. A stab of pain made him grimace.

"Sacramento Park is the most likely place to find horse breeders," he said.

"That's a large area to cover."

"Phone the police detachment. Ask for Sergeant Carl Shandy, an old buddy of mine."

"I didn't know you had any cop friends left," Ryan said, checking Marleau's cell phone directory to find the number.

When Ryan called, he heard Sergeant Shandy's crisp voice. After introducing himself, Ryan asked, "Do you happen to know any Arabian horse breeders in the Sacramento Park area?"

"I sure do. These folks live on a ranch about a twenty-minute drive from here. They have some fine Arabians. My daughter, Suzie, is crazy about horses. The owners, Mr. and Mrs. Garzi, let her pet, feed, and ride them."

"Are the owners from the Middle East?"

"The Garzis are brown-skinned, if that's what you mean, but otherwise they're no different from your average, blue-eyed, blond North Dakotan."

"Can you describe the Garzis?"

"Mrs. Garzi is a real looker with a gorgeous set of tatas, brown eyes that could lead a monk astray, and silky black hair. Her husband is thickset and balding, the kind you wouldn't mess with or want to meet in a dark alley. Why are you interested in these folk?"

Ryan was reluctant to tell him in case Shandy decided to carry out an investigation of his own.

"I've a client who wants to buy Arabians," he said.

"He's in luck. They're for sale. He'll have to be prepared to part with a hundred thousand buckaroos a pop. These nags have foot-long pedigrees."

"Do you happen to have Garzi's address?"

"Just a minute, it's a rural route." Ryan heard him put down his cell phone, and Ryan listened to distant squad room chatter about golf. When Shandy came back on the line, he gave Ryan precise directions on how to reach the horse breeder's acreage.

"Thanks, Sergeant, you've been most helpful."

He switched off the cell and turned to Marleau. "We've got them." He headed for the exit. "I'm going there now."

"What about backup?"

"I'll check the place out and then decide what I need in the way of reinforcements."

Marleau had a wounded look on his face. "Make sure you don't wreck my wheels, the way you did the Maxima."

"Don't worry. I'll take good care of the Yukon."

"Not a scratch, understand?" Marleau pushed himself up on his hands. "Watch your back, partner. Any way you slice it, he's a bad dude."

While Ryan drove to Sacramento Park, Joanne picked up the phone in her study, expecting to hear Ryan's voice. Greg Duluth was on the line. He sounded breathless and asked for Ryan.

"Ryan's out. What can I do for you, Greg?" she asked.

"Can't you guess?"

"Nothing off the top of my head."

"You'd better tell your crazy man to come in and see me. Tell him to drag in Belanger as well."

"As I said, Ryan's not here and neither is Marleau. Maybe I can help you?"

"You know as well as I do they're implicated in a downtown high-speed car chase that involved the firing of automatic weapons. The multiple collisions and traffic pileups took police officers five hours to sort out."

"This doesn't sound like a caper the guys would be mixed up in, Greg."

"The fire department put out a blaze of what's left of Ryan's Maxima." His husky voice sounded dry. "Don't pretend you're not aware of this little escapade. Where are they?"

"I don't know, exactly. I'm sorry, I can't contact them, Greg. Both Ryan and Marleau are out on a 24-7 surveillance job."

"That doesn't sound like Ryan. He hates working nights." She heard his sharp intake of breath. "I think you're lying. Another thing, I know they're involved in an explosion beside a house in Moorhead that destroyed the place."

"I can't help you on that one either, Greg. I wish I could be more obliging."

"The arson squad found what was left of a van that was packed with explosives. Investigators matched tire tracks to the pickup involved in the chase. Although no one was killed, the fire caused over half a million dollars in damages, and that's just a conservative estimate."

"I'm sorry, Greg, but I'm really not able to assist you."

"There's more. A sales clerk in a tattoo shop claimed two men, matching Marleau's and Ryan's description, asked her questions about tattoos at the same time the artist was murdered. The sales clerk said these two men then pursued the killer."

"It sounds far-fetched. How could Ryan and Marleau possibly be involved in these multiple crimes?"

"Far-fetched or not, you better tell him to phone me the moment he gets home and to be prepared to do some explaining on exactly what they've been up to over the last twelve hours."

"I'll pass along this information to Ryan."

"This caper has his stamp written all over it." Greg cleared his throat. "You can tell him that from now on if he's crazy enough to cause this mayhem, he's going to either get his PI license pulled or end up in a body bag."

"Thank you so much for calling, Greg."

"Don't hang up, Joanne. Listen to me very carefully. You are seriously pissing me off. By deliberately withholding information on Ryan's activities you may be getting yourself into deep trouble."

When he hung up, Joanne felt heated, and she went to the bathroom and washed her face in cold water. While she looked at her dripping face in the mirror, she felt her body tense. She dried her cheeks and began to massage the cramp out of the muscles in her neck.

Feeling edgy, she went outside to sit on the deck and listen to the beat of her heart. A searing wind from the south caused small swells on the river, and the moonlight's reflection looked like slivers of silver trapped in dark water.

Gary strolled up from the dock, a robe over his pajamas.

"Can't sleep?" he said, glancing at her flushed face. "What's up?"

Joanne continued to look at the river while she hugged herself as if seeking comfort from the feel of her arms wrapped around her breasts.

"Is it that bad? Ryan involved?" her son asked.

"Right on both counts," she said, letting out a long sigh. "Greg Duluth was on the phone."

"What did the staff sergeant want?"

"To speak to Ryan and Marleau about a downtown car chase, involving firearms."

"Wow! It sounds crazy."

"That's not all of it. After the chase, a bomb exploded that leveled a house in Moorhead."

"Did Ryan and Marleau cause all that havoc?" He stopped twisting his cell phone. "I wonder where they are now."

The night air felt warm and moist, and the sky was clear above the spruce and oak trees on Red River Road. Gary watched his mother, her face crisscrossed with thought.

"I wish Ryan would call; I've tried to get him on his cell, but he's switched it off."

When the phone rang, the musical sound made her jumpy.

"Ryan!" she said and then listened at length without interruption. Only occasionally did she nod and offer encouragement. Gary stood beside her, chewing on a hangnail. When she switched off the cell, she didn't speak immediately, as if trying to organize her thoughts. "Ryan's found Habib's ranch. The stables are empty. They're gone, cleaned everything out and left nothing but a few sticks of furniture."

"Where are they?"

"He believes they're heading south."

"Where?"

"He doesn't know exactly, but he thinks they'll carry out an attack and use the horses as a cover."

Unconsciously, Joanne brushed her hand against the checkered grip of her handgun in her pocket.

"Why can't we go to the cops?" Gary said.

"Without proof, they won't listen. Besides, Greg wants to question Ryan and Marleau about the mayhem. He'll want to hang them out to dry, keep them in custody for a while, and by that time it may be too late."

"Too late for what?"

"Ryan suspects Habib will soon launch his terror attack."

"Are you going with him?"

Joanne didn't let herself dwell on the choices she had to make. Her hands clenched and unclenched at her side.

"Yes, of course," she said in a quiet voice. "Marleau's out of commission. He'll want backup. You two will stay in the house until we get back."

"No way, I'm coming. Charlene will think the same."

"That's not for you to decide. Meanwhile, I have to phone Tamara Ravenstein before Ryan gets back From the ranch. I'm convinced she has a rough idea where Moe and his family are going with the horses."

CHAPTER 28

I T HAD BEGUN TO RAIN when Carl answered Joanne's call in his den. He was watching Piers Morgan on CNN while he ate from a bowl of roasted peanuts.

"Sorry to bother you so late," she said.

"It's no trouble, Joanne," he said.

"Ryan has found where Moe's parents lived in Sacramento Park, but they've pulled up stakes."

At first, he ignored her, continuing to eat the nuts.

"I'd tell him to leave it alone, Joanne," he said. "This whole business bothers me deeply. It should be in the hands of the feds."

Through the open blinds, he saw his garden quiver with light whenever thunder was poised to roll across the Red River Valley.

"I need to talk to Tamara," she said.

"I don't want you to harass my daughter at this late hour." He sucked in his cheeks. "She's in no condition right now to talk to anyone."

"Ryan is trying to prevent Habib and his wife from carrying out an attack."

"Everything connected to this so-called terrorist sleeper cell, in my opinion, is pure supposition."

"They murdered Sanjay because he discovered Moe's connection to extremists bent on some sort of strike from their base of operation in Sacramento Park."

"That's all in the realm of fantasy," he said, the heat in his voice rising. "Sanjay was nothing more than an arrogant Hindu with an inflated attitude about his own self-importance."

"You're wrong. He was a well-respected international security adviser."

"I did some background checks on him. His Bengali parents made a fortune in a lucrative antiquities smuggling operation. They looted sacred Hindu artifacts from temples and tombs and peddled them in Europe and North America."

"What has this to do with Sanjay's murder?"

"Everything! Sanjay's father was grooming him to take over the family firm when Interpol eventually caught up with Sanjay's father and the Indian authorities stripped him of his property and wealth. Sanjay and his sister managed to bribe immigration to jump the cue and settle in North Dakota. Sanjay meanwhile under the guise of being a security expert moved his smuggling antiquities business to Afghanistan where he pillaged the country's heritage in a trade that's nearly as lucrative as narcotics."

"I don't understand how—" Joanne began.

"Listen to me. I'm sorry I ever recommended him. Judging by what the police have discovered, I wouldn't be surprised if he switched to heroin trafficking, a trade that corrupts and ruins our youth, when the supply of artifacts started to run out from smuggling centuries-old Buddhist art." His eyes turned abstract, faking concentration as though the brief refuge of sharing fear with her didn't cancel the realization that the shadow of death hovered over him and may have already lodged inside his pupils. "I won't have you implicating my daughter in any of this. Do I make myself clear?"

"Tamara may know some clue—" Joanne insisted.

"Tamara's on Nardil," he said, curling his fingers against his palms.

"I'm sorry. I didn't know that, Carl."

Carl stood up and paced his book-lined den with a stiff gait as though his knees pained him.

"We desperately need to find out where they've gone. I'm sure it has to do with the horses. After all, Moe did take his riding gear with him."

The arthritic pain in Carl's knees made her wince. "You can't talk to Tamara. She's depressed for God's sake."

He put Joanne on hold while he closed the blinds and turned off the overhead lights. He sat in the air-conditioned gloom, his hand motionless on his mahogany desk, half listening to Piers Morgan prattle on about terrorism. Why did Tamara have to fall in love with the wrong man?

But like all fathers who raise teenage girls, he knew that at some juncture in her life she would meet a man she thought was special. Moe was handsome, better educated than she was, and wise in the world's ways. Why had she decided that he was the one she would give her whole heart and soul to?

Carl switched off the hold button. "She did tell me that Moe talked about going to the Annual American Arabian Horse Show and Gymkhana in Rapid City that begins on Friday. He mentioned that just before he disappeared. They were both crazy about horses, you know."

After she hung up, Carl stepped outside on the front steps.

The rain had stopped, and his ivy-covered mansion was encased in shadow. He shivered but not from the damp cool air. What other secrets and private unhappiness did the house contain? He wondered if he would ever know them all. He saw the face of his murdered ex-wife, Aimée, float in the air in front of him like a chimera. He saw the furtive look in her eyes, the plastic surgery that had smoothed her brow and tightened her skin, and her puckered lips that hid the smirk that flickered across her face. The cloud shifted, and thin light shafts from a crescent moon hung like shattered silver flames in the night sky.

CHAPTER 29

G RAIN ELEVATORS IN THE TOWN of Millsburg stood like sentries on Route 29 south of Watertown. The thin moon brightened fields of ripe wheat, and to the southeast thunderheads billowed into the sky.

Joanne lifted a strand of hair off the glasses she wore for driving before handing the cell phone to Ryan.

"It's Marleau," she said.

He opened the window and took a deep breath of damp air.

"I'm being discharged this morning," Marleau said.

"That's great news. How's slim treating you?"

"Julie is doing a fine job keeping me nourished and entertained." He cleared his throat. "Deirdre's visited a couple of times. She thinks my wound is a real bummer."

"If we were back in the squad room, you'd be the butt of every joke."

"I'm glad you haven't lost your sense of humor." He started to cough, and Ryan heard gurgling as he drank from a straw. "I wish I could be of some use instead of lying flat on my stomach."

"Look at it this way. Being laid up for a few more hours means you won't be gravitating to trouble for a while."

"Well, you are." He hesitated and then came out with it. "I have to get the hell outa here. I'm as restless as a polecat in a henhouse."

"Wait until you're discharged, and then get back to finding Aimée's killer, which of late you've been neglecting."

"I should be helping you guys prevent a bunch of psychopaths from obliterating some target in South Dakota."

"We'd like to have you along." Ryan's face stretched with impatience. "But what you're doing pays the bills. For the time being, keep a low profile as far as the WFPD is concerned. Greg's on the warpath."

"I'll hold the hounds at bay while you hunt down the terrorists." He breathed in hard. "Where exactly are you heading?"

"Habib is expected to unload the Arabians at the Rapid City horse show tomorrow morning. Then, I suspect unencumbered he'll carry out a strike somewhere in South Dakota." He glanced out of the window at the stands of a stampede ground. "We're passing through Tecumseh, so it won't take us long to catch up."

"A convoy of horse trailers with North Dakota license plates should be easy to spot."

"He has a head start, but he can't move too fast. He'll have to make pit stops to water and exercise the Arabians."

Ryan heard Marleau clear his throat. "I thought I heard other voices in your vehicle. Are just the two of you heading for Rapid City?"

"We've taken the kids."

"So you'll use them as cover."

"They'll be kept well out of harm's way."

"Any idea what his target is?"

"The Dakotas are bristling with military facilities, but I'm not sure."

"Good hunting. Going after this guy is like having razor blades mixed in with your oatmeal. If you get the chance, close this sicko's file."

Joanne took over the driving again somewhere west of Sioux Falls, past fields of sunflowers. The early morning sun hung suspended over the rolling hills like a red diamond, the low-lying clouds turned

211

a rich purple. Ryan snored beside her, his chest rising and falling under his sports shirt. Her mind was racing. None of the events of the last two days had made much sense.

She began to have second thoughts about Charlene and Gary coming along with them. The idea of putting the kids even close to danger made her tense. Ryan wanted leave them in a hotel in Rapid City, but she knew they would never agree to stay behind. Her eyes drifted to the rearview mirror. She could see them dozing. They looked young and vulnerable, heads almost touching. A flood of emotion gripped her. She and Ryan had gutsy teenagers, and she loved them.

Ryan's shoulder twitched, and his eyes snapped open, glazed over with sleep. She watched him turn to face her, the tension now drained from his face to make him look almost boyish.

A semitrailer roared past, and the displaced air rocked the Range Rover. Joanne removed her sunglasses, and in the hazy sunlight, her contact lenses had darkened her blue eyes to the color of sky before a storm. She fixed her gaze on the rolling prairie on either side of Route 90. The rolling plains of South Dakota stretched out before her to remind her of how much she loved the prairies. She knew she would never want to live anywhere else.

The sky had turned heavy with dark clouds by the time she drove over Box Elder Creek on the outskirts of Rapid City. Suddenly, she pressed her fingers on her mouth and braked hard.

Ryan glanced at her, a questioning look on his face.

"Why are we stopping?" he asked.

When the Range Rover's tires crunched to a halt on the shoulder, she remained silent. She stared at a billboard dwarfed by the dark humps of clouds that shrouded the looming Black Hills.

"I think I've solved the riddle," she said.

"You've done what?"

He followed her eyes to the billboard's Mount Rushmore silhouetted by a red sun. Opening the door, he climbed out to stretch.

"Substitute presidents for kings; it's often the obvious that's overlooked," she said.

"Why destroy the monument?" he asked, joining her.

"It's symbolic of everything that is noble about America."

"Blasting these four presidential heads doesn't make much sense, except for its emblematic value, but it will rile up a lot of people and cause an enormous backlash."

"Blowing up the memorial will terrify people and ratchet up security at other landmarks."

Ryan used his hand to wipe sweat off the back of his neck. "When we catch up to them at the horse show, I'll plant a tracking device on his vehicle that'll lead us directly to their base camp that I suspect he's already set up near the monument."

"If we're right about Mount Rushmore, how will Habib destroy the presidents?"

"In Afghanistan, the Taliban used *plastique* packed in holes to obliterate giant statues of Buddha carved out of the rock faces of sandstone cliffs. Relatively easy to do when compared to bringing down massive presidential heads in granite on top of a mountain."

"How could he do it?"

Ryan propped one foot on the bumper and stared hard at the billboard. "If four suicide bombers packed with explosives attempted to scale the mountain, they'd be spotted even at night. Besides that, they wouldn't be able to carry on their backs enough firepower to do more than superficial damage." He walked toward the billboard and gazed at the presidential heads. "They'll need some sort of airborne device to bring the heads down."

Beside him, she listened to wind puff the cottonwood trees and the traffic's steady hum like a well-oiled machine.

"What if they use missiles?" she asked.

"They're good at ground-to-air demolition, but I doubt they could pull off a missile attack undetected. Light aircraft packed full of explosives might work, but it's risky."

"What they need then is a guided airborne contraption capable of flying below the radar."

"Let's assume Habib's pilots fly ultralights full of fuel and explosives into the four heads simultaneously; the explosions would be enough to obliterate them. The heads would be irreparable."

"Is it easy to fly those flimsy machines?"

"As Brits flying spits would say, 'It's a piece of cake.' If that's the case, I wonder where his pilots learned to fly." He took his iPhone out of his pocket. "I'll call Marleau and ask him to contact local flight-training schools and get descriptions of recent grads."

They climbed back into the Range Rover where Charlene and Gary were playing chess. After Ryan made his call to Marleau, they drove toward the haze-covered Black Hills with every mile growing more suspenseful, more sinister.

CHAPTER 30

THE SUN DIPPED BEHIND THE foothills, a red-hot spark between two ridges, turning the valley a deep purple. El Joey's, a Mexican restaurant in Rapid City, was packed with tourists. Joanne had changed from gunmetal blouse and slacks to a gossamer silky outfit, her hair down to her shoulders.

"You've killed men before, haven't you?" she asked, toying with the stem of her wineglass. When he didn't reply, she shook her head at his offer of more Chardonnay. "When I am out with you, like this evening, I forget you are a dangerous man."

"Blood and violence excite some women," he said. "That's why the Roman Colosseum attracted them in huge numbers."

"You think I'm like those Roman matrons?"

"I can't say for sure. I haven't taken you to any NHL games lately."

She smiled and examined his face. "I know I am drawn to strong men, but that's only part of the reason I find you so attractive."

The room was ablaze with the sun's last rays. The red light colored the deep-blue tiled floor, the cane deck chairs, tables, and yellow cushions the color of blood.

"What are your others reasons?" he asked.

"You have a deceivingly smooth voice and a quiet manner. You're strong, yet you have a streak of tenderness. When we make love, you are gentle, yet I can sense an undertow of brutality and power held in check like a mastiff on a short leash." She gazed into his face for a moment. "Sometimes when I see your eyes, reflected in a certain light, they look both compassionate and cruel."

"Is that why you find my eyes appealing?"

"They have a magnetic quality."

"Violence doesn't make a man strong."

She bit down on her taco and stared at him, a pensive look on her face.

"I have to admit being drawn to your physical presence and toughness," she said.

"Confess! What you really admire is my tight butt."

"That is definitely one of your most appealing *assets*."

He grinned and gave her a loving look. During the meal, she continued in a bright, talkative manner. Only when they ordered coffee did her face tighten as she switched thoughts.

"Before we get in too deep, don't you think we should at least share what we know with the local bureau office?" she asked.

"It could be too late by the time we'd convinced anyone to listen to us," he said.

Ryan knew there was no easy way out. From the beginning, finding the terrorists reminded him of a raft trip on the fast-flowing Colorado River. When the raft tipped, he found himself caught in an undertow. Tugged below the churning white water, it took him a minute before he reached the surface and sucked in air, only to feel wrenching force tug him underneath the tumbling water again. He barely managed to swim ashore.

"If we sit back and do nothing, we'll see a replay of before 9/11 when a memo warning the feds about suspicious Middle Eastern pilots training in Phoenix got stuck on someone's desk." He leaned across the table and covered her hands with his. "Our only hope of saving the monument is if we can find a way to stop him."

He heard sirens blaring outside the restaurant and then the noise diminished, replaced by chatter and knives scratching on plates.

Ryan signaled to the server for the check.

"We're really on our own, aren't we?" she said.

He gazed at the almost-perfect symmetry of her face, the smoothness of her cheeks, her big-city good looks, and the extraordinary serenity of her eyes.

"From now on, we have to focus on catching this monster," he said.

"In the process of finding him and saving the monument, I hope we don't destroy ourselves," she said.

"Pour me another coffee, my love."

A few hours after sunset, Arrak heard the squeal of trailer brakes. He sat up and rubbed his eyes. He had woken up from a short nap on some straw beside al-Tikriti and feedbags containing aero engines wrapped in plastic. He wondered why they hadn't taken the more direct route to Rapid City on Interstate 90 instead of meandering along side roads. An abrupt left turn jolted the stallion, and he strained against his tether. Arrak peered through the ventilation screen at a deserted stretch of highway somewhere west of Wall.

Why were they taking another detour? It was too early for a rest stop. He stroked al-Tikriti's nose, and the stallion sniffed his hands. When the truck drove over a series of ruts, he had to hang on to the side of the swaying trailer. When the trailer came to a halt, Arrak stretched, raised his arms above his head, and arched his back, unconsciously mimicking the horses in the stalls.

In the early morning twilight, Arrak could see a weed-encrusted road leading to a barn beside a half-collapsed farmhouse. Smashed windows stared out at him like empty eye sockets. Puffy clouds filled the sky, and the wind smelled of damp grass from a recent shower. The horses brushed against the sides, itching to get out.

He heard rapid footsteps and recognized Habib's heavy stride. He watched him swing open a double barn door to disturb roosting pigeons. A light came on in the farmhouse, and three men tumbled out and started to load kit bags into the back of the pickup.

Arrak felt frustrated at not knowing why they had stopped beside the farm buildings. Habib had kept him out of the loop on the exact travel plans. When Arrak heard a wrench uncouple the trailer, he squeezed past the rumps of the horses to the door and flung it open.

"What's going on?" he shouted to Habib, whose chest heaved. "Why are you unhitching the trailer?"

Behind Arrak, horses nickered, and the first sunlight left an orange haze above the distant hills. Arrak sensed something had gone terribly wrong.

Habib pinched his nose with his thumb and forefinger. For a few minutes, he remained silent, while Arrak's frustration mounted.

"Take the horses to the barn and tie them up," he said finally.

Arrak's mind went into a tailspin.

"Aren't we selling them at a public auction in Rapid City at the horse show?" he asked, climbing out of the trailer.

"Change of plan."

Arrak glanced around at the dirt road and the dilapidated farmhouse. "Surely we can't leave them in this dump? Have you any idea how valuable these animals are?"

"They've served their purpose. They're worthless to me now."

Arrak's mouth fell open; his eyes focused on Habib's thumb that stroked the tip of his .38 Magnum with a silencer. Habib's gaze fixed on him like a fist as he leaned forward, twisted his fingers into Arrak's hair, and pushed his head back against the side of the trailer.

"Shoot them," he said, offering him the gun's handle.

Arrak could feel his body tremble. Sweat poured down from his forehead and into his eyes. When Habib relaxed his grip on his hair, Arrak broke loose, pressed his back against the trailer, and tried to shrink away from him.

"Please," he whispered, clutching his chest as pain clamped down on his heart. For a moment, he thought he might have had something like a stroke. "Are you telling me to—?"

"Don't refuse me," Habib said.

Arrak's face twitched as though Habib had slapped him.

Habib holstered the gun, grabbed Arrak by the throat, and squeezed until Arrak's vision started to blur.

"Do it."

Arrak wheezed out rapidly. "I can't."

"Obey me, now." Habib lips twisted in a grin. "Don't force me to turn you over to Rashid. He has ways to prolong pain."

When Habib released him, Arrak gasped for air. He felt his lips part, but no sound came out, his voice clotted with a crust in his dry mouth. He had never been on the receiving end of Rashid's torture, but he knew the terror he could inflict.

"Your affection for these animals is a noble kind of love, similar to that a jihadist has for his brothers," Habib said in a soothing voice.

Arrak glanced at a bank of thunderheads forming over the Black Hills. The clouds pulsed and flickered with sheet lightning. He became aware of the faces of the newcomers fixed on him. One of them lit a cigarette with a lighter, and the smoke drifted in his direction. The horses sensed the tension and began to scrape the floor with their hooves.

"You don't want to refuse my director order," Habib said.

"I'll do it," Arrak whispered, feeling as though he had toothpicks wedged in his windpipe.

He led the Arabians to the barn lit by a hurricane lamp. The stale air smelled of bird droppings, mildew, and moldy straw. As he tied them to posts in the barn's four corners, a weight crushed against his heart. He hung his arm around al-Tikriti's neck. When he pressed his face on his hide, his tears dampened the stallion's mane. The stallion shivered and started nickering.

Out on the periphery of his vision, Arrak saw a figure move along the barn wall and step out of the shadows. Rashid reached out with his hand like a blind man and touched Arrak's face. Arrak jerked his head back from the rancid smell of Rashid's fingers.

Rashid thrust Habib's handgun with the pearl handle at him.

"Shoot the motherfuckers at close range in the temple behind the eye." He cackled a guttural sound that echoed off the ceiling. "That way, you won't waste bullets."

Arrak took the butt of the pistol and avoided Rashid's eyes. He heard Rashid slam the doors.

As if in a nightmarish dream, he strolled to Naborr. She sniffed the floor for stray pieces of straw. He aimed the pistol at the mare's head and pulled the trigger. Blood spurted out of the wound and drenched the pistol's barrel and his hand. She stumbled but still stood. He panicked when he thought he would have to shoot again, but after a few seconds, she faltered, staggered, and hit the floor with a thud. He stared with a stupid grin at his bloody palm. In a trance, he shot the other two horses.

He stood for a moment and wept.

As he approached al-Tikriti, the stallion smelled the blood, and his eyes widened in terror. He rose up on his hind legs and whinnied.

When the stallion calmed down, Arrak's eyes darted around the barn. At the far end, he spotted missing wallboards. Arrak felt a surge of raw rage rise in his soul.

He untied al-Tikriti and dragged him to the rear. He slipped the lariat off his neck and slapped him hard on the rump to encourage him to squeeze through the wall gap. He watched the stallion scramble over broken fence rails.

He waited until al-Tikriti trotted into an arroyo. The stallion looked back once and then disappeared into a deadfall.

CHAPTER 31

E ARLY THE NEXT MORNING, RYAN leaned on the Jefferson
Hotel's balcony rail. He gazed at the rounded Black Hills,
cool and misty in the dim dawn light. He punched his partner's cell
phone number and waited.

Marleau mumbled, his voice thick with sleep, "Greg sends you
a message: 'Tell that crazy son of a bitch to turn himself in or I'll
issue an APB and have him arrested.'"

"How could he do such a nasty thing to the best man at his
wedding?"

"It's time to call his bluff. By the way, I hit pay dirt with the hang
glider and ultralight set. This spring, an instructor who belongs to
Aerial Adventures with Attitude based at the Steinbach Municipal
Airport in Manitoba trained four young men to fly ultralights. One
was American, the other three East Indian pilots with Cockney
accents, who claimed to be from Mumbai. Get this, the instructor
remembers the American had prancing horses tattooed on his
right arm."

"Did he remember the guy's name?"

"Ron Bailey. It's phony."

"What sort of ID do these flying clubs ask for before enrolling student pilots?"

"A driver's license."

Ryan groaned. "Good Lord, no wonder we think our Canadian friends are a weak link in continental security." A satisfied smile spread across his face. "You've done a lot of legwork despite having a sore ass."

"I'm on my second wind."

"What gave you this jolt of energy?"

"Deirdre's moved in." Ryan heard him breathing hard into the receiver and someone giggling in the background. "By the way, she's become really interested in Aimée's murder case. She figures I should concentrate on family members. She believes most murders are committed by close relatives or friends of the victim."

"She's right. It's time to put her on the payroll."

"She already is. When I persuaded her to go to Ravenwest on the pretext of applying for a job, she picked up all kinds of gossip from a talky receptionist. Cole is turning into a real nutcase. His girlfriend has left him, and he is now sleeping at the apartment of some female employee from the office. He rarely goes to work. When he makes an appearance, he's as crazy as a coot."

"It sounds as though Cole has some serious issues." Ryan felt his jawbone tighten. "Find out why he's gone off the deep end."

When Ryan switched off his cell phone, his mouth felt dry, and his hair was damp with sweat. He went inside the hotel suite, made coffee, and returned to the balcony. The rain during the night had slackened, and shafts of sunlight shone through the clouds.

Even though they now had a compelling clue on the target, finding Habib's base of operation was going to be tenuous and speculative to say the least. After breakfast, Joanne planned to check out the American Arabian Horse and Gymkhana grounds and place homing devices on their vehicles.

When he straightened up, he realized Charlene had been watching him ruminate.

222

"Are they really out there, Dad?" she asked, staring at the Black Hills, painted mauve in the early sunlight.

"We presume, as soon as they're rid of the horses, they're going to a base in the hills."

His daughter wore a silk kimono over her pajamas, and her hair hung loose on her shoulders.

"What would you do if you met Moe's dad face-to-face and he was armed?" she asked.

"I'd tear up his check," he said in a low voice.

"Is that when you forget who you are?" she asked, stretching her back to her full height.

"You're perceptive." He turned back to her and held her soft hands in his. "You and Gary are to remain in Rapid City."

She pulled her hands away and turned to watch the sun brighten the foothills in a golden light. "As I've told you before, I'm not afraid."

"You'll both be safe if you stay in this hotel."

He glanced at her and saw her open her eyes wide as though she had just woken from a long sleep. "Gary and I have talked this over, and we agree there's no way we are going to stay behind."

CHAPTER 32

LATER THAT MORNING, CARL'S MAJORDOMO, Bertrand Sapergia, told Marleau his boss was having lunch at Maxwell's with the governor. Marleau parked outside the restaurant, the rain steaming on the Yukon's hood. Deirdre sat beside him and puckered her lips in the visor mirror to apply ruby-red lipstick.

"I don't know why you have to drag me along," she said.

"Having you adds an air of respectability," he said.

"I'm glad to be useful."

"Ryan said you did a good job of finding out about Cole's bizarre behavior."

"Oh, that was easy, and I don't mind doing things you rope me into, even though some of the work you do is dangerous. But you can forget it if you think I'm going to be like Joanne and start dodging bullets."

"I'll protect you. Let's go."

She hesitated and fluffed up her auburn hair. "For starters, you can open the umbrella. I'm not getting a single raindrop on my hair."

He opened her door holding an umbrella over her head. They went inside the foyer. The restaurant was doing a brisk noon-hour business, and servers in black dresses and white aprons took orders and brought in trays of food.

"There's Carl, on the right," Marleau said, nodding to a corner table.

She whispered, "Why, Carl's elderly. Go easy on him."

"There isn't time. I can't cut him much slack."

The maître d's eyes locked on Marleau then shifted to Deirdre beside him.

"I need to talk to Carl Ravenstein now," Marleau said to the maître d'.

"I don't like to pull a guest away from the table unless it is absolutely necessary," the maître d' said, patting his slicked-down hair. "After all, he is lunching with the governor."

"Just tell him Marleau Belanger needs to see him on urgent business."

"I'll relay your message, Mr. Belanger, but if Mr. Ravenstein doesn't want to be disturbed, you'll have to wait here until he's finished lunch."

Terrorists plan to blow up a national monument tonight, and he wants me to cool my heels, Marleau thought.

"I don't give a damn if he's with Jack Tyler." Marleau grabbed the front of the maître d's starched shirt. "Take me to him now, or I'll knock you down on your fat ass."

"But, sir, you can't—" he spluttered.

"Want to bet?"

"Better do as he says, sir," Deirdre said.

When Marleau released him, the maître d' straightened his bow tie. His face had turned red and was slicked with sweat.

"This is most irregular. Come this way," he said, leading them into the restaurant.

They walked through the dining room to a corner booth where Carl sat opposite Governor Jack Tyler, who wore a well-pressed suit and had a healthy glow from a summer tan.

The maître d' whispered in Carl's ear.

"What burning issue needs my attention?" Carl asked, looking at Marleau and Deirdre as though they were worms in the salad.

"Who are you?" the governor said, lowering a fork of rare steak on the way to his mouth.

Marleau ignored him.

"Ryan has identified the target the terrorists are going to attack," he said.

"You've been hired to find out who murdered my ex-wife."

"Oh sure, Carl, meanwhile a major monument—"

"If you and Ryan continue to pursue this obtuse, dim-witted obsession that's caused me and my family nothing but grief, I swear I'll pull you off the case." He got up and bumped into a server. "Now get out of here and stop harassing me."

Governor Tyler waved at the maître d'. He came running to the table, bowed, and offered apologies. Deirdre tugged at Marleau's jacket sleeve, and she half dragged him out of the restaurant.

Joanne sniffed an unmistakable verdant smell of horses as she adjusted her sunglasses in the harsh morning sunlight while she examined the canvass banner stretched across the entrance of the outdoor arena that announced the Fourteenth Annual American Arabian Horse Association's Gymkhana and Auction in Rapid City. Rain during the night had turned the slopes of the hills a dark green, but the morning was cool and full of blue sky.

She carried a slim briefcase and wore a headscarf and a tan pantsuit that she hoped would help her blend in with the horsey set. She headed for a trailer marked Registration. Inside the office, she approached a willowy woman in jodhpurs seated in front of a laptop.

"I'm interested in buying Arabians," she said. "The ones that caught my eye in your catalogue are four from Sacramento Park near Fargo."

The woman gave her a breezy smile. "I suppose you found out about them on the net," she said, straightening her horn-rimmed glasses as she typed, focusing on the screen. "Are they listed with the North Dakota Arabian Horse Registry?"

"I believe so."

"Do you know the owner's name?"

"Sorry, no."

"There's only one Fargo breeder listed: James and Jane Bellingham from Sacramento Park. They have four young Arabians for sale, two stallions and two mares."

"That's exactly what I'm looking for."

"Are you from out of town?"

"Minneapolis."

"The Bellingham's thoroughbreds have solid pedigrees, three- and four-year-olds in excellent condition. They haven't won any major trophies, but they look magnificent in the videos the Bellinghams sent us." She stared hard at the screen. "There'll be a lot of interest in these animals." She ran her finger down a list beside her on the desk. "The names of the horses are al-Tikriti and Euphrates, the stallions, and Naborr and Daurita are the mares."

"When can I preview them?"

"Now if you like." She glanced at her watch. "I'm not too busy. Why don't I show them to you?"

"That would be lovely."

"My name's Gloria Katzenbach," she said, offering her hand.

"Judi McNally," Joanne said, shaking her slim fingers.

Gloria slipped on a blue blazer and led the way past an outdoor stadium decked with flags. In the distance, Joanne heard a brass band warming up.

"We're only a regional show, not as large as Scottsdale, Albuquerque, or Louisville," Gloria said. "But the good news, Judi, is we are growing."

As they neared the stables, Joanne shivered. If she came face-to-face with Moe, she hoped he wouldn't recognize her. Sunlight flared off the side of an aluminum horse trailer, prompting her to put on dark glasses. She walked alongside Gloria and half listened to her patter.

"Even the big boys of the Triple Crown are now beginning to sit up and take notice of us," Gloria said.

"How many entrants do you have this year?" Joanne asked.

"We've attracted a record three hundred."

Joanne kept her sunglasses on when they entered the long wooden stables with stalls on either side. She took a swift glance at a thickset buyer. His hands ran down a horse's fetlock, and he straightened up to make notations on a clipboard. Out of the corner of her eye, she spotted a man with black hair and a dark complexion stride toward them, his boots kicking up loose pieces of straw.

When he glanced at her, Joanne's breath quickened, and a flush spread across her face. She averted her eyes and studied the names of horses on the opposite side of the stables. He paused as if he wanted to talk to Gloria, then changed his mind and walked on.

Wondering if the man she had just seen was Moe's father, she almost bumped into Gloria who had made an abrupt stop in front of a stall. Gloria rubbed her cheeks as if trying to comprehend something that had gone wrong.

Beside her, Joanne took a deep breath of fresh straw and horse sweat. She buried her hands in her pockets.

"That is strange," Gloria said, craning her neck to look over the tops of the doors of empty stalls, twenty-three to twenty-six.

She consulted her list. "I could've sworn the Bellinghams had checked in. Never mind, I can show you tons of other Arabians in a similar age and sex range."

Gloria turned at the sound of running footsteps, the crack of straw on the cement floor. When she spun around, her polished riding boots squeaked. She raised her eyebrows, and her mouth froze open as she watched Judi McNally run out the door, her legs pumping.

CHAPTER 33

A T THREE O'CLOCK THAT AFTERNOON, Ryan and Joanne took off in a bubble-shaped Bell 47 helicopter for an hour flight over the Black Hills. As the chopper only had room for two passengers, Charlene and Gary remained at the Rushmore Helicopters ticket office in Keystone.

Following Ryan's instructions, the chopper pilot whisked them above the treetops and began to make a wide circle around the monument.

"We're looking for large buildings or warehouses where Habib could store the ultralights," he said to Joanne, raising his voice above the roar of the rotors.

"We also need to look for a cleared area for a runway," Joanne said.

"They'll more than likely attack at night and want the pilots to fly a low flight path along a valley so they won't be easy to detect."

He examined the crowns of the heads of the four presidents like round domes towering over the amphitheater. He could clearly see the two main parking lots, the avenue of flags, terraces, and footpaths.

The helicopter followed the circular highway around the monument and flew over Hill City and Keystone.

"To have any impact, they'll have to carry out a frontal attack," he shouted.

She studied the topographical map and photographed possible sites through the plastic bubble. She wrote down coordinates on a pad of lined yellow paper.

The sky was a brilliant cobalt blue and dotted with puffy clouds. The pines on the slopes of the hills had turned velvet green. She pointed out the Chief Crazy Horse monument to him, the outline of the chief's noble horse, head, and outstretched arm, facing toward the eastern plains. Ryan, his features shadowed by a baseball cap, searched for warehouses through binoculars.

The pitch of the rotors changed when Ryan asked the pilot to descend.

"There's a resort that's close enough to the monument," he said, pointing to a complex surrounded by pine trees. "Look, there's a valley that gives them a clear flight path to the presidents."

Joanne jotted down the location of the cabins, a main office, and a warehouse on her sketched-out map. Below them, needle rock formations jutted above the pines, and beyond distant Great Hogbacks formed an outer ring.

Joanne squeezed Ryan's hand. "It's hard to concentrate on finding his lair when the scenery in the Black Hills is so breathtaking," she said.

While Habib half listened to patriotic piped-in music, he put down his coffee cup on a stone bench and gazed at the four heads carved into the mountain.

He smiled as he visualized his eagles roar into Washington's prominent chin, strike just below Jefferson's nose, crash into Roosevelt's mouth, and explode into Lincoln's beard.

Using binoculars, he examined the stone faces laced with rock veins, a crisscross of scars as though the presidents had suffered terrible facial wounds. He noted how the sculptor, Gutzon Borglum, hollowed out the eyes so they appeared as though they stared right at him.

He thought it ironic that one of the reasons Borglum had carved the heads on Mount Rushmore's summit was a bid to safeguard the carvings from mutilation. According to a guidebook, Borglum had read how in the 1800s British artillery in Egypt had used the Sphinx for target practice.

He lowered his binoculars and shifted his gaze to the canyon below the monument, strewn with the debris left by hard rock miners. The view reinforced his plan for an aerial assault as the only way to succeed. Any other alternative would have failed. It would have been impossible to carry backpacks of high explosives over loose shale or somehow dangle them attached to ropes from the summit. Even at night, they could never scale the floodlit mountain unnoticed.

He laced his fingers over his stomach and smiled to himself. Homing in on the heads from the air would take guards by surprise. Around midnight, his eagles would skim above the pine tops in the canyon to seek out and destroy this so-called Shrine of Democracy.

He would have his revenge for all the destruction and desecration Islamic countries had suffered in the hands of Americans. Images of the Abu Ghraib prison, west of Baghdad, of prisoners abused by American guards, had stiffened his resolve. He stretched out his short, muscular legs, and his hatred shifted to Americans who supported Israel while his fellow Palestinians slipped deeper into poverty and despair. His revulsion of Americans had grown for the way US corporations had exploited the Arab world's oil wealth. By international influence and military threats, Americans had stolen Arab oil at paltry prices. He regarded this theft as the biggest act of pilfering ever witnessed by humankind in the history of the world.

For a while, he continued gazing at the memorial with fire in his eyes. Once his pilots had shattered the four heads, this bold act would galvanize the Islamic world in an ironclad jihad. He dreamed of a united Muslim hegemony, under strict religious rule, that would hail him as its leader. He and his followers would sweep

231

away those in command, who had grown too old, too complacent to fight.

His leadership would use open societies as a springboard for Islamic agents with cells in Bosnia to fan out from the Balkans into Russia and Eastern Europe. His next step would be to call for a holy war against the West. He would begin by exhorting young Muslims to join the insurgency in Iraq and Syria. He would hail the nineteen jihadists who died in the World Trade Center attacks as brave warriors and call on Muslims to give the infidels a 9/11 day after day after day.

The prospect of bringing down capitalism along with the collapse of Western political systems gave him a narcotic rush like a semitrailer that roared to the center of his brain loaded with Afghan heroin.

Nothing could stop him now.

The steady throb of helicopter blades interrupted his thoughts. For an instant, the sun's reflection off the helicopter's bubble stung his eyes. He felt a sudden chill run down his back as though a wintry wind had blown over his tomb.

Why did the helicopter make him feel uneasy?

He pulled the brim of his hat at an angle over his eyes. His lips parted, and he curled his fingertips against his palms. He watched the helicopter hover overhead like a giant dragonfly. He felt disturbed by the chopper's presence until it disappeared behind Mount Rushmore.

CHAPTER 34

L ATE THAT SAME AFTERNOON, MARLEAU caught up with
Ricky at the food court in the West Acres Shopping Mall.
His quarry was sitting at a counter, eating stirred New York fries
saturated in thick gravy. As Marleau limped across the food court,
he felt confident he was close to solving the case, but he needed to
eliminate Ricky from his list of suspects.

As he approached Ricky, he noticed the ex-Ravenstein pool
attendant used his fingers to stuff the mushy fries into his mouth.
When he stood beside him, Marleau punched Ricky's shoulder.

Ricky choked on a mouthful of fries.

"Surprised, Ricky?" he said, thumping him hard on the back to
dislodge the blockage in his throat.

"Why can't you leave me alone?" he asked, wiping his thick lips
on a paper napkin.

"Hey, Ricky, what's up?"

Ricky chewed his regurgitated fries, looked sideways at
Marleau, and said nothing.

"I'm interested in the company you keep, my man," Marleau
said, poking a finger into his ribs.

Ricky opened a penknife, used the point to clean black dirt under his nails, and then wiped the crud on the table's edge.

"I'm having a hard time having you sit next to me," he said.

"Am I making you uncomfortable?"

"You hit me in the face," he said, rubbing his nose as though the blow was still fresh.

"Are you the type who wants to square a grudge?"

"No, I don't hold a beef against you for what you did."

"Then you won't mind if we go for a drive and have a private chat."

Ricky combed his fingers through his thick hair, while his gaze followed two ponytailed teens. The girls looked at him as if he were catnip, before sashaying past them in pants that exposed the tops of creases, dividing their swaying buttocks.

"I ain't going nowhere with you," he said.

"Oh yes, you are." Marleau swung round on the stool, put his hand inside his pocket, and pointed a snub-nosed handgun at Ricky.

Ricky stared wide-eyed at the taut barrel-shaped mound inside the pocket of Marleau's tan slacks.

"It's loaded," he said.

Ricky shrugged. "You wouldn't shoot me in this crowded mall."

"Don't tempt me. Now get up slowly."

Before rising from the stool, Ricky paused to scan shoppers passing by as if searching for a rescuer. Marleau held on to Ricky's shoulder, removed the revolver from his pocket and dug the handgun into the small of Ricky's back. He quick stepped the boy to the exit.

Outside the mall, blistering afternoon heat wafted across Marleau's face. Once inside the Yukon, he lowered his backside on an inflated cushion in the shape of a doughnut.

As they drove out of the parking lot, Ricky asked, "Where are you taking me?"

Marleau ignored his question and headed west on Interstate 94. Once he was out of city limits, he turned left on a gravel road until he passed the heads of ripened wheat ruffled by a breeze. He drove down a side road and parked beside a coulee where a couple of mallards swam in among the cattails. He turned off the ignition. Beyond the flat fields, storm clouds gathered, flickering cool white sheet lightning.

Marleau swung around and brought his face so close to Ricky's eyes that he squirmed against the locked door. "I understand you've developed a cozy relationship with the Sinise brothers. I want to know about it, okay. I think you and your pals are connected not only to Aimée Ravenstein's murder but to the death of a colleague of mine, Sanjay Sinha."

The coolness from the air-conditioning evaporated and turned the inside of the SUV as humid as a wet sauna.

"If you don't talk, I could damage your face again, and this time, I'd leave ugly marks that will affect your social life. No girls will want to look at you ever again," he said. "You wouldn't like that, Ricky, would you?"

Ricky blew out his breath and looked wanly at mosquitoes on the windshield probe the glass with proboscises, searching for a way to get in to feed. The thunderheads yawned open, and the sun's red light shone like rivers of fire through cracks in the clouds.

"Get the cement out of your mouth, Ricky," Marleau said.

Ricky leaned back and stretched his muscular, hairless arms, his long fingers bent like talons. He ran his fingers through his shaggy, blond-tipped hair. He took off his reversed baseball cap and used the crown to mop his forehead.

"I heard some towel head was goin' down," he said.

"When?"

"Mark Sinise talked about it when I went to pick up a delivery."

"What exactly did this shithead say?"

"That's all I know, man."

Ricky's face was shiny with sweat. It started to drizzle, and moisture condensed into steam clouds enveloping the SUV's hood.

"Are you a mule for the brothers?" Marleau asked.

"So what?"

"Where do you make the deliveries?"

Ricky was silent while he swiveled a toothpick in the corner of his mouth.

"Where do you take the scag?" Marleau asked.

"A house in Moorhead."

"The one that exploded?"

"Yeah."

"Who did you contact at the house?"

"I'd never met this dude before."

"Can you describe him?"

"He was tall and had arm muscles like slabs of meat. He was white, but they called him Arrak. I remember because his name sounded like the country."

"Any distinguishing tattoos?"

"Yeah, on his arm, two ponies on their hind legs."

A wave of heat swept over Marleau. He felt himself tumble out of the humidity inside the vehicle and into a cool place where the distant thunder over the prairies was only the harmless echo of exploding car bombs, long since muted by the drift of sand and time.

"What else can you tell me about this dude, Arrak?" he asked.

"Nothin' much. I smoked a few joints and passed out." His eyes started to water; he looked sideways at the branches of chokecherry bushes lift in the breeze. "What do I know? Fargo's a weird town. When I woke up, I heard Arrak talk in some foreign language to brown-skinned, dark-haired dudes."

"What happened next?"

"Arrak shoved me into my truck. On the way home, I hit an old man, walking his dog. I just clipped him, but he got my license number, and the police charged me with drunk driving and leaving the scene of an accident."

"While you were in custody, let me guess, you called Paul Sinise's legal counsel, Mark Sokolov. Am I right?" Ricky put his face in his hands. "I bet Skippy didn't waste any time to grease the wheels of justice to get you out on bail."

Marleau spotted a tattoo on Ricky's arm and lifted his sleeve to examine Arabic script on his biceps. He asked, "You converted to Islam or what?"

Marleau saw him try to suppress a twitch of anger from flooding his face. "They did it to me while I was out cold." He started pounding the window with his fists. "I can't stand being cooped up in this heat."

"Knock it off," Marleau said, restraining his arm.

"God, I hate talking to you."

"Just a few more questions and I'll open the windows and turn on the air."

Ricky's hands cupped the crown of his head to expose sweat stains that swelled under his armpits.

A sudden burst of rain made a steady beat on the roof but did nothing to cool the heat inside the Yukon.

"Does Cole Ravenstein owe money to the Sinises to pay off gambling debts?" Marleau asked.

Ricky wiped his palms on the front of his shirt but remained silent.

"Cole's in bed with the Sinises," Marleau continued. "He's linked to international drug cartels, biker gangs, and contract killers. Am I right?"

Ricky twisted his face away from Marleau and stared out the passenger window at the rain, his lips as tight as the stitched mouth of a shrunken head.

When Ricky hesitated to reply, Marleau added, "Why are you protecting him?"

"Man, I can hardly breathe," he said, biting his lower lip. "Okay, this is what I heard. Aimée stopped bailing Cole out by paying off his poker debts, so he borrowed money from loan sharks. When he couldn't pay them back, they said they'd kill him. Paul Sinise provided Cole with the money to pay off what he owed."

"In return for what?"

"A stake in the company, I guess. That's all I know, honest to God!"

Marleau turned the ignition key and switched on the air-conditioning. The rain stopped, and the sky cleared. When he opened the windows, Ricky gulped in fresh air, squeezed his eyes shut, and used his fists to wipe away moisture.

"If you want to know who killed Aimée, Chris Chisholm is your man," Ricky said.

"How can you be so sure?"

"Chris has become a liability. The bros want to put him away in case he talks to the feds."

Marleau poured Ricky cold water from a thermos into a paper cup and opened a box of doughnuts.

Ricky drank so fast he choked. After his paroxysm died down, he stared at the open box of doughnuts.

"Have as many as you want," Marleau said.

Ricky wolfed down two chocolate doughnuts, and the sugar made words tumble out his mouth. "Chris is both mentally and emotionally sick and seems determined to bring down Cole. Who loses if he sinks? Who loses if the feds find out he's involved in the Sinise's schemes?"

"So you think Chris is the key to unlock the gate to the truth," Marleau said.

"He's capable of shooting Aimée or having someone do it for him."

The window let in the heavy, warm fragrance of ripe wheat, the smell of chemical fertilizer, and the odor of a dead animal in the swamp.

Ricky was quiet for a while until he asked Marleau for the time because his watch had stopped.

"Where are your folks?" Marleau asked.

"Don't have none," he said with his mouth half full. "Bein' on my own hasn't been easy, man."

Ricky swallowed and stopped eating to stare up at seagulls circle in the clearing sky above a field. Then he set another doughnut down on his knee and licked the chocolate off his fingers. "My mother never told me who my father was. She was a prostitute, for Christ's sake. A man tried to rape her behind the bar at the Wakefield Hotel, and she stabbed him to death."

"Is she doing time?"

Ricky looked at him in an odd way, a smear of chocolate on his mouth. "She's in the Dakota Women's Correctional in New England and won't be coming out for a while," he said.

Marleau laced his hands behind his head, flexed his neck muscles. He glanced at Ricky. For the first time, he felt an undertow of regret for the harsh way he had treated the boy.

He thought Ricky must feel trapped in a whirlpool, buffeted on all sides without any way out. He considered apologizing to him, then thought the best thing to do was to be quiet. He put the car in gear, turned around, and headed back to town.

Before he left the gravel-surfaced side road, he felt a sudden nausea almost overcome him. He stopped for a moment. Beside him, Ricky had fallen asleep.

Marleau wondered if Carl Ravenstein knew the truth about his son or if he really cared. Greed and guilt obviously had a powerful grip on Cole, eating away at his soul like cankerworms.

Although he didn't have children of his own, the thought of Ricky, sucked down into a maelstrom of evil, went somewhere beyond his emotional reach. He shifted his butt to relieve the pain. He then thought about Ryan and Joanne in a battle with a man determined to reduce a noble monument to rubble.

He wanted to be in the Black Hills to help them prevent the destruction of the presidential heads, but if he went, he knew he would end up being a liability. As soon as he dropped Ricky back at the mall, he'd call Ryan with the update on Ricky's connection to Arrak and the links between Habib and the Sinises. When he drove toward the city, he could feel a dark mood coming on similar to the gray clouds that scudded across the wide horizon.

CHAPTER 35

I N THE BUFFALO DINING ROOM at the foot of Mount Rushmore, Ryan and Joanne pored over topographical maps of the Black Hills. The cafeteria-style restaurant had long rows of tables under a high ceiling. Middle America patrons, straight out of Norman Rockwell's illustrations, packed the tables and filled the room with a steady hum of chatter.

Ryan stared in frustration at the smooth surface of the four presidential heads carved from granite as gnarled and twisted as driftwood.

Was it time to let go, to leave the fate of Mount Rushmore to the feds and simply walk away? Through the open window, the pines were bursting with birdsongs. Why anguish over the assumption of a terrorist attack that was still as hard to pin down as a badlands dust devil?

Ryan's cell phone rang, and he stood up to answer it. Marleau told him about his confrontation with Carl at Maxwell's and his subsequent meeting with Ricky.

"What made Ricky decided to cooperate?" Ryan asked.

"It took a bit of arm twisting." Ryan heard Marleau clear his throat. "We're right about the Sinises in bed with the terrorists?"

"Afghan heroin for American dollars makes everybody happy."

Ryan had arrived at this conclusion so quickly that he didn't want to trust it.

"Does Carl have any idea of how deep Paul has his hooks into Cole?" Ryan asked.

"I doubt it. Carl's cut himself off from the real world."

"I'll break the news to him when I get back."

Ryan stared at the monument bathed in a nearly flesh-colored light from the afternoon sun. He leaned his head back and closed his eyes. "From what you've told me, to solve Aimée's murder, the best place to find her killer is the weak link—Chris Chisholm. His lifestyle is too lavish for a retired Ravenwest employee living on a company pension. He's supplementing his retirement income big time."

"You want me to bring him down?"

"Get the old fraud to spill his guts?"

"Like any corrupt bastard, Chris is a moving shit storm. It shouldn't be difficult."

"I expect you to have this case wrapped up by the time we get back."

"Yeah, as sure as a snow blizzard in July."

Ryan's eyes burned from the sun's reflection on the glass, and he looked away.

"Are you close to finding Habib's hideout?" Marleau asked.

Ryan glanced at Charlene, her cheeks hot and streaked with color. She was trying to get his attention with her eyes. He held up his hand to ask her to wait.

"Nothing concrete so far," he said.

"What's Habib's real beef for wanting to blast a mountain?"

"My guess is he'll use his role as the destroyer of an honored American symbol to rally support of the radicals and wage a propaganda war against America and the West. After the attack, I suspect he'll escape to Afghanistan to rally the troops. Meanwhile, we keep searching for his base of operation. It has to be somewhere close to the monument."

"I don't want to see the results of his handiwork on CNN."

"We're due for a lucky break."

"Bon chance, mon ami."

As soon as Ryan switched off his cell phone, Charlene seized his arm. For an instant she couldn't speak.

"What's the matter?" he asked.

"The guy looking at the presidents through the telescope is the one who broke into our house," she whispered.

Ryan stared at her in amazement.

"Are you sure?" he asked.

She nodded.

Ryan studied the tall, clean-cut man in a blue suit and tie at the telescope. He stood up to get a closer look. He recognized his long angular face topped with a thatch of black hair as that of the driver of the red pickup during the city car chase. When the man glanced up, his high cheekbones and narrow chin looked unreal, as though constructed by a plastic surgeon.

"He's the guy Marleau and I tracked down to the Moorhead house he blew up before leaving."

"We now know for sure Habib and his gang are here," Joanne said.

Gary turned his reversed baseball cap the right way and pulled down the bill, while Charlene pretended to study the map. Ryan reached under his jacket to feel the comfort of the .257 Magnum's handle in its shoulder holster.

"Why is he spending so much time studying the heads if he isn't planning to obliterate them?" Charlene asked.

"His presence proves they're here," Joanne said.

"Let's not forget we're outnumbered, up against professional killers, a determined bunch of fanatics who want to sacrifice their lives to destroy this mountain," Ryan said.

"The question is, do we try to stop them by ourselves?" Joanne said.

"You've been quiet, Gary," Ryan said. "What's your opinion?"

"After all we've found out so far, we'd be crazy if we didn't try to find his base," he said.

"I know the odds may be stacked against us, but there's one thing that really bothers me. We're the only ones who have a chance of stopping him," Charlene said.

"I'm betting on him striking tonight," Ryan said. "The longer they wait the more likely they are to miss a window of opportunity. The weather forecast is for clear skies tonight and then thunderstorms predicted for the next few days."

Gary drained his cola can through a straw, making a gurgling sound. "One thing's for sure," he said, crumpling the can in his fist, "Habib's managed to keep two steps ahead of us. If we don't destroy his ultralights, those four heads will be nothing but rubble tomorrow morning."

Joanne wrapped her arm around her son's shoulder and squeezed, until he squirmed away. "Even if we find evidence and phone the authorities, their immediate reaction will be to treat us as a bunch of crazy cranks. Even if they do decide to follow up and we leave the search in their capable hands, we risk being too late." Her hand shook slightly as she put her cup of herbal tea down on the table. "It's like when families are involved in some disaster, and then on a TV newscast you see plenty of men in suits or uniforms milling around, gathering evidence, talking to reporters. They always arrive after the event has taken place, when it is too late to save those who are dead or prevent the traumatized from suffering. If we let this happen, we will blame ourselves and have to live with the knowledge that we didn't act."

"The only way to make this come out a happy ending is if we go for it," Charlene said.

Ryan took a deep breath and stared hard at his daughter and Gary. "I'm proud of you both for what you've said, but I'd like to clarify the 'we' in this situation. Right from the start, it's been decided you two are going to have to remain behind, while we make any forays into Habib's secret airbase. It will be our job to disable the ultralights."

Out of the corner of his eye, Ryan spotted Arrak pull on a knapsack and head for the parking lot.

"I'll tail him," Ryan said, getting up.

"Don't take any unnecessary risks," Joanne said.

"I'll be careful," he said, leaning over to brush his lips on her cheek. "Adios."

Later that evening, Marleau climbed behind the Yukon's wheel, took his Beretta Cougar .32 semiautomatic out of the glove compartment, and put the handgun in his pocket.

He tried to think his way through the case.

After his meeting with Ricky, he had eliminated him as a suspect in Aimée's murder. Ricky had pointed the finger at Chris Chisholm or her son, Cole, as her possible killer, but Marleau still didn't believe the young punk.

He thought that when most people talked to police, private investigators, crime perpetrators, and victims of crime, they felt they had to lie at some point, either to protect themselves or somebody else or to ensure that someone got punished.

He was convinced the Moorhead house where Ricky delivered drugs and ended up getting stoned with the jihadists was central to Sanjay's murder. He believed that Chris Chisholm and the Sinise brothers had forged the links between drug dealers and terrorists and to some extent with the coroner, Dr. Roberts. How did this arrangement link to Aimée's murder?

Greed characterized all the players apart from Moe's father. Habib had a different agenda. The presence of the jihadist gave the investigation a veneer of international intrigue. Marleau believed Ryan was right about the cell's leader. Habib was out to destroy a beloved icon to build a political base within the Arab world and become the leader in a Pan-Islamic movement whose sole aim was to punish America.

When Marleau phoned Chris Chisholm's house, Chris's wife told him her husband was at a watering hole in the old part of town. Marleau found Chris in a bar called the Fartsie Angel. The band was putting away its instruments, and the place was almost deserted.

Marleau sat down on the stool next to Chris and ordered a club soda. Chris's bloodshot eyes swiveled sideways, a slight crease forming in his forehead.

"Haven't we met someplace before?" Chris asked, rubbing his smooth-shaven chin. His leather bomber jacket smelled of cigarette smoke even though the bar was a smoke-free establishment. "You look like you're a couple of beers short," Chris added.

"It's been a long day."

"Aren't you the guy they booted off the WFPD for excessive boozing?"

"This straight up, for real. I'm a recovering drunk, Chris. So this gives me a certain amount of leeway when I meet up with human garbage like you."

"If you're here to insult me, get the hell away from here."

Marleau leaned closer. "Your wife never inherited a dime, and the cash you've been so busy spending to upgrade your property is drug money. Ever heard of the Afghan connection?"

Chris glanced at the other patrons, sitting around tables. "Are you afraid you're up against something you can't handle? Because you should be. I've got powerful friends."

"I'm going to bring you down one way or another. I've never been a guy that follows the book. I work outside of the law without the niceties of doing procedures by the numbers." Marleau cupped his hands on his footballer knees. "You have a cute granddaughter, Chris. I know a guy who owes me a huge favor. He's actually a nutcake. You know the kind? He likes to hang around school yards and talk to kids at recess."

In seconds, Chris's face went from contentment to rage. "You keep the hell away from her," he said.

"Not unless you start by answering some questions about your dealings with the Sinises."

"I thought someone would catch up with me sooner or later," he said. His voice had lost its certainty, replaced by a guttural echo. "Although, I half expected it would be Moar, your partner. He always struck me as a smart young cop with a career path ahead of him."

"You think so."

"Yeah, I never figured he'd go private."

"Well, this friend of the smart ex-cop figures you're somehow involved in the killing of Aimée Ravenstein."

Chris put a cigarette in his mouth and fiddled with the lighter.

"Can't smoke in here, mister," a deep-voiced bartender said behind him.

Chris glanced at the bartender, a thin man wearing a bow tie and stained white apron.

"This place ain't private enough for me," Chris said. "Let's find a McD's. I'm hungry for a Big Mac and fries."

"That's okay with me."

Chris walked outside, his body bent at the middle, his expression as rigid as a presidential head carved in stone on the side of a mountain.

CHAPTER 36

T HE SUNSET DIED ON THE far side of the mountain range, and
Rashid looked down at the valley below hazy with shadow.
The sky was a dark blue, tinged with the sun's pink afterglow, the
moon as thin as a wafer over the tops of the pines.

The weather forecasters predicted clear skies until midnight
with a chance of thunderstorms later. The revised forecast had
prompted Habib to leave for the cave to prepare for the attack
before the weather turned sour. Rashid was finally alone in Habib's
bedroom.

Rashid tugged on a cord of a small desk lamp, and the bulb
reflected off his new expandable backpack on the bed. He twisted
a dial to open a safe embedded in the cabin's wall and scooped
bundles of US dollars, euros, and British pounds into the backpack.

The feel of the money in his hands left him unsatisfied, like the
moment after a car bomb failed to explode.

Then he whispered in Arabic to the dark corners of the office,
"With money, I can do anything."

He went to the window to look at the onyx sky now speckled
with stars. The piles of cash prompted him to recall growing up

in a Sunni neighborhood of Baghdad. His parents had to feed a growing young family, and they agonized over where the next meal would come from. He turned his thoughts from grim memories of an empty stomach to images of what he would do back home with his pockets full of cash.

A Porsche 911 Carrera and smart clothes could attract women in a way the scars on his face had never made him popular. Would money help women overlook dark eyes that brimmed with madness, fingernails grimed almost black, and oily hair smarmed down with his own body grease? He grinned to display a mouthful of yellow, uneven teeth. If money couldn't get women to forget ugliness, he'd have cash to satisfy his passion for slot machines.

Now with the attack less than three hours away, a new tension filled him.

What use would the money be if the authorities caught him after the attack? He hated the thought of spending decades behind razor-sharp wire at Guantanamo Bay where he'd be subjected to water boarding.

He didn't care about the survival of the others; he despised them all.

How could Habib be so stupid not realize it would be easy for Rashid to figure out the combination of the safe and steal his money? Rashid also couldn't understand why Habib seemed gripped by this intense fanaticism. Why spend so much time and treasure to destroy giant heads carved out of a mountain face?

The bravado of the pilots annoyed him, particularly Gulbuddin, who taunted Rashid in front of the others for not joining them in martyrdom. Earlier this evening, at supper, the pilot had accused him of being a craving mongrel.

For this insult, Rashid vowed to get his revenge. He stashed the money in his backpack. To succeed with his plan to punish Gulbuddin and escape, he needed to create a diversion, stir the pot to a dangerous boiling point.

That afternoon, Rashid had pounded Mohammed for straying in the forest. The black eye Rashid had given him had unnerved

Habib. If Rashid destabilized the situation further, it would make it easier to get away without anyone seeing. The added stress of another disruption would make Habib malleable, less focused.

He decided to lie to Habib that he had overheard Gulbuddin talking on the phone to a federal agent. During the ensuing chaos, while Habib dealt with Gulbuddin's betrayal, Rashid could simply melt into the background.

He wrapped his arms around himself, as if trying to contain his excitement.

It was past ten when Ryan drove the Range Rover down a narrow dirt road to cabins perched on the side of a steep hill off Highway 16, east of Hill City. Joanne, Gary, and Charlene were with him. He felt frustrated that Arrak had managed to shake him off so easily in the multilevel parking lot earlier. The only hope of finding Habib's base of operation, along the highway that looped around the monument, was to continue testing clues from their aerial survey in a time-consuming search of likely locations.

The Range Rover's headlights reflected off half a dozen log cabins belonging to the Golden Spike Resort and Crystal Cave nestled among aspens and pines. Ryan slowed down on the rutted road and scanned the area. There was no traffic, no close resorts or cabins. The Golden Spike was off the beaten track, free from prying eyes. He pulled up in front of plastic slides, swings, and bikes that littered the lawn beside a wading pool.

"This place looks harmless enough," Joanne said, shuffling maps to get at her ballpoint pen and notepad. She had made a list of resorts they had visited so far: Sitting Bull Motel, Presidential Lodge, Horse Thief Guest House, Rushmore View Resort, and Big Thunder Chalets.

"While I take a look around, Gary, go to the front desk and ask if there are any available cabins for rent," Ryan said, climbing out of the car. "Be casual."

Ryan waited until Gary strolled to the office strung with baskets of petunias and Christmas lights. Ryan then skirted to the back of the cabins made of pine logs and river stones. No lights shone behind heavy drawn curtains.

The darkness among the pines mingled with a chilling stillness. Hugging the tree line, Ryan picked his feet up and put them down with care to avoid making any noise by stepping on dried twigs.

He recalled the manager of the nearby resort and campground telling him the Golden Spike had recently changed hands. The new owners kept to themselves. It struck the manager as unusual that in the last few days, he had seen vehicles drive in, but none of them stayed. He suspected the new couple had jacked up the cabin rental rates even at close to the end of the season.

When Ryan crept up a slight incline, he noticed how the resort, tucked in among the trees, appeared shielded from the highway by rocky outcrops. Behind one of the cabins, he spotted a pale light coming through a crack in the curtain of a rear window. His eyes narrowed when the dim yellow light reflected off a speck of chrome buried under pine branches.

As he crept closer, he made out the hulk of a truck. He pushed aside branches and ran his hand over the red polished metal surface of the familiar Ford pickup with a dent on the rear mudguard.

The getaway vehicle, he thought. *I'll disable it.*

Ryan stuck his Swiss army knife into all four tires, and the pickup sank with a sigh.

He hurried back to the Range Rover, crouching crablike as he ran through scrub and trees. When he reached the vehicle, he tapped on Joanne's window, and she rolled it down.

"We've come to the right place," he wheezed, feeling as though the proximity to Habib had robbed him of air.

"Oh my God," she whispered.

Joanne removed a Browning Baby .25 from the glove compartment and slipped the semiautomatic pistol into the pocket of her leather jacket.

"The red pickup they drove in Fargo is parked behind one of the cabins," Ryan said. He could see fear creep across her face.

"Gary's still inside the office," she said. "If they recognize him, they'll know we're onto them."

"Give him a few more minutes," he said, climbing into the driver's seat.

Joanne buried her face inside Ryan's jacket. "I hate waiting," Joanne said with sudden force.

Ryan opened the door and climbed out. "I'll go."

The neon sign threw an eerie red light across the beaten path that led to the office. The door screen squeaked, and Ryan felt a wave of relief when Gary sauntered out, his hands locked in the hip pockets of his jeans.

"What a rip off," Gary said. "They want five hundred bucks a night—" Gary's grin vanished when he noticed Ryan's wrinkled brow.

"Get in the car now," Ryan said.

"This place gives me the creeps," Charlene said.

Ryan switched on the engine and jammed the vehicle into reverse, spinning tires and rattling loose gravel.

"Who did you talk to?" Ryan asked.

"I spoke to a woman I've never seen before behind the counter," Gary said.

"Can you describe her?"

"She had dark, curly hair, big hips, and—"

"Habib's wife, Zahara."

He pulled onto the highway, drove until they were out of sight of the drive, and parked in an empty lot beside a lake. Ryan opened the window and breathed in a draught of cool air, letting the fresh pine smell seep into his lungs.

"Why are we parking here?" Charlene asked.

He turned around and faced Charlene and Gary.

"You two stay inside the vehicle until we get back," he said.

"Dad, are you sure you know what you're doing?" Charlene said.

He glanced at the sky speckled with stars and the lake's surface riffled in the gentle breeze.

"Joanne and I are going to find the ultralights and disable them," he said.

From outside the vehicle, Ryan heard the sound of a small night animal skittering in the dry leaves.

"What happens if you don't come back?" Charlene asked.

"Don't worry. We will," Joanne said, getting out.

"If we run into anything we can't handle, we'll phone the police in Keystone," Ryan said.

"Hey, that's funny," Gary said. "Call the Keystone cops."

"This isn't a laughing matter," Ryan said, handing Gary a handgun. "The Magnum's loaded. You know how to use it. There's extra ammo in the glove compartment."

"While we're gone, don't do anything stupid like following us," Joanne said.

On the way to McDonald's, Chris Chisholm lazed against the passenger seat and watched the traffic go by, his eyes half shut.

"You stay awake, you hear me," Marleau said, nudging him in the ribs with his elbow.

"I ain't murdered nobody," he said.

"You haven't convinced me of that."

Chris stared at the neon signs; his face twitched as the beer wore off. The night's gloom waited for him like a pack of hyenas.

At the all-night restaurant, Marleau found a secluded booth, and they sat down. After he ordered black coffees, Big Macs, and fries, he sat opposite from Chris.

"I've tagged you for Aimée Ravenstein's killer," Marleau said.

Chris rubbed his thick stomach.

"You think I did it?" he asked.

"You're a sick, violent bastard."

"I need to go to the washroom."

"Stay cool. When you get back, I'll ask you a few questions, and if your answers are to my satisfaction, you'll be in a taxi on your way home."

While Chris stumbled toward the washroom, a woman wearing a headscarf turned to Marleau.

"Is your friend all right?" she asked, looking toward the washrooms. "He looks as though he's lost his best friend."

"He's okay. He's going through a messy marital breakup."

"I'm sorry."

"Don't be. He's better off on his own."

A few minutes later, Chris lurched back to his seat and started wolfing down his Big Mac.

"Does the name Habib mean anything to you?" he asked.

"Spell his name for me."

"H-a-b-i-b."

"What's so special about Habib?"

"He's a psychopath who's in bed with you and the bros."

Chris covered his mouth to choke down laughter.

"Are you a comedian or what?"

"Does the description of a thickset, bald-headed Middle Eastern guy mean anything to you?"

"I've never heard of him."

Marleau scratched the back of his neck. "Maybe Habib isn't our man. How about a tall, scrawny kid with a black beard and two prancing ponies tattooed on his left bicep?"

Chris tried to hide the knowledge in his eyes by removing his bifocals and wiping them on a paper napkin. "Is he Aimée's contract killer?" he asked, clipping his glasses back behind cauliflower ears.

"I'm asking the questions. Where did you meet this jihadist?"

"What?"

"Never mind." Marleau leaned forward and grabbed Chris by his collar, pulling him across the table until his shirt sopped up ketchup on the side of his plate, leaving a bloodlike stain. "Where did you meet him?"

"Let me go," he spluttered.

When Marleau released his grip, Chris grabbed a wad of paper napkins and started to wipe ketchup off his shirtfront.

"You don't want to do time in the North Dakota State Penitentiary, do you, Chris?" Marleau said. "Ryan and I have enough evidence against you to put you away for good."

"Why am I getting rousted out by you private guys? Is Ricky locked up? Why isn't Paul sitting in prison? Of course not. They're both on the loose, free as hawks. If it weren't for guys like me, you PIs would be out of a job."

"Cut out the violins; you're breaking my heart."

Chris arched his back as though seeking a challenger.

"Tell me what I need to know, or I'll unleash that psychopath I told you about earlier," Marleau said. "He has photos of Connie."

Chris opened his eyes wide, a smirk breaking at the corners of his mouth. "I have a sister in Canada. I'll send her there."

"He'll find her."

He watched Chris's face shrink and become hard and tight like the skin of an apple.

"The guy who killed her lives in East Riverview, north of Moorhead," he said.

"Do you have a street number?"

"Not off the top of my head, but I can tell you how to get there."

After Chris gave him a detailed description, Marleau helped him into a cab. Before leaving the restaurant, Marleau limped to the washroom to rinse his hands and face. His rear end felt raw and enflamed. He blew into the mirror and fogged the glass with his breath. He could feel his heart pumping adrenaline throughout his body. It felt as if the head of a full-grown male deer had come into focus inside the telescopic sights of his hunting rifle.

CHAPTER 37

S EALED WITH THIN CLOUDS, THE jagged rim of the Black Hills had the sheen of silk that hinted rain. Seated on the patio at the back of his cabin, Habib glared at Rashid, his eyes narrowed in the remoteness of a man who has moved into another dimension. The dim porch light reflected off the sweat on Rashid's torso and tapered down to his camouflaged military dungarees. Rashid sat shirtless with one muscular buttock propped on the edge of a brick barbecue pit, his legs crossed, and his face a molten mask of fury.

"What did you just tell me?" Habib whispered.

"Gulbuddin has betrayed us," Rashid said.

Habib felt his body convulse. "How?" he asked.

"I overheard him on his cell phone talking to some federal agent."

A band of sweat formed on Habib's forehead. He wanted to get his hands on the young man's throat. He pictured himself staring into his eyes while his massive hands cut off blood and oxygen to his brain. He would take his time to strangle Gulbuddin, to watch the gradual life force ebb out of him.

"What did he say?" he asked.

"He told them he had information on an impending terrorist attack. Before he had a chance to reveal to the agent where and when, he heard my footsteps. He then ended the conversation and went back to washing dishes."

Habib's red-rimmed eyes seemed to brim with energy. Had he survived a possible disaster? No matter what went down, he had to concentrate on the attack less than an hour away.

"You caught him in time," he said.

Rashid nodded several times, staring down at the deck's grease-stained boards. "I kept an eye on him in case he tried to use his phone again."

"How could a brother betray us?"

"From the time he joined us, he's always had a bug up his butt." Rashid rubbed the pimples on the back of his neck. "What do you want me to do?"

Habib hated the thought of executing Gulbuddin. He admired the young fanatic for his passion and puritanism. He had recruited him along with the other British lads of East Indian origin from the Finsbury Park Mosque in North London. At the time, they belonged to al-Muhajiroun, a strong fundamentalist group. Using false Canadian passports, he had arranged for them to fly Air Canada from Heathrow to Winnipeg. After completing flying training in Steinbach, they had sneaked across the border at night and then hitched rides to his ranch.

Habib went inside the cabin and closed the drapes to shut off the view of the valley. Rashid pulled on a sweater and followed him. He was standing close enough for Habib to smell a combination of Egyptian tobacco and dried sweat.

Habib squeezed his eyes tight, breathed out so it sounded like a fizz from a cola bottle. "You'll execute him."

"Yes, my master." Rashid's eyes roved over Habib's face, and a tiny laugh rose out of his throat like a bubble. "You'll need another pilot."

Habib began breathing hard as though he were swimming against the tide.

"Arrak?" Rashid ventured.

"I need him to coordinate the jihad."

"He still sulks over the death of the horses."

"He'll get over it."

"What about your son? You told me he's a good pilot."

For an instant, Habib felt as though a gust of wind made him slip on the rope ladder to the cave that stored the ultralights. He imagined he had swung out in a wild arc away from the moss-encrusted granite face and looked down into the rock-strewn abyss.

After the initial shock of realizing the possibility of his wayward son replacing Gulbuddin, he felt in control, stronger, and more determined.

"Think of the headlines, the prestige." Rashid twisted his thick lips in a lopsided grin. "You've always wanted him to be a martyr."

Habib paced the floor; the boards creaked under his weight. He raised his finger for added emphasis. "He will fly in Gulbuddin's place," he said.

Rashid put a cigarette between his lips, lit it with his butane lighter, and exhaled smoke in front of his face as though he wanted to put a screen between himself and Habib.

"Excuse me for bringing this up, Habib, but your wife is still angry for my punishment of Mohammed for trying to escape," he said. "She will fight you like a cat to stop you from sending him to fly into the mountain."

"Leave Zahara to me." Habib forced a high-pitched laugh even though the idea of a confrontation with his wife caused a wave of dread to tug at his heart. "She will do as I say," he added.

Habib zipped up his jacket and tucked a .45 semiautomatic under his belt. "Where is Gulbuddin?" he asked.

"He's playing cards in the main cabin with Ayman and Nadir."

Rashid turned his gaze to the screen door where the crescent moon hovered above the horizon. The branches in the wind made moving shadows on the lawn.

Then Habib added, "Takeoff nears; they'll soon be at prayer."

The night air was cool and smelled of rain, and the thin moon whitened the tips of the pines. In the east, smoke from smoldering forest fires billowed into the night sky.

At the forest edge, Joanne tucked her hair inside her cap. She felt the underbrush tug on the pants of her camouflage suit. When they reached the clearing, she didn't see any movement inside or outside the log cabins. She made a mental sketch of the layout of the resort with its wide expanse of lawn in front.

A light came on in a large A-frame cabin ahead of them, and she trained the night-vision binoculars on the screen door.

A man came out, the tip of his cigarette glowing in the dark. From her recollection of Sanjay's photo of Habib, he looked as though he had the same height and build. His bald head with sprouting hair at the temples and broad features reinforced her recollection of him in the family portrait.

"That's our man," she said, handing Ryan the binoculars.

She watched Habib walk along a path until he went behind a cabin and disappeared down the slope to the valley.

"He's smaller, stouter in real life," Ryan said. "I bet he'll lead us to the hangar where he stores his aircraft."

Joanne followed Ryan as they circled the cabins before going into the forest along a deer track. He told her he didn't know if this was the right way, but the direction they were going felt right.

Joanne froze when she trod on a dead branch, the snap sounding like rifle fire.

"Sorry," she whispered.

"We'll slow the pace a bit," he said.

After a few minutes, he halted beside an outcrop encrusted in dried moss. She crouched down beside him as he stared through binoculars at a cliff face.

He handed her the binoculars. "There appears to be a ledge below the stunted pine."

Joanne focused on the twisted pine with roots that clung to the rock face. She lowered the binoculars when she spotted the ledge hacked out from the side of the cliff.

"What's above?" he said.

She adjusted the binoculars until she pinpointed a different texture in the granite face as though a giant fault had penetrated the rock.

"There's something not quite right," she said. "A part of the cliff looks too smooth, too artificial."

As they approached the cliff, she felt reluctant to leave the cover of the trees. When a faint light shone from above the ledge, they took cover behind a boulder. A thin young man opened a flap and looked out at the valley below him. They waited until he tossed out the dregs of a coffee cup.

When he went back inside, Ryan studied the cliff.

"If we climb to the ledge, we could get a peek at what's on the other side of the ridge," he said.

"I'm ready," she said.

Joanne followed his lead as he hauled himself up with roots and tree trunks. Once they reached the ledge, she heard the faint hum of a generator.

"This is it," he whispered.

As they crawled along the ledge, Joanne could see pinpricks of light from the cabins below. In the distance, George Washington's prominent nose jutted out into space.

Ryan climbed in between needle-shaped rocks and took her hand to haul her up. On the other side, the slope was clear of trees, reminding her of a ski run. At the end of the clearing, the ground disappeared into a deep gorge.

"Why didn't we see some indication of the runway from the air?" he asked.

She pointed at piles of pine branches stacked up on both sides. "They covered it up during the day," she said.

After climbing back on the ledge, Joanne stopped to listen. Above the hum of the generator, she heard a low chatter of men's voices.

At the sound, the skin of her face tightened. When the voices stopped, the silence continued to make her uneasy. Why hadn't her fear subsided?

By instinct, she sensed Gary was in trouble, a sensation she hadn't felt since a year ago when her son had been kidnapped in Seattle and imprisoned on one of the Gulf Islands.

Crouching on the windswept narrow ledge, in the cool light of the slender moon, she promised herself that if he was in danger, she wouldn't allow Habib to hold any claim on his life. No force on earth could cause her to break her vow.

CHAPTER 38

Z AHARA WIPED A DAMP TOWEL across the bruises on her son's face with slow, tender strokes. A white scarf with black trim covered her head. She heard him moan while he slept. The bruises where Rashid punched him had turned an ugly purple. She then washed blood off the scrape on his temple where he had fallen on a tree stump. She was relieved his breathing remained deep and steady.

She straightened up and dabbed at bloodstains on her lavender blouse and gray slacks with a damp towel. His eyes flickered and snapped open.

"I'm glad you're awake," she said.

At first, he appeared disoriented. "Where am I?" He ran his fingertips over his swollen face. "Am I hurt?"

"Don't worry," she said. "I didn't find any bones broken."

He tried to roll over on his side but stopped midway. "Ouch, that's painful," he said.

His mother lifted the blanket to examine bandages around his abdomen. "Lie still," she said. She blinked her eyes, fighting a wave of fatigue.

"Why does Rashid hate me?" he asked.

"He's afraid your father would blame him for not keeping a closer eye on you. Why did you give him the excuse to beat you up by straying from the cabins?"

"It was such a beautiful evening; I loathed being cooped up. I just went for a stroll in the forest to cool off. I had no intention of running away."

"Your father doesn't want anyone to leave the grounds."

Mohammed opened his eyes wide, somehow vulnerable, reminiscent of a frightened child. "Why did Rashid punch me so hard?" he asked.

"He hates anyone who is better educated or is any way superior to him."

"I'm no better than he is."

"Of course you are; you're a Kadir," she said.

She couldn't help but admire the outline of Mohammed's muscular body under his T-shirt. His thick arm muscles glistened with sweat.

"I'm proud of you for fighting back," she added.

"I blame Father for this beating," he said.

"Your father wrestled Rashid to get him off you."

"He took his time."

She leaned over him, the light catching tiny scars on her round face.

"He's on edge now that the attack begins in under an hour," she said.

He sat up on his elbows. "How can you defend him?" he asked.

"I'm on your side; you must believe me." She straightened up in front of him, her hands on her hips, blocking the overhead light. "I would give my life for you."

Joanne felt cramps in her knees from crouching on the ledge. She glanced at her watch. "It's getting close to eleven fifteen. Shouldn't we—"

Ryan was about to reply when two men flung open a flap attached to the rock face. Wearing camouflage jackets, they shouldered AK-47 rifles and climbed like monkeys down a rope ladder.

Below her, Joanne listened to their boots scrape on shale.

"What the hell's going on?" Ryan said.

The valley was quiet except for the wind in the dry aspen leaves. In the distance, she saw white light from lightning in the west.

For a moment, she felt paralyzed again by some unknown, indistinct fear.

"I have a terrible feeling something's happened to the kids," she whispered. "We have to go back."

"With those guards out of the way, we have a chance to disable the aircraft."

She reached in her pocket for her cell phone. "Can I call them?"

"What if someone hears you? We're so close, Joanne, almost within touching distance of the ultralights." With the curiosity of a hunter, Ryan surveyed the spot where the men had exited. "It won't take long to dismantle them."

CHAPTER 39

Z AHARA DOZED IN THE CHAIR beside her son's bed. When she
heard a muffled shot, the noise jerked her awake. At first,
she thought it was some sort of target practice or drill. Then, she
realized it could be something more sinister.

"I have to find out what's going on," she said, getting to her feet.

Zahara felt exhausted; her sleep deprivation over the last few
days was huge. She stood with her eyes half open. All her life, it
seemed, she had lived to endure pain.

Her son reached for his jeans at the end of the bed. "I'm going
with you."

"Wait, before I go, I've something important to tell you."

He lay down, and Zahara pulled the blanket over him. She
returned to the edge of the bed and tried to keep her mind calm.
Even in the event of some emergency, it wasn't too late to put an
escape plan into effect. She didn't have much time.

"After the attack, I don't trust your father to get us out safely,"
she said.

Her son sat up. "After the launch, he's told us we'd escape with him."

"I suspect he has other plans for us."

"What do you mean?" he asked.

"He doesn't want excess baggage."

"He plans to kill us?"

"Possibly." A slight tremor shook her hands. "I've devised our own plan to escape. Just before the attack, we'll leave in the pickup."

"Where will we go? Without his network, we'd be caught."

The breeze from an oscillating fan ruffled her hair. She cleared her throat and widened her eyes, like a woman trying to stretch fatigue out of her face.

"We'll simply vanish, disappear inside the walls, so to speak, for a while until this whole business blows over; change our names, identities," she said in a voice sounding like a guttural echo inside a drainpipe. "We have family on my side in California. They will take us in, no questions asked." She leaned over and pecked the crown of his head with her lips. "We'll survive. You're stronger than you think. I saw that when you fought back after Rashid first punched you in the jaw."

"It was nothing, Mother."

Her face was as blank and stark as a minaret under starlight. "I'm going now alone."

Zahara stepped out into the night and closed the cabin's door. She took a deep breath and headed to the back door of her husband's cabin. On her way, she spotted Habib armed with a .45 automatic. Did he mean to kill them now?

She raced back to the cabin, slammed the door shut, and locked it. She heard Habib knock and then try the door handle. When he found it locked, he bellowed as he kicked the door with such force that the locked hatch came out the jam and a piece of splintered wood fell on the linoleum.

"How dare you lock me out?" he said, stepping beside the shattered door.

"I'm sorry, Habib. I heard shots; I was afraid," she said.

"Gulbuddin is dead," he said.

"How did he die?" Mohammed asked, coming out of the bedroom, zipping up his jeans.

"He attempted to betray us, so Rashid executed him."

Zahara fished in her pocket for a paper tissue and blew her nose. "Gulbuddin is incapable of treachery. He loves you as if you were his father."

"Rashid overheard him talking on the phone to a federal agent. Fortunately, Rashid interrupted the call in time."

"I don't believe Rashid. He's an odious, evil fiend."

"He's absolutely loyal."

"If he ever lays a hand on my son again, I'll shoot him."

Habib reached forward and brushed Zahara's rouged cheek with the back of his hand. She spun away from him as if he had slapped her.

"Listen to me," he said, shaking his fist. "You're my wife. You do as you're told and never again threaten my men."

Zahara took a deep breath and blew it out like air that had escaped from a hot air balloon.

You must control your tongue, she told herself. *Don't get him riled up. He mustn't suspect you of having a plan for you and your son to be free of him.*

"I apologize. I didn't mean what I said about Rashid," she said in a mild voice. "He carried out your orders."

"He had no reason to beat me up," her son said.

Habib stroked the pistol's barrel. "It was for your own good," he said, his voice guttural.

"What have you done with Gulbuddin's body?" she asked, trying to distract him from his verbal assault on her son.

"The pilots and Arrak are digging his grave."

Habib clapped his broad hand on a mosquito on the back of his thick neck and stared at the blood smear on his palm.

Habib walked over to the table where Zahara now stood. He grabbed the front of her blouse and planted the barrel of the handgun on her forehead.

"You're both coming to the cave before the attack on the monument," he said, his voice harsh and guttural.

Zahara's face clouded over; her eyes had the same fear of a deer trapped in a snowdrift before wolves moved in for the kill.

"You promised me we could stay in the cabin," she said. "Why do you want us to watch you destroy some worthless pieces of carved rock?"

Habib released his hold on her blouse. He slapped her across the face. The sound of the flat of his hand striking her cheek resounded off the log walls.

"You do what I say, or you join Gulbuddin in hell."

Zahara rubbed her inflamed cheek and then licked blood on her lips. "Are you going to kill us?"

"No, but Mohammed will take Gulbuddin's place."

"You told me you needed my computer and Internet skills to organize your jihad," his son said.

Zahara swept her hair from the front of her sullen face and held the curls back with her hands for a moment. "Your son is not like the others. He doesn't want to be a martyr."

Habib tried to snag her eyes, but she looked away from him. Depression at the possibility of losing Mohammed sucked her down and pulled her into a dark place.

Habib must have seen the look of horror on her face, as his expression softened. He lowered the gun and put it down on the table.

"God commands him to be a true warrior," he said.

Zahara's gaze turned inward, her fingernails curled around the ring of keys on a nickel-plated handle in her pocket.

"Surely his life is too important to waste on blowing up stone heads," Zahara said.

"It is the will of God. Mohammed must obey me," he said.

She raised her chin to expose her neck. "How much more blood must you spill? How many tears will I have to cry? How many more times will you maim my heart?"

Mohammed turned to his father.

"You promised me after the training that I'd never be one of your suicide pilots," he said. "Besides, I'm not a good flier."

"Good enough to join the others on this mission."

"No, no," Zahara said.

She jerked the keys out of her pocket and swung them like a sock full of metal shavings across his cheek.

Habib reeled back in shock and traced a jagged welt below his eye with his fingertips. He bellowed with rage as he reached out and grabbed both her hands. Forcing her back against the log wall, he squeezed her knucklebones until Zahara screamed. He spat in her face.

Mohammed picked up Habib's revolver from the table and aimed it at his father.

"If you ever hit my mother again, I'll kill you," he said.

"Put the gun down, Mohammed," Habib said.

Mohammed remained silent and gripped the gun with both hands.

Habib released his hold on Zahara. She backed away as if she thought him contaminated by a deadly disease.

Mohammed placed the gun on the table.

Habib knew the time before an attack would be loaded with tension. He had dismissed the two guards in the cave. He wanted them to escape well before the pilots blew up the monument. After he had told the pilots about Gulbuddin's execution, in the stark light inside his cabin, Ayman's and Nadir's faces had looked as though someone had painted them with wet ash.

"Arrak can fly in Gulbuddin's place," Zahara said. "You arranged for him to learn to fly in Canada in case you needed a spare." When her husband remained silent, she added, "Would you rather kill your flesh than a foreigner, who has no blood ties?"

Habib ran fingertips over the welts the keys had made on his cheek. He felt an unexplained twinge in the back of his neck. His eyes traveled over Zahara's face, down to her breasts and stomach, hips and thighs. He knew no matter what happened between them, he would always love her.

"All right, Arrak will fly," he said.

Her face fell apart, and tears streamed down her cheeks.

While Habib waited for them to get ready to accompany him to the cave, he felt suffocated inside the cabin. He made an abrupt turn, went out the door, and let the night surround him and lock him in a cool embrace. His eyes picked up a slight movement inside a deadfall of pines. He caught sight of a deer venture out into the open ground and standing still. His hard breathing disturbed the doe, and she darted back into the trees.

I either kill or betray those I love and trust, he thought.

When his wife and son joined him, they walked like ghosts along the path at a funeral-march pace of slow and measured steps.

CHAPTER 40

GARY CLIMBED OUT OF THE Range Rover and started to pace on the road. He was annoyed that his mother and Ryan had excluded him from the mission to disable the ultralights. Charlene watched him from an open car-door window.

"Get back inside. You're making me nervous," she said.

"It's late, and there's no sign of them," he said.

Gary tossed a stone into the lake. "It's a dumb idea of your dad's to call Keystone."

"Why, Mr. Know-It-All?"

"The cops in a resort town don't know squat. They handle nothing more dangerous than drunken students on a Saturday night toot. By the time they arrive, it'll be game over."

"He meant the feds, meathead."

Gary wandered along the lakeshore and dipped his hands in the cool water.

"Where do you think you're going?" Charlene shouted, thrusting her head outside the car window.

Gary crouched down and skimmed a few flat pebbles on the still lake's surface. "While I'm away, stay inside and keep the doors and windows locked," he said.

"You're going nowhere without me."

"Wanna bet?"

"I'm coming with you, and that's final," she said.

"It'll be dangerous. Jihadists don't fool around."

"I don't care."

He coughed deep within his throat. "Stay put."

A faint police siren wailed in the distance where dark clouds rose above the hills. Then he heard her slam the car door, followed by the sound of her runners slap concrete as she jogged to catch up to him.

"Keep behind me, and be as quiet as you can," he said.

"Yes, *buana*," she said, using the Swahili term for master.

As they approached the resort, Gary saw the cabins were dark except for an A-frame. He crept around to the lighted window and peered through lace curtains into a bedroom. On the unmade bed, he spotted a backpack stuffed full of money. The sight of the hundred-dollar bills intrigued him. The other cabins seemed deserted. It would be easy to sneak in and stuff bundles of bills in his pockets. He climbed some stairs and found the screen door open.

Behind him, Charlene was breathing hard.

"I'm going inside," he whispered.

"Are you crazy?"

He entered a kitchen crammed with old appliances where the smell of fried chicken assaulted his nostrils. A shiny blue fly beat against the window. In the book-lined living room, the glassy eyes of stuffed pronghorns on the walls glared down at him. He broke into a sweat when he saw a burning cigarette in a saucer. The scratched paneling had a scrawled outline of a head and shoulders that looked as if someone had practiced knife throwing at the life-sized figure. In among the bedroom's crumpled sheets and pillows lay the tantalizing pile of cash.

Charlene tapped him on his arm, and he jumped, startled.

"What are you doing?" she whispered.

She saw he had unzipped the backpack on the bed.

"Wow! Unbelievable!" he said.

"Don't touch it."

Gary's heart pumped when he heard a toilet flush.

They raced for the door. On the back steps, Charlene stumbled and fell. Gary caught her. She limped a few steps to test her foot to see if it would take the weight. Behind a tree, he took off her runner and probed for swelling with his fingertips.

"It's sore," she whispered.

Gary ripped his shirttails, tore them into strips, and wrapped them around her ankle.

"Ouch," she said as she tried to squeeze her swollen foot back into her runner.

"Go barefoot. We'll take it slow," he said.

Gary shivered when he heard a dry cough behind him. It was then that he noticed the pain in her eyes replaced by a new and unknown terror.

In the darkness, he heard soft footfalls on dried leaves. His first instinct was to bolt. Despite the need for flight, he could never leave her behind.

When he straightened up, he stared into the barrel of a revolver held by a thickset man with narrow, dark eyes set beneath the hard line of his brow. The knuckles of his fingers wrapped around the trigger looked as big as quarters.

His broad shoulders stretched the back of his sweater. The coarse skin of his face flushed and dilated with his own heat.

The man with the gun rammed the revolver in Gary's ear.

"Move a muscle and your brains come out your nose," he said.

CHAPTER 41

A S SOON AS RYAN STEPPED inside the cave, the smell of aviation fuel assaulted his nostrils. He scanned the cave, his handgun in a two-handed grip. The cave appeared empty. At the entrance, a series of partitioned rooms contained cots. Beside the sleeping quarters, a makeshift kitchen had piles of greasy plates and a portable burner. Almost hidden behind wooden crates and round aviation fuel barrels, Ryan spotted a workshop that he suspected Habib used to assemble the aircraft. At the far end of the cave, the dim light from naked bulbs reflected off three ultralights lined up like giant dragonflies. Above him, the lights reflected off embedded crystals in the roof.

"Why three ultralights for four heads?" Joanne asked.

Ryan pictured in his mind the arrangement of the four presidential heads.

"If they decide on a full frontal attack, they could use two ultralights for the outer heads, Washington and Lincoln, while the third aircraft blew up the inside ones that are closer together, Jefferson and Roosevelt," he said.

He examined the nearest ultralight's two-stroke engine behind an open cockpit. The aircraft had a camouflaged V-shaped wing and a rudder hinged to a vertical stabilizer. In front of the pilot's canvass bucket seat, a control stick and two rudder pedals were connected to wing-mounted spoilerons. Two rear wheels jutted out behind the cockpit with a third wheel in front.

"If we slash fuel lines or cut cables, it'll look too obvious they've been sabotaged and too easy to repair," he said. "We need to damage something harder to detect that's lethal."

"I'll look around," she said.

In the kitchen, she rummaged in a cupboard beside a coffeemaker. She spotted a sugar bag on the same shelf as tools and spare parts. "Someone has a sweet tooth."

That's it! His mind screamed. *That's it!*

"We'll put sugar in the fuel tanks to clog the filters," he said. "They'll take off but won't fly for long before the engines seize up."

"What a sweet idea."

Ryan opened the fuel caps of two ultralights and poured sugar into the white plastic fuel tanks. The fuel cap of the third ultralight in the rear refused to budge.

"This one's stubborn; find a wrench," he said.

He froze when he heard voices, and they dived for cover behind a row of fuel barrels. Ryan crouched beside Joanne and waited. Two men strolled into the cave. They shouted at each other in Arabic. Ryan recognized Habib but not the clean-shaven younger man in a flying suit. The young pilot had a thin body that looked as though it was made of whipcord, his hair thick and black, combed back in ducktails.

When the sound of their voices receded, Ryan noticed the young man unlock and slide open hangar doors that revealed the short runway.

"We have to somehow disable the third ultralight," Ryan whispered.

He had a terrifying vision of watching the first two ultralights take off and crash while the third carried enough firepower to destroy the two central heads and disfigure the outer presidents.

Ryan knew they would never get a second chance to save Mount Rushmore.

CHAPTER 42

A T THE SAME TIME WHEN Ryan and Joanne were agonizing over how to sabotage the third ultralight, Habib ran his hands over the taut canvass of the rear ultralight's wingspan. In fifteen minutes, his eagles would soar and then descend to fly along a narrow, protective valley to the monument.

For most of the morning, his pilots, disguised as hikers, had walked along the valley to become familiar with every outcrop and jagged rock spire.

Beneath the ultralight's port wing, he discovered a filtered cigarette butt. How could one of his pilots be so stupid? His stomach knotted, and his breath came faster. A smoldering butt in spilled fuel could turn the cave into a fiery furnace and transform his precious birds into charred skeletons.

His stomach tightened when his thoughts turned to Gulbuddin's bullet-ridden body. What other disaster could happen to scramble his plans? He was so keyed up he wondered if he could stand any more imaginary or real threats so close to launch time.

No matter what else happens, he thought, *it ends soon.*

While Habib flicked a fuel gauge with his forefinger, Rashid burst into the cave, his breath ragged with exertion.

"I found a couple of kids outside your cabin," he said.

Habib reeled back in sudden surprise as though hit in the face with a fist. His jaw sagged.

Rashid gulped in air as he stared at his boss's jagged facial cuts. "What have you done to your face?"

"It's nothing. I scratched my cheek on a low branch." Habib took a deep breath to control his racing heart. "What have you done with the kids?"

"They're tied and gagged and locked in your cabin."

"Anyone else penetrate the grounds?"

"Everything is secure. They claim to be hikers, who took a wrong trail."

"Do you believe them?"

He grinned. "If you ask me, they're just looking for a place for some serious coupling."

Habib rubbed his hand across his forehead, feeling ridges forming there. He forced himself to sound jocular. "They are an insignificant wrinkle in a flawless plan."

When Habib heard thunder, he strolled over to the open hangar doors. A shimmer of sheet lightning hovered over the western horizon. The storm brewing seemed far away.

"Once the birds are in the air, we'll tidy up loose ends and then follow our escape plan," he said. "Meanwhile, bring the kids to the sleeping quarters for questioning."

After he left, Habib stood motionless as he watched Arrak kneel on a prayer mat. He could feel his heart hammering in his chest. He was sorry to have to sacrifice such a warrior, a young man who had grown to be more like a son to him.

He glanced at his watch and signaled to Ayman and Nadir. The pilots followed a preflight checklist. They wiggled the control stick, maneuvered rudder pedals, and examined fuel lines to the engine.

Habib poured himself a cup of black coffee with plenty of sugar. He noted that the sugar bag was half empty but thought nothing of it.

Feeling restless, he strolled out on the ledge to have one last look at George Washington's profile. He had selected this base close to the memorial with considerable care. He had bought the resort from a retired couple from Fargo. He had transported ultralight parts from his Fargo warehouse to the Black Hills embedded in the walls and ceilings of horse trailers for assembly inside the cave.

Habib let his mind ease back over the events of the day. After morning prayers, he had grilled the pilots by making them go over several times the topographical features of the flight path to the monument. For maximum impact, the pilots had to fly in formation to attack the heads at the same instant. In the early afternoon, Zahara had cooked them a last supper, a traditional meal of hummus, kebab, pita bread, yogurt, and sweet tea.

He stirred his cup of sugary black coffee with his finger. The day had seemed segmented as though weeks had passed instead of hours. He knew he would win in the end despite Gulbuddin's betrayal, the quarrel with Zahara, and Rashid's discovery of two teenagers in his cabin.

While looking out onto the valley, he couldn't help gloat at the thought that the four presidential heads would soon be turned into scorched, scarred holes in the side of Mount Rushmore.

CHAPTER 43

RYAN SAT ON HIS HAUNCHES and stared through a gap in the fuel barrels at the aircraft ready for takeoff. His face was twisted with irritation at his inability to sabotage the last ultralight in the lineup. Joanne leaned against the cave wall and stared at what she could see of the sleeping quarters.

"Who do you think the two prisoners are?" Joanne whispered to Ryan.

"I've no idea but Habib went inside and closed the door. He is probably questioning them to find out if they pose any threat prior to the attack."

It was quiet in the cave except for the hushed sound of wind and the steady beat of the generator. As she watched the pilots wheel the ultralights to the double steel doors, she wrapped her arms around herself as if trying to contain her anxiety. The pilots took care to prevent the wingtips from grazing the cave's walls.

The night air was cool and smelled of pine needles, dried leaves blowing in the wind, and the sulfurous odor of lightning that licked across the dark sky.

She shifted her attention in the direction of the sleeping quarters partly blocked from view by packing crates. A wave of nausea rose into her mouth. Was it possible that the two prisoners could be Gary and Charlene? She didn't want to even consider this a possibility. What if they had strayed to the resort and wandered into a trap?

Habib closed the door and stared down at the boy hog-tied on the cot. He had a hostile, sullen look that marred his handsome face. Habib tore the duct tape from his mouth, peeling off pieces of skin.

"We don't mean you any harm, sir," the boy said. "We're on vacation, and my girlfriend sprained her ankle, so we just went inside the cabin to rest up."

"Are there just two of you?"

"Yes, sir. Please let us go. We're really sorry. We took the wrong turn in the trail and lost our way."

Habib didn't believe him, and he had no time to waste. He would start with the girl. She looked softer and more easily frightened than the boy, who had a cocky manner despite his efforts to be subservient.

He hit her across her mouth with the back of his hand, but the tape muffled her scream.

"I think you're lying. Where are the others?" he asked, tugging the tape off her lips.

"There's no one else," she said, her tongue probing for blood on her mouth. "We're two friends on a hiking trip."

"That's right, sir, honest." Gary glanced at Charlene. "Please don't hit her again."

Habib gave Gary a savage punch in the stomach. He squirmed and tucked himself into a tight ball.

"You are here to spy on us," he said.

"No way! We're telling you the truth," the boy said.

"How did you get here?" he asked.

"We hitchhiked from Rapid City," he said.

Habib's expression hardened.

"The name of the man who tied you up and dragged you here is Rashid Lihham," he said. "Do you know what his last name means in English?" Although bloodied from Rashid's beating, the boy still had a look of defiance on his bruised face. "The literal translation in English is 'butcher.' He is well acquainted with the torturer's finer arts. All I need to do is call him in here, and he'll beg me to allow him to practice his grisly trade. He knows where the most sensitive parts of a woman's body are and where a man is most vulnerable." Doubt and fear crossed the boy's face. "You have a few seconds to think about it before I unleash Rashid's special brand of terror."

Habib glanced down at his watch. It was time to launch his birds. He looked around for Rashid, but he had slipped away.

Habib went outside to the ledge to see if Rashid had gone for a leak, but he was nowhere in sight. Despite his annoyance at Rashid's disappearance, he tried to force himself to relax.

He frowned at the dark clouds. Suddenly, they parted, and the moon appeared. The cold light on the jagged peaks reminded him of winter moons in Damascus.

On his way to signal the pilots to take off, he opened the door to take a last look at the two young people, cowering on the cots. They would die soon. His gaze drifted to streaks of lightning on the horizon from the approaching storm.

"Time to free my eagles," he whispered through his teeth to the wind.

CHAPTER 44

JOANNE TRIED TO CALM HER thoughts of the possibility that the two prisoners dragged into sleeping quarters by the heavy built newcomer were Gary and Charlene. She breathed slowly, the way she taught her students to do prior to going on stage to perform.

Her thoughts shifted back to disabling the third aircraft.

"Why don't we try to cripple that plane while we have the advantage of the element of surprise?" she said.

"Let's think this through," he said, his eyes flickering around the cave. "How many people are there in here? At this moment, there are the three pilots, Habib, Moe, Zahara, and the recent arrival of that big guy who dragged in the prisoners. The only weapons we have are our sidearms, while they have AK-47s and semiautomatic weapons. I don't care for those odds."

Through the steel doors, she saw storm clouds blot the sky. She could smell the loamy odor of the cave, taste the acrid fuel smell on her tongue, and hear the throb of the generator drown out the beat of her heart.

Her voice sank to scarcely a whisper. "What if the two prisoners are our kids?"

Ryan reached out to touch her hand. He managed a thin smile almost lost in the dim light of the naked bulb.

Gary tried to calm his mind and consider their options. Habib had tightened the ropes around his wrists and ankles so hard he could feel the cords dig into his flesh. The tape hadn't been stuck back over his mouth, so he could talk to Charlene on the cot beside him. A trickle of blood running from a gash on her lips had stained her blouse.

When she opened her eyes, he gave her a reassuring smile.

"The folks aren't tied up here with us, so we can assume they haven't been captured," he whispered.

"I hope they can save us in time," she said.

"You think they'll kill us?"

"Undoubtedly."

"What do you think of me now that we're about to die?" he asked, grinning.

"You're the best," she whispered.

"Really? No kidding. I thought you placed me somewhere in between Frankenstein and Darth Vader."

"By any measurement, you're a ten."

He shook himself as much as the ropes would allow. "If we get out of this jam, will you still have this high opinion of me?" he asked.

She gazed at his broad shoulders and sculptured arms. "You're kind of good looking, in a goofy sort of way, and you have enough courage to take on all of al-Qaeda."

"Wow! It's worth getting tied up for a compliment like that from you."

She glanced up at crystals in the ceiling shimmering above her like constellations of stars.

"You didn't run off when you had the chance to escape," she said. "You stayed to protect me."

Habib felt a surge of confidence as he supervised the pilots strap on thick white belts of explosive. When Ayman complained that the belt made him look pregnant, Nadir forced a laugh. His face a blank, Arrak examined the two triggers dangling from his belt.

Habib couldn't predict what Arrak would do. Did Arrak still hate him for forcing him to shoot his beloved Arabians? Habib felt a twinge of remorse for sacrificing the young man, who was a born leader, a keen fighter.

After the attack, Habib had made sure his story would be spread via the Internet, television, and the myriad of Arab newspapers. His name would be famous throughout the world.

He glanced at his watch. It would end in minutes.

With mounting excitement, he ordered Nadir and Ayman to wheel the ultralights to the apron, the cleared staging area from which they would take to the air.

Before the flyers climbed into their cockpits, Habib kissed each pilot on both cheeks.

"Your names, my brothers, will live forever," he said.

CHAPTER 45

WHILE THEY WATCHED HABIB AND pilots preoccupied with takeoff preparations, Joanne and Ryan emerged from behind the barrels. In the dim light, they arose like phantoms with handguns drawn. When he heard Moe's and Zahara's voices nearby, Ryan poised as a panther frozen in midstride.

As they slunk back for cover, Ryan placed a restraining hand on Joanne's shoulder. "Out in the open and not knowing precisely where they are, we'd be dead. Zahara is sure to have a weapon, and we'll have to assume Moe is armed. That big guy could be lurking around somewhere." In the weak light, Ryan's tanned face seemed almost translucent. "We'll wait until they're distracted by the first two pilots taking off."

"We'll know soon how good we are as saboteurs," she said.

When she moved closer to Ryan, she tried to think of something to say to him that wouldn't reflect possible failure.

"If we succeed, you could be a hero," she said.

He twisted his body so that he could see more of her face. "That'll cramp my style," he said.

"They'll name schools after you." She could feel his body heat as she burrowed into his jacket. "Your picture will be on the cover of *Time*." She curled further against his side and put her fingers in his hair. "If we survive, what are you going to do?"

"Not breathe a word to anyone about this caper."

"What else?"

"Apart from finding Aimée's killer, I'm looking forward to fishing trips with Gary in the fall."

"What if Habib survives? He'll want to kill us."

"I hope to take him out of the equation, but if I don't, we'll tighten our seat belts; we're in for a bumpy ride."

Ryan pressed his forefinger to his lips. There was a long silence broken by Zahara saying something in Arabic to Moe.

Joanne froze when Zahara came closer to their hiding place to pour coffee in a paper cup. Zahara's eyes looked turquoise from the light, her skin the color of dust-speckled putty. She tilted the cup, took a long drink, let the coffee revolve on her tongue, and then crinkled her eyes as though the coffee tasted bitter. She rummaged in a cupboard until she found the sugar bag. She poured some grains into her cup and swigged more coffee. Her face stiffened. Joanne held her breath. Had Zahara somehow become aware of their presence? Instead of coming toward them, Sahara turned around with a snort and disappeared in the direction of the sleeping quarters.

Through the open steel doors, Joanne could see the first ultralight face the runway in position for takeoff.

"When they're airborne, I'll shoot the third pilot and then eliminate Habib," Ryan said.

"What do you want me to do?"

"Cover my back by taking care of Zahara and Moe."

Her hand shook as she reached over and took his tapered fingers. She pulled herself close to him so she could hear his heartbeat and taste his breath.

"You're a mighty cool customer, sweetheart; it's not every day I see you take human lives," he said.

She remained silent.

Ryan shifted his weight so he could get a better view of the launch area. "What the devil is holding them up? I would've thought the lead pilot would've started his engine and be airborne by now."

Nestled in his arms, she could feel a blast of cold wind work its way into the cave. It was then she decided to tell him that apart from their own survival, she was worried about someone else's safety.

"The reason I have no qualms about protecting your butt is that someone very close and precious to me—apart from you—is at risk," she said.

Ryan shook his head and smiled. "What are you talking about, sweetheart?"

She let the silence fill between them. Should she have mapped out what she had said more clearly? She let her eyes scan over the packing cases, workbenches, and barrels. Why had she decided to hint about her news to him now?

His face remained puzzled and confused, until his eyes glanced down at her belly. "Don't tell me you're pregnant?" he said, a flood of confusion and surprise crossing his face.

She let that question hang in the air for a moment and then grinned. "Are you pleased?"

The look of shock on his face drifted to one of pleasure. "Of course I am, but why didn't you tell me sooner?"

"I only found out three weeks ago."

"If I'd known, I'd never let you come along on his escapade. You picked one hell of a time to make your announcement," he said.

CHAPTER 46

A T THE SAME TIME THAT Ryan and Joanne waited for the ultralights to take off, Marleau drove through North Moorhead. He glanced at moonlight reflecting off the rows of houses on spacious, well-treed lots. Elm branches stood out in stark contrast to the sky speckled with stars. The night had turned the road into a primeval place that reminded him of when he went trick-or-treating as a boy in his east Fargo neighborhood and imagined seeing ghosts and goblins in every shadow.

He followed Ricky's instructions and turned right at an old wooden Norwegian church. He braked when he came to a small clump of elm trees that ringed a two-story brick farmhouse. He parked on a side road outside the grounds.

He could feel tension well up inside him as his boots crunching on gravel joined other night sounds: frogs croaked love songs in ditches, owls hooted in nearby trees, and small animals scrabbled in the bushes.

When he stopped in front of padlocked wrought-iron gates, he wondered if the puzzle pieces were about to fall into place.

If he could find evidence to convince counterterrorist authorities there was indeed a plot to blow up Mount Rushmore, he had a chance to help save the monument. He suspected the house would only hold threads that would end up being illusive, fragmented dead ends.

He scrambled through a gap in a hedge and walked across a wide expanse of lawn wet from dew. He took out his snub-nosed .38 semiautomatic and checked the chamber to make sure it was loaded. In the distance, he heard dogs bark.

Without warning, his ankle twisted on a rolling object, and he staggered to keep his balance. The contortion sent shooting pains to his butt wound.

The barking grew shriller and more feverish. Lights came on behind the house to illuminate a wire-mesh pen. Inside the run, Dobermans snarled and clawed at the wire.

The back door swung open, and a man bellowed at the dogs, "Cut it out!"

When the Dobermans quieted down, the door slammed. In the floodlights, Marleau checked to make sure he had switched off the safety on his sidearm. He crept around the house and tried the back door handle. It opened, so he tiptoed into the kitchen.

"Come on in, Ricky," Cole said, his voice coming from a room to his left.

Holding the revolver in a two-handed, outstretched grip, Marleau followed a crack of light from a half-opened door. He kicked it wide open.

He recognized the back of Cole's head. He was sitting in front of a plasma TV, his eyes glued to CNN. Cole swung around, and when he saw Marleau, he half screamed in surprise and shock.

"What the hell are you doing here?" he asked.

Marleau pointed the pistol at the middle of his wide pale-blue tie and cocked the hammer back.

"That's the question I want to ask you," Marleau said.

Cole narrowed his gaze, sweat beads popping up on his tanned forehead. Marleau could see him struggle to organize his thoughts.

The room was silent except for the tick of an antique clock on top of a bookcase and the uneven banter of a CNN political panel, coming from the television.

"Put that stupid thing down, Marleau," he said. "You didn't come here to shoot me, did you?"

"Place your hands on the armrests where I can see them," he said.

Cole gripped the armrests, his wrists corded with veins. Marleau positioned the pistol's barrel on the back of his head where his ash-blond hair was cut short, shaved at the neck.

"You've got a lot of gall threatening me." Cole pivoted in his chair to face Marleau. "My father hired you and Ryan to find my mother's killer."

"Turn around," Marleau said. Cole swung back to face an open window and stared out at streaks of yellow floodlights that lit a bleak, weed-choked garden. "The advantage of having a gun is that I ask the questions. Why are you here? Doesn't this house belong to Paul Sinise?"

"He's my landlord."

"Isn't the mansion big enough for you?"

"At times, I prefer a more solitary life. Being away from my family helps me keep my sanity."

"You mean living at home cramps your style, particularly when you make arrangements for multimillion-dollar drug deals with terrorists."

Marleau glanced over his shoulder at CNN's Anderson Cooper doing a newscast from Kabul, the shell of a pockmarked parliament building in the background. "The news you're hoping for wouldn't happen to originate from Mount Rushmore?"

Cole cleared his throat and glanced sideways at the door as though he needed someone to come in and rescue him.

His face seemed to shrivel when he heard the weakness in his own words. "I need a smoke." He picked up a joint from an ashtray, put the stogie between his lips, and fired the stub with a silver lighter the shape of a pot-bellied stove.

He sucked in breath, and his cheeks hollowed. He blew out a stream of sweet-smelling smoke, and a thin layer of sweat coated his forehead like icing on a glazed doughnut. He huffed in air and smoke along the paper until the red glow almost singed his mouth.

"Been to any AA meetings lately?" Cole asked.

"I'm the one asking the questions," Marleau said, stepping closer until he could smell Cole's raw fear. He shoved the gun barrel in his ear.

Marleau was used to seeing Cole in natty business suits, self-assured and confident. Now Cole looked pathetic hunched over in the chair in a sweat-stained T-shirt.

"Apart from Ricky, who keeps you pumped up?" He slapped him across the cheek. "Give me their names."

Cole wiped his lips and closed his eyes for a moment as if trying to block out Marleau's question. The smeared blood on his mouth gave him a grotesque painted-on smile like the Joker in the Batman comics.

"Word on the street is you owe the brothers big time," Marleau said.

"I've paid it back."

"Maybe you have and maybe you haven't. All I know is Paul wants a piece of the action at Ravenwest. To keep Paul off your back, you're involved in a Middle East drug operation that provides an unlimited supply of Afghan heroin you sell at a huge profit in the Midwest. These transactions give you cash to bail you out of this financial jam. So far, this deal with the devil hasn't proved as lucrative as you'd hoped. Have you told your father that his company is threatened to be taken over by slimeballs?"

Marleau could see something in Cole's eyes that wasn't exactly fear but more like bewilderment, as though Marleau had revealed something astonishing.

"This jihadist you're in bed with happens to have a bizarre obsession. He get his kicks out of blowing up monuments."

Cole's face went blank and stark as a still winter lake in the moonlight.

"Your sister's been shagging the son of this Osama wannabe," Marleau said. "How am I doing so far, Cole?"

"Everything you've said is pure supposition and conjecture," he said, rubbing his eyes.

Marleau slapped him again. "Apart from you and the Sinises, who else is behind this elaborate import-export scheme?"

Cole ran his fingers through his greasy, long hair trying to regain control of his agitation. He remained silent for a moment before mumbling, "Is that all you can come up with? It's pathetic."

"I've only scratched the surface. You think your mother's death was nothing more than a nasty domestic dispute that got out of hand?"

Cole shrugged. "Is that what you call it?"

"At the police training college, instructors taught us killers are remorseless, murderous psychos created by their environment. On the other hand, there are those who are born possessing killer instincts. They have some minute deformation in the gene pool."

Cole widened his eyes as though trying to stretch sleep out of them.

Marleau cleared his throat and continued, "I think the latter describes you best. You killed your mother not only because she refused to give you more money to pay off debts to the Sinises, but she symbolized in some weird way everything that you think is wrong in your world."

"Since when did you think of yourself as my shrink?" Cole said, "I had absolutely nothing to do with my mother's death."

Marleau leveled the pistol at an oil painting of an eagle soaring above snowcapped mountains. He fired, and the bullet shattered the glass and showered Cole's head with tiny shards.

Cole rocked in his chair as he brushed glass off the shoulders of his jacket and out of his hair.

A dark smile split Marleau's face, and his eyes turned to ice. "It's time for answers, Cole." He lowered the gun and took aim at Cole's cowboy boots. "If you're don't talk, I swear I'll blast off your big toe off and then keep shooting higher."

"Stay cool, man," Cole said, tucking his feet under the chair. He looked pale. He closed his eyes for a moment and leaned back in his chair.

Marleau aimed the pistol at his kneecap. "Last chance or I blast both knees to pulp," he said, listening to Cole's sharp intake of breath.

"Okay," he whispered.

"When did Paul start applying the screws to you for the money you owed him?"

"It was after my father resigned, about the time I took over."

"How much do you owe the brothers?"

He shifted his weight, and his two-tone cowboy boots scraped on the polished hardwood floor. "I don't know exactly, but it is close to nine million. I got myself hooked on online poker. Paul threatened to wipe me out if I didn't pay him back or give him a piece of the company. I couldn't go to my father. Mother was my last hope."

"Hadn't she paid your gambling debts before?"

"Yeah, but this time she said no."

"Did you inherit money after her death?"

"Sure, a few hundred thousand, sufficient to tide me over, but not nearly enough to keep the brothers from breathing down my neck."

Marleau raised his weapon and aimed in between Cole's eyes. "I'm curious to know if Habib told you anything about his plans to attack Mount Rushmore."

Cole bunched up some tissue from a box on the desk and blew his nose, then wiped his nostrils and upper lip before throwing the wad on the floor.

"Do you have any idea where he plans to launch this attack from his base in the Black Hills?" Marleau asked.

"He never told me about any attack, only that he planned to shut down his Sacramento Park horse ranch for good."

"When I came in, I figured you were anticipating some sort of news announcement on CNN." Marleau dug the barrel into the sensitive spot between Cole's head and shoulders. "Chris Chisholm told me you had all the answers."

Cole hesitated until Marleau raised a hand as if to slap him again.

"I can give you the names of the players if you let me take a folder out of my safe," Cole said.

"Including the jihadists?"

Cole stared with a narrow, angry gaze, as though he was trying to gain control of the situation. He then cleared his throat, wheezed, and fished around in his pocket.

"Get your hands up where I can see them," Marleau said.

Cole pulled his hand out, revealing an atomizer. He opened his mouth wide as if to spray the back of his throat but then slowly slid the atomizer back in his pocket after seeing Marleau's cold gaze.

"Does this file give me enough names, phone numbers, addresses, and background data to convince the feds that the attack is real?" Marleau asked.

"Yeah."

"Get up slowly and unlock the safe. Try anything stupid and you'll end up in a wheelchair."

Cole used his feet to roll the chair's wheels until he reached the safe embedded in the wall. "It's the real deal, honest."

"Let me determine whether it's worth anything," Marleau said.

Cole revolved the combination lock until the safe swung open. He reached inside and rummaged in among neat piles of cash before he removed a red leather briefcase, which he placed on the desk.

Marleau told him to open it. Cole said he kept the briefcase locked. He dug inside his pocket. Instead of keys, he whipped out the atomizer. He pointed the atomizer at Marleau and sprayed mace in his face.

CHAPTER 47

H ABIB REACHED DEEP INTO THE dark reservoir of his soul in an attempt to ignore gusts of wind, rain, and the rumble of an impending storm. The pilots had complained that the wind speed was too severe to fly. Habib knew, despite the foul weather, that he couldn't delay the destruction of the monument any longer.

During training sessions, he had instructed his pilots to visualize taking off on an uneven runway, climbing to about two hundred feet, and making a sharp left turn to descend into a narrow canyon. He had asked them to store in their mind's eye every jagged peak, needle rock, outcrop, deadfall, and pine copse until they approached the massive carved heads that he had purposely selected for destruction, a monument embedded in the American psyche.

He faced the storm and realized the moment had arrived when success or defeat depended on whether he could instill in his *shahids* enough courage to fly the aircraft into the unexpected, cursed rain and wind.

Cole Ravenstein spat a grain of marijuana off the tip of his tongue and laughed as Marleau reeled in pain from the full force of the pepper spray at close range in his eyes. Cole snatched Marleau's revolver from him after his hands flew to protect his stinging eyes.

"I've met some miserable miscreants in my life but never anyone who relished killing his mother. You must've really hated her," Marleau said, his blinded eyes stinging.

"She may have been a mean bitch, but I didn't shoot her," Cole said, pointing the gun at Marleau's chest.

"You kept company with killers, but you never struck me as being one. What did she do that nudged you over the edge?"

The room lit by the light of the desk lamp and the glow from the television was quiet for a moment.

"Did she treat you cruelly when you were young?" Marleau continued.

Cole's tone betrayed a sense of personal hurt. "Before she and my dad reconciled, we lived in California for a while, and some of her psycho boyfriends abused me."

"So you have deep scars?"

Cole's body appeared to shrink. His mouth gaped open, but he didn't reply.

"Did you blame her for the shoddy way these men treated you?" Marleau asked, trying to make out the blurry impression of the young man in front of him. His eyes watered as though he had drunk three fingers on a glass of whiskey. "On the night she died, did you use the gun to scare her into giving you money?"

Cole's lips stretched back in an effort to smile.

"After you shot her, did you phone Paul?" Marleau asked. "Did he send his cleanup crew to sweep away any evidence, so you walked away, without fear of prosecution?"

Cole glanced at his watch and stared for a moment at the flickering TV screen. A new story about an undiscovered frog species was unfolding.

"Put the gun down, Cole; it's over. When I first came in, didn't you expect to see a shocking news story that would electrify the world?" Marleau's eyes cleared enough to glance at the TV. "Why are CNN news cameras focusing on a tiny pregnant frog instead of on Mount Rushmore?"

"The show is about to begin."

"All I can hear is the excited voices of anthropologists in a Madagascar rain forest going gaga over a tiny frog the size of a dime. I think you rather anticipated cries of anguish and rage from a nation mourning the destruction of a beloved monument."

Cole's annoyance spread across his face like an attack of poison ivy.

"The longer we wait, the greater the odds that Ryan and Joanne have prevented this attack," Marleau continued.

"I'll make you a deal," Cole said. "Before you phone the cops, give me a head start, and I'll hand over this briefcase full of information on drug shipments and transactions. It'll make the feds salivate."

"It's a deal."

Cole pushed the briefcase across the desk. He then scooped piles of dollars and euros from the safe and stashed the cash in a backpack.

Marleau wiped tears out of his eyes as he tried to open the briefcase. "It's locked."

Cole tossed him a set of keys.

"Which one?"

"You figure it out."

"Where are you going?"

"To a safe, warm, tropical place where you'll never find me." He paused at the office door. "By the way, I did shoot my mother. I did enjoy filling that bitch's body full of lead."

Marleau heard the back door slam and the dogs bark. He raced to an adjoining bathroom and washed his stinging eyes out with cold water. Back in the office, he tried different keys in the lock. The third key turned in the lock with a click, and he wrenched open the case. Inside he found a single red three-ring binder marked "Confidential." He opened the binder and his watery eyes began to scan the document.

"You lying bastard!" he shouted in anger.

The pages contained financial data of Ravenwest's next quarterly report. He slammed the binder shut.

He phoned the Moorhead Police Department and told them who Aimée Ravenstein's killer was. He walked with a stumbling gait to the door, and he lumbered across the lawn. At the back of the house, he watched the rear lights of a pickup disappear down the drive.

He tried to reach Ryan on his cell, but he didn't answer.

"Wherever you are, old buddy, I hope you're alive," he said aloud.

CHAPTER 48

WHEN THE WIND DIED DOWN, lead pilot Ayman started his engine. He had a dark complexion with shoulder-length hair tucked into his crash helmet. He paused for a moment, his green eyes staring ahead at the narrow strip that disappeared at the end into the canyon's steep drop.

By an act of God, Habib thought, *the winds have calmed*.

Watching the *shahid* steel himself for flight, Habib thought the handsome young fighter would make a good model on an al-Qaeda recruitment poster.

Ayman taxied into a crosswind and aligned his aircraft in the center of the strip. He swung around to give Habib a V sign, before he brought the engine up to full power. When the ultralight started to roll, Ayman applied slight pressure on the rudders to keep the aircraft straight. As soon as he reached flying speed, he pulled back, and the aircraft lifted into the air.

Habib watched the night swallow the ultralight as the sound of Ayman's engine grew fainter.

"Get ready," he shouted to Nadir, who would fly into the rock face between Thomas Jefferson and Teddy Roosevelt. As

Nadir taxied to the runway, Habib signaled Arrak to start his engine.

While waiting, Habib pictured himself—after the destruction of the monument—in the hills of Kunar province on the border between Afghanistan and Pakistan surrounded by tribesmen, who proclaimed him the new supreme leader.

Images of this vision diminished when Habib turned his attention to Ayman, who had reached his climbing speed and was making a shallow bank, while Nadir bounced down the runway close to flying speed.

He had expected to hear Arrak's engine by this point. In the dim light, he heard only silence. Why hadn't Arrak taxied into position? Instead, the pilot had switched off his engine and climbed out of his cockpit.

Habib tumbled from triumphant daydreaming into a sudden, horrifying reality. Something was terribly wrong with Arrak. The pilot had his hands in his pockets, and he stared at the angry sky.

"Have you gone mad?" Habib asked as the wind started to pick up and tug at his jacket. "There's no time to waste. Start your engine and get airborne."

Arrak appeared not to hear him, his mind elsewhere. Habib lashed out with the flat of his hand several times across the stubble of Arrak's cheeks.

"Take off now and join the other *shahids*," he said.

Habib felt heat boil deep in his core, and he aimed his handgun at the pilot's helmeted head.

"If you don't take off, I'll shoot you like a mongrel dog," he said.

Arrak raised his gloved hand skyward and waited for his life to end.

"Look up at the sky, my master," he whispered, when Habib didn't shoot.

Habib glanced up in the direction of Arrak's hand to the airborne ultralights. Ayman's aircraft seemed to slow down, falter like a wounded bird. His ultralight stalled, nosedived, and went into a spin. The wing of Nadir's aircraft dropped, and the nose pitched down.

Habib heard the roar of the ultralights crash into the forest in a flash of flames. He could hardly breathe. For a moment, he felt as though all the dizzying thoughts and plans had flown away from him to be replaced by a pool of darkness.

As Habib's mind raced in turmoil, he shrieked commands to himself. *Act! Get revenge! Escape!*

The blazing pines where the ultralights crashed lit up the night sky.

"Come with me," he said, gripping Arrak's arm.

He staggered back into the cave where his wife and son waited for him.

"Where is Rashid?" he said.

"He left," Zahara said.

His son rubbed stubble on his cheeks as he watched rain dampen the fires set by the disabled aircraft. "What's happened, Father?" he asked.

Habib's eyes wrinkled in the corners as if he tried to squeeze meaning out of his son's question. Habib's lips and the skin around his mouth moved without words.

Arrak went inside the sleeping quarters, and when he returned, his eyes widened and his voice turned high-pitched. "I know the two prisoners," he said.

Habib tried to swallow, but his mouth had gone dry. The thunderstorm broke, and rain almost obliterated the view of the runway.

"Who are they?" Habib asked, turning to his son.

"The girl is the private investigator Ryan Moar's daughter, and the boy is the son of his whore Joanne Sutter," he said.

"Moar must have sabotaged the aircraft," Zahara said. "If you kill the children, you'll have your revenge."

"Lock the hangar doors, Arrak," Habib whispered.

"Yes, my master," he said.

"After you lock the doors, Arrak, use your bedouin knife to silence them both."

CHAPTER 49

CROUCHING BEHIND THE BARRELS, JOANNE could hear her own breath, loud and raspy. After the two explosions and flashes of light, she did a couple of silent high fives with Ryan.

She had waited for the sound of the third aircraft's engine, but the ultralight remained on the ground. Did the sight of the two ultralights crashing and exploding discourage the third pilot from taking off?

"Is it time to make a break for it; shoot our way to the door?" she said.

"We can't," he whispered, lowering his binoculars he had pointed at the sleeping quarters' open door. Ryan removed the Magnum from his holster. "The prisoners are our children and I expect they mean to kill them."

She straightened up and the light from the overhead bulb wove its way into her hair. All the goodness and beauty seemed to drain from her face. Then her body began to stiffen, the muscles of her back hardening. Her eyes closed for a moment, her face growing tight and tense as though she was balancing on the tip of a precipice. The pain and rage caused by Habib dissolved and broke into a single purpose to kill him.

Using a two-handed grip on her handgun, she followed Ryan away from the protective cover of the fuel barrels. She stepped forward, took a deep breath, swinging her handgun from side to side, ready to fire at anything that moved. On her way to the sleeping quarters, she thought only of keeping both her son and unborn child alive.

When she heard gunfire, she threw herself against the sharp contours of the wall. She heard bullets ricochet and whizz close to her cheek. She lifted the gun to the ready position and saw Habib's rigid face in the light of a single bulb. For an instant, she saw a machine pistol in his hand swing around toward her. Joanne fired and then ducked behind a vise embedded in a worktable. Habib's bullets dug gouges out of the woodwork and showered dust and splinters in her hair.

Where is Ryan? Why isn't he firing? she thought. She had a dreadful feeling that Habib had killed him with his machine pistol.

She screamed as a bullet tore into her calf, and she fell back on the floor. She saw blood flow from her left leg. She leaned down, and blood seeped through her fingers. Then she heard muffled cries. She rolled over and fired a wild series of shots.

She saw Habib jump back and shield his face as bullets pummeled the wall behind him.

Habib fired the machine pistol and stitched the air with death. He was surprised that Joanne was still alive. He thought he had killed Ryan Moar. The shots from behind the barrels where Ryan had taken cover had stopped. Habib could feel a massive bellow of anger well inside him that the woman continued to keep him pinned down.

He could feel his hand twitch to fire again, but he had to conserve ammunition. In his haste to seek cover, he had separated himself from his spare clips.

He aimed at her exposed shoulder.

"Die," he shouted above the sound of the machine pistol.

His bullets gouged holes in a cupboard where he had pinned her down. He needed some cover so he could finish her off.

Where were Zahara and his son? They were both armed. He didn't see Arrak anywhere either. Did his absence mean he was slitting the throats of the children as easily as if he was slicing roast beef?

Habib cursed when he realized the magazine was empty, and he tossed aside the useless weapon.

When the bullets shattering the rock face inches above him suddenly stopped, Ryan snaked along the floor to find cover. Then a bullet thumped into his thigh, making a rubbery sound like a boxing glove striking flesh. Pain flooded his leg, and blood soaked his pants.

Reaching for a discarded rifle, he used the weapon as a crutch to hobble on the uneven floor. Before he reached the wall, he cringed at a sustained explosion of fire. Bullets in front of him shattered the thin partition wall that separated the sleeping quarters from the rest of the cave. While he inched his face around the door, he suppressed panic when he spotted both Charlene and Gary tied up and lying motionless on cots.

He pointed his handgun in the direction of Habib's last hiding place. He squeezed off shots, and his bullets stitched a series of holes in packing cases. He heard a scream, and he stopped firing. He hoped he had wiped Habib's slate clean.

Even as a young patrol officer, he had wrestled with the fear of exercising the power of life and death over another human being, but Habib belonged in a special group who lived in his nightmares.

Habib reeled back as bullets bounced off the rock face and showered him with shards of granite. He flung himself behind a crate as another volley ripped the air around him. In the dim light, he spotted Zahara sprawled on the ground with bullet holes stitched in her chest. The sight of his wife's blood caused rage to boil up inside him that spread like galloping gangrene.

He scanned the suddenly silent room. His son's fate was unknown. There was no sign of Arrak. Habib felt confident he had wounded or killed both Joanne and Ryan, but he couldn't be sure if they were dead or were poised like maimed wolves to kill him.

If I find them alive, I will take my time to kill them so the pain will be excruciating, he thought.

During a lull in the shooting, Ryan staggered to where Charlene and Gary lay tied up on the cots. Habib surprised him when he rose from behind a pile of wooden crates like a ghoul, and Ryan experienced a momentary sense of bewilderment. Ryan aimed his weapon and fired, but his bullets didn't stop Habib's ferocious headlong rush.

Habib held a knife high above his head. When he crashed into Ryan, Ryan wrapped his fingers around Habib's wrists. Ryan lost his balance and brought Habib down with him. They rolled on the floor in a tight embrace, the knife's blade inches from Ryan's throat.

As Ryan summoned superhuman strength to force him back, Habib howled. The sound chilled Ryan. He sensed Habib's growing strength as he tired. Locked together, Ryan steeled himself to glance at Habib's bull-like eyes. Ryan sensed his madness. He shivered deep in his core. Habib's knife seemed poised to slice its way down his throat.

Ryan heard bullets whistle above his head, and Habib froze for an instant. Ryan hit him in the face with such force that the knife went flying. Habib released him and staggered back.

A great, wild sense of relief charged through Ryan like an electric current. He watched Joanne fire at Habib, who scrambled to his feet and disappeared in a dark patch near the door.

CHAPTER 50

Habib groped for a toolbox he had left by the exit door, leading to the ledge. Inside the box, he unlocked an inner compartment and set charges to go off in fifteen minutes. He then reached for a switch to turn off the generator.

In total darkness, he made his way like a bat along the memorized direction of the door that led to the ledge. When he opened the door, bullets whistled over his head. His body shuddered when another bullet grazed the side of his temple and almost knocked him over.

Regaining his footing, he slammed the exit door shut. He locked the door from the outside. He took in a deep breath of moist night air. He wiped sweat that stung his eyes. He jogged along the narrow ledge like a circus tightrope walker.

A flash of lightning made him flinch, and he missed his footing. He began to fall sideways, and he teetered close to the edge. He managed to grab a tree root to maintain his balance. A hundred feet below him, he stared down on jagged rocks. He lunged for the rope ladder. As he climbed down the cliff, his boots kicked up an explosion of dust and dislodged small stones that rattled and clattered onto the valley floor.

When his feet hit the uneven surface below the cliff, he stumbled across open ground. He angled for the cover of pines. Once under the protective branches, he scrambled up the deer trail. He felt battered and shaken by the failure of the attack on the monument.

Forcing his bone-weary legs through the undergrowth, he could think of nothing but collecting his money from the safe. Then he planned to drive the pickup to a safe house in St. Paul.

"I can't be beaten," he yelled at the top of his lungs as he flung open his cabin door.

Inside his bedroom, he put in the combination to open the safe. When he saw the safe empty, he bellowed in frustration. Rashid must have stolen the money. He caught a glimpse of his rage and pain reflected in a shaving mirror. His burning eyes reminded him of a man who had lost his soul.

Without money, he felt vulnerable, but he could still get away in the pickup. He looked at his watch. In five minutes, SEMTEX, a Czech-made plastic explosive, would go off inside the cave. He imagined a ball of fire would melt Moar's flesh off his bones before the cave imploded and brought down rocks to obliterate everything inside.

He laughed a guttural sound that came from deep within his throat. He could still be a thorn in the side of America, never really eradicated. He would wait for the right time to resurface and attack again. He hurried down a path to the pickup buried under branches.

After the lights went out, Joanne switched on her pencil flashlight. The beam played over the locked door and the steel toolbox standing beside it. She guessed Habib had escaped. Her flashlight's beam played over Zahara's blood-splattered body. Where was her son? Was Arrak still a threat?

Overwhelmed by the need to find Ryan, she shouted his name. She heard him cry out, "Over here!"

She followed the sound of his voice. Near the doorway of the sleeping quarters, her flashlight caught the third pilot armed with a knife. She fired at him and missed.

Then she heard a crash of bullets come from behind her. The shots picked up the pilot and dumped him backward onto his buttocks. Blood fanned out across his chest. For a moment, he looked surprised as though the bullets had done something unexpected. The shooter fired again, and this time he spun around and landed in a twisted, misshapen heap near the cot where Gary lay tied up.

Joanne hugged the partition wall when she heard Charlene's feeble cry, "Help me."

Habib thrashed about in the undergrowth until he found the pickup. He removed the branches. He climbed into the vehicle and felt secure in the leather seat. He switched on the ignition and listened to the soft purr of the engine.

The powerful headlights startled an owl that flew into the overcast sky. The windshield wipers swept away dried leaves and twigs to give him a clear view of the resort.

In a few hours, he would be far from the Black Hills.

When he shifted the automatic gear to drive, he felt a momentary confusion when the pickup shuddered and shook. He pressed farther down on the accelerator. The vehicle lurched forward like a wounded elephant. The Ford appeared held back by some unseen hand. He yelled in frustration, the sound of his voice drowned out by the thump of flat tires.

He eased up on the accelerator and slammed his fists on the steering column. He turned off the ignition and climbed down to examine the slashed tires.

He glanced at his watch and twisted his mouth in a crooked smile. In minutes, he would hear the muffled roar of explosives from inside the cave, and Moar's family would be crushed to pulp under tons of rock.

CHAPTER 51

INSIDE THE CAVE, JOANNE KNEELED on a prayer mat beside Gary's cot. She used her Swiss army knife to cut the ropes around his wrists and ankles. He struggled to his feet and shook his legs to start the blood flow. She then shone the flashlight on Charlene's blood-streaked face.

She said a silent prayer while Ryan stood on one leg and sliced the ropes around his daughter's arms and legs. Joanne hugged them, feeling the ebb and flow of tidal waves of relief.

"Oh, come on, Mom, I'm okay," Gary said.

She released them and tried to control her shakes.

"Thank God you're alive," she said.

"Is the man with the big knife dead?" Charlene asked, glancing at the cots strewn with rumpled bedding.

Joanne shone the flashlight on the third pilot's body. Blood oozed from multiple wounds in his chest.

"Who shot him?" she asked.

"I did," said a voice from behind her. "Don't shoot."

She spun around, the flashlight's beam on Moe, his hands above his head.

"Your mother's over beside those crates," she said, shining the flashlight on Zahara.

Moe's mother was sprawled legs akimbo on the floor, blood trickled from multiple wounds on her chest but her eyes blinked in the bright light. Moe staggered over to her and cradled her in his arms.

Joanne turned her flashlight's beam on her husband. Blood flowed from his hip. Charlene tore up some bedsheets, and Joanne wrapped them around his thigh.

"Where are the others?" Ryan asked.

"Zahara's is dying, Habib escaped, and Moe saved our lives by shooting the surviving pilot," Joanne said.

"I know that guy," Gary said, leaning over to examine the dead pilot. "His name is Arrak and he broke into our house."

Gary then wrapped Ryan's arm around his shoulder, and Ryan hopped along on his good leg.

Joanne heard footsteps and shone her flashlight on Moe, his mouth open in a silent shout of despair.

"She's gone," he whispered.

"I'm so sorry," she said.

His eyes registered nothing but bleakness.

"Before she died, she warned me that my father has a timer set for explosives to go off inside the cave any minute now," Moe said.

Joanne tried the door handle. She shouted in frustration when she found the door locked.

She banged the steel surface with the flat of her hands. "Open it up! We don't want to die!"

Gary spotted the toolbox and red glow of the explosive timing device's numbers. "We've only got one minute and forty-nine seconds."

"My mother has a ring of keys," Moe said.

"Get them, man, go now!" Ryan said in a harsh whisper.

Joanne gave Moe the flashlight. As they waited in the dark, holding each other, the seconds flashed by in her mind like sparks in a fuse, and she braced for the explosion.

Moe seemed to take forever to find his mother's key ring.

When he returned, Gary shouted that thirty-nine seconds remained. Moe aimed the flashlight on the keyhole and shoved a key into the lock.

Would he know the right one? Joanne could see sweat plaster his face and stain his collar. Her dry lips moved in prayer as she listened to a steady drip of water from within the cave like the last seconds of her life ticking away.

She heard Moe shout as the lock opened.

A cold breeze tugged at her as the iron door swung wide. Moe helped Ryan hop outside. Ahead of her, she saw Gary and Charlene hold hands on the narrow ledge.

"Get a move on," she shouted.

Moe hoisted Ryan over a rockfall. She heard a boom and expected the cave to explode and blast them off the ledge. Then she realized the bang was a clap of thunder. Rain began to pelt her face and sting her eyes. She felt her boots slip on the ledge, and to keep her balance she clung to the wall.

Gary gripped her arm. "The ladder's below."

While she climbed down, Moe and Gary eased Ryan down the rungs. He leaned on his good leg while they propped him up on either side to lower him down.

"Hurry! Hurry!" Joanne yelled.

Above her, a rumble deep within the cave brought down showers of pebbles and soil on their heads.

When the explosion died down and the dust cleared, Joanne felt a momentary confusion when her feet touched loose shale at the foot of the cliff. Beside her, Ryan was perched on one leg, his arm around Gary's shoulder. Charlene had locked her hands around Gary's neck, her cheek pressed against the stubble on his face.

She felt her heart swell with triumph that both her family and the monument were safe.

CHAPTER 52

B EFORE DAWN, THE SKY OVER the valley was heavy with rain
clouds that blocked out the stars. A cold wind rattled loose
shingles in the log cabin's roof. Inside Habib's bedroom, Joanne
wrapped bandages around Ryan's thigh.

"Thank God it's only a flesh wound," she said.

"How's your calf doing?" he asked.

"The gash is deep enough to leave a memorable scar," she said,
rolling up her pant leg to show him the bandage. "It isn't serious
enough to interfere with my tennis handicap."

"Are Charlene and Gary all right?"

"They're fine. Charlene's ankle is swollen, but it won't take long
to mend."

Ryan sat up and swung his legs over the bed to the floor. He
heard Charlene's giggle in the kitchen. "What brought on this
sudden mirth?"

"Charlene's so thankful for what Gary did. After she sprained
her ankle, he took care of her. That's when Rashid caught them."

She examined the bandage on his leg and then stood back to
admire her work.

"Not bad, huh?" she said, tweaking his cheek. "So you feel strong enough to drive us home?"

He gave her a sly look.

"I've got bruises on my lips that need urgent attention," he said.

"Are you implying the cure is for me to plant my lips on yours?" He nodded.

"I'm not falling for that ruse," she said, arching her eyebrows. "Cool your engine, mister." She ruffled his hair. "There's nothing like a good old-fashioned adrenaline rush—"

The door opened, and Moe stuck his head around the jamb.

Ryan's eyes hardened to granite. "What do you want?" he growled.

"To go back to Fargo with you," he said, stepping uninvited into the room.

Ryan paused as if to search for words. "Apart from blasting the monument, you wanted to kill us all."

"I had nothing to do with any of—"

"Don't tell me you weren't involved in this attack?"

"If I didn't join him, my father threatened to expose me. I'd be sent back to Syria to be tortured."

"You expect us to believe you?"

Moe turned to Joanne, his eyes pleading. "Please give me another chance."

Joanne turned to Ryan. "I think we should."

Moe's eyes brimmed with hope as he stared out of the window at the first smudge of dawn brighten heavy rain clouds.

"Your father and Rashid are still at large." Ryan's expression darkened. "How do we know they won't murder us?"

"They can't harm you now."

"Isn't revenge in your blood? Each time we kill one of your kin, are you not honor-bound to kill us?"

"My father and Rashid are preoccupied; they're trying to escape to Damascus."

Ryan gave him a wry look. "Not exactly an assurance that they won't want to slit our throats."

Ryan tested his weight on the injured leg.

"Please, Ryan, I'm begging you," Moe said, clasping his hands together.

Ryan avoided his eyes. He craned his neck to look out at the deer trail that led down to the ravine to the pile of shattered rock where the cave once stood.

"No way," Ryan said.

Moe stared at him wide-eyed with fear.

"Moe talked to Tamara on the phone. She's so happy he's coming home," Joanne said.

Ryan listened to noises inside the cabin. The woodwork creaked in the wind. He heard chatter in the kitchen and a fridge door close. He stared at short hairs on his toes. "I think we should turn you over to the authorities," he said, his face rigid.

Moe wiped his forehead with the back of his hand.

"He saved our lives," Joanne said, dusting off a dried leaf from Moe's leather jacket.

"He'll cause us all kinds of security and immigration problems."

"Not if we pass him off as one of the family. He's young enough to be your son."

Ryan laughed without humor. "Yeah, right."

"Come on, Ryan," Joanne said, sitting down beside him to tuck her arm inside his. "Don't you want them to be happy?"

Ryan glanced at Joanne, and she nodded. He turned to Moe. "Go pack your things."

"Thank you," Moe whispered. He went off to load his kit bag in the back of the Range Rover.

Charlene limped into the bedroom. "When are we going home?"

"We'd better leave right away before the neighbors realize that the banging last night wasn't all thunder," Ryan said.

While he closed the cabin door, Ryan thought about Habib's obsession to blow up statues. As he climbed into the Range Rover, he paused to stare at the distant profile of George Washington. The magnificent carved head of the first president made him question if there was any way to explain the folly that caused humans to undo the great wonders the world.

SHARK

Michael D. Hartley

A RYAN MOAR MYSTERY

Turn the page for a preview of *Shark*, the next
novel in the Ryan Moar Mystery Series ...

J OMO WILLOW DISMISSED HIS DRIVER and hurried through brass-studded wooden Arab doors to an enclosed courtyard. The life of the teacher of economics at the State University of Zanzibar ended when he decided to stop for a beer after work at the seafront Mbuyuni pub on Mizingani Road.

He glanced up at thin clouds building up in the Mozambique Channel. They filtered the sunlight to bathe the pub's pillars in dull silver. Purple bougainvillea hanging over the courtyard's walls contrasted with the orange rust on the cast-iron roof and in the rain gutters. The evening air was dense with a strong smell of sun-bleached carcasses of fish beached in the stagnant water of tidal pools beside sand traced with crawl lines of crabs.

Inside the pub's thick walls that once housed a former sultan's harem, Jomo removed his sunglasses and broad-brimmed hat. He used a handkerchief to mop sweat off the top of his clean-shaven head. His broad mouth was surrounded by a trimmed beard. He ordered a Serengeti lager from a tall bartender wearing an embroidered pillbox-shaped hat. The bartender's skin was coarse and wrinkled like a tortoise's neck.

Jomo sat on a stool, stretched out his muscular legs, and laced his fingers across his flat stomach. The professor had reason to celebrate. He had finished his new book on African economies, and life with his wife, Renée; two young children; and a one-eyed cat was for him a timeless vision. They lived in an Indian colonial-style house painted white with gray trim. In his garden, he had an ornamental pool frequented by water snakes that dined on frogs. He tried to distance his home life from university politics, which were far too often inhabited by academic charlatans and greedy civil servants.

Even though window fans sucked out stale air, the Mbuyuni pub reeked of cigarette smoke, curry, and the ammonia-like smell from behind glass-beaded curtains that shielded the stone trough-shaped urinal in the *choo*.

Above the bar, neon signs advertising Tusker beer reflected off the sweaty faces of two men who had hard, compact bodies, square teeth, pronounced facial bones, and hair in dreadlocks. Their faces, coarsened by the sun and the wind, had mixed features that combined African tribal brutality with the cruelty of Arab slavers.

Jomo noticed they had curved knives tucked into their belts, and he suspected they belonged to gangs of drug dealers from the mainland. Their eyes had a ferocity that mirrored the threats contained in the e-mails he'd been receiving recently.

The frenzy of hatred in the notes focused on his proposal to expand fiber optics on campus. Some colleagues and corrupt officials opposed the Internet as an unnecessary evil, but Jomo had never anticipated such a severe backlash to his commitment to change.

Jomo lit a cheroot and puffed smoke through his nose. He could feel the skin on his face shrink and grow hot whenever the two goons glanced in his direction. Could those who opposed his plan to modernize communications at the university have dispatched these two to intimidate him? If so, it was time for him to leave. He drained his beer, paid for his drink, and headed for the exit, trying to be inconspicuous.

Outside, a sea breeze rattled banana leaves, and a ship's horn wafted in from the bay, but he also heard the gangsters' low voices behind him. Jomo threw away his cheroot and ground the butt into the pavement. He cursed his driver for not waiting outside the pub for him. He sensed the narrow obsidian eyes of the criminal pair boring into the back of his head.

In the square, where he waited for his car, two boys kicked a soccer ball, and an elderly woman in a black shawl sold mangoes from a pushcart. Almost unnoticed, a thin European sidled into the square and leaned against a rain-streaked coral wall, his gaze fixed on the two men at the pub's entrance. He wore a Panama hat and a wrinkled, cream-colored tropical suit. The pale exposed skin on his freckled face, neck, and hands reminded Jomo of a fish's belly. The man's stare appeared innocuous but oddly menacing.

Above the sounds of the waves and the soccer players' chatter, Jomo strained to hear the soft purr of his Mercedes, but there was no sign of his driver. The European stood erect, his left hand wrapped around the butt of a handgun equipped with a silencer. He aimed the revolver at the two men, and Jomo scrambled behind a wall of shattered masonry.

The assassin's first muffled shots sounded like the pops of damp firecrackers. The shooter killed the nearest hoodlum with a bullet through the heart. The hoodlum's companion withdrew a handgun hidden in his pocket, but the killer was too quick for him. The European fired two shots into his shoulder, and the wounded man dropped his weapon and clutched at the bullet holes while blood flowed through his fingers. His pleading sounded like the squeal of a warthog caught in a steel trap. Jomo heard another shot, and the man's cries ended.

When the shooter paused to examine his handiwork, Jomo felt enormous relief that perhaps the two men who had left the bar at the same time as he did were the intended target.

His throat went dry when he heard the crunch of the shooter's crocodile-skin, needle-pointed boots on loose gravel, coming toward him. Jomo glanced at the shooter's sunken cheeks and reddish pencil-thin moustache that glowed in the yellow light. The intense glare of his milk-blue eyes made a cold vapor wrap around Jomo's heart. The assassin pointed the handgun at his head, fired two bullets, and Jomo's skull exploded like a coconut.

3

In the square, the gunfire scattered gulls feeding in the drain. Sprawled behind mangoes in the old woman's cart, the soccer players heard the soft sound of bullets pierce the professor's skull. While the boys listened to their chattering teeth, the white man pocketed the handgun and melted into the warren of narrow streets, whistling an Irish ballad through gapped teeth, his eyes fixed on the red band of light in the west.

A flock of cormorants skimmed across the turbulent surface of the muddy Red River north of Fargo; the sigh of wind in the poplars mingled with the honk of geese. In spring, when the fish spawned in the cattails and the floodwaters seeped in among the elms, the river's damp, clawing smell made Ryan Moar think that the water's spring odor was possibly the same as when silt-laden waters first flowed north in narrow channels to Lake Winnipeg at the end of the Ice Age.

His hands thrust in his pockets of his leather jacket, Ryan strolled beside the levee in front of his property on Red River Road. He needed time to think about what he was going to say to his wife, Joanne Sutter, about his trip to East Africa. Joanne's cairn terrier barked when she came out on the deck of the cedar-log house they shared with two teenagers.

The evening sun coated her smooth cheeks and blonde hair that brushed her shoulders. Her face relaxed in repose was a rarity as she usually had an actor's animated expressions of laughter, surprise, skepticism, or compassion. His favorite was a wicked grin that gave her the look of a mischievous child. Her pregnancy accented a languid sensuality beneath the surface like an underworld fire.

"I recognize that special look," she said as he climbed the steps to greet her.

There was no point in trying to disguise his resolve to go to Zanzibar to solve the murder of his friend Jomo Willow, a former economics professor at North Dakota State University. Before leaving to teach in East Africa, Jomo had married Renée, Ryan's first wife's younger sister.

4

"Renée needs me to sort this out," Ryan said, reaching out to touch Joanne's hands on the deck's railing. "It won't take long."

"You never know the time a murder investigation will take." Joanne's face burned with irritability. "Besides, I want to go with you."

"Won't it be dangerous in your condition?"

"The baby and I will be just fine," Joanne said.

"You're only two months away," Ryan replied, a lopsided grin spreading across his tanned face.

"I'll take all the shots."

"Apart from the heat, think about tsetse flies, yellow fever, malaria, beriberi, sleeping sickness."

"Maybe you're right." She sighed. "Promise me you'll be back in time for the baby's arrival."

"I won't want to miss it."

Her face twisted in a frown. "According to Fodor, Zanzibar's a dodgy place. You know nothing about the island's politics or crime scene."

Ryan turned to the turbulent river that mirrored his thoughts. "I'll probably discover it's nothing more than a straightforward case of mistaken identity."

The Kenya Airways 737 broke through a layer of cumulus on a circuit downwind. Ryan spotted the steel skeleton of the half-completed Zanzibar airport off the starboard wing. On the port side were palm-tree-fringed beaches with glistening white sand. The graceful curve of the rotating lantern sails of dhows skimmed on the ocean's surface.

During the landing, Ryan remained absorbed in the pilot's maneuvers until the aircraft came to a standstill opposite the terminal building and the whine of jet engines came to rest. He followed passengers down the aisle before stepping out of the air-conditioned cabin into the late afternoon's heat that hit him like a blast furnace.

After hauling his luggage off a carousel, he scanned the airport terminal for Renée in among the passengers and waiting loved ones. There was no sign of her in the crowded terminal where people wore head scarves and turbans, business suits and flowing robes, and spoke languages he didn't understand. The last time they'd met was ten years ago at his first wife Kathy's funeral.

At the service, Renée had worn her hair as short as wheat stubble, and she had sported a black stud in her nose. Her slim build and tiny hands had given her the appearance of being younger than in her early twenties.

At the terminal exit, Ryan's cell phone chimed.

"Ryan, I'm afraid," Renée said a muffled voice.

He could feel a muscle spasm building inside him. "Renée, what's going on?"

He heard children's voices whine, beg for attention.

"We've had to move into the Al Mutlaq Hotel," she said.

"Are you and the children in any danger?"

"We're alive," she whispered.

"What happened to you?"

"I'm too exhausted to talk now. I'll see you at the Al Mutlaq tomorrow morning."

She disconnected the line.

While Ryan waited for a taxi to take him to his hotel, a boy of about fifteen caught his eye and half raised his hand in a salute. He had dark, curly hair and the wispy beginnings of a beard on his square chin. He wore scuffed tennis shoes, and his pressed khaki cargo pants were held up by a belt with a shiny buckle.

"You want a taxi?" he asked, taking the handle of Ryan's rolling luggage.

"Sure, what's your name?" Ryan said, following his suitcases and the boy.

"Bari Khan."

"Do this for a living, Bari?"

6

"Yes, bwana," he said, the boy's broad smile displaying rows of white, well-formed teeth.

The boy released his grip on the luggage so he could swing his arms in a wide gesture that culminated in a clasp of hands with Ryan, followed by the holding of thumbs and a second handshake. Bari's boyish round face beamed, his thin shoulder muscles flexed under a yellow T-shirt emblazoned with a Tanzanian flag, five diagonal stripes of green and blue sandwiching a black strip fringed by yellow.

The boy leaned over the curb and stuck two fingers in his mouth to whistle. A rust-flecked Renault drove ahead of waiting cabs and slid in beside them.

Bari glanced at the luggage tags and clasped his arms across his chest to do an exaggerated imitation of shivering. He loaded the bags in the trunk and opened the Renault's door.